THE F~~A~~
HOUSE OF
ÆTHELFRITH

By

H A Culley

Book five about the Anglo-Saxon Kings of
Northumbria

Published by

Orchard House Publishing

First Kindle Edition 2017

Text copyright © 2017 H A Culley

Cover Image: © iStock/Jarih

TABLE OF CONTENTS

List of Principal Characters **5**

Place Names **8**

Glossary **11**

PROLOGUE **13**

PART ONE - ECGFRITH 16

Chapter One – The Disputed Throne **16**

Chapter Two – The Battle of the Two Rivers **40**

Chapter Three – Æthelthryth **62**

Chapter Four – The Isle of Man **71**

Chapter Five – The Battle of Loidis **96**

Chapter Six – Two Weddings **117**

Chapter Seven – The Last Days of Rheged **132**

Chapter Eight – The Division of the Diocese **148**

Chapter Nine – The Battle of the Trent **162**

Chapter Ten – Wilfrid **187**

Chapter Eleven – The Invasion of Hibernia **194**

Chapter Twelve – The Battle of Dùn Nectain **214**

PART TWO – ALDFRITH 229

Chapter Thirteen – Two Funerals **229**

Chapter   Fourteen – Wilfrid's Rise and Fall **263**

Chapter Fifteen – The Battle for Cumbria **287**

Chapter Sixteen – Disaster in the North **312**

Chapter Seventeen – The Return of the Exiles **331**

Chapter Eighteen – The Usurper **358**

PART THREE – THE LAST OF THEIR HOUSE 385

Chapter Nineteen – The Boy King **385**

Chapter Twenty – Border Warfare **397**

Chapter Twenty One – Swefred the Hereræswa **418**

Chapter Twenty Two – Death of a Tyrant **433**

Chapter Twenty Three - Cenred **453**

Chapter Twenty Four – Osric the Good **464**

Chapter Twenty Five – Epilogue **481**

Author's Note **485**

Other Novels by H A Culley **492**

About The Author **494**

List of Principal Characters

(In alphabetical order)

Historical characters are shown in bold type

Æthelbald – Eldest son of Alweo, later King of Mercia

Æthelfrith – King of Bernicia from 593. First King of Northumbria. Reigned 604 to 616. Father of Oswald, Oswiu and five other children. Founder of the ruling house of Northumbria

Æthelwald Moll – King of Northumbria from 759 until 765 when he became a monk. His background in this novel is fictitious.

Alchfrith – Oswiu's son by Rhieinmelth. *(NOTE: Spelt Ehlfrith in earlier books but changed to the alternative spelling of Alchfrith in this book to save confusion with his brother Ecgfrith)*

Aldfrith – Oswui's eldest son (illegitimate)

Alaric – Catinus' elder son

Alweo – Son of Eowa and nephew of the late King Penda of Mercia

Ælfflaed – Oswiu's daughter by Eanflæd. Abbess of Whitby

Ælfwine – Oswiu's younger son by Eanflæd. Later Sub-king of Deira

Æthelthryth – Ecgfrith's first wife

Bruide – Son of the King of Prydenn, later High King of the Picts

Benoc – Ealdorman of Jarrow

Beorhtmund – Behrtfrith's son

Beornheth - Cuthbert's younger brother, the Eorl of Lothian

Behrt – His elder son

Behrtfrith – Beornheth's younger son

Catinus – Briton born in Mercia who became Ealdorman of Bebbanburg

Cenred – Son of Cuthwin, later King of Northumbria

Coenred – King of Mercia from 704 AD

Conomultus – Catinus' younger brother, Bishop of Abernethy in the Land of the Picts

Cuthbert – Prior, later Bishop, of Lindisfarne

Cuthburh – Aldfrith's wife, Queen of Northumbria

Cuthwin – A thegn and descendant of King Ida of Bernicia

Domangart – King of Dalriada until 660

Drefan – Catinus' body servant

Drest – High King of the Picts

Eadstan – Catinus' military commander

Eata – Abbot of Lindisfarne

Ecgfrith – Oswiu's son by Eanflæd. Sub-king of Deira 664 - 670. King of Northumbria 670 - 685

Edyth – Daughter of Benoc, Ealdorman of Jarrow

Elfin – King of Strathclyde

Eochaid – Son of Ruaidhrí and Edyth; named after his grandfather, King Eochaid of the Ulaidh.

Eormenburg – Second wife of Ecgfrith, possibly his mistress prior to their marriage

Ethelred – Penda's third son. Later King of Mercia. Also spelt Æthelred in some sources

Godwyna – Daughter of Benoc of Jarrow. Edyth's younger sister

Heartbehrt – Son of Alweo and Hereswith, captain of Eochaid's warband; later King of Man

Hereswith – Catinus' daughter, wife of Alweo

Kendra- Behrtfrith's daughter, later Swefred's wife

Leoflaed – Catinus' wife and mother of Hereswith, Alric and Osfrid

Lethlobar – Son of the late Eochaid, King of the Ulaidh in Ulster

Mael Duin – King of Dalriada

Morcar – Reeve of Bebbanburg

Morleo – King of Ardewr

Octa - Hereræswa of Northumbria after Redwald

Osred – Aldfrith's eldest son

Osric – Aldfrith's youngest son

Osfrid – Catinus' younger son

Osthryth – Oswiu's daughter by Eanflæd. Later married to King Ethelred of Mercia

Otta – Aldfrith's middle son, actually named Offa but the name has been changed in the novels to save confusion with King Offa of Mercia who appears later in the series

Rægenhere – Wilfrid's younger brother and chaplain to Alchfrith

Redwald – Hereræswa of Northumbria

Ruaidhrí – The bastard son of King Eochaid of the Ulaidh and half-brother of Lethlobar

Sigmund – Leader of Osfrid's gesith

Stepan – Ealdorman of Cumbria

Swefred – Osfrid's younger son

Wilfrid - Bishop of Northumbria

Wulfhere – Penda's second son, later King of Mercia

Uurad – A Pict. Catinus' body servant, later commander of Osfrid's warband. Also the name of his son, the captain of Swefred's gesith.

Place Names

(In alphabetical order)

I find that always using the correct place name for the particular period in time may be authentic but it is annoying to have to continually search for the modern name if you want to know the whereabouts of the place in relation to other places in the story. However, using the ancient name adds to the authenticity of the tale. I have therefore compromised by using the modern name for places, geographical features and islands, except where the ancient name is relatively well known, at least to those interested in the period, or else is relatively similar to the modern name. The ancient names used are listed below:

Amorica – Brittany and part of Normandy, France
Béal Feirste – Belfast, Northern Ireland
Bebbanburg – Bamburgh, Northumberland, North East England
Bernicia – The modern counties of Northumberland, Durham, Tyne & Wear and Cleveland in the North East of England. At times Goddodin was a subsidiary part of Bernicia
Berwic – Berwick upon Tweed, Northumberland
Bremetennacum – Ribchester, Lancashire
Caerlleon – Chester, Cheshire
Caer Luel – Carlisle, Cumbria
Caledonia - Scotland
Cantwareburg – Canterbury, Kent
Dalriada – Much of Argyll and the Inner Hebrides
Deira – Most of North Yorkshire and northern Humberside
Duboglassio – Douglas, Isle of Man

Dùn Add – Dunadd, near Kilmartin, Argyll, Scotland. Capital of Dal Riata.

Dùn Barra - Dunbar, Scotland

Dùn Breatainn - Literally Fortress of the Britons. Dumbarton, Scotland

Dùn Dè – Dundee, Tayside, Scotland

Dùn Èideann - Edinburgh

Dùn Nectain – Location disputed but probably Dunnichen in Angus, Scotland

Eoforwīc - York

Elmet – West Yorkshire

Frankia – The territories inhabited and ruled by the Franks, a confederation of West Germanic tribes, approximating to present day France and a large part of Germany.

German Ocean – North Sea

Glaschu – Glasgow, Scotland

Gleawecastre – Gloucester

Goddodin – The area between the River Tweed and the Firth of Forth; i.e. the modern regions of Lothian and Borders in Scotland. Later called Lothian.

Gwynedd – North Wales including Anglesey

Hibernia - Ireland

Isurium Brigantum - Aldborough in Yorkshire

Kinneddar – Lossiemouth, Moray, Scotland

Lindocolina – Lincoln, Lincolnshire

Loidis – Leeds, Yorkshire

Luncæster – Lancaster, Lancashire

Lundenwic – London

Mamucium – Roman name for Manchester

Mercia – Roughly the present day Midlands of England

Northumbria – Comprised Bernicia, Elmet and Deira. At times it also included Rheged and Goddodin

Orcades – The Orkney Islands, Scotland

Pictland – The confederation of kingdoms including Shetland, the Orkneys, the Outer Hebrides, Skye and the Scottish Highlands north of a line running roughly from Skye to the Firth of Forth

River Twaid – The river Tweed, which flows west from Berwick through northern Northumberland and the Scottish Borders.

Rheged - A kingdom of Ancient Britons speaking Cumbric, a Brythonic language similar to Old Welsh, which roughly encompassed modern Lancashire, Cumbria in England and, at times, part of Galloway in Scotland

Rhumsaa – Ramsay, Isle of Man

Strathclyde – South east Scotland

Wintan-ceastre – Winchester, Hampshire

Glossary

Ætheling – Literally 'throne-worthy. An Anglo-Saxon prince.

Birlinn – A wooden ship similar to the later Scottish galleys. Usually with a single mast and square rigged sail, they could also be propelled by oars with one man to each oar.

Brenin – The Brythonic term by which kings were addressed Wales, Strathclyde and the Land of the Picts.

Bretwalda - In Anglo-Saxon England, an overlord or paramount king accepted by other kings as their leader

Ceorl - Freemen who worked the land or else provided a service or trade such as metal working, carpentry, weaving etc. They ranked between thegns and slaves and provided the fyrd in time of war

Currach - A boat, sometimes quite large, with a wooden frame over which animal skins or hides are stretched and greased to make them waterproof

Custos – A guardian or custodian, the word was used in a variety of contexts including to mean one left in charge in the absence of the lord or king

Cymru - Wales

Cyning – Old English for king and the term by which they were normally addressed

Eorl – A noble ranking between thegn and members of the royal house. In the seventh century it meant the governor of a division of the kingdom. Later replaced by ealdorman, the chief magistrate and war leader of a shire, and earl, the ruler of a province under the King of All England; for example, Wessex, Mercia and Northumbria

Gesith – The companions of a king, usually acting as his bodyguard

Hereræswa – Military commander or general. The man who commanded the army of a nation under the king

Knarr - A merchant ship where the hull was wider, deeper and shorter than that of a birlinn

Seax – A bladed weapon somewhere in size between a dagger and a sword. Mainly used for close-quarter fighting where a sword would be too long and unwieldy

Thegn – The lowest rank of noble. A man who held a certain amount of land direct from the king or from a senior nobleman, ranking between an ordinary freeman and an eorl

Ulaidh - A confederation of dynastic-groupings that inhabited a provincial kingdom in Ulster (north-eastern Ireland) and was ruled by the Rí Ulad or King of the Ulaidh. The two main tribes of the Ulaidh were the Dál nAraidi and the Dál Fiatach

Uí Néill – A Hibernian clan who claimed descent from Niall Noigiallach (Niall of the Nine Hostages), a historical King of Tara who died about 405 AD

Settlement – Any grouping of residential buildings, usually around the king's or lord's hall. In 7th century England the term city, town or village had not yet come into use

Síþwíf - My lady in Old English

Stipend – (in this context) Income received from a diocese or a monastery

Weregeld – In Anglo-Saxon England, if property was stolen, or someone was injured or killed, the guilty person would have to pay weregeld as restitution to the victim's family or to the owner of the property

Witan – The council of an Anglo-Saxon kingdom. Its composition varied, depending on the matters to be debated. Usually it consisted of the Eorls and the chief priests (bishops and abbots in the case of a Christian kingdom), but for the selection of a king or other important matters, it would be expanded to include the more minor nobility, such as the thegns

Villein - A peasant (tenant farmer) who was legally tied to his vill

Vill - A thegn's holding or similar area of land in Anglo-Saxon England which might otherwise be described as a parish or manor

PROLOGUE

604 AD

'You must flee. King Æthelfrith is nearly at the gates and our men are too frightened to deny him entry.'

Ethelric, King of Deira, was indecisive at the best of times and his younger brother, Edwin, lost patience with him.

'I am leaving here with my family before it's too late; if you're sensible you'll come with us.'

'But I can't abandon Eoforwīc. If Æthelfrith captures our capital he'll crown himself King of Deira.'

'He'll do that anyway. We've been defeated in the field and we don't have the men to hold the place against him. He'll find it a lot easier to be recognised as king if you're dead.'

Ethelric shuddered. He was well aware that he was no warrior and he should have listened to Edwin when he told him he was walking into a trap two weeks ago when he advanced to defend his borders. As it was Æthelfrith, the king of neighbouring Bernicia, had out manoeuvred him and his army had been routed.

He might not be a good commander but he was a proud man and his conscience wouldn't let him abandon Eoforwīc. Edwin looked at him with exasperation.

'Good luck, brother. I must go. At least one of us must live to recover our birth right in more propitious times.'

The two men embraced before Edwin left Ethelric sitting on his lonely throne.

After a while Ethelric stirred from his lethargy and called for a servant to summon the captain of his gesith and the hereræswa of his army. The boy, one of the few who had remained at his post in the king's hall, looked bewildered.

'Cyning, don't you remember? They were both killed at the Battle of the Tees.'

The king looked at him in incomprehension for a minute. Then he remembered and he started to sob. This unnerved the boy even more.

'Is there anything else I can do, Cyning?' the boy asked nervously.

'Do you know who is in charge of the garrison now?'

'No, Cyning. I'll go and find out,' the boy said brightly, glad of the excuse to leave the presence of his pathetic king.

However, the boy did no such thing and joined the rest of the population in their flight through the southern gates. When Æthelfrith rode in from the north he found the place deserted. Like all large settlements the streets were ankle deep in filth and mud. The stench of rotting matter, urine and faeces was pungent but he hardly noticed. He hadn't washed for days and his tunic, trousers and byrnie were stained black with other people's blood.

He dismounted outside the king's hall and, accompanied by his gesith, he entered. Ethelric had remained sitting on his throne at the far end and barely looked up as the group of armed men entered.

Æthelfrith marched up to his fellow king and, without a pause, he thrust his sword into Ethelric's chest. The proud king of Deira toppled from his throne, rolled down the three steps of the dais and lay spread-eagled on the straw covered dirt floor, blood seeping from the gaping wound to stain the front of his white tunic a deep crimson. A great cheer went up from the Bernician warriors who had crowded into the hall.

'All hail, Æthelfrith, King of Bernicia and Deira,' one called out.

'No, not Bernicia and Deira; not any more. King of all the lands north of the River Humber,' he corrected him. 'King of Northumbria.'

'May your house rule Northumbria for many centuries,' one his eorls called out.

'Nay, your house is doomed.'

The voice came from behind the throne and an old woman hobbled into view, bent over and leaning on a stick.

'Be warned, Æthelfrith, you are a regicide and you will pay for your crime for three generations. Brother will kill brother and uncle will kill nephew until your house becomes extinct.'

The king recoiled from the old crone's curse and a deathly hush descended on the hall. Then, from the front ranks of the watching men, an arrow flew to strike the harridan in the throat. She gurgled and tried to pull it free but it was a mortal wound and she dropped dead beside Ethelric.

PART ONE - ECGFRITH

Chapter One – The Disputed Throne
Summer 670 AD

The ealdorman's hall sat on top of a gentle slope within its tall palisade on the rock overlooking the German Ocean. Today the wind was a strong breeze from the east with the occasional gust that whipped the white horses on top of the waves into streamers of spume.

The sentry in the watch tower of the fortress known as Bebbanburg was relieving his boredom by letting his eyes feast on a pretty laundry girl as she carried the clean clothes she'd just dried up towards the hall. When she disappeared inside he reluctantly turned his gaze to check that no-one was approaching from the landward side before turning back to survey the empty grey sea.

Except it wasn't empty. From nowhere sails had appeared from over the horizon to the south east. He quickly counted them and made it seven but then he saw more behind them. He swore, blaming his own negligence on a pretty face and a pair of shapely breasts, before frantically ringing the alarm bell. He could now count twenty sails and so many ships could only mean trouble.

The first man to reach him, panting from having run up the ladder to the platform at the top of the tower, was Ruaidhrí, his watch leader. He was a Hibernian prince who'd taken refuge in Northumbria when he was a boy. His half-brother and he were rivals to inherit the throne of the Ulaidh in Ulster and their father feared for his life had he stayed there. In the end his brother also had to flee when the leader of a different clan of the Ulaidh seized the throne upon their father's death.

Ruaidhrí was closely followed by Catinus, the Ealdorman of Bebbanburg, and Eadstan, his military commander.

Ruaidhrí had opened his mouth and was about to say 'Why did you sound the alarm?' when he saw the fleet heading towards them.

'Alchfrith,' hissed Catinus.

'Are you sure, lord?' Eadstan asked.

'Who else? We know he was putting together an invasion force to challenge Ecgfrith for the throne.'

'But why here?'

'Because he thinks, if he can take Bebbanburg - the ancient fortress of the Kings of Bernicia - others will take his claim to be King of Northumbria seriously.'

Bernicia was the original realm conquered by Ida and his sons, the ancestors of the two half-brothers who were now squabbling over who should succeed King Oswiu as ruler of Northumbria. The kingdom had expanded over the intervening years until it now included, Lothian, Deira, Rheged, and Elmet as well as Bernicia.

'Well, no one has ever captured this fortress so I wish him luck, however many Frankish mercenaries he's brought with him,' Eadstan replied.

'Perhaps,' Catinus muttered, 'but when besieged in the past the garrison had warning of the attack because it came overland. They had the time to stock the store huts. We've had no warning and we've scarcely got enough to last us three weeks, much less if we give refuge to the inhabitants of the vill down there.'

He nodded in the other direction towards the collection of huts, church, thegn's hall and, further away, isolated farmsteads that made up the vill that shared the name of Bebbanburg.

'You can't think of refusing them sanctuary, surely?' Leoflaed asked as she joined them.

His wife was the sister of the local thegn and she had grown up amongst the families who lived in the shadow of the fortress.

'No, of course not,' Catinus said swiftly to reassure her. 'I was merely highlighting the paucity of our supplies if we are besieged.

In fact he had been toying briefly with the idea of letting the local people fend for themselves before he realised that wouldn't be acceptable to either Leoflaed or those of his warriors who had families living in the vill.

'Is there no chance that they are headed further north?' Ruaidhrí asked.

'I doubt it very much. Where would they be headed in such strength? There must be a thousand men, more if some of those ships are knarrs. Not Lindisfarne; it's a holy shrine to Saint Aidan and that protects it, even if its status as a monastery isn't enough by itself. What lies to the north? Lothian? Capturing the northernmost province of the kingdom wouldn't be as significant as taking Bebbanburg. Besides both Dùn Èideann and Dùn Barra are formidable strongholds, both of which he'd find just as difficult to capture as here. No, this is Alchfrith's target.'

'I'll call everyone to arms.' Eadstan said, heading back down the ladder.

'And send messengers to the vill, to Alweo as he is the closest ealdorman, and to the king at Eoforwīc,' Catinus told him.

After he'd departed Catinus kissed his wife on the cheek.

'You had better go and inform the reeve. He'll need to find room for the people from the vill and their animals and then plan to husband our supplies for as long as possible.'

'Huh, it would be easier to do it myself.'

She regarded the new reeve as incompetent and a ditherer. She would have to take charge herself if anything was to get done.

'He's going to be more of a hindrance to me than a help. You need to get rid of him and find someone better.'

Her husband nodded. He knew he should have done it earlier but he'd kept him on in respect to his father, who had been the reeve for decades before he died a few years ago.

Once everyone had departed, Catinus and the young sentry watched as the ships sailed past the fortress and turned into Budle Bay just along the coast to the north.

The ealdorman and the sentry grinned at each other. Alchfrith had timed his arrival badly. The tide was out and they'd get stuck fast in the mud just under the surface of the water. They wouldn't be able to float off and make it to the beach before the middle of the night. If they tried to wade ashore before then his men, especially those in chainmail byrnies, would get bogged down in the heavy, cloying mud. At least Catinus had until dawn to get ready.

~~~

Ragenhere had been persuaded to accompany Alchfrith as his chaplain when he crossed the sea to invade Northumbria, but he did so unwillingly. He was well aware that his elder brother Wilfrid, Bishop of Northumbria, was backing Alchfrith's attempt to seize the throne and he wondered what Ecgfrith would do if he found out. Exile would probably be the mildest punishment his brother could hope for.

As the unwilling channel of communication between the two, he was also vulnerable to a charge of treason. In his case exile would be unlikely; Ecgfrith wouldn't be too worried about upsetting the Pope or the archbishop if he executed a priest, brother of a bishop or not. He would probably be quietly disposed of. He was convinced that Ecgfrith was going to win the struggle for the throne – he was more competent and a stronger character for a start - and Ragenhere got more and more worried about his future.

He agonised over the problem all night, tossing and turning unable to sleep, much to the annoyance of the others he was sharing a tent with. They were used to their companions snoring and farting but restlessness was somehow worse. When he eventually went outside at three o'clock in the morning someone gave an ironic cheer.

The night was clear and the hills around the bay were bathed in the silvery light of the new moon. The wind had died down and now a gentle breeze caressed his face and helped to calm him.   As he stood there looking across the bay his indecision faded away and he started to walk towards the north.

'Who's that? Where are you going at this time of night?'

The gruff voice speaking Franconian startled him; he'd forgotten that there would be sentries patrolling the perimeter.

'Er, I need to have a crap.'

It was the only reason he could think of for leaving the camp.

'Well, don't go too far. Those bastards in the fortress could have patrols out.'

'Good point, thank you.'

He went to squat a little distance away but in sight of the sentry, who spat in disgust and turned away. As soon as he did, Rægenhere got up and quickly made his way towards the road that led to Bebbanburg. Half an hour later he'd reached the sea gate, guided there by the torch that burned in front of it to illuminate anyone approaching.

'Who's there? Show yourself or you'll get an arrow in your chest.'

'I'm a priest, Father Rægenhere. I've come to see Ealdorman Catinus.'

'Wait there. If this is a trick to get us to open the gate so it can be rushed you'll be the first one to die.'

'No trick. I'm on my own.'

'Stand by the torch then, where we can see you, and wait there.'

Rægenhere bit his lip in his anxiety until he tasted blood. He stopped, trying to compose himself.

One of the two gates opened a foot and two men came and unceremoniously yanked him inside as the gate slammed shut again.

'I'm Catinus,' a voice said out of the darkness. What does Wilfrid's brother and Alchfrith's chaplain want with me?'

'Can we go somewhere private, lord, and I'll explain.'

'Are you an emissary, Rægenhere? If so, you're wasting my time. There is nothing Alchfrith could offer me. I'm loyal to Ecgfrith.'

'No, not an emissary.'

'Check him to make sure he's unarmed.'

When one of the gate guards had done so without finding anything, Catinus told him to follow him and he set off uphill towards his hall. However, instead of taking him inside, he turned left before they got there and entered the small timber church.

The only illumination came from the sanctuary candle and, as Catinus stood near it, its pale light lit half his face, making it look like a disembodied ghost's head.

'Well, why am I missing my sleep?'

'I don't want any part in this mad escapade of Prince Alchfrith's. In my humble opinion it's doomed to failure. Oh, he has some support amongst the nobles, but not enough, and those who do favour him do so clandestinely. In the main they'll wait and see, not take sides openly.'

'You're not telling me anything I hadn't already guessed. You still haven't explained why you've come to see me.'

'I don't want any part of it. I'm loyal to Ecgfrith too. When I became Alchfrith's chaplain he was King of Deira. I went with

22

him into exile willingly but I draw the line at what he's doing now.'

'Forgive me, Father, if I don't entirely believe you. I suspect that you have concluded that you've chosen the losing side and want to jump ship to save your own skin.'

Catinus couldn't see Rægenhere's face turn red in the darkness but he sensed that he'd hit the mark.

'I'm not blaming you,' he continued, 'but you'll need to do more than just join us. I want to know Alchfrith's strength, how good his warriors are and what he intends to do.'

'Yes, I understand. Very well, I'll tell you all I know.'

'Good. In that case, welcome to Bebbanburg Rægenhere. I don't know about you but I need my sleep these days. We'll talk again in the morning. I'll show you to the priest's hut. You can sleep there tonight.'

~~~

Rægenhere confirmed what Catinus had guessed: Alchfrith had twelve hundred men with him, all Frankish mercenaries except for his own gesith. Some were experienced warriors with the scars to prove it but over half were youths, full of bravado but with little or no experience of fighting.

But he did have one piece of information that caused Catinus concern. He claimed that Alchfrith had men inside the fortress who would open the gates to let his army in.

'Who are these men? I know most of the garrison personally and they have been with me for some time. Even the young warriors and those still under training grew up here.'

'Are there none who joined you recently?'

'No, not really. Not in the last year certainly.'

'What about the local inhabitants who you gave refuge to?'

Catinus thought for a moment. He knew most of them but not all. It was possible that enemy agents had slipped in with them he supposed. The people who would know them all were Leoflaed and her brother, Bryce.

'Can you and Bryce check them without arousing suspicion and let me know if there are any who you don't recognise,' he asked her. 'Alchfrith would hardly have used Franks so they must be members of his gesith, so be careful.'

'There's one family who claim to have been travelling south who nobody knows,' she told him later. 'They said that they were pilgrims who had visited the shrine to Saint Aidan on Lindisfarne.'

'A family? Not just men?'

'Bryce said that there were two brothers, two older boys and a woman.'

'I suspect we've found our infiltrators then. The woman could be a slave or just someone brought along as cover.'

'What will you do?'

'I'm not sure. I don't understand why they haven't made their move before this. Alchfrith can't want to spend more time than necessary besieging us; it just gives Ecgfrith more time to muster his army. For now let's just keep an eye on them.'

The reason for Alchfrith's delay became obvious the next afternoon when another army appeared over the crest in the ridge to the west. At first Catinus and the garrison were elated, thinking it was Alweo with a relief force, but many of his men would be mounted and only a few of the new arrivals had horses. Furthermore, he wouldn't have been able to raise so many in such a short time.

As the host came closer Catinus recognised the banner being carried amongst the leading riders and his heart sank. This wasn't, as he'd hoped, a relief force who'd come to reinforce him; they were the warriors of Rheged. This was the province of Northumbria which lay to the west, sandwiched between Mercia in the south and the Caledonian kingdom of Strathclyde in the north. Oswiu had been Alchfrith's father but his mother, now long dead, had been his first wife, Rhieinmelth, the last of the royal house of Rheged. The new arrivals had evidently come to join her son.

~~~

'Alchfrith's agents are on the move,' Ruaidhrí said a trifle breathlessly as he rushed into the ealdorman's hall, his face flushed with excitement. 'Just the men and the youths, not the woman.'

He had just turned twenty but, despite one or two harrowing experiences, he seemed to have retained the irrepressible youthfulness that Catinus had taken an immediate liking to when they had first met in Ulster nine years ago.

Catinus had estimated the number of besiegers at some three thousand and he had expected an attack for the last two nights. However, this was the first night when the moon had been hidden by clouds.

'Good. Time for us to finalise our little surprise for Alchfrith. Go and tell Eadstan.' He paused. 'And Ruaidhrí.'

'Yes, lord?'

'No need to run.'

The young man grinned and walked quickly out of the hall.

'Where do you think the woman is?' Leoflaed asked.

'Probably lying dead in their tent, if she was just a slave they were using to give credence to their cover story. I suppose it's just as well to check.'

After he had sent one of the sentries on duty outside the hall to confirm his suspicion he walked unhurriedly towards the north gate - the main entrance to the fortress. It was wider that the sea gate and was the obvious entrance for an enemy to storm. However, he had a surprise up his sleeve for the attackers.

'Good evening Eadstan. Everything going to plan?'

'Yes, the gate guard have been withdrawn and the four infiltrators have nearly reached the gate.'

Catinus nodded and climbed the short flight of steps onto the mound where the stronghold's small church stood. The east side of the mound had been cut away and the earth was held back by a stone retaining wall, along the inner side of which a walkway ran. Below the wall was the paved roadway that led from the outer gates, sloping upwards to join the plateau containing the church and the ealdorman's hall after a distance of a hundred yards.

Outside this roadway stood a double palisade – the inner was four feet from the outer and a walkway ran between the two. Anyone entering the fortress would therefore have to make their way along the roadway between the wall on one side and the double palisade on the other.

In doing so they would have to run the gauntlet of arrows, rocks and any other missiles the defenders could throw at them. If they were in sufficient numbers they would eventually reach the open area at end of the entrance road, albeit at the cost of significant casualties. Once there Bebbanburg would inevitable fall. There was no way that Catinus could hold it with the enemy inside the fortress, outnumbered as he would be by perhaps thirty to one.

He had seen this as soon as he first arrived as custos of the fortress and he'd taken steps to correct the weakness in its defences. His improvement had never been put to the test for real, though it had occasionally been checked to ensure it would work if ever needed.

The puzzled agents – two brothers and their sons who were, as Catinus suspected, members of Alchfrith's gesith – couldn't understand why the gates were deserted. After checking the area, they lifted the two heavy bars and pulled the gates open. The approach road was even steeper than its continuation inside the gates. Consequently using a battering ram to break in wouldn't have been feasible.

They swung the heavy gates open one at a time and then one of them took the blazing torch from its sconce outside the gates and waved it to and fro three times. The four ran back inside the gates, no doubt anxious to get out of the way of the army which would come racing in through the entrance any minute now.

They didn't get very far before they ran into half a dozen of Catinus' warband. The roadway was illuminated by torches spluttering in sconces high up above them. Three of the warriors charged with their shields held before them, knocking the agents aside, before turning around so that the four were surrounded by fully armed men whilst they only carried daggers. A minute later the last one died just as the leading group of Alchfrith's men reached the open gates.

The six warriors fled back up the roadway. At the end they ran through the curious structure that Catinus had installed. It consisted of two very tall tree trunks that looked like ships' masts with a length of palisade secured in mid-air between the top half of the masts.

What few realised was that the length of palisade was held in place by two stout chains, the lower ends of which ended in two small huts at the base of the masts. These were kept locked in order to conceal the windlasses they contained. Now their doors were open and, as soon as the six men had run past, the windlasses let out the chains slowly and the length of palisade descended until it rested on the roadway.

Secured in place by the two stout masts behind each end, it blocked the exit from the roadway which had now become a killing zone. As the invaders ran into the fortress those in the lead realised the danger, but those behind them, eager to kill, rape and plunder, crowded in until the press of men was a solid mass. Those still trying to get through the outer gates didn't realise what the delay was and, in their eagerness, they pushed all the harder at their fellows in front of them.

Then the killing began. Arrows, spears and javelins rained down on the trapped men from Frankia and Rheged. Some of the former wore chain mail or thick leather jerkins but few of the latter possessed them. Panic set in as men died and more were crushed to death, unable to move. Then rocks rolled down chutes set at intervals along the wall and the palisade above them, each one pulverising scores to death.

Finally word reached those at the rear about the trap that they'd fallen into and the pressure suddenly eased as the rearmost ranks stopped pushing and fled down the hill. Those still alive inside the killing zone picked their way over the piles of corpses whilst still being bombarded with arrows and spears before they too disappeared back into the darkness.

'How many dead?' Catinus asked Eadstan the next morning.

'Three hundred and seventy two.'

'And wounded?'

'None. The throats of those still alive were cut during the night.'

Catinus grimaced. The bodies would have been looted of any armour, weapons, silver arm rings and anything else of value they might have been wearing or carrying. It wasn't surprising that the wounded would have been killed in the process. No doubt fingers would have been cut off to get at rings too.

The two men walked down to the gate accompanied by Rægenhere, who had been invited along to see if he could identify anyone. The corpses had been dragged outside the gates and laid out along the hillside for the enemy to come and reclaim for burial.

'Most of the dead are the Franks I think, though it's difficult to be sure as they've been stripped of everything except for tunics and trousers. The Britons of Rheged don't wear ribbons tied around their lower legs though, and most of these do.'

'Do you see anyone you recognise?'

'He was one of the Frankish captains and so was he,' the priest replied.

29

'I suppose it's too much to hope that Alchfrith is one of the dead?' Eadstan asked.

'No, I can't see him. It's not his style to be at the forefront of the fighting though. He'd have waited until the fortress was secured before venturing inside.'

Catinus went back inside and climbed back up to the top of the watchtower. He studied the enemy encampment and smiled grimly when he saw most of the Franks were taking down their tents prior to heading back to the ships. They'd evidently had enough. Mercenaries expected to suffer some casualties, but to lose a third of their number in a single night was not what they had signed up for.

As he watched Alchfrith appeared from his tent and appeared to be arguing with one of the Franks, presumably their leader. The man brushed past the erstwhile prince, who stamped his foot in frustration.

Even more encouragingly, the warband and fryd from Rheged also started to dismantle their camp. Catinus wouldn't want to be in their shoes. The mercenaries could sail back to Frankia, enlist with another leader and be safe from Ecgfrith's reprisals; not so the Britons from Rheged, unless they too fled abroad.

By mid-afternoon the only sign that Bebbanburg had been under siege was the mud and detritus where the camp had been and the unburied bodies by the main gates. Even Alchfrith and his gesith had fled westwards. Catinus sent four of his best scouts to track them and see where they went whilst he set about organising every available man to dig a deep pit. The bodies were covered in oil and burned and then covered in quick-lime before being covered over with earth.

The burial of the dead had been unpleasant work and a sombre mood descended on the fortress. The thegn and his people went back to repair the damage done by the invaders to their homes and recover the livestock they had taken up into the hills whilst Leoflaed told the reeve to get the roadway by the gate washed clean of blood. Even so the stench of death seemed to hang over the area until heavy rains completed the job.

Three days after Alchfrith had left Ecgfrith arrived with Alweo and a hundred and fifty mounted warriors.

'You seem to have managed very well without me, Catinus.'

'Thank you, Cyning. However, it wasn't difficult once we realised that there were enemy agents in our midst. I'm most grateful to Rægenhere for making me aware of the plot.'

'Rægenhere? Wilfrid's brother? I thought he was Alchfrith's chaplain.'

'He was, but he argued with him when he knew he was attempting to seize the throne.'

It was embroidering the truth somewhat but he owed the priest that much at least.

'I see. Well it seems that I too am in his debt in that case. I'll have to see what I can do for him as he is presumably now without employment.'

Catinus thought that, like many powerful men, he made promises he fully intended to keep but then forgot. He was therefore pleasantly surprised later on when Rægenhere was given the post of prior at a new monastery that Ecgfrith had decided to pay for at Jarrow.

Four days after the king arrived Catinus' scouts returned.

'Cyning, your brother had fled north into Pictland.'

31

'Where exactly?'

'King Drest told us that he had refused him sanctuary and that he's now sought refuge with Bruide, King of Penntir.'

'Catinus, you and your man Ruaidhrí know Penntir well. I want you to go there and demand that Bruide sends me Alchfrith's head.'

'Cyning, I spent two years on Lindisfarne with Bruide and I was his closest councillor when he became king. He's ambitious, totally ruthless and reacts badly to threats. If Catinus and I go there to demand your brother's head, it'll be ours that Bruide sends back to you.' Ruaidhrí said before Catinus could respond.

'What do you suggest then? I cannot rule with the threat that he may repeat his attempt to seize the throne hanging over me.'

'Offer to pay him for your brother,' suggested Catinus.

'Yes, that might work; not that I want Alchfrith back alive, just his head will suffice. It was your suggestion so you can take the offer to Bruide.'

~~~

When he had left four years before, Catinus had hoped that he would never ever see the jetty at Kinneddar again; yet here he was back once more. Uurad, his body servant, viewed the place with mixed feelings. He had been born and spent the first dozen years of his life there. However, his family had fled with the rest of the fisher folk when King Morleo of Ardewr and Ruaidhrí had escaped from Bruide's clutches.

Morleo had returned with help from King Oswiu and regained his kingdom from Bruide, something that was hardly likely to endear Oswiu's successor to him.

The place was even more run down than when Ruaidhrí had last seen it. There was one knarr tied up to the jetty and a few fishing boats on the nearby beach but there were few people about, and those that were visible disappeared as soon as the birlinn sailed into the river mouth and moored alongside.

The men he sent out came back to report that there were no horses to be had, only a few ponies. They would need those to carry equipment, so Catinus was forced to set out on foot for Bruide's capital at Elgin, six miles upriver. He was saddened to see that the prosperous settlement he had built when he was the regent during Bruide's minority had turned into the dilapidated ruins he now saw around him. He left the crew behind to guard the birlinn and set out with Uurad and his gesith for Elgin.

They had disembarked just after noon but it was mid-afternoon when they arrived near Elgin to find their progress barred by a warband of some fifty warriors.

'Who are you and what do you want?' a man standing in front of the Pictish warriors asked in a language that was like Hibernians Gaelic but which wasn't too dissimilar to the Brythonic tongue spoken in Strathclyde and Rheged.

'I'm Ealdorman Catinus, emissary of King Ecgfrith of Northumbria. You should remember me, Oengus, from when I ruled here during King Bruide's minority.'

'Eorl Catinus? I wouldn't have recognised you. You look old now, your hair and your beard have turned grey.'

'It wasn't that many years ago, Oengus, but I grant you that my hair is turning white now. I'm no longer an eorl but an ealdorman.'

'I don't understand the difference but it's good to see you again; whether my cousin Bruide will be as pleased to see you is another matter. I take it, as you come here as the representative of Ecgfrith, that it's about his half-brother Alchfrith?'

'He is here than?'

'Yes, worse luck. The man's a pain. He does nothing but complain about everything. If he doesn't like the way we Picts live he can piss off somewhere else,'

Catinus laughed and he followed Oengus through Elgin to the king's hall. The place hadn't changed much since he was last there. He'd seen pig sties that looked cleaner and smelt better.

However, Oengus' blunt comment about his aging appearance had troubled him. He was only forty two but he looked much older. His swarthy face was now lined and his cheeks were hollow, something his salt and pepper beard hid to some extent, but the overall impression was of gauntness. He'd lost weight too. His sons were only ten and six and he worried that he might die before one of them was old enough to inherit as Ealdorman of Bebbanburg.

He doubted now that it would be the eldest, Alaric. He made no secret of the fact that he wanted to be a monk. On the other hand Osfrid couldn't wait until he was old enough to start training as a warrior. If he was to be his father's heir Catinus would have to live another dozen years.

Bruide's welcome was less than friendly. He sat on a throne twice as big as he was on a platform raised six feet above the level of the rest of his hall. Access was via steps guarded by four warriors whose visible areas of skin were completely covered in tattoos. Most Pictish men had some, but not in such profusion. The area under the platform was curtained off and Catinus presumed that was the king's bedchamber.

The place stank of sweat, body odour, urine and stale beer. This was masked to some extent by the smoke from the central hearth which had failed to find an exit through the small hole in the roof.

'Catinus, I had hoped never to see you again.'

'Brenin, I come in peace as the emissary of King Ecgfrith. May we speak in private?'

'No, we may not. I have no secrets from my nobles and warriors.'

'It's a rather delicate matter concerning one of those present.'

'If you mean Alchfrith, say so. No doubt Ecgfrith wants me to kill his brother for him. How much is he prepared to pay?'

Catinus saw Alchfrith tense. He went to say something but evidently changed his mind.

'I've brought a chest of silver with me, Brenin.'

Two of his gesith carried a small chest and put it down at Catinus' feet.

'Silver or gold?'

'Silver,' Catinus replied surprised.

It was the common precious metal in use; gold was available but its use as currency was rare. It was mainly reserved for jewellery and the ornamentation of other precious artefacts.

'What weight?'

'Fifty pounds, Brenin.'

'Not enough. Two hundred is my price.'

'I fear that is all I'm authorised to pay you and all I have brought with me.'

'Then you had better send for more.'

Catinus stood there, uncertain whether the audience was over.

'Well what are you waiting for? Get out.'

'Are you not offering us hospitality?'

'No, why should I? I didn't invite you here. You can camp outside Elgin, but you had better have left to get the rest of the silver by the time I get up in the morning.'

When Catinus had left Bruide turned to Alchfrith.

'Don't worry. When, or perhaps if, he comes back with more silver I'll up the price again for keeping me waiting.'

Alchfrith smiled wanly, not at all convinced that Bruide wouldn't sell him to his brother eventually. He was beginning to realise that taking refuge with him had been a bad idea.

That night he got drunk in an effort to forget his problems. Perhaps he should have paid attention to the youth who kept topping up his goblet with more and more ale, but he was too absorbed in thought.

~~~

Uurad helped the drunken Alchfrith to a quiet corner of the hall near the door. It wasn't a popular spot to sleep because of the draught so they had the area to themselves. He was fifteen now and no one who had known him when he was twelve would have recognised the runt he was then as the brawny youth of today.

As soon as the hall grew quiet, except for the inevitable night time sounds made by a dormitory of single men, Uurad cautiously unsheathed his dagger. He'd already undone Alchfrith's fancy short cloak and laid it between them. If the prince felt the dagger's point as it entered his throat, he gave no sign. Uurad had sharpened it especially and it took less than a second to cut through one of his carotid arteries and his windpipe.

Alchfrith made no sound and Uurad used the cloak to soak up the sudden outrush of blood from his neck. It soon ceased when his heart stopped. It took him a lot longer to cut surreptitiously through the spine, sinews, muscles and other blood vessels in the neck but eventually the head rolled clear of the torso.

Uurad wrapped it in the blood stained cloak and made for the door. Luckily no one stirred as he opened it and slipped outside.

The two sentries outside turned as he emerged between them.

'Gonna puke,' Uurad told them in a slurred voice as he staggered down the steps.

One of the sentries sniffed the air as he passed them.

'What's that smell,' he asked.

'Smells sort of metallic,' the other replied.

'It's blood!'

By then it was too late. The boy had disappeared into the darkness. They thought of chasing after him but they would be whipped if they left their post, so they did nothing. It was a decision that would cost them their lives in the morning when Bruide found out what had happened.

'Who's there?' the sentry outside Catinus' camp challenged him.

'Me, Uurad. I've got a little present for the ealdorman.'

'What are you doing out of the camp?'

'Making sure we don't go back empty handed.'

'Go on then.'

'Lord, wake up.'

'What is it? Oh, it's you Uurad. What do you mean by rousing me in the middle of the night?'

'We need to get out of here, and quickly.'

'Why? What's happened?'

The boy didn't reply but unwrapped the bundle he was carrying.

Catinus stared at the gory head with its matted hair and sightless eyes uncomprehendingly for a second or to, then leapt to his feet.

'Alchfrith's head! How did you get that?'

'Cut it from his body,' Uurad replied, grinning.

'Well done, lad. You can tell me about it later but, you're right, we need to get moving back to Kinneddar. Go and tell Eadstan to get the men ready to depart, silently mind.'

'What about the tents and the supplies?'

'We'll have to leave them behind. The ponies too. Tell the men to bank up the fires at bit. I want it to look as if we are still here. It's five hours until dawn; by then we should be back on board the birlinn.'

When Bruide found out what had happened he was apoplectic with rage and swore to have his revenge on Catinus and Ecgfrith.

Chapter Two – The Battle of the Two Rivers

671 AD

Catinus and Leoflaed were visiting Alweo and their daughter, Hereswith for the baptism of the latter's first child and the former's first grandchild when the summons from Ecgfrith arrived. The baby boy had just been named Æthelbald and was being dipped into the river by Alweo's chaplain when the messenger rode up. The letter he carried was for Alweo as Catinus' would have gone to Bebbanburg.

Greetings,

I have dire tidings from north of the River Twaid. It seems that Drest, High King of the Picts, has played me false. Despite re-assuring me that he recognised my title to the Kingdom of Prydenn, he has invaded and slaughtered my vice regulus, Eorl Hunwald, and his warband at Dùn Dè. At the same time he, or perhaps Bruide, has invaded Ardewr and I'm reliably informed that they have killed its king, Morleo.

As if that was not bad enough, it seems that Drest and Bruide have embarked on a deliberate campaign to murder all Anglo-Saxons living in Pictland. I gather that Conomultus, Bishop of Abernethy, was only spared because he was a Briton by birth.

This means that between them these two now rule most of the Land of the Picts. They are strong enough now to threaten

both Lothian across the Firth of Forth and also Strathclyde. I
have written to King Elfin asking him to mobilise the men of
Strathclyde and to meet me and our army at Stirling, which
thankfully my garrison still holds.

My priority this summer had been to teach Rheged a lesson
for supporting my brother Alchfrith against me, but that will
have to wait. The Picts take priority.

Muster your horsemen and your fyrd and make all haste to
Stirling.

Ecgfrith,
King of Northumbria and Bretwalda of the North

'It's a proud claim to have succeeded Oswiu as bretwalda
but, by the sound of it, only Strathclyde and perhaps Dalriada
recognise him as such,' Alweo said after handing the letter to
Catinus to read. 'At least it sounds as if your brother is safe.'

'Yes, but for how long once we invade?'

'Hopefully he'll have the sense to go back to Iona.'

'I hope so.'

Catinus was deeply troubled by this turn of events. Not
only was he concerned for his brother but, if the Picts invaded,
Lothian could be lost. The Britons who lived in what used to be
called Goddodin had revolted against rule by the Angles in the
past. If Lothian was lost it would bring a hostile frontier down
as far as the Twaid, and that was only thirty or so miles north of
Bebbanburg.

As a reward for bringing him his brother's head, Ecgfrith had
given him the title to the fortress. Although it was his home,
officially it had been a royal stronghold and Catinus was merely

its custos. There had been nothing to stop the king installing another custos there at any time. It wouldn't have affected his status as an ealdorman but he would have had to build a new home somewhere else on his lands. He hadn't thought it likely in his lifetime, but it was far from certain that one of his sons would have become custos when he died. Now his son would inherit it and hold it in his own right.

Uurad had also been rewarded. Ecgfrith had given him a silver arm ring and Catinus had done the same, as well as making him a member of his warband. He had been sorry to lose him as a body servant, especially as he'd got rid of his replacement within the first week. He was idle, sullen and had a habit of never being around when Catinus needed him. He'd ended up becoming a kitchen boy instead, a fate few would have envied.

Now he had an orphan who Uurad had found for him. His name was Drefan, which meant trouble, but he was far from that. Catinus was dubious at first as the boy was only nine but he was eager to please and desperate to be his body servant as his mother had recently died, leaving him destitute. He had no idea who his father was.

They set off the next day to return home. It was not the best of days, a chill wind blew from the east and occasionally it pelted them with near horizontal rain. The road was no more than a muddy track which the recent rain had turned into a quagmire. By the time that they camped that night at Warren's Ford they were mud splattered, wet, tired and cold. Catinus was proud of his two sons. Eleven year old Alaric bore the discomfort stoically whilst his younger brother kept telling him that warriors had to suffer far worse hardship. Eventually

Alaric's patience with Osfrid wore thin and he dropped back to ride beside Drefan, who was leading two of the pack horses.

'Do you like serving my father?'

'Very much, and I'm not just saying that because you're his son. He's demanding but fair. Many masters are the former but few are the latter. He doesn't treat me like a chattel either.'

'A chattel?'

'Yes, someone he owns. Will you be going to Lindisfarne soon?' he asked, changing the subject.

'Yes, in the autumn. I can't wait to meet Brother Cuthbert.'

'I thought that Eata was the abbot.'

'He is, but it's Cuthbert who is the healer and the prophet. He even saved the life of King Oswiu years ago.'

Drefan was silent. Someone who could cure the sick and foretell the future sounded too incredible to be true. He didn't say so though. People in Northumbria worshipped Cuthbert and he would be ostracised, if not worse, if he expressed any doubts.

Catinus meanwhile was discussing the problem of replacing the reeve with Leoflaed. They had ridden a little ahead of the rest to avoid being overheard.

'I could dispense with his services but I don't like to leave you without support and I don't have the time to find a new one before I leave for Stirling.'

'So you don't think I'm capable of managing without a man to help me?'

'I didn't mean that.'

'I rather think you did. I'm also quite capable of finding a suitable replacement.'

'But it's my job to appoint the reeve!'

This discussion wasn't going the way either of them had intended. Catinus knew how capable Leoflaed was but he couldn't believe that she would manage on her own without male support.

'Fine; I'll do without until you get back, but we're not keeping that useless man in post until you do. I can assure you that I can cope quite well on my own.'

They rode the rest of the way to the campsite in a silence that was far from companionable.

~~~

Catinus arrived at Stirling with thirty mounted men and a hundred and twenty spearmen and archers. He and Leoflaed had maintained a slightly frosty relationship until the morning of his departure. When he awoke he turned to her and apologised and she burst into tears. After a bout of gentle love making he agreed that she should appoint the new reeve.

He told the old one brusquely that he'd failed to live up to expectations and he was to be gone by the end of the day. By the time that the astonished man had thought to question his dismissal Catinus had mounted his horse and was heading towards the gates.

He stopped beside Godwald, the aged warrior who now commanded the garrison and told him that he'd dismissed the reeve and he was to make sure that he'd left before the gates were shut at nightfall.

As he rode down the hill and followed the road to the west he was honest enough to admit to himself that he'd taken the coward's way out. He should have pointed out the reeve's shortcomings to him before this; that way his dismissal wouldn't have come as so much of a shock. He should have also given him more time to pack but he didn't want Leoflaed to have to cope with a surly reeve after his departure.

An hour after his small army had left the blue sky disappeared, replaced by ominously grey clouds and shortly after that the rain started. Strangely he welcomed the discomfort as penance for his reluctance to resolve the reeve situation properly.

Ecgfrith hadn't brought the nobles and warriors of Deira with him. He'd made his nine-year old brother, Ælfwine, Sub-king of Deira and left him under the guardianship of the Eorl of Elmet to defend the border with Mercia whilst he was away. The contingent from Rheged was also noticeable by its absence. The province was in turmoil by all accounts, fully expecting Ecgfrith to exact retribution for their support of Alchfrith.

Many of those who had taken part in the abortive siege of Bebbanburg had already fled with their families to Hibernia, where they'd taken service with several of the petty kings that littered the island as mercenaries. This had left Rheged with little enough manpower to look after the livestock and the crops and raids by the men of Strathclyde had taken advantage of the situation. For the moment Ecgfrith was disinclined to take these raids up with Elfin, whose support he was trying to enlist against Drest and Bruide.

'Catinus, I'm splitting your men up between Alweo, who's in charge of my horsemen, and Redwald the Hereræswa, who's in command of those on foot.'

'What does that leave me to do, Cyning?'

'I want you to go and see Elfin as you know each other well. He seems reluctant to join me and I want to know why. If he won't commit himself, then you're to ensure he stays neutral. I don't want to find myself with an enemy at my back when I advance into Hyddir.'

'I understand Cyning. I assume that I may take my gesith with me?'

'Of course, although if you fail I can't see that twenty or so men will save you from Elfin's warband.'

Catinus cautiously approached Dùn Breatainn along the north bank of the River Clyde. Besides Eadstan and his gesith he had only brought Drefan and four other boys to serve the members of his gesith. Their tents, cooking utensils and provisions were carried on four packhorses led by the servants. It had taken them two days from Stirling, staying at the monastery founded by Saint Mungo near Glaschu overnight. No doubt the abbot had sent a messenger to Elfin to warn him of Catinus' approach because he found a welcoming party awaiting him at Dùn Tochter, a small fort five miles from Dùn Breatainn at a point where the Clyde estuary narrowed to become the river.

'It's good to see you again Catinus; that is, if you come in peace?'

'I do indeed Lulach. I'm pleased to see you too.'

Lulach had been one of those who had captured Dùn Breatainn with him, Elfin and Lethlobar of Ulster when they'd killed the previous King of Strathclyde.

The two men rode together under the pleasant afternoon sunshine and Catinus tried to ignore the incessant biting insects that swarmed around them now that there was no wind to blow them away.

'This is a bad business; about Drest I mean. He seems intent on uniting the Picts into one nation. That's not good news for us either.'

'Hmmm, I'm not so sure that it's Drest's idea. I suspect that Bruide's behind him pulling the strings.'

'You think so? Well you know Bruide better than we do. The rumour is that he's killed Morleo of Ardewr as well as your Eorl of Prydenn.'

'I believe that to be more than rumour. Excluding Cait, which is too far north to bother much about, that means he now controls more of Pictland than Drest does.'

When they arrived at Elfin's fortress his gesith set about camping on the shore of the Clyde whilst Lulach escorted Catinus and Eadstan up to meet King Elfin.

'Brenin, greetings,' he said in the Brythonic language. 'I rejoice at seeing you in good health. I come at the behest of King Ecgfrith. I suspect that Lulach has already briefed you on what I know about the current situation in the Land of the Picts so I won't waste time on repeating it.'

Elfin laughed. 'You've become more of a diplomat since I last saw you, but you still don't waste time on small talk.'

Catinus frowned. 'I'm a warrior not an envoy, though I seem to be used as one more and more. I assure you it is not of my seeking.'

'No, perhaps not, but you make a good one. I hear that if you are denied what you ask for you just take it anyway. What did Ecgfrith do with his brother's head by the way?'

Catinus blushed. It seems the tale of Alchfrith's death had even reached Elfin's ears.

'He buried it in the graveyard at Bebbanburg.'

'At least part of him had a Christian burial then. I hear that Bruide fed the body to his dogs.'

'Sometimes such stories are apocryphal but it sounds typical of Bruide; to vent his anger at being deprived of a valuable hostage in that way I mean.'

'Quite. Now I assume that Ecgfrith didn't send you all this way to discuss his late brother?'

'No, Brenin. As you will have guessed, he intends to advance into Hyddir and Pobla and bring Drest to battle. He must be made to pay for his actions against us. He hopes that you may join him in this enterprise.'

'And Dalriada too?'

'I have no instructions about Dalriada.'

'So he's not bothered to enlist Mael Duin's support? I think that's an error if he intends to claim to be Bretwalda of the North, as his father was.'

'You think he should?'

'It ensured peace on Oswiu's northern border for most of the time he was on the throne of Northumbria. I valued the security and prosperity it brought me. However, it has probably run its course. If what you say about Bruide is true, he seeks chaos and conflict as a means of increasing his own power.'

'Does that mean that you'll bring your army to join Ecgfrith at Stirling?'

'What does Ecgfrith hope to gain from this war?'

'To defeat Drest and secure his northern border, no more.'

'I have a border with Hydirr in the north-west and Uunnid in the north-east. I will advance through these two kingdoms as far as Stirling but no further, provided that Ecgfrith will allow me to keep the land I conquer. It will give me a buffer between my people and Pictland.'

'I have no authority to agree such terms, Elfin.'

'Then go back to Ecgfrith and return when you have the authority.'

'And if he says no?'

'Then I shall probably take the land anyway.'

'That would be a mistake. Even the suggestion is likely to antagonise him.'

'Then I leave it to your diplomatic skills to phrase it more acceptably.'

~~~

'Did he say what he would do if I refused his terms?' Ecgfrith asked.

It was the question that Catinus had been dreading.

'There is nothing to stop him taking the lands anyway. After you defeat Drest the Picts will be in no position to contest his encroachment, and I suspect you might not want to go to war over the issue.'

'You suppose correctly. Of course, it would be a different matter if he had openly threatened to annex the land.'

Catinus studiously avoided meeting the king's eye. Ecgfrith was no fool and he was grateful that Catinus had found a way to phrase it so that it didn't become a matter of dispute.

'Very well, I agree, but only as far as Endrick Water and the Carron Valley. The rest of Hyddir, Uuynnid and the whole of Pobla will become mine.'

Catinus returned to Elfin the next day and he accepted the limitation, albeit unwillingly. As a token of good faith he lent Catinus fifty of his most experienced warriors, all mounted, but on hill ponies. They could move more swiftly than a man on foot, but they would be no use as cavalry.

Nevertheless, Ecgfrith allocated them to Alweo and Catinus joined him as his second-in-command. With his gesith, this brought the total of mounted warriors up to over a hundred and fifty.

The past week had been fine, although the sun had been obscured by white clouds for much of the time. On the day that the army broke camp to march up Strathallan towards the head of the Firth of Tay the weather deteriorated. A cold wind swept down the glen from the north east bringing with it gusts of rain and even the odd shower of hailstones. Although it was only the beginning of autumn it felt more like the start of winter.

Catinus wrapped his cloak around the lower half of his face and pulled the hood down as far as possible over his eyes. He was wearing his leather arming cap but his helmet hung from his saddle and he wore his shield slung on his back. Normally Drefan would have carried both helmet and shield on his pony until they were required, but today he had a feeling he might need them urgently.

Alweo had sent six men ahead to scout and another six rode along each slope of the hills lining the glen. It was their job to make sure that the main body weren't ambushed. They had reported seeing Picts shadowing the army's progress from the crest line above them but there had been no attempt to attack them – so far.

Thankfully the weather had improved as the day wore on, and although the sky overhead remain grey, there was no more rain or hail and the wind had moderated.

They were half way along Strathallan, heading for the junction with Strathearn, when their advance was blocked by a sizable body of Picts. The muddy track they were following crossed a river known as Allan Water via a shallow ford at that point and their enemy had taken up a position on the far side of the river.

'How many of them are there,' Ecgfrith asked Catinus when the latter had ridden back to tell him.

'No more than a thousand. Alweo and I suspect that there are more hidden somewhere waiting to descend on our flanks as soon as we are committed to attacking the lot blocking the ford.'

'He's got scouts out looking for them?'

'Yes, but they need to proceed carefully or they risk riding into a trap.'

'Good. We'll wait here until we know more.'

'In that case it may be a good idea to deploy flank guards, Cyning.'

'Very well, Redwald, will you see to it?'

The hereræswa nodded brusquely and left. He resented being told to do the blindingly obvious. He watched Catinus mount up and ride back to the vanguard with narrowed eyes. He was one of those who thought that the late king had raised Catinus too high, though he had never said so. Now the wretch had made him look as if he didn't know his job. It was time the jumped-up Briton was taught a lesson. It was a decision which was to have dire consequences.

An hour later Alweo's scouts returned.

'They're waiting for us in the Glen of the Eagles, lord,' they told him. 'About two thousand of them.'

'As we suspected, thank you.'

Catinus wasn't a fool; he realised that he shouldn't have suggested putting out flank guards. He knew that Redwald would have taken it as an insult; it was something he'd have done automatically once they'd halted. Catinus had a plan but he was sure that it would be more acceptable to the proud Redwald if it came from Alweo. So this time his friend rode back to talk to Ecgfrith and his hereræswa.

Unseen from the Picts blocking the river crossing, Redwald led half of the spearmen up the re-entrant to their right. It took them up behind the hill between them and the waiting Picts in the Glen of the Eagles. Meanwhile Alweo and Catinus led the horsemen back the way they had come to cross Allan Water two miles further down Strathallan. The king took command of the rest of the footmen, including the archers, and sited the latter where they could see their foes on the opposite bank of the river and the entrance to the Glen of the Eagles.

To spring the trap a fire was lit on the summit of the mountain behind which Redwald waited with his men. As soon as they saw it, he led them to the saddle between two hills and down the Glen of the Eagles. The surprised Picts panicked when they realised that their ambush had been foiled and, instead of turning to face the onrushing Northumbrians, they fled down the glen.

As soon as they came within range of Ecgfrith's archers volley after volley of arrows darkened the skies and score of the routed Picts fell dead or wounded. Those behind the leaders tripped over the bodies and chaos resulted. Then Redwald's men hit them in the rear.

The other body of Picts, seeing their comrades' plight, started to cross the river to go to their aid. That was when Alweo's horsemen charged into their right flank. They speared as many as they could before the Picts recovered and started to form a line facing them. The horsemen disengaged and then charged again, this time throwing their spears at the Picts and wheeling away.

Suddenly a horn blared forth over the noise of battle and the Picts started to disengage, running away to the north-east where the glen joined Strathearn. Ecgfrith had won an easy victory and he could have sent his men to chase the fleeing enemy, but dusk was approaching and it got dark quickly in the mountains.

Alweo looked for Catinus to congratulate him on the success of his plan but he couldn't see him. Then he spotted a group of men clustered around someone lying on the ground. It wasn't until he recognised the crowd gathered around the casualty that he became worried. They were all members of Catinus' gesith.

His friend had been hit by two arrows: one in the shoulder and one in the thigh. The former didn't look too serious but the thigh wound was bleeding copiously. It was only then that he realised that the arrows were not the type used by the Picts, who only had hunting bows. These were longer arrows that must have come from a war bow. It meant someone on their own side had tried to kill his friend.

~~~

Catinus gritted his teeth as the wounds in his shoulder and leg were dealt with. Both arrows had barbed heads which had to be cut out. Luckily the one in his leg had cut a vein rather than an artery but he had still lost quite a lot of blood before one of the infirmarians travelling with the army was brought to tend to him.

He was already feeling faint with the pain and, when the wounds were cauterised with a hot iron, he passed out. When he awoke the next morning he found the monk who had treated him examining his wounds.

'The wounds appear to be clean. You may limp when you recover but otherwise it's just a question of time. I'll get you a place on one of the waggons taking the other wounded back to Stirling.'

'You'll do nothing of the sort,' Catinus yelled at him. 'Get me my horse, I need to catch up with the army.'

Alweo had to leave him when Ecgfrith continued his advance at dawn but his gesith had stayed on the assumption that they would escort him and the convoy of casualties back down the glen.

'You are in no fit state to ride, lord,' the monk told him.

'Why? I don't need my leg to ride, or my shoulder, if my horse is led. Drefan, do as you're told boy; go and get my horse and tell Eadstan that we're leaving.'

'Yes lord.'

'You're too weak. If you try to ride you'll fall off.'

'Then one of my men can ride either side of me and make sure that I don't.'

'Well, if you won't listen to my advice I can't stop you being an idiot. Good day to you, lord.'

The first problem was getting him up on his horse. Eventually they made a seat from a log and some rope and hoisted him up using the branch of a nearby tree. He grimaced in pain and some blood seeped through the bandage on his thigh, but it wasn't until the horse started to walk that he realised that it just wasn't possible for him to ride very far. Eventually he had to settle for sitting in a small cart.

Meanwhile the rest of the army had reached the River Earn and had turned eastwards along the south bank. They were following a trail of abandoned equipment and Picts wounded on the previous day who had either been too weak to continue or who had died along the way.   This trail led Alweo and his vanguard to a ford over the Earn.

'They must be trying to escape along the west bank of the River Tay into the mountains,' Redwald said when Alweo told Ecgfrith about the ford. 'Cyning, if we send Alweo and his men north to hold the crossing over the River Almond the Picts will be forced to turn back. We can then trap them on the peninsular where the Earn enters the Firth of Tay.'

Neither Alweo nor Ecgfrith knew the geography of the area as well as Redwald evidently did, so he impatiently sketched a rough map in the earth with his sword.

'Here's where the Firth of Tay narrows and becomes the River Tay. The Earn enters the Tay at that point. Between the two rivers there is a triangular tongue of land about two miles wide narrowing down to a point at the junction. There is a small hill running east west which slopes down to the river on each side. If we can bottle up the Picts in this area we can annihilate them, especially if we can capture the high ground. But we need to act quickly or they'll get away.'

Alweo arrived at the ford over the Almond a few miles north of the River Earn and saw Picts streaming across it. However, only a few hundred had already crossed, judging by the numbers on the open plain to the north. Each of his men were riding double with an archer clinging on for dear life behind them. They charged across the ford, scattering the fleeing Picts and then turned and dismounted. His men formed a shield wall to hold the crossing whilst the archers strung their bows and sent several volleys into the packed mass of Picts now forming on the southern side of the ford.

The Picts significantly outnumbered the Northumbrians and, had they wanted to, they could have easily forced the crossing. But they were tired, dispirited and disorganised. They chose the path of least resistance instead and retreated back the way they had come. Those coming up behind them saw them retreating and, on being told that their enemies were holding the ford, also turned back.

Alweo harried them all the way to the Earn and, after they'd crossed onto the south bank, they found the Northumbrian army drawn up to the west of them. Rather than face them, they turned and headed east into the triangle formed by the Tay and the Earn.

Many were aware that they were being herded into a spit of land with no escape but their warnings went unheeded and they were swept along with the rest. King Drest finally managed to restore some form of order to his army once they could retreat no further and his men were hectored and bullied into a rough formation across the gap between the two rivers by their leaders. Unfortunately for the Picts, they had gone beyond the low hill onto the flat ground beyond and Ecgfrith was able to send his men to secure the hill.

It was now late in the day and Ecgfrith was anxious to finish this before his foes had the opportunity to use the darkness to escape. He sent his archers forward to fire into the Picts. Many of the latter had thrown away their shields during their flight and so had nothing with which to protect themselves. Most arrows therefore scored a hit and the more casualties they suffered, the more enraged the Picts became.

Finally their discipline broke and they charged forward in a disorganised mass to be met by an unyielding shield wall. Many more died in that reckless charge and, when they withdrew to reform, the Northumbrians advanced, pushing them backwards into the narrowing spit of land.

Some tried to escape by swimming across one of the two rivers and were swept away into the firth and drowned. The fight went out of the Picts and they started to surrender. Soon it was all over. There were over a thousand casualties amongst the Picts, as opposed to just a few hundred on the other side, and there were six hundred captives. One of the dead was Drest, High King of the Picts.

Redwald felt elated at their success and was being praised by Ecgfrith when Alweo arrived with a thunderous look on his face. His men held two archers between them who were struggling to get away.

'Cyning, you will be well aware that Ealdorman Catinus was badly wounded by two arrows during yesterday's battle. Those arrows came from our own archers. These two wretches to be precise. Several other archers saw them deliberately aim at Catinus and will swear to it.'

Ecgfrith looked as if someone had slapped him in the face. 'Our own men? Why would they do such a thing?'

'Because they were paid to do it.'

'Who would want to try and kill Catinus?'

'First, Cyning, ask whose men they are.'

The blood had drained from Redwald's face when Alweo had arrived with the two archers in tow but now he spoke up.

'If they were paid, it doesn't matter whose men they are, anyone could have bribed them.'

'You say that, Redwald, because they are your men.'

'Is this true?' Ecgfrith looked stunned.

'Catinus is no better than a serf and a Briton to boot. He has no right to be an ealdorman and be telling his betters what to do.'

'So you ordered him killed.'

'No, Cyning. They are good archers. They were told to wound him only, which is what they did.'

'The infirmarian saved his life. He would have died otherwise,' Alweo spluttered.

'It's not the point. You ordered your men to wound or kill another noble. The rest is irrelevant.'

Ecgfrith had a steely glint in his eye that Alweo hadn't seen before.

'As of now you are no longer my hereræswa and you will be deprived of your lands and property. You and your family will go into exile. You have three weeks to make the necessary arrangements.'

Redwald's jaw dropped open in disbelief.

'I have served you faithfully, and your father before you, for many years. You cannot do this to me.'

'I've just done it. And you will pay Catinus weregeld for his injuries.'

'Never!'

Redwald went to draw his sword but Alweo was too quick for him. As the hereræswa's hand grasped the hilt, the point of Alweo's seax ripped through the chainmail covering the man's belly and cut into his guts. Redwald collapsed onto the floor frantically trying to hold his intestines in place. It was no use; he would be dead in less than twenty minutes but his scream of agony brought men running to where he lay. Ecgfrith realised it was a dangerous situation. Redwald had been their commander for years and he was well liked.

'Redwald is a traitor,' he cried holding up his hands. 'He tried to kill me and Alweo saved me.'

'Why would he try and kill you, Cyning,' a man called out, voicing what many others were thinking.

'Because he paid these men to kill Ealdorman Catinus and, when I banished him, he went to draw his sword to attack me, an offence punishable by death. These men will attest to Redwald's guilt.'

'You will or you'll hang for sure,' Alweo whispered to them.

'It's true. Redwald paid us to kill Catinus.'

'Why?'

'No one seems to know; perhaps Catinus offended him in some way.'

'Who killed Redwald, Cyning?' another man asked.

'Ealdorman Alweo saved me.'

At that there was an angry buzz in the crowd. Alweo was popular with his own men but others, especially the older warriors, tended to remember that he was born a Mercian ætheling and that his father had been the hated Penda's brother.

Beornheth, Eorl of Lothian, stepped forward and looked down at the writhing Redwald.

'Cyning, the rogue is in his death throes. It little behoves us to prolong his agony needlessly. May I end it?'

'Thank you, Beornheth, I would be grateful.'

He drew his sword and thrust it into Redwald's neck. The former hereræswa twitched once and lay still. A sigh of relief went up from the watching crowd.

Several other eorls and ealdormen had forced their way through the crowd and now surrounded the young king.

'Cyning, no one doubts that Redwald deserved punishment for his actions and we would have supported his banishment, but did he deserve to die?' Beornheth asked. 'He hadn't actually drawn his sword, if I have understood matters correctly. Why didn't Alweo prevent him from doing so, if necessary by threatening him with his seax? Did he need to use it? Furthermore, he drew a weapon in your presence, which is forbidden.'

'I acted to save the king's life,' Alweo responded heatedly. 'If I'd waited to assess the necessity or otherwise of my actions King Ecgfrith would have been dead.'

'Stop!' The king's voice drowned out what was about to become a general argument with others joining in on one side or the other. 'We will continue this in my tent later when all eorls and ealdormen are present to form the Witan.'

Catinus limped into the tent leaning on a hastily made crutch. His bandaged shoulder and thigh were an eloquent testimony to the perfidy of Redwald. Many still didn't like the fact that he was not born a noble, or even an Anglo-Saxon, but they grudgingly admitted that he was a skilful military commander and had faithfully served Northumbria for nearly all his life.

The debate about Alweo's action in slaying Redwald was heated but the upshot was that Alweo was exiled. It was decision that Catinus took badly and he and Alweo took a ship back to Bebbanburg as soon as they could, leaving their men to make their way home overland. From Bebbanburg Alweo rode back to his home; a week later he, his wife and their baby son Æthelbald left with a few servants and those members of his gesith who had decided to continue to serve him and travelled to Towcester where he hoped to find his cousin, King Wulfhere of Mercia.

He wasn't sure of the welcome he would receive but he had no alternative.

Chapter Three – Æthelthryth

672 AD

Ecgfrith stayed in the Land of the Picts for the next three months. He annexed the former kingdoms of Hyddir, Pobla and Uuynnid and created two new eorldoms out of them, which he called Strathearn and Fife. He now had a buffer zone between Northumbria and the rest of the Land of the Picts. Elfin was also pleased as Strathearn also separated his kingdom from that of the Picts.

The one regret that Ecgfrith had was that Bruide had escaped and he had now managed to get himself recognised, not as High King, but as King of a single Kingdom of the Picts. In truth, there were no monarchs left to contest his rule over what had been Ardewr, Penntir and Prydenn. Only Cait in the north remained outside his control and its king seemed content to ignore what was happening in the south.

Details took time to trickle down to Eoforwīc, Ecgfrith's capital. Over time it emerged that Bruide had consolidated his control over the former three kingdoms of Ardewr, Penntir and Prydenn by dividing them into four regions, each governed by an eorl, except that wasn't the title the Picts used. They called them mormaers. The regions were called Atholl, Moray, Buchan and Angus. It was a clever move. It would be difficult now for anyone to claim the throne of one of the old kingdoms as it didn't exist anymore.

After the Battle of the Two Rivers, as the defeat of the Picts on the land between the Tay and the Earn was being called,

Ecgfrith had needed to make two new appointments; that of hereræswa and master of horse. He would have liked to make Catinus the former. He was a good commander and tactician but, even if he wasn't still recovering from his wounds, such an appointment would never be acceptable to the Witan. He therefore decided on Beornheth, the Eorl of Lothian.

Catinus would have been the obvious choice as master of horse too if it wasn't for his wounds. In the end his choice fell on Ruaidhrí. He also made him an ealdorman and gave him Alweo's old territory. Although he was a Hibernian, he was a prince and he was a popular choice.

The one problem the king was left with, at least for now, was his wife. Æthelthryth continued to spend more time in the monastery at Threekingham in her native East Anglia than she did at Eoforwīc. Even when she was with him she continued to refuse to allow him to sleep with her as husband and wife. This frustrated Ecgfrith beyond endurance, both because she was attractive and he desired her and because he needed an heir.

'Wilfrid, I insist you convince Æthelthryth that it is her Christian duty to lie with her husband. How can we have children if she doesn't? My patience is wearing extremely thin.'

The two men were sitting in Ecgfrith's private chamber in the king's hall at Eoforwīc. This had been extended since the new king had come to the throne and contained a small office as well as a sleeping room. It was in the office that they now sat with a brazier under the one window to take the chill off the bitter February air. The room had been designed better than most of its type. The window faced south so that the prevailing easterly wind sucked most of the smoke out of the room.

'I will do my best, Cyning, but the queen is very devout and sees fornication with anyone, including her husband, as a sin,' the Bishop of Northumbria replied.

'Well, it's up to you to convince her otherwise.'

Privately Wilfrid thought that, even if by some miracle he did persuade Æthelthryth to sleep with Ecgfrith, he wouldn't be able to sire an heir. He'd been having an affair with a girl called Eormenburg for a couple of years now and there was no sign of her getting pregnant.

'Very well, Cyning. I will travel to Threekingham and see what I can do.'

'You can tell her that, if she fails to return to me and carry out her proper duties as my wife, she must become a nun so that I can remarry.'

~~~

'That's what he said?'

'Yes, Síþwíf. Exactly that.'

'If I were to become a nun I would only do so as an abbess; that would mean that Ecgfrith would have to pay for me to found a new monastery.'

'I see. Where would you want this monastery to be?'

'At Ely in the Fens. Half the people there are still pagans and I would make it my life's work to convert them.'

Wilfrid returned to Eoforwīc only to find that Ecgfrith was no longer there. He'd gone to Bebbanburg to visit Catinus before travelling on to Dùn Èideann to see his new hereræswa, Beornheth.

The bishop sighed. He disliked the discomfort associated with riding a horse everywhere and had debated whether to obtain a cart fitted with padded seats in which to travel. However, he feared that it would make him a laughing stock; only women and young children used such carts. He consoled himself with the thought that, if he rode north to see the king, he would be able to visit his monastery at Hexham on the return journey and check for himself how the building work was progressing.

He was convinced that all workmen were lazy and overcharged for their labour and materials so he liked to keep an eye on them. In any case, as the abbot, he needed to show his face there occasionally. The same applied to Ripon where he was also the abbot.

The journey north to Bebbanburg took five days. It was now early April. Wilfrid had put off leaving until after Easter in the hope that the weather would be more clement. It wasn't. The last few days in March had been unusually warm, almost balmy, but April had been ushered in by a return of wintry showers and a chilly wind from the east. To add to his misery he suspected that Ecgfrith would have moved on further north by now.

He breathed a sigh of relief when Bebbanburg, on top of its rock, hove into view. He climbed wearily off his horse outside what was now called the ealdorman's hall and looked around him. Apart from several stable boys, who came to take his horse and that of his escort, and two sentries who looked down at him with indifference from the top of the steps leading into the hall, no-one seemed to be about. No doubt they were all sheltering from the gale force wind that brought with it the occasional shower of hail off the German Ocean.

He stomped off towards the hall just as the door opened and a woman appeared with a boy of about seven. This must be Catinus' wife and youngest son. He racked his brains but their names escaped him. He forced himself to smile just as his chaplain sidled up to his side and whispered 'Leoflaed; the boy's name is Osfrid.'

The bishop nodded imperceptibly to acknowledge his chaplain's help and went to meet his hostess.

'Lady Leoflaed, it's a real pleasure to see you again. This must be your youngest boy, Osfrid.'

'Bishop Wilfrid. This is unexpected surprise. We had no word that you were coming.'

It was a less than fulsome welcome but Wilfrid ignored the implied complaint.

'I have urgent business with the king. Is he still here?'

'Yes, he's gone to Lindisfarne with my husband to see Abbot Eata and Prior Cuthbert. Will you travel after them if the matter is so urgent?'

Wilfrid wanted to get in out of the cold but Leoflaed showed no inclination to invite him into the hall. If he hated Eata, he loathed Cuthbert and the awe in which everyone seemed to regard him. Eata had been responsible for his expulsion from Lindisfarne when he was a young novice and he'd never forgiven him.

'No I don't think so. When are you expecting them back?'

'The tide is coming in at the moment so the island will be cut off in a couple of hours. By the time it goes out again it will be dark, so I expect that they will stay there for the night.'

'I see. Well, it seems that I will need to beg hospitality from you until tomorrow then.'

'Oh, that might be difficult, bishop. We are full to bursting as it is with the king and his entourage and you seem to have brought a lot of men with you.'

'The king is on Lindisfarne. Surely that will free up some room.'

'He only took my husband, his brother, Ælfwine, our eldest son and two men as escort. You're not suggesting that you should sleep in the king's bed or with me in my husband's I hope.'

Wilfrid was alarmed until he noticed the glint of mischief in the woman's eyes.

'No, of course not. My men can camp outside the fortress, if necessary, but I'm sure you can find a suitable bed for the Bishop of Northumbria.'

'Apart from the bedchambers for the king and our family, there is only the guest chamber. However, that is occupied by the Eorl of Lothian, who has come here to confer with the king to save him travelling all the way to Dùn Èideann. He's out hunting this afternoon but he will return soon. The married men live in the huts with their families and the rest either sleep on the ground in the warriors' hall or in the ealdorman's hall. Perhaps you could share with Catinus' chaplain though. Father Isen has a small hut of his own.'

'I see. Where is this chaplain?'

'He's out hunting with Eorl Beornheth.'

'What? That's scandalous! A priest has no business hunting, least of all in the company of an important noble.'

'Why not?' Leoflaed laughed. 'He's his cousin after all.'

'Oh, I see. Still, it's not an appropriate pursuit for a priest.'

'Well, you had better tell him so when you share his hut. In the meantime you'd better come in out of the cold.'

As Wilfrid made to follow her into the hall, thankful to get out of the icy wind at last, she turned back to him.

'Aren't you going to look after your men first? They can sleep in the warriors' hall; it's very crowded but it will be warmer in there than sleeping in their tents.'

Wilfrid looked as if he'd been struck in the face.

'Surely your reeve will take care of them.'

'He's out hunting as well. Unless you expect me to do it of course?'

Grumbling the bishop turned back to his men who had returned from the stables carrying their tents and equipment.

'You are to sleep in the warriors' hall apparently,' he said in a tone that indicated that he couldn't care less where they went.

'Where is it?' the leader of his escort asked, somewhat disgruntled at being kept standing around in the cold.

'No idea. Ask someone.'

With that he hastened into the hall, rubbing his hands together to restore some warmth to them. Despite his thick leather gloves they felt as if they were lumps of ice.

~~~

'Wilfrid, I hope that you're the bearer of good news,' Ecgfrith said as he entered the hall and spotted the rotund bishop warming himself at the central hearth.

68

'Cyning, I came all this way to bring you the news myself. Queen Æthelthryth has agreed to become a nun.'

'At last! I was beginning to think she was refusing to take her vows just to spite me.'

Wilfrid, who suspected that was exactly what Æthelthryth had been playing at, coughed and hurriedly added the condition that she had stipulated.

'The queen wishes to become an abbess; she feels it is only appropriate in view of the fact that she is the daughter of one king and wife of another.'

'Abbess? Is there a vacancy in Northumbria then? If so, I wasn't aware of it.'

Both his aunt Æbbe, Abbess of Coldingham, and Hild of Whitby were elderly but they showed no signs of dying soon.

'No, Cyning, your wife would like you to found a new monastery for her at Ely in the Fens.'

'What? If I'm going to fund a new monastery it would be in my kingdom, not in East Anglia.'

'I'm afraid that Queen Æthelthryth was quite specific. Perhaps you would like to consider her proposal at your leisure, Cyning.'

Ecgfrith gave the smooth talking prelate a glare that would have made other men look at the floor, but not Wilfrid. He continued to smile at Ecgfrith until the king dismissed him.

'If Æthelthryth thinks I'm going to build her a monastery in Ely she'd mistaken,' he ranted later when he was alone with Beornheth and Catinus.

'Why don't you say no and continue with your present arrangement,' Beornheth asked.

Ecgfrith looked at him sharply. He fondly imagined that no one was aware that he had taken Eormenburg as his mistress; in fact everyone at court knew about it.

'Because I need to sire a legitimate heir.'

'Then, Cyning, I suggest that you have little choice. The queen has been intransigent so far; this is the first time she had offered to give you what you want. Either you should take the opportunity she offers, or she'll stay married to you.'

Ecgfrith looked upset but after a while he nodded slowly.

'You're right. But I want a solution now. She can go and join my aunt at Coldingham until her damn monastery is built at Ely. She needn't think it'll be anything grand either; a simple timber church and huts will suffice.'

Two months later, in mid-summer, Ecgfrith married Eormenburg. He was twenty seven and she was nineteen.

'Much good may it do him,' Beornheth said quietly to Catinus at the wedding feast. 'If he hasn't managed to get her pregnant in the last five years I doubt he's going to now.'

'Then we must hope that Ælfwine is more fertile.'

Catinus looked down the table to where the king's brother sat on the other side of the new queen. Ælfwine was nearly twelve and about to depart for Lindisfarne to be taught by the monks for two years before beginning his training as a warrior.

Although nominally King of Deira, it was merely a courtesy title. The boy had no power or even land of his own. He and Ecgfrith were very close, but the king had learnt the lessons of the past. Catinus wondered if their intimacy would last as Ælfwine grew to manhood, or whether he would become resentful at his dependence on his brother. He sighed. Only time would tell.

Chapter Four – The Isle of Man

672 - 673 AD

Wulfhere looked down on Alweo from where he sat on his throne on a raised dais in his hall at Tamworth. His brother Ethelred sat on one side of him and his queen, Ermenilda of Kent, sat on the other. Alweo's wife, Hereswith of Bebbanburg, stayed at the back of the hall with their baby son, Æthelbald, and his wet nurse.

'Well, cousin, have you finally remembered that you are a Mercian and not a wretched Northumbrian? Or are you here because Ecgfrith has kicked you out.'

'Neither, Cyning. Because I slew the treacherous Redwald in the king's presence he thought it sensible for me to leave Northumbria rather than stand trial.'

'Well, you had better not draw a sword in my presence or I shan't be so forgiving.'

'Of course, cousin. I only acted because Redwald was trying to draw his own sword to attack Ecgfrith.'

'So what do you expect me to do with you?'

'I was King Oswiu's master of horse for many years, as well as being an ealdorman. I was hoping that I might be able to serve you in a similar capacity.'

At that Ethelred leaned over and whispered something in his brother's ear. Wulfhere evidently thought that whatever the suggestion was it merited consideration because he nodded agreement before turning his attention back to Alweo.

'Well, cousin, it seems that I might have an appointment for you worthy of your talents. The Isle of Man has been Mercian territory for many years but recently it has become the haunt of Hibernian pirates and outlaws. They killed the King of Man last year and now control the whole island. As they also murdered his family, there is a vacancy and I am considering giving Man to you as my vassal. The only slight drawback is that you'd have to drive out the Hibernians and re-establish control over your new domain. Are you up to it?'

Alweo thought quickly. About twenty of his gesith had elected to go into exile with him but he had no other warriors to call upon. He would either have to buy the services of mercenaries or persuade someone to help him. It didn't sound as if Wulfhere would do so. He could hardly go back to Ecgfrith to ask for his assistance, especially as Man lay off the coast of Rheged and Northumbrians had always felt it should be part of their kingdom.

On the other hand, what other prospects did he have? If he turned this down Wulfhere would undoubtedly wash his hands of him and he and his family would be homeless.

'Thank you cousin, that is most generous of you. Of course I will need sufficient men to drive out the Hibernians...'

'Good, that's settled then,' Wulfhere interrupted before he could finish his plea. 'You and Hereswith must join us this evening.'

With that the king moved onto the next matter awaiting his attention and a servant showed Alweo and his family to a small hut that had been set aside for their use.

'You'll need some help to recapture Man,' Ethelred said to him as he thrust another chunk of venison into his mouth.

'Yes, I'm well aware that I'm hardly likely to get very far with just my gesith,' Alweo replied gloomily.

'If we share the plunder, with three quarters going to me, I may be able to assist you.'

'Why would you do that?'

'Mainly because of the gold and silver that the pirates have captured from passing ships, but also because I'm keen to see Man back in Mercian hands.'

'How many of these Hibernians are there? What sort of army will we need?'

'It's not just a matter of having enough men, we also need birlinns. Otherwise the rogues will escape back to Hibernia and then come back again later.'

'Do you have any birlinns?'

'No. My estates are all inland, but your friend Catinus does.'

Alweo dare not return to Northumbria himself so he sent one of his gesith, a young man named Thored, to Bebbanburg with a letter. Thored made the two hundred and sixty miles from Tamworth to Bebbanburg in eight days, only to find that Catinus and his family had gone to Alnwic for the marriage of Alweo's replacement as ealdorman, Ruaidhrí.

Thored debated whether to wait where he was for Catinus to return or to go on to Alnwic. As it was July and the weather was fine he decided to go on to Alnwic and set off again the next morning. His decision was helped by the fact that his father was the thegn of a nearby vill called Eglingham and it would give him the chance to see his family again. As there was an old Roman road from Berwic to Hexham that passed close to both Eglingham and Alnwic he headed west over the hills to find it.

It was a calm day with scarcely a cloud in the blue sky. The only people he saw was the odd shepherd watching over his flock and, with nothing else to distract him, he started to daydream. His mind wandered back to the first girl he had made love to in Eglingham when he was thirteen and she was twelve. He'd been a fool and he was lucky she didn't get pregnant. Nevertheless he still thought about her from time to time.

There had been others since of course, but somehow that first time was special. She was married now, to the blacksmith. When he had left with Alweo she had been expecting her first child and the pregnant woman of twenty had looked nothing like the sweet twelve year old he'd seduced eight years before.

He was jerked out of his nostalgic reminiscence when he came across the paved road. It had deteriorated over the centuries since the Romans had departed, of course, but the broken and weed strewn cobbled surface still made travelling easier than the dirt tracks that normally served as roads.

He hadn't gone more than ten miles down the road when he encountered a large group travelling north. There were about thirty horsemen surrounding an enclosed cart, in which presumably women and young children were travelling. The cart had been constructed with a curved roof and sides constructed of vertical planks with small openings to allow air in. There was no door, merely an open archway in one side.

He had ridden off the side of the road to allow the convoy to pass when he noticed the banner borne aloft by a warrior immediately behind the cart. It was a black wolf's head on a red background. He had found Catinus.

The ealdorman was riding beside a boy of about eight on a pony and Thored assumed correctly that he was Osfrid, Catinus' younger son. When the pair drew level Thored dug his heels into his horse and fell in alongside them.

'Please forgive my intrusion, lord, but I was looking for you. I have a message from the Ætheling Alweo.'

Catinus was puzzled for a moment. He'd almost forgotten that his friend was a member of the royal house of Mercia.

'Alweo? What does he want with me? You realise, of course, that he is banished from Northumbria? I hope that he hasn't been so foolish as to have returned.'

'No, lord. That is why he has sent me as his messenger. My name is Thored of Eglingham.'

'One of his gesith who went with him into exile I assume?'

'Yes, lord.'

'Very well. You've found me but I don't intend to stop here and read Alweo's letter. Follow us back to Bebbanburg and I'll see you as soon as I've bathed and changed my clothes.'

'So he expects me to furnish him with six birlinns does he? Even if I could find so many, what makes him think that I'd lend them to him? Is he providing the crews, or does he expect me to do that too?'

'I think that he was hoping that this would be a joint venture and that you would lend him the birlinns fully manned, lord.'

'And I am meant to pay for all this?'

'He offers you part of the plunder, lord.'

'Plunder? I thought he was to govern Man for Wulfhere. Is he planning to start his rule by plundering his own people?'

This wasn't going as well as Alweo had led Thored to believe it would.

'No, lord. Man is a nest of Hibernian pirates at the moment and, although it is Mercian territory, Alweo will need to expel them before he can sit on the throne. The Hibernians will have acculumated...'

He got no further before Catinus interrupted him.

'The throne? You mean he is to be the King of Man?'

'As Wulfhere's vassal, yes.'

'I see. You were saying, about the plunder.'

'Yes, it is to be divided between Alweo and Ethelred, who is providing the army to help capture the island.'

'And my share?'

'Yes, lord. Alweo will pay for your birlinns from his share.'

'And how much will that be?'

'We don't know, but the pirates are said to have amassed considerable treasure.'

'Which Alweo and Ethelred intend to keep, rather than return it to their original owners?'

'That would be impractical, lord. How would anyone know who they are?'

'Very well, and what is my share to be?'

'Alweo wasn't specific, lord. He thought you could come to an arrangement later.'

'No, if I'm to be involved in this venture I will need two things: permission from King Ecgfrith, who will also need payment I'm sure, and an agreed percentage of the plunder for me. After all, I will have to pay my men and fit out my ships ready for sea.'

'I don't have the authority to agree that, lord.'

'Well then you had better go back to Tamworth and see what sort of specific deal Alweo is offering. Meanwhile I'll go and see King Ecgfrith and explain the situation.'

~~~

It had taken months to make the necessary arrangements, including securing Ecgfrith's agreement to his involvement and that of King Elfin of Strathclyde to establish a camp on part of his land opposite Man. It was early April before everything was ready, by which time the risk of winter gales had passed.

Catinus had managed to gather together seven birlinns which had sailed north up the east coast of Pictland, passed south of the islands called the Orcades and thence down the west coast to Legacæstir in Mercia. From there they escorted Ethelred's hundred warriors and Alweo's gesith north, packed into two hired knarrs and landed them on the beach near the fishing village of Stranraer in Strathclyde where they made camp.

They had been forced to sail past the Isle of Man but Catinus was confident that the Hibernians wouldn't attack such a strong fleet. Now they waited.

Just after dark had fallen Thored and four other men from Alweo's gesith were landed by one of Catinus' birlinns on a beach midway between the two main settlements - Rhumsaa and Duboglassio. Their task was to climb the highest mountain on the island, Snaefell, and kill the men who kept watch there.

The pirates had a simple system for capturing the knarrs that carried merchandise across the sea between Hibernia and England. The lookouts on Snaefell would wait until a knarr had passed the southern tip of Man and then light a signal fire. The smoke would alert the birlinns at Rhumsaa and Duboglassio and those beached at the former would sail north whilst others from the latter sailed south to trap the knarr between them. Even if they tried to flee towards the Hibernian coast the sleeker birlinns with many more rowers would usually catch them up before they got there.

Even if the knarrs sailed in convoy or were escorted by a birlinn the six ships on Man were normally more than a match for them.

If the watch could be eliminated, then the Hibernians would have no warning of the approach of Catinus' fleet. If they sailed close to the Rhins, the westernmost part of Galloway, they would be over the horizon from Rhumsaa and they could then land men on the beach which Thored had used.

Thored led his small group up the hillside towards the peak of Snaefell. None of them were familiar with the island but they could see the top of the mountain when the clouds parted and its black silhouette stood out against the moonlit sky. It was harder going than they'd expected and he began to worry about getting to the summit and killing the watch in time.

Then the man in front of him held his hand behind him and pushed Thored back. Thankfully it was a period when the clouds had parted so the others could see him gesture for them to hide in the thick gorse bushes which grew alongside the faint trail they were following. They ignored the painful picks and lacerations of the thorns on their bare arms and legs and waited silently.

At first it was a faint murmur but they could distinctly make out speech and laughter coming from a little distance away. Thored felt a fool. Of course, there was no point in keeping a lookout at night; they were undoubtedly today's watch heading down to either Rhumsaa or Duboglassio. Sensing the direction that sound came from at night was difficult and he had no idea whether the men were to his left or his right. However, it didn't matter. He would never find them at night on the side of an unfamiliar mountain. He and his men would have to set up an ambush for the next day's watch as they ascended the mountain.

As a precaution they disassembled the beacon set ready to light and settled down for the night, leaving one man on guard. As soon as the rising sun gave him enough light Thored scouted the summit. Apart from the narrow trail they had followed there were two other tracks, but one showed signs of much greater use than the other. The grass had been worn away down to the bare earth and some branches growing on the shrubs beside the path had been broken at the end.

Thored sent two men down the track to hide until the men had passed. Their task was to prevent any escaping back down the mountain. He and the other two hid just over the crest. The men climbing the mountain were quieter than those who had descended the previous evening, but that wasn't surprising given the steepness of the slope.

'Those bloody bastards have dismantled the beacon! Sod them; we'll have to re-build it.'

Thored suppressed a chuckle. Evidently they thought that
the previous watch had done it as a joke. He signalled to the
two men with him and all three rose from the ground and
walked a few steps up the far side of the summit until they
could see the four men who had started to gather the scattered
wood. All three had strung bows with an arrow nocked ready
for use. Two of the Hibernians fell dead and the other was
wounded in the shoulder. None wore any form of protection
and, as they weren't expecting trouble, were only armed with
seaxes and daggers.

The fourth turned and ran back the way he'd come, straight
onto the spear of one of Thored's men who was waiting a
hundred yards below. Another of his men went to cut the
throat of the one with an arrow in his shoulder but Thored
stopped him.

'Let's see what he can tell us.'

He jerked the arrow out and the Hibernian screamed in
agony. Blood started to pour from the hole and Thored put his
foot on it and twisted it, making the pain far worse. It was then
that he realised that the captive was only a boy, fourteen at
most. Looking around he saw that two of the others were little
more than boys, only one was a man and an old one at that.
Obviously the Hibernians used those who would be little use in
combat as lookouts.

'How many men are there at Rhumsaa and how many
birlinns?' Thored asked in Gaelic.

When the boy merely glowered at him and spat Thored
reapplied pressure to the wound. The boy screamed again and
passed out. Thored grabbed the water skin he'd been carrying

and splashed it over their captive's face. The boy spluttered and stared at Thored with unfocused eyes.

'Now we can do this the hard way and you'll eventually talk before you die, or you can co-operate and I might even let you live.'

He went to stamp on the shoulder again but the boy held up his other hand in a gesture of surrender.

'That's better. Now what's your name?'

'Padraig,' the boy said sullenly.

'Very well Padraig, how many birlinns are there at Rhumsaa and how many at Duboglassio?'

'I don't know about Rhumsaa; I live at Duboglassio.'

'How many at Duboglassio?'

'Three.'

'Good. And how many warriors are there?'

'Hundred? A hundred and fifty? I'm not sure. More than enough to kill you anyway.'

'And how big are the birlinns? How many oars?'

'Two have twelve a side and Lugh's has fourteen.'

'Is Lugh your chieftain?'

'King of Man, yes.'

'A hundred men to crew them would make sense.'

'What about Rhumsaa?'

Padraig shifted uncomfortably and groaned.

'Answer my question and we'll do something about that wound.'

'Three smaller birlinns,' he answered through gritted teeth.

'How many oars a side?'

'Ten, I think.'

'What's he saying?' one of the other men asked Thored as none of the others spoke Gaelic.

'It sounds as if he may be telling the truth,' one of Thored's companions said after he'd given them the gist of what Padraig had told him. 'The ships at Rhumsaa are lighter and faster so that they can drive the knarrs towards the bigger birlinns.'

'How many men at Rhumsaa?' Thored asked, renewing his interrogation.

'I don't know, just enough to crew the three ships I think.'

'Probably seventy or eighty then.'

'Right lad. Drink this, go on get it down you. It'll dull the pain.'

So saying he gave the boy a leather flask full of strong mead. Padraig choked after the first mouthful but then managed to get half of the flask down before he passed out.

'Aren't you going to kill him?' one of the men asked, surprised that Thored was taking the trouble to deal with the wound in Padraig's shoulder.

'No, Alweo has promised me enough land to establish a vill once he's king here and I'll need slaves to work the land. This is the first of them.'

'So you've ambitions to be a thegn? What about the rest of us?'

'You can be my warband if you want,' Thored replied, grinning at them.

One of the men spat a gob of phlegm onto the ground.

'I want my own farm thanks.'

'You can have it and be in my warband as well.'

'I'll think about it. We've got to take the bloody place first. If this lad's right, we're facing nearly two hundred hairy-arsed Hibernians with half that number of our own warriors.'

'Get a small fire going, just use dry wood though; we don't want any smoke.'

Thored watched until he was satisfied that what little smoke it produced was dispersed by the wind before it could be seen and then wrapped a cloth around the hilt of one of dead Hibernian's seaxes. He stuck it in the hottest part of the fire and then applied the red hot tip to the boy's bleeding shoulder. The smell that emanated from the wound was a mixture of roasting meat and acrid burning.

He threw the seax away and then pissed on the cauterised flesh, both to take away the heat and to kill any infection. After binding the wound with a strip of cloth torn from one of the dead Hibernians' tunics, he picked Padraig up and put him over one shoulder. The lad was thin and small for his age. Thored would have been surprised if he weighed more than six stone.

An hour and a half later they were back on the beach where a fishing boat was waiting for them. They were too small to attract the interest of the pirates on Man and so it was the ideal boat to take them over to the Galloway coast where Alweo, Catinus and Ethelred met them.

'What have you got there Thored?' Alweo asked as they stepped ashore, Padraig draped over the muscular warrior's right shoulder.

'A Hibernian boy who has been very helpful, lord. I was going to kill him but I've decided to keep him as my slave.'

'What did you learn from him?

'There are three birlinns at Duboglassio manned by about a hundred men and three smaller birlinns at Rhumsaa crewed by about seventy. The watch party was composed of three boys and one old man so I suspect that no warriors are left behind when the birlinns take to the sea, just old men and warriors in training like this one.'

'He doesn't look like a boy training to be a warrior to me, more like an urchin whose scarcely been weaned from his mother's teat,' Ethelred scoffed.

'I can assure you he's like a wildcat when he's awake, lord. Don't underestimate the Hibernians, they're doughty fighters.'

The Mercian ætheling looked far from convinced but he said nothing more. By now it was mid-morning and they needed to put their plan into operation before the missing watch was discovered and the Hibernians were warned.

~~~

Leoflaed had watched her husband depart with misgivings. He was now in his mid-forties but he seemed to think that he was still a young man. He'd wanted to take Osfrid with him as a ship's boy but she'd put her foot down. He was only nine and far too young to be risking his life in her opinion. It was bad enough worrying about Catinus without losing sleep over Osfrid as well. She thanked God that her elder son, Alaric, was a monk on Lindisfarne and out of harm's way, even if she didn't see anything of him now.

Catinus had been gone a month when she realised that she was pregnant again. This would be her fourth child and she didn't need anyone else to confirm what her body was telling her. In the past she had known she was going to have another baby about seven months before the birth and she didn't think that it would be any different this time. That meant that the child would be born sometime in November. With any luck her husband would be back long before then.

At least she wouldn't have to undergo the rigours of pregnancy alone. When Alweo had left Tamworth for Caerlleon he'd sent Hereswith and their two-year old son Æthelbald to stay with her mother at Bebbanburg until Man was secured. The little boy was now walking and getting into all sorts of mischief. Much to her surprise, Osfrid made time each day to play with him for about an hour. Normally Anglo-Saxon boys refused to have anything to do with their juniors, let alone one who was seven years younger and barely walking.

With the Picts subdued and a treaty with Mercia that seemed to be standing the test of time, Northumbria was prospering. Catinus had commissioned a number of knarrs and had built a small harbour a couple of miles south of Bebbanburg from which they could operate. The vill below the castle had expanded and now contained two blacksmiths, two armourers, a goldsmith, a leatherworker, a shoe maker, three tailors and a jewellery maker. The items they manufactured were exported down the coast to East Anglia, Lundenwic and Kent as well as across the sea to Frisia and Frankia together with wool and hides from the farms.

The knarrs' captains and the merchants who used them had grumbled when Catinus had taken all his birlinns for the invasion of Man because that hadn't left any to escort his knarrs when they sailed across to the Continent, a journey that was dangerous without a birlinn or two as escort because of

Friesian pirates. Nevertheless, the demand for weapons, chainmail, helmets, jewellery and leather goods continued unabated all down the East Coast of England.

Of course, there were many other centres of craftsmanship but Bebbanburg had established a reputation for quality. In return, they imported iron, silver, gold and cloth. Bishop Wilfrid had even ordered a new jewel encrusted gold cross and chain from the Bebbanburg jewellery maker. It was so heavy that everyone wondered why a man would want to wear something like that around his neck.

Leoflaed didn't understand why her husband had felt it necessary to take charge of his fleet himself. There were plenty of other men who could have commanded his ships. She didn't think it was because he wanted to get away from her; if anything they were more in love now than they'd been when they'd first wed. Their relationship had matured and deepened over the years.

She had asked him about it before he'd left but all he'd said was that Alweo needed him and he felt duty bound to help his friend. It was Hereswith who told her why he'd gone.

'All men need some excitement from time to time to make them feel alive,' she'd said, and then added, 'except monks and priests of course.'

~~~

Alweo led his gesith and another forty men provided by Ethelred north from where they'd landed towards Rhumsaa, whilst the main body set off towards the south and

Duboglassio. Meanwhile Thored and his three men took the path back up Snaefell to the summit.

By the time that they had gathered the wood and lit the beacon it was early afternoon. As expected the six Hibernian birlinns set out from their respective harbours into a choppy sea with a brisk wind blowing in from the west. They expected to sail around to the west of the island to trap some unsuspecting knarr or two. Instead they were confronted by Catinus and his fleet.

The three smaller birlinns from Rhumsaa were the first to realise that they'd been tricked. As they headed for the northern tip of Man they saw three much larger birlinns waiting for them. The wind was from the west so neither fleet had an advantage as far as that was concerned, but the smaller birlinns were faster. They tacked through one hundred and eighty degrees and headed back for the safety of Rhumsaa.

Meanwhile Alweo and his men had arrived at the northern settlement and had entered it without any resistance. The Hibernians had felt so secure in their base that they hadn't bothered to repair the palisade when parts of it had fallen down. A few old men and boys had appeared with weapons when the alarm had been sounded but they'd been quickly killed or captured.

The local populace had welcomed the new arrivals as their saviours. It was evident that the Hibernians had treated them as slaves, or worse. Leaving six men to search the place and make sure that there were no Hibernians in hiding and four more to guard the captives, he led the rest to the quayside just as the three birlinns returned.

The leader of the pirate ships was now in a quandary. If he tried to tie up and disembark his men he would be attacked by Alweo and his fifty men. Although he had more warriors, they would be disorganised as they tried to get ashore, whereas Alweo's men were already formed up as a shield wall. On the other hand, if they tried to go back out to sea the three large birlinns would be waiting to grapple their ships and board them.

Further south things were not going so well for Ethelred. He had arrived at Duboglassio to find that the settlement was surrounded by a tall palisade. He had expected the gates to be open at this hour so that they could rush them as soon as the beacon was lit, but they remained firmly closed. When people arrived seeking admittance, or when someone wanted to leave, the gates opened for them and were then shut again.

When he saw the smoke from the signal fire he waited enough time for the Hibernians inside to have left in their birlinns, and then he led his men forward to assault the settlement. He'd hoped that he could get his men over the palisade by the simple tactic of two men lifting a third up so that he could pull himself over the top, but the palisade proved to be too high. Furthermore, there were several archers on the walls and, after losing several men, he retreated.

Half an hour later he returned to the attack; this time using a felled tree as a battering ram against the gates. Whilst some used their shields to protect those carrying the makeshift ram, his archers tried to keep the heads of the Hibernian bowmen down. The gates were stout and at first the ram made no progress. Ethelred began to worry that the pirates would have encountered Catinus' ships and fled back to the settlement, in which case he would be outnumbered.

He need not have been concerned. Lugh, the Hibernians' leader, didn't flee at the first sight of Catinus' ships. However, the Ealdorman of Bebbanburg hadn't let Lugh see that he was opposed by four birlinns; he'd only sent two forward initially to draw the Hibernians into a trap. As the three pirate ships closed on the two Northumbrian birlinns, the other two of Catinus' ships appeared, one from the east and one from the west.

At first Lugh didn't react. Catinus worried that he'd flee back to their base, in which event they would be formed up and ready to oppose his men as they disembarked unless the Mercians had been successful in taking the place. Thankfully Lugh wasn't a man to avoid a fight just because he was outnumbered.

One of his birlinns turned to engage the one approaching from the east and another headed for the one coming in from the west. Lugh himself continued on course to meet the two approaching from the south.

Catinus watched Lugh's ship carefully. If he was Lugh he wouldn't place his birlinn in the middle of two enemy ships. Although Lugh's birlinn was a little larger than either of Catinus', with two more oars a side, he was bound to be overwhelmed by the combined Northumbrian crews.

'What do you expect him to do?' Catinus' helmsman asked.

'Turn at the last moment to run down the side of one or other of our birlinns, sheering off our oars so we'd be immobilised,' Catinus replied. 'Then he could attack and take our second ship before we could go to its aid.'

The helmsmen nodded in understanding.

'Be ready to pull in your oars on my order,' he shouted to his rowers.

Catinus' second birlinn was now closer, ready to trap the Hibernian ship between them. He waited until they were within hailing distance and then warned them what he expected the enemy to do. He didn't need to explain what he wanted the other birlinn to do, they had practiced the manoeuvre several times.

When Lugh was a hundred yards away his helmsman put his steering oar hard over. The rowers on his port side backed their oars whilst those on the starboard side give one last pull and then raised their oars. The birlinn turned sharply to port ready to run down the starboard side of Catinus' ship.

However, both Northumbrian birlinns swung to starboard at practically the same time, taking Lugh by surprise. Once Catinus' birlinn had passed in front of the Hibernian ship his helmsman swung the steering oar hard over to starboard and the oars on that side pulled harder. At the same time the port side rowers pulled in their oars and grabbed their weapons and shields.

The port side of the Northumbrian birlinn smashed the oars on the port side of the pirate, crushing the rowers' ribs and breaking bones as it did so. A little later the second Northumbrian ship did the same to the starboard side. This time some of the enemy rowers had managed to pull their oars inboard in time but many hadn't. With half his crew incapacitated and with two birlinns secured to his ship with grappling irons, the outcome was a forgone conclusion.

Catinus still limped from the wound to his thigh so he wisely left the fighting to others. Eadstan therefore led his warriors onto the enemy ship. As he landed, seax in hand as it was much better for close quarter fighting, he was faced with a giant Hibernian wielding an axe. Eadstan stumbled as he landed on the walkway between the rowing benches, which saved his life as the axe whistled over his head.

The axeman had expected his weapon to connect with Eadstan's body and, when it didn't, he had trouble keeping his balance. Eadstan seized the opportunity to thrust his seax into the giant's belly. At first he thought that his thrust hadn't done much damage as the man gave a roar of fury and raised his axe to chop Eadstan's head in two. But then his eyes glazed over as he looked at the seax buried up to its hilt in his guts. He roared again, this time in pain and toppled off the walkway down into the space where the rowers sat.

Eadstan drew his sword as his seax was now out of reach and looked around for his next opponent, but the only fight still in progress was on the aft deck where the helmsman stood. Lugh was the last of the enemy standing. He had managed to kill two men but then, as Eadstan watched, one of Catinus' warriors put a spear through his throat.

The wounded and those injured when the ships had come together were quickly dispatched and then, leaving half a dozen men and two ships boys as a skeleton crew to take the birlinn back to Duboglassio, Catinus sent the other birlinn to help the one that was engaged with a pirate ship to the east whilst he set sail for the battle taking place to the west.

By the time he got there it was all over. The Northumbrian birlinn had been bigger than the Hibernian and, although they'd lost ten men with another half a dozen wounded, they had managed to capture the Hibernian ship.

'Catinus, our other ship is in trouble.' Eadstan pointed towards the last Hibernian birlinn and he saw that his fourth ship had managed to ram it, but now both ships were slowly sinking. A fierce battle was raging and, to his dismay, he saw that it was taking place on his birlinn. The ship that had been with him initially was coming towards them but they were headed into the wind and were reliant on the rowers only. They arrived just as the holed Hibernian sank, pulling the other ship, which was lashed to it, under as well.

When they got there they rowed around rescuing the survivors from the sunken Northumbrian birlinn although, as pitifully few could swim, there weren't many of them. By the time that Catinus had arrived the others had picked up ten in all out of a crew of over thirty. Their foes were left to drown.

When his three birlinns and the two captured ones arrived at the jetty at Duboglassio he found a grinning Ethelred waiting for him. He had lost a few men but eventually the battering ram had broken the bar holding the gates closed and they had swarmed into the settlement. It had taken them over an hour to root out and kill or capture the defendants and now his men were busy rounding up the Hibernian families to be sold into slavery.

Just at that moment Alweo arrived on one of the birlinns from Rhumsaa. Leaving most of his men to clear up, he'd decided to see how things were going at the main settlement.

'Well, I suppose I'd better call you Cyning now,' Ethelred laughed, throwing his arm around the new King of Man.

'Thank you both of you. I've brought the treasure we found in Rhumsaa with me. I suppose we had better start to decide what constitutes the various shares. Have you found much plunder here?'

'We have, not just silver and a little gold and a few jewels, but fine cloth and even some spices. However, that can wait,' Ethelred said. 'I'm so thirsty I could drink a barrel of ale in one go. Let's celebrate our victory first.'

It took another month to scour the island for fugitives and impose Alweo's rule over all of the Isle of Man so it was early June before Herewith arrived with their son and her servants. She brought Headda, Bishop of Lichfield, with her to crown Alweo and the ceremony took place two days after that.

However, by that time Catinus had returned to Bebbanburg with his birlinns, taking Lugh's captured ship to replace the one he'd lost. He'd managed to recruit a few young men and several boys to partly replace those he'd lost but he still couldn't man all the oars for the return journey. Therefore they made slow progress when the wind was against them.

On the other hand Ethelred had no reason to hurry back to Mercia and so he decided to stay and travel back with Headda after the coronation. The ceremony took place in the king's hall; a timber building of a design that was peculiar to Man. The walls were made of upright logs with a mixture of straw, mud and dung forced into the gaps between the logs to keep out the wind. Outside of the walls there was a colonnade of timber columns which supported the roof frame. This was made of curved timbers with horizontal battens to produce a cylindrical frame onto which panels of woven twigs had been tied; finally cut sods of turf had been laid on top.

The door was located in the long side that faced away from the prevailing wind and the hall's few windows had been cut into that side. There were shutters but they weren't generally needed if it rained as the timber colonnade sheltered the windows.

The interior was one big space, except for two rooms partitioned off along the far wall. These were a store room and the king's private chamber. Smoke from the central hearth escaped from the hall via a square chimney built into the apex of the roof. This consisted of a pyramidal roof supported on four short uprights. The wind blew across the hole in the roof, drawing out the smoke, whilst the capping prevented most of the rain from entering. Ethelred thought it was a clever idea and intended to suggest that Wulfhere copy it when he returned to Tamworth.

Alweo entered dressed in clothing made from the cloth which had been stolen by the Hibernian pirates. He was followed by Herewith, also wearing a new robe made from the same bolt of cloth as her husband tunic, holding little Æthelbald's hand. The robe had been made a little fuller than her others as she was expecting their second child. The bishop and Ethelred, representing King Wulfhere, brought up the rear of the little procession. It took its time to reach the dais at the north hand end of the hall as Æthelbald could only take small steps but he'd refused to be carried.

Alweo took the throne in the centre and his wife the chair beside it. Their son sat at her feet. Headda picked up the Manx crown, which had been recovered from the Hibernians' hoard and lifted it above Alweo's head.

At the moment that the bishop crowned the new King of Man Catinus was on the last stretch of the long voyage around the north of Britain back to Bebbanburg. As Alweo took the oaths of his newly appointed thegns in the hall at Duboglassio, the fortress appeared out of the thin mist that hung over the sea, standing proudly on its rock. However, this time the elation Catinus always felt when he saw his home again was tempered by an uneasy feeling that all was not well.

Chapter Five – The Battle of Loidis

674 AD

It had taken Catinus a long time to get over the death of Leoflaed. The baby had been born prematurely and it had been a breech birth. Her women had been unable to staunch the bleeding and she died ten hours later. The baby girl had stopped breathing almost as soon as her mother had breathed her last. They had been buried together in the same coffin on a cold, wet day in early May when Catinus was still on Man. A messenger had been sent to tell him but he'd arrived after Catinus had sailed.

Catinus sank into despondency and it seemed that nothing interested him anymore. He had asked his chaplain why God had taken her from him but the priest had no answer. No one seemed able to comfort him. His daughter Hereswith was far away on Man and, although his elder son was given leave by Abbot Eata to leave Lindisfarne to visit him, Alaric failed to elicit much of a response from him.

Osfrid had tried to talk to his father once but Catinus had rebuffed him and told him to leave him alone. He didn't try again. The nine year old boy had taken the rejection badly and he hardened his heart against his father.

Whilst Catinus was away Leoflaed had conducted the business of the shire, assisted by the new reeve, a young man called Morcar, and the captain of the garrison, Godwald. When she died Osfrid announced his intention of taking over, including presiding over the shire court. Many had laughed at the idea of a young boy sitting in judgement over them but they soon found out that he was clever, astute and fair.

When his father had shut himself away to mourn his wife, Osfrid continued to run the shire and the fortress, assisted by the Morcar, Godwald and now that he had returned, Eadstan.

'Lord, it's been six months since we returned and it'll soon be winter,' Eadstan told Catinus one day. 'We need to make preparation or people will die. Osfrid has done a remarkable job of managing the shire for you so far, but you need to help your thegns prepare for the coming winter. We also need to organise a wolf hunt or they'll come down from the hills when they're starving and decimate our livestock. We can advise Osfrid but it isn't our responsibility, or his. It's yours.'

'Osfrid has been acting as Ealdorman?'

'Who else, lord? Morcar, Godwald and I have done what we can to help but he has had to make the decisions. When I've asked you a question all you do is tell me to do what I think is best. I'm the leader of your gesith, I'm not a noble, nor would I wish to be one.'

'Where is my son?'

'He's in the hall organising the collection of taxes.'

'Send him to me when he is finished.'

'Yes, lord. And don't forget he's not yet ten and he's missing his mother just as much as you're missing your wife.'

Catinus nodded and engaged in some hard thinking whilst he waited for his son.

'I'm sorry, Osfrid. I didn't mean you to have to bear the burden of my duties. I just didn't think about it.'

'No, you didn't,' the boy replied coldly. 'You were so absorbed in your own grief that you never thought about me and what I must be feeling. You neglected your responsibilities but I couldn't. Consequently I felt duty bound to step in when mother died, but I expected you to take over when you returned. Instead I had to carry on acting as the ealdorman. I needed you to lift the burden from my shoulders and help me though my grief, but you did neither of these things.'

The stare he gave Catinus showed more than any words how resentful he felt.

'I know I was selfish and wrapped up in self-pity, but I loved your mother and I couldn't bear living without her.'

'And you think I didn't?'

'No, of course not.'

'I'd just lost my mother and when you came back I thought that you would comfort me. Instead you treated me as if I didn't exist. Do you know what that did to me?'

'Yes, I can imagine. It's no good telling you how sorry I am. All I can say is that I now realise that I need to pull myself together and be a proper father to you. Despite what you might think, I do love you. I can understand how bitter you feel at the moment; I can only hope you'll find it in your heart to forgive me in time.'

'I take it that I no longer need to act the ealdorman and that you'll take over?' his son said, his voice devoid of emotion.

'Yes, most certainly, but I'll need your help. I need to know what the current problems are and anything else you think I should know.'

His son's detachment hurt him nearly as much as his wife's death had.

Osfrid was a strong character and he didn't readily forgive his father for his neglect, but by the time he turned ten they were beginning to behave towards each other like father and son again. Then the messenger from Ecgfrith arrived.

'Osfrid, you need to hear this. Repeat what you have just told me.'

'Yes lord, King Ecgfrith sends you his greetings and ...'

'No, not all the usual preamble, just the nub of the message.'

'Sorry, lord. King Wulfhere has broken the truce that he had agreed with King Oswiu and has crossed into Deira to support a pretender to the Deiran throne. Ealdorman Catinus is to move with all speed to join King Ecgfrith with his warband at Eoforwīc and instruct his fyrd to follow on as soon as possible.'

'Does that mean you are going to leave again?' his son asked despondently.

'I don't have a choice, Osfrid. I must do as the king commands.'

The boy nodded, his misery evident in his face. Catinus was going to ask him to take charge of the shire and the fortress whilst he was gone, but the rift between them was all too recently healed. Morcar and Godwald would just have to manage on their own whilst he was away.

'Well what are you waiting for, boy. Go and get ready, and don't forget to have the armourer sharpen your seax.'

'You mean I'm to come with you?'

'Of course, being ealdorman isn't all sitting in judgement and collecting taxes. How else are you going to learn how to command warriors?'

The smile that lit up his son's face gladdened Catinus' heart and gave him reason to hope that his son had managed to put the past behind him.

~~~

In the same way that Ecgfrith had agents in Mercia and several other kingdoms in the south, so Wulfhere had agents in Northumbria. A rumour had recently been circulating in Eoforwīc that Ecgfrith had decided that it was time to take action against the Britons of Rheged in retaliation for their support of Alchfrith three years previously. The rumour was that he had ordered his Bernician and Lothian eorls and ealdormen to muster their men at Yeavering ready to strike into Rheged.

The first part of the rumour had some foundation in fact; Ecgfrith had been discussing with his Witan how to deal with the rebels in Rheged. However, no firm decision had been reached, no plans had been made and no muster at Yeavering had been ordered.

The Mercians crossed the border and headed north east towards Loidis and Eoforwīc. The Deirans were outnumbered but they fought a series of delaying actions to give Ecgfrith the time to mobilise his army. By the time that Ecgfrith had assembled his nobles and their war bands, together with the fyrds of eastern Deira, Wulfhere was besieging his brother, the thirteen year old Ælfwine, in Loidis. Ælfwine should have been at Ripon Monastery, where he was being educated with the novices, but he'd gone to the capital of the kingdom of which he was the titular ruler for the funeral of the Eorl of Elmet.

'Cyning, it would be better to wait until your full army has assembled,' Octa, Redwald's replacement as hereræswa, advised Ecgfrith.

'I can't wait. My brother is in Loidis. I won't risk him being killed or captured.'

Ecgfrith and Ælfwine had always been close and the king worried about him when they were apart, even when he wasn't in danger as he was now.

'I understand, but at least wait until Ruaidhrí gets here with his horsemen. We need his trained scouts.'

Ecgfrith nodded. 'How many men do we have here already?'

'About fifty horsemen, four hundred warriors and nine hundred in the fyrd.'

The king sighed. 'And you say that the latest reports put Wulfhere's strength at two thousand?'

'Yes, but I'd rather wait for reports from Ruaidhrí's scouts. The estimates we have now aren't very reliable. Some say no more than fifteen hundred and other over three thousand.'

'Do we know how many men my brother has in Loidis?'

'His gesith and warband together number about seventy and there are three hundred member of the fyrd.'

'Not many to hold off two or three thousand.'

'No, but there is only a palisade around the king's hall and the warrior's hall, so they will have a much smaller perimeter to defend.'

Ecgfrith hoped that the general population had managed to flee before the Mercians had arrived. Those that stayed would not have been treated gently by the invaders. Then he had a thought.

'How many riders do Ruaidhrí and Catinus have between them?'

'Perhaps a hundred and fifty.'

'Send messengers to intercept them. I want them to go direct to Loidis and harass the Mercians as much as possible. They are to kill their forage parties and launch night attacks on their camp to keep them on edge. If we can disrupt the siege it means that Ælfwine has a better chance of holding out until I can get there.'

~~~

Ruaidhrí had been a boy of twelve when he'd first met Catinus and the ealdorman had been his mentor when he was growing up. He respected him, both as a military commander and as a man, so he had no compunction in asking him to command their combined force when they met up some thirty miles from Loidis, even though Ruaidhrí was Ecgfrith's Master of Horse and had brought more horsemen.

They found a wooded hill with a nearby stream some five miles from Loidis to use as their base whilst the scouts reconnoitred the area.

'Lord, there are some one and half thousand men camped around Loidis but there are many more inside the settlement so it is difficult to calculate their total numbers, but our estimate is about two and half thousand,' the chief scout told the two nobles. 'There are few horses so we don't think that they can have more than fifty mounted riders, allowing for packhorses and the horses belonging to the Mercian king and his nobles.

'Perhaps fifteen or sixteen hundred are members of the fyrd. The other thousand will be trained warriors.'

'That's a lot more warriors than Ecgfrith will have been able to muster quickly,' Catinus muttered after the scout had left.

'Yes, and they apparently use the fyrd to forage so we can't even the odds much by killing the foragers.'

'No, but if forage parties disappear it'll affect the fyrd's morale and they'll all go hungry: whether warband or fyrd.'

Ælfwine stood on the walkway on top of the gate in the palisade that ran around his hall. He was wearing a byrnie that was slightly too large for his slim body and a borrowed helmet that required a lot of padding underneath it to keep it sitting firmly on his head. One of the armourers in Loidis had presented him with a short sword that he'd made for his own son and he carried a shield that was too big and heavy for a thirteen year old to carry for too long.

A gap of fifty yards separated the two halls and their surrounding palisade from the nearest huts. At the moment the only occupants of the space were the dead and wounded from the last assault the Mercians had made. A hundred of the garrison defending Ælfwine's stronghold were archers and they had taken a deadly toll as the Mercians had crossed the open space carrying their hastily made ladders.

He could see movement between the nearest huts and he called out in his high treble voice 'here they come again.' The cry was repeated all along the walkway and the weary defenders scrambled to their feet.

This time the leading Mercians were archers, each with a man beside them with a shield to give them protection.

Ælfwine's archers started to pepper the running attackers with arrows but this time several of them were hit by the Mercian bowmen. A few moments later the first Mercians reached the fifteen foot high palisade and lifted their ladders into place.

A large man with a pitchfork grinned as the first Mercian appeared at the top of his ladder before thrusting it forward so that the prongs lodged in the topmost rung and he gave a mighty heave. The ladder toppled backwards taking the man at the top and four others climbing below him with it. They crashed into the men waiting their turn to climb and several screamed in agony with broken bones.

However, elsewhere the Mercians had got a foothold on the walkway and were engaged in fierce hand to hand fighting. A group of Mercians ran along the walkway to where Ælfwine was standing with several of his gesith, killing all who stood in their way. Several of his warriors pushed past the King of Deira to defend him and three of the Mercians fell into the compound below with wounds from the gesith's spears.

Ælfwine got increasingly angry when he saw his gesith being cut down by the Mercians who, although taking casualties, were gaining the upper hand. One of the Mercians managed to dodge past the defenders and came face to face with Ælfwine. He blocked the man's thrust with his shield and brought his sword round to strike the other's shield. The next blow from the Mercian's sword jarred his left arm and he had to struggle not to drop his guard. Despite the numbness, he forced his shield back into position and stepped back to give himself room to swing his sword.

With a cry of triumph the Mercian stepped forward but then stumbled as he tripped over the body of one of the dead.

Ælfwine seized his opportunity and thrust his sword through the exposed neck of the Mercian before he could recover. As he pulled the blade out blood gushed over him. The young king didn't let that distract him and he barged into his dying opponent with his shield, sending him off the walkway to crash onto the ground below.

Ælfwine turned to face his next opponent but the Mercians were retreating. He stood there for a moment, his chest heaving whilst he struggled to get his breath and then one of his surviving gesith grabbed his arm and pointed. A wedge of horsemen were cantering across the open space, scattering the attackers and cutting them down as they went. They completed one circuit around the palisade and then disappeared just as suddenly as they'd appeared.

They left behind them scores of dead and wounded Mercians for the loss, as far as Ælfwine could see, of three men and two horses. Someone who had kept a clear head shouted for the archers to shoot into their disorganised foes and several more Mercians died before they could retreat into the cover provided by the huts.

'They lost two hundred and thirty men, Cyning,' the garrison commander told Ælfwine later.

'And how many did we lose?'

'Twenty nine killed and forty too badly wounded to fight again for the foreseeable future.'

The loss of a quarter of the defenders was a serious blow, whereas the Mercians had probably only lost a tenth of their number. Such a high rate of attrition was unsustainable.

'Did you see who our saviours were?' Ælfwine asked.

'I recognised Catinus' banner of a wolf's head.'

'Probably just my brother's horsemen then. Men on foot will take a lot longer to reach us.'

'Don't despair, Cyning. It must mean that King Ecgfrith is on his way.'

The commander smiled affectionately at his young king and put a hand on his shoulder.

'You fought well today and you killed your first man in battle. It has boosted the men's morale no end.'

'Thank you. I suppose I should be pleased, but another attack like that will finish us off,' he said gloomily.

There was nothing further to be said. Ælfwine was correct.

~~~

Osfrid was fuming at being left behind with the servants to guard the packhorses. Why had his father brought him to war if he was to be kept out of sight of the action? How would he learn anything from that? He was even angrier when Catinus had told Drefan to look after him. The boy was only ten, just a few months older than he was, and he was a servant.

He waited until all the warriors had ridden off and then re-mounted his little mare.

'Where are you going?' Drefan asked as soon as he saw Osfrid preparing to ride after the men. 'Your father said that you were to stay with me.'

'Get lost, Drefan, I don't take orders from servants.'

Drefan stared resentfully at Osfrid's back as the young boy rode off through the trees following the path the horsemen had taken.

Osfrid stopped at the edge of the trees and carefully surveyed the ground between him and the buildings at the edge of the town. From where he sat he couldn't see any movement, then he spotted some of the Northumbrian horsemen in gaps between the huts as they moved carefully through the streets.

Off to his left lay the Mercians' camp, which appeared to be deserted apart from a few boys and unarmed servants. He rode just inside the trees until he was close to the nearest tents. Someone had left a fire burning, presumably to cook food on, and so he cantered forward and, jumping from his horse, he picked up a stick which was alight at one end. Before anyone could challenge him he rode back out of the camp.

Some of the tents were made from leather but most were thick cloth impregnated with fat and grease to make them waterproof. Back in the safety of the trees Osfrid used his seax to cut off a few strips of cloth from his oiled cloak and tied them to half a dozen of his arrows. Then he lit each in turn from the flame.

Drawing back his hunting bow as far as he could, he sent all six of his fire arrows into the upwind part of the camp. He waited until he saw flames flickering and smoke billowing upwards, to be whipped away by the wind, before he retraced his steps to his camp.

Ælfwine had stayed on the parapet despite being urged to get some rest whilst he could. He was the first to spot the smoke and then the flames as the wind spread the conflagration from one side of the enemy camp towards the centre. The Mercians had abandoned the town to go and fight the flames and Ælfwine took the opportunity to order two thirds of his men to get something to eat and drink and then sleep. They were all exhausted and he prayed that it would be some time before the enemy returned to the attack; time enough for the other third of his men to get some rest at any event.

As a boy being educated at Ripon he was treated like any other novice and so he had no personal body servant. However, one of the boys serving the members of his gesith brought him some bread, cheese and a flagon of ale.

'You need to sleep Cyning,' the boy told him firmly. 'My master says that you will be no good to anyone if you're exhausted.'

Ælfwine was about to cuff the boy for his impudence but instead he nodded and sat down with his back to the palisade to get a few minutes rest. It was four hours before he awoke to find it was now dark. One of his thegns was kneeling by him and gently shaking his shoulder.

'I'm sorry to wake you Cyning, but two of the sentries reported movement near the east side of the palisade.'

'Thank you, I'll come.'

Five minutes later he joined the garrison commander.

'What's happening,' he asked in a whisper.

'We're about the illuminate the area.'

A minutes later he gave an order and men threw earthenware jars full of oil and fat from the walkway to land several yards from the palisade. Seconds later several fire arrows plunged into the places where the pots had shattered and walls of fire leaped up. By the light of the flames the defenders could see that the Mercians had nearly reached the palisade with their scaling ladders.

Volley after volley of arrows rained down on the attackers and they fled back into the darkness, most of them dropping their ladders in their haste to escape. By the light of the dying flames Ælfwine could see that at least sixty men had been killed or badly wounded. A few tried to crawl away but they were sitting ducks for the archers. By the time that the flames died down none of the fallen were moving.

Catinus had been furious when he returned to find his son missing. He blamed Drefan and roundly cursed him until he calmed down and realised that he was being unfair. The boy had never seen Catinus so angry and he cowered expecting to be beaten, though that had never happened before. In the end all he received was a tongue lashing but that was bad enough.

When someone drew his attention to the smoke rising above the trees he remounted his horse and he and Ruaidhrí went to investigate. They met a grinning Osfrid on the way. Catinus was about to vent his fury on him when Ruaidhrí put his hand on his arm.

'Is that your doing, Osfrid?' he asked.

'Yes, lord. I sent a few fire arrows into their camp and now the blaze is spreading nicely.'

Catinus bit his tongue. He was glad that Ruaidhrí had stopped him but he needed to make his son realise that he'd been reckless as well as disobedient; however, now was not the time. Then he realised that, without many of their tents, the Mercians would billet themselves in the huts in the town. Men sleeping in small groups would be vulnerable.

The following day was uneventful. The Mercians sent out patrols but Catinus' men withdrew five miles, only to return in the late afternoon. That night the weather changed. The dry, sunny days had lasted for nearly two weeks, but now conditions changed with a vengeance. Clouds scudded across the sky as dusk fell and an hour or so later a violent thunder storm arrived from the west. The heavy rain soon turned the dusty ground into a quagmire and the night was lit up by forked lightening accompanied by the crash of thunder.

Ælfwine had returned to his post on top of the gates. He stood with the hood of his cloak pulled up to keep off the worst of the downpour whilst watching the open ground. No one thought that the Mercians would make a night attack again but Ælfwine thought it was possible. Hopefully his brother's army was on its way by now. If so, Wulfhere would want to capture Loidis before it arrived.

When the next flash of lightening lit up the sky he thought he saw movement, not in the cleared ground between the huts and the hall, but at the edge of the town. He shrugged; it was probably a few Mercians seeking shelter from the storm.

The next morning dawned bright and clear. The only evidence of the previous night was the puddles of water that dotted the ground. However, the discovery of nineteen men with slit throats in the huts nearest the perimeter of the town further demoralised the Mercians. Ælfwine knew that something had happened to disturb them, but he didn't know what.

He was feeling confident that he could hold out until his brother came to relieve Loidis when that confidence was dashed. Some five hundred more reinforcements arrived under the banner of the Middle Anglians. Just before dusk several hundred more arrived, this time bearing that of the East Saxons. They more than made up for the losses that Wulfhere had suffered and Ælfwine grew despondent.

~~~

Ecgfrith had advanced as far as Tadcaster when Catinus' messenger arrived with news of the reinforcements. Instead of halting for the night he decided to push on. Loidis was only a dozen miles from Tadcaster; they could be there by midnight and camp nearby, ready to do battle the next day.

As his men settled down for the night Ecgfrith called a war council. It was held in the open as erecting tents had been pointless. What time was left before sunrise was better spent sleeping rather than erecting and dismantling the camp. Apart from Octa the Hereræswa, he was joined by five eorls, Catinus and Ruaidhrí, who had ridden with their men to meet the king.

'We have just under three thousand men in total, whereas the Mercians have perhaps three and a half thousand now that they have been reinforced. However, we have another few hundred bottled up in the fortress. The Mercians are camped along the River Aire two hundred yards from the perimeter of the town. Catinus will explain their disposition in more detail.'

'Thank you Cyning. Before we arrived the Mercians left their camp and baggage train virtually unguarded whilst they went into Loidis to try and breech the walls around the king's hall. They changed tactics when my son burned half their tents down single handed.'

It was evident how proud Catinus was of Osfrid by the fact that he had singled him out for mention.

'Now they always leave a strong guard on the camp. Furthermore, we attacked and wiped out three of their foraging parties. They are short of food and so they are forced to forage in much stronger numbers. Our estimate is that this reduces the numbers engaged in attacking the hall by perhaps five of six hundred.'

'My plan is to capture their camp and take up a position between it and the town. I expect Wulfhere to withdraw his men and to try and recapture his camp. There isn't room to deploy them properly if we take up our position in the space between their camp and the nearest huts. This will force him to attack us piecemeal. We will force them back into the streets of the town where a detachment of our warriors will be waiting for them. I also want some of our archers on the hut roofs to add to the chaos.'

'What will the horsemen be doing, Cyning? They are not suited to fighting in enclosed spaces,' one of the eorls asked.

'A few scouts will be deployed to make sure that we are not surprised by either more reinforcements or the returning forage parties. The rest will give Wulfhere a little surprise.'

~~~

Ælfwine watched in dismay as the Mercians swarmed up their scaling ladders and managed to drive the defenders back from a section of the palisade. More and more Mercians climbed up to join their fellows and they inexorably drove his men back. A few of the attackers ran down the steps into the compound and started to slaughter the unarmed men, women and children who had taken refuge with him.

Then a horn rang out again and again. The assault on the fortress ceased in an instant and now the enemy was retreating back into the streets of the town. Those left stranded on the walkway around the palisade and in the compound tried to flee but the Northumbrians were in no mood to let them escape.

Ælfwine yelled for his men manning the palisade elsewhere to join in the fight against the Mercians on the walkway whilst he led twenty men down into the compound to deal with the enemy there. The first warrior he encountered was a boy only a couple of years older than he was. The boy had evidently only just completed his training as he made the thrust with his spear in the manner taught to all new warriors.

There was a standard defence against it and no doubt his opponent expected Ælfwine to use it; he didn't. Instead of deflecting it with his shield and making a counter thrust he let go of his shield, leaving it hanging in front of him by the strap around his neck and, grabbing the spear haft with one hand, he pulled the boy towards him and thrust his seax into his groin.

The boy yelled in agony and fell to the ground clutching his wound with both hands. Ælfwine left him to bleed to death, and pulling his shield in front of him again, sought another opponent. Most of the Mercians in the compound had been killed by this time. A few had tried to surrender but they had been cut down. The Northumbrians were in no mood to spare those who had killed women and children in cold blood.

Only one man with a battle axe remained. He swung it around him like a man possessed and had already cut down two of Ælfwine's best warriors. The young king looked around him and spotted an archer up on the palisade.

'Kill him,' he yelled, pointing at the axeman.

The archer nodded and nocked an arrow to his bowstring. The axeman was too preoccupied keeping his foes at bay to be aware of the archer. The arrow flew true and struck his chest, penetrating his leather jerkin and lodging close to his heart. It wasn't enough to kill him but it distracted him sufficiently for two spearmen to get past his guard. One point entered his neck and the other entered his eye socket and ended up in his brain. The man dropped as if pole axed.

The only Mercians left on the walkway were dead and so Ælfwine gathered the two hundred of his men who could still fight and they made their way out of the gates towards the sound of battle.

~~~

Ecgfrith had drawn his men up in five ranks with his archers in front after they had captured the camp and the baggage train. All but the most valuable items were put to the torch and it was the smoke from the conflagration that had alerted Wulfhere to the presence of Ecgfrith and so saved Ælfwine from defeat.

The Mercians came running into the open space to find their foe drawn up a mere hundred yards from them. The archers were even closer and they poured a rain of arrows into the horde of Mercians as they ran into the open. Some two hundred died before the rest were able to seek shelter behind the huts.

Then archers on the rooftops began to single out the lords and best equipped warriors for death. The heavily armed men couldn't climb onto the roofs easily and so it was the less well protected that tried to get to grips with the archers, who turned and jumped across the short space from roof to roof in the densely packed town. They paused now and again to send an arrow into their nearest pursuer. Eventually the Mercians realised that they were dying to little purpose and gave up the chase. When they climbed down into the street they were confronted by groups of Northumbrians who made short work of killing them.

Wulfhere eventually managed to restore order and his men advanced out of the town in formation to engage the main body of the Northumbrians. At first he seemed to be gaining the upper hand as the latter slowly withdrew. Then Ælfwine led his two hundred in a mad attack on the rear of the enemy centre.

Coincidentally Catinus appeared on one flank of the Mercians and Ruaidhrí on the other. It couldn't have worked better if it had been planned. Each group of seventy horsemen threw their spears into the packed rows of warriors and then withdrew. This, coupled with the attack on their rear, unnerved the Mercians and the less experienced of them at the rear turned to flee into the town.

Many managed to escape but scores didn't, falling to either Ælfwine's men or the hunter packs sent in by Ecgfrith and his archers.

Ecgfrith's shield wall advanced and, now weakened, Wulfhere's men were forced back. Then the cry went up that Wulfhere had fallen. Ethelred did his best to rally those

Mercians who hadn't fled, but it was hopeless and, after another quarter of an hour in which he lost two hundred more men, he surrendered.

Chapter Six – Two Weddings

675 AD

Ecgfrith was overcome with emotion when he saw that his brother was not only alive and well, but carrying a battered shield and a sword from the end of which a few drops of blood still dripped.

'You took your time,' Ælfwine greeted him with a grin.

Ecgfrith didn't reply but jumped down from his horse to embrace his brother.

'You don't know how much I wanted to race here to rescue you but Octa convinced me that to do so would have been suicidal until I'd mustered enough men. You can't imagine how relieved I am to see you alive and well.'

Then he noticed the blood on Ælfwine's byrnie and face.

'You're wounded?'

'No, it's not my blood; just that of the men I killed.'

He grinned, inordinately thrilled that he'd killed his first two men.

'It seems that my little brother has grown up to be a warrior.'

Ecgfrith was proud of his brother but he was also worried about him. Ælfwine had always been reckless and seemed to have no fear, either of death or anything else. He wished that he had a cooler head. He had an uneasy feeling that sooner or later it would lead into a situation that he wouldn't be able to escape from unscathed. He sighed. It was no good trying to talk some sense into the boy. He would nod in agreement and assure his brother that he would take more care in future and then completely forget about his promise when some other adventure presented itself.

The Mercian invasion had been a disaster. The pretender to the throne of Deira had been killed and, if Wulfhere wasn't dead, he was severely wounded and might yet die. Dark had descended soon after the rout of the Mercians so at least they were spared immediate pursuit. Ethelred sent his brother back to Mercia in a cart that had survived the attack on their camp with what remained of the king's gesith as escort.

Meanwhile he did his best to round up his army and led them back along the old Roman road that ran from near Loidis to the ruins of Mamucium. Here he halted. Officially he was still in Northumbria but, as the people of Rheged had revolted against Ecgfrith's rule and, as yet, he hadn't sought to re-impose his rule on them, Rheged was an anarchistic land with the local nobles acting as they pleased. Consequently there was no organised resistance to his occupation of the area.

Gradually other survivors of the Battle of Loidis trickled in. Of course, some had headed for their homes, but in the end Ethelred managed to gather two thousand men; enough, he thought, to be able to negotiate with Ecgfrith.

Ecgfrith had followed up the Mercian retreat and was at the ruins of Rigodunum, ten miles from Mamucium, when Ethelred's messenger found him.

'What does Wulfhere say, Cyning?' Octa asked.

'Not Wulfhere, he must have been more seriously wounded than first reports suggested. The message is from his brother, Ethelred. He proposes a meeting to discuss a truce.'

'Huh, not surprising. He's outnumbered, his men are discouraged and we've got him on the run. I say we invade Mercia and ravage the land, as he's done in Elmet.'

'Yes Ecgfrith. We can subject Mercia to your rule, as our father did twenty years ago,' Ælfwine chimed in, his eyes alight with excitement.

'Calm down. You're getting carried away and not thinking things through. Even our father couldn't hang onto Mercia for long. Besides, I still have the problem of Rheged to deal with. No, it would be far better to agree a lasting truce with Mercia.'

~~~

The negotiations were entrusted to Bishop Wilfrid for Northumbria and the Mercian Bishop of Lichfield, Seaxwulf. Ecgfrith's instructions were quite clear. He wanted to secure a lasting peace with Mercia, just as his father had done. As evidence of good faith he wanted a royal hostage but Wulhere's son, Coenred was only three months old. Wulfhere's nearest relatives after his brother and his son were his cousin, Alweo, King of Man, and the latter's two sons, four-year-old Æthelbald and one year old Heartbehrt.

His other demand was appropriate recompense for the destruction wrought in Elmet. This was a simpler matter. Lindsey had originally been an independent kingdom until a Northumbrian noble had become king. For a time it was a client kingdom of Northumbria until Penda conquered it and made it part of Mercia. Ecgfrith wanted it back, even though it was south of the Humber.

It was Wilfrid who suggested a compromise. Instead of demanding a suitable Mercian hostage he suggested that the two royal houses should be bound together through marriage. Ecgfrith's sister Osthryth was now twenty nine and still unmarried, a condition she was quite content with. However, she had refused to become a nun and so had remained a spinster. At thirty, Ethelred was almost the same age as Osthryth and so Wilfrid proposed that they should marry.

Neither party was very keen on the idea, but politically it made sound sense. The negotiations dragged on for over a month, by which time Wulfhere had recovered from his wounds sufficiently to take over the reins of government again. He pressured Ethelred to agree to the match and so the wedding was arranged for the early autumn.

If Ethelred was unwilling to marry someone as old as he was, he was even more unwilling to give Lindsey away, but Wulfhere saw little alternative. Mercia was now too weak to resist Ecgfrith if he decided to invade and there was more trouble on his southern border. Raids from Wessex were increasing in frequency and severity. He needed peace with Ecgfrith urgently so he could turn his attention to the immediate problem.

It was a fine but chilly day in late September when a sulky Ethelred and an equally unwilling Osthryth were married in the monastery church at Lichfield by the two bishops, Wilfrid and Seaxwulf.

Catinus and his son Osfrid had been invited, along with most of the nobility of both Mercia and Northumbria. Although the church was as large as any in Northumbria, it was still crowded and Catinus had given in to the pleas of Osfrid, now eleven, that he be allowed to sit on his father's shoulders so that he could see. Catinus realised that it was a mistake several minutes after giving way to his son. His thigh had healed well enough but it still troubled him and now, with the additional weight of Osfrid placed upon it, it threatened to give way.

Catinus lifted him off his shoulders and told him curtly to push his way to where he could see the altar. As far as he was concerned he couldn't care less whether he witnessed the ceremony or not. Given his short stature compared to most men present he would have to have been right at the front to see anything. Whereas his slight son might be able to worm his way there, a man as stout and broad shouldered as he was couldn't do so without creating an uproar.

He'd only come because Ruaidhrí wanted someone to accompany him. Although Master of the King's Horse and an ealdorman, Ruaidhrí didn't feel part of the nobility of Northumbria. Catinus realised that, underneath his confident outward façade, his friend was actually quite nervous amongst strangers.

The Ulsterman was now twenty six and about to get married himself. His choice had fallen on a daughter of the Ealdorman of Jarrow, whose lands adjoined his to the south. She was called Edyth and she was ten years younger than Ruaidhrí. They had met when her father had brought her to Alnwic to buy her a new riding horse a year ago.

He bred horses mainly for the king's warriors and taught them to fight on horseback, but he also bred a few horses from stock he owned for private sale. Ruaidhrí had fallen for Edyth during that first meeting and she seemed equally smitten by the handsome young Ulsterman. The problem was that, although their estates were next to each other, Alnwic was in the north of Ruaidhrí's lands and Jarrow lay on the River Tyne, a dozen miles south of the River Wansbeck which separated the two domains.

Catinus had eventually persuaded his friend that he needed to grasp the bull by the horns and eleven months ago, immediately after he'd returned from the battle against the Mercians, he'd ridden south with just his body servant and two men as escort to see Edyth's father. He needn't have worried; her father was delighted to see his third daughter married to an ealdorman. His two eldest girls had chosen a thegn and the church, which wasn't what he'd hoped for them. He also had two other children, a boy of thirteen being educated at the monastery near Jarrow and another girl.

If Catinus hadn't particularly enjoyed Ethelred's wedding itself, he certainly enjoyed the feast afterwards, as did Osfrid. For the first time in his life the boy had been allowed to get drunk and he celebrated his new found freedom by being violently sick. Unfortunately the recipient of his puke had been the fifteen year old son of a Mercian noble who'd been sitting next to him.

Amongst the general rowdiness of the feast the altercation didn't attract too much attention, but the unfortunate Mercian boy had leaped up from the table in revulsion and had taken considerable exception to the ruination of his brand new tunic and trousers. He had drawn a dagger on Osfrid when a calmer head next door to him clamped his hand down on that of the offended boy.

'We've all drunk too much in our time, boy. Let it pass and go and get changed.'

'Do you know who I am?'

The boy's eyes glittered dangerously and for a moment the man thought that he might be foolish enough to attack him.

'No, do you know who I am,' he said putting emphasis on the I.

'Some insufferable thegn who's poking his nose in where it has no business,' he replied heatedly.

The man laughed. 'I'm no thegn, boy. Your father knows who I am well enough. I'm Wigestan. The commander of Prince Ethelred's gesith,' he added when comprehension didn't dawn on the boy.

'Oh,'

'Yes, oh. Now go and get changed.'

Wigestan glanced down at Osfrid, who was now snoring loudly, and smiled. The boy would never know how close he came to being gutted.

~~~

Osthryth awaited the arrival of her new husband after the feast with considerable trepidation. She knew what had happened between her sister Alflæd and Ethelred's elder brother, Paeda. He had treated her brutally until she'd had enough and she slowly poisoned him to death. She prayed that Ethelred wouldn't be like Paeda.

She cowered in the bed, pulling the furs up under her chin when he entered, calling out some bawdy comment to his friends who'd come with him to the door of his chamber. He came and sat on the bed beside her when he saw how afraid she was.

'What's this?

His mind was a little befuddled by drink but not so much that he didn't soon realise why Osthryth was afraid of him.

'Don't worry,' he laughed softly. 'I'm nothing like Paeda; I don't think you'll have to resort to poison in my case.'

'You know?'

'Yes, I know and Wulfhere knows. We chose to keep quiet about it because we were ashamed of how Paeda behaved and we didn't want it to become the subject of idle gossip amongst the common people.'

He gently stroked her shoulder and then bent down to kiss her gently on the lips. Somehow she knew that Ethelred would treat her well and perhaps she might even come to love him in time.

~~~

Once again Ruaidhrí felt nervous, this time because it was his own wedding day. Unlike the fine weather which had graced Osthryth's marriage to Ethelred, the weather was foul. The sky wasn't even grey, it was black, and snow fell with flakes as big as the opal mounted on the hilt of his dagger, a wedding gift from Catinus.

Thankfully most of the guests had arrived before the weather had worsened. Everyone said that they had never seen snow like it so early on, after all it was only the middle of November. Men were out clearing a path from his hall to the church, but the snow fell as fast as it was cleared.

Everywhere was a blinding universal white, not that anyone was able to see very far through the swirling flakes. He trudged through the snow, thankful he was wearing leather boots instead of shoes, and kicked the accumulated snow from them before he entered the small timber church. His body servant took his thick, oiled riding cloak from him as he entered and he walked down the aisle between the throng of people standing on either side.

Catinus smiled at him as he reached the front and Osfrid gave him a cheeky grin. The priest officiating had arrived at Bebbanburg the previous week and had travelled down with Catinus and his son. His arrival had caused something of a stir. Catinus' brother, Conomultus, had been left without a home when Bruide had replaced him with a Pict as the Bishop of Abernethy. Conomultus had been lucky to have just been exiled.

He had fallen out with King Oswiu years ago and had fled Northumbria; however, now that Oswiu was dead, he felt that it was safe to return and had taken passage on a knarr as far as his brother's fortress. He had thought of retiring to Lindisfarne as a monk but Catinus had persuaded him to stay at Bebbanburg as his chaplain.

When his previous chaplain had died, the priest from the nearby vill had fulfilled the role pro tem. It was a step up in status from being a local priest but he seemed pleased by Conomultus' appointment. Catinus wasn't surprised. He was an idle man and would have no doubt welcomed the reduction in his responsibilities.

Edyth arrived in a covered cart to protect her finery from the snow as much as possible. She looked radiant as she walked down the aisle, keeping her eyes demurely downcast. When she reached her husband-to-be she looked up and smiled at him before looking at Conomultus, waiting for him to begin.

When the ceremony was over and mass had been celebrated the couple stood in the doorway and looked in dismay at the falling snow. The path that had been cleared was a foot deep again so Ruaidhrí sent for the cart and travelled back to his hall in it with his new bride. The rest would have to make their own way as best they could.

This time Osfrid was a little more circumspect about how much ale and mead he consumed and only became pleasantly merry. Besides, he didn't want to show himself up in front of the young girl he was sat next to, Edyth's youngest sister Godwyna. She was eleven years old and Osfrid thought that she was the prettiest girl he had ever seen. Godwyna was flattered by his obvious interest in her and she unconsciously flirted with him. By the time the meal finished Osfrid knew he was in love.

Of course his father told him it was merely infatuation but Osfrid knew better. Had they both been a few years older Catinus would have encouraged the match. Not only was her father, Benoc, an ealdorman, but he was also descended from Ida, just as Ecgfrith was, although through another branch of the family.

It had taken five days before the weather had improved sufficiently for everyone to leave Alnwic after the wedding. Ruaidhrí was getting worried by this stage as feeding so many guests for so long had seriously depleted the food he'd stored to see them through the winter, so Catinus proposed a hunt before everyone left.

Rather than leave Osfrid with the women and other children, Catinus decided to take him on the hunt; a decision which made his son's eyes light up, Godwyna forgotten for the moment.

They split into four parties, each heading in a different direction. As his domain started the other side of the River Aln, Catinus led the hunt going north.

'Keep close beside me and if we encounter a boar or a stag keep behind me.'

'Yes, father,' Osfrid said dutifully.

If he had the opportunity to make a kill he intended to take it, never mind what his father had said. He hefted his spear in his right hand, judging its weight and point of balance.

The going was tough. In some places the drifted snow had yet to thaw and, where it had, it was a morass of mud. The hounds found no scent at all until they entered the woods that ran alongside the river about two miles north of Alnwic. Then they got excited and the huntsmen had to run to keep up with them.

'Boar, I'll be bound,' one of thegns riding beside Catinus said.

Not counting Osfrid, there were six mounted nobles and two huntsmen on foot, each with two hounds. One pair were used to track the quarry and the other pair brought it to bay so that one of the nobles could make the kill. Two boys followed on with pack horses to bring back the kill.

It was evident from the spoor that they were tracking a boar and, as it turned out, a wily one. He led the dogs into a clearing but then circled back through dense undergrowth. The first that Catinus knew of his presence was when the beast erupted from a bush and charged at the thegn riding beside him.

It happened so fast that the man was totally unprepared and the huge boar thrust his pointed tusks into the underbelly of the horse. It fell to its knees and then collapsed onto one side trapping its rider's right leg underneath it. The man was totally helpless as the boar drew its head back to rip its tusks into the thegn.

Catinus thrust his spear down into the body of the animal but the only effect that had was to enrage it further. Osfrid was immediately behind the thegn and reacted quickly. He jumped down from his horse and aimed the point of his spear at roughly where he thought its heart should be. Thrusting with all his might he pushed the spear point through the hide covered in rough, matted hair and into its flesh. It was much more resistant than he expected and, before he could reach the heart, the boar had twisted round to face him, the thegn forgotten.

Osfrid found himself looking straight into the boar's small red eyes as the spear was torn from his grasp. He thought he was about to be gored to death as the boar lowered its head and went to impale him on its tusks. He felt the animal's fetid breath on his face just as he jumped to one side a split second before it reached him.

He rolled and came up crouched ready for the beast's next attack, drawing his dagger as he did so; but it wasn't necessary. He had bought the others enough time to react and now the boar was in its death throes with three new spears in its side.

Osfrid felt drained and sick. His father reached him just as he was about to collapse and threw his arms around him, nearly crushing him to death in his relief at the boy's narrow escape. Catinus knew he should scold him for disobeying him but, had he not acted when he did, the thegn would have died. He returned to Alnwic to be hailed as a hero at the feast held that night. He basked in all the praise but the most important thing to him was the admiration in Godwyna's eyes. Then his heart sank as he realised that they would both be leaving in the morning and heading their separate ways.

To take his mind off the girl Catinus decided to take his son on a tour of his shire. It comprised an eighth of the original kingdom of Bernicia. It extended from the River Twaid in the north to the Aln in the south and as far west as the mountains called simply the Uplands. This area stretched for over thirty miles from east to west and divided Bernicia from the Caledonian Kingdom of Strathclyde. It was uninhabited except for a few people who recognised no lord.

They departed in early January after the Christmas celebrations were over. Conomultus came with them as did Eadstan and Catinus' body servant, Drefan. Eadstan wanted to bring all the gesith as escort but Catinus told him that the group was to be kept small. In the end they just took Leofric and Uurad, his two former body servants who were now skilled warriors. The cold spell over Christmas had ended and the weather was comparatively warm for early January. A brisk south easterly wind, coupled with the absence of any rain for over a week, had dried the ground and so travelling was relatively pleasant.

His domain might only comprise twelve vills but they were spread over a vast area. By the time that they returned January had turned into February and the weather had turned much colder with occasional wintery showers. Both father and son were glad to reach Bebbanburg again and made straight for the hearth to warm their chilled bodies.

No sooner had they begun to thaw out than the reeve entered.

'Morcar, what is it that's so urgent that it can't wait until I can feel my fingers again?'

'Oh it's not urgent, lord. But I thought that Osfrid would like to see the two gifts that have arrived for him whilst you've been away.'

Osfrid opened one package then the other with numbed fingers. The first contained a magnificent seax with a leather hilt inlaid with gold wire and surmounted by a wolf's head fashioned from gold. The note with it said that it was from the thegn whose life he'd saved.

Catinus whistled when Osfrid showed it him.

'That must have cost a quarter of his annual income,' he said, turning the weapon over in his hand.

Not only was the hilt expensive and finely made but the tempered steel blade was engraved with a wolf's head on both sides near the hilt. The scabbard was equally noteworthy being made of wood encased in red leather dotted with small silver studs. The chape at the end was also made of silver. He doubted if even the king had a weapon as fine.

Osfrid had never seen anything so impressive and he couldn't take his eyes off it, swishing it through the air and admiring it until his father reminded him he had a second gift to open.

Once he'd done so he forgot all about the magnificent seax. It was simple silver brooch to fasten his cloak with but it was special because it was a gift from Godwyna.

'There's a note inside the wrapping for you father,' he said handing it over without taking his eyes off the brooch. Godwyna must have had it made especially because it too featured a wolf's head, the emblem of Bebbanburg.

'It's an invitation from Ealdorman Benoc for us to visit his family in Jarrow. Apparently Godwyna won't shut up about you.'

'Really? When are we going?'

'When I've thawed out and taken care of all the routine business that will have piled up in my absence.'

'I can help you with that,' his son said eagerly.

The reminder that his son had been forced to cope with everything whilst he had shut himself away to mourn Leoflaed saddened him and he determined to travel to Jarrow just as soon as possible.

But it wasn't to be. Two days later a summons came from Ecgfrith ordering him to muster his men for the invasion of Rheged.

Chapter Seven – The Last Days of Rheged

676 AD

Ecgfrith's nobles stirred uncomfortably after the king had finished speaking. The Witan was meeting at Loidis the day after the muster of the army was complete. The weather was set fair; the sky was uniformly blue, dotted with the odd fluffy white cloud, and for early April it was unseasonably warm. However, the mood inside the church, where the Witan was meeting, could not have been darker.

The uneasy silence was broken by Ælfwine.

'You make it sound as if you want to exterminate the Britons of Rheged.'

'You've obviously been listening then,' his brother replied caustically. 'That's exactly what I've been saying. Our forefathers drove the Britons out of Bernicia, Deira and Elmet and now we must do the same to the faithless inhabitants of Rheged.'

'Cyning, I know that they supported your brother's claim to the throne but isn't what you propose a little extreme?' Beornheth, the Eorl of Lothian, asked. 'After all the Goddodin are a British tribe who inhabit Lothian and we co-exist peacefully with them.'

'But they are loyal and have been part of Lothian since before my uncle Oswald was king. They are integrated into Northumbria and many Angles have settled there, even some

132

Saxons, and they've intermarried so that now they are one people. That isn't true of Rheged. They lived under the rule of an Anglian eorl appointed by Oswiu to represent him but they murdered him, his family and his gesith before joining Alchfrith's revolt. It's not the same as Lothian.'

'What will you do when you have driven out or enslaved the Britons of Rheged?' Bishop Wilfrid asked.

'Divide it into two shires, each ruled by a Northumbrian ealdorman, and new Anglo-Saxon settlers will be given the land.'

'Then I hope that you will consider establishing new monasteries following the Roman rule to replace the Celtic ones at Caer Luel and Heysham, Cyning'

'Perhaps, but if so I won't be appointing you as abbot, Wilfrid.'

The bishop tried to look affronted at the suggestion but the laughter of the other members of Witan indicated that the king's barbed remark had hit home. Wilfrid was already abbot of three monasteries and was said to be much richer than even the king in consequence.

A few more nobles and several churchmen spoke against the king's strategy, but in the end the Witan acquiesced to his plan.

~~~

Catinus had debated what to do about Osfrid. Unsurprisingly the boy had wanted to go with him but he was now nearly twelve, the age when Catinus had arranged for him to go to Lindisfarne to be educated alongside the novice monks. Osfrid was less than keen, especially as the Master of Novices was his brother. Alaric was young, at sixteen, to be chosen for such an important role but he had already made a name for himself as a scholar and got on well with the novices. He was both liked and respected, two qualities that didn't always go hand in hand.

Abbot Eata had wanted to send him to Rome or to Frankia to improve his education further but Prior Cuthbert was concerned that the other candidates for the task were less well suited. They either had a tendency to bully their juniors or they were poorly educated themselves. In the end Eata gave way in return for a promise from Cuthbert that Alaric would be allowed to travel to the Continent once an acceptable candidate to take over the novices was available.

'But father, if I can't go with you, I should stay here and manage the fortress and the shire, as I've done before.'

Catinus had winced at the reminder of the months he'd shut himself away from the world.

'I'm sorry, Osfrid, but you need to learn more about the scriptures and how to read and write better. Besides you'll be with boys your own age; it's time you were allowed to grow up more slowly than hitherto.'

'Huh! They'll think like children. I'm passed that stage.'

'More's the pity. No, it's no good continuing to plead with me. My mind's made up.'

'Then who will be in charge here?' Osfrid asked, thinking he'd played his trump card.

'Your uncle, Conomultus. Don't forget he's been a bishop and is a very able administrator.'

'Oh, won't you want him to go with you?'

'Normally yes, of course, but he can serve me better by remaining here.'

Whilst the last of his men were travelling to the muster point for the shire at Yeavering, Catinus and Conomultus rode to Lindisfarne with a sulky Osfrid and Drefan. The fact that the servant boy was excited about going to war with his father made Osfrid even more irritable.

'I'd advise you to snap out of your current mood before we arrive at the monastery. The first impression you make on your fellows is important. Unless, of course, you want to be friendless and miserable for the next two years,' Conomultus told him sternly.

'Don't care.'

'You're behaving like a spoiled brat instead of the mature youth I know you can be,' Catinus added. 'We're stopping here.'

'Why?'

'Because I know that Drefan is getting on your nerves with his exuberance and both of you need to be taught a lesson. Now get off your horses.'

Puzzled, the two boys did as they were told. The two men did likewise and Conomultus took the reins of the horses.

'Now you are to wrestle until one of you has pinned the other to the ground. Best of three. Now go.'

The two boys looked at each other dubiously. Drefan was a year younger than Osfrid and smaller, but he was wiry and could move quickly. The problem was that he was a servant and his opponent was his master's son. His natural deference made him hesitant.

Osfrid was well aware of that and his innate sense of fairness prevented him from taking advantage. They circled each other but made no move to get to grips. Exasperated, Catinus kicked his son hard on the bottom, sending him cannoning into Drefan. The other boy hadn't seen the kick and thought that he had made his move. He sidestepped and stuck his leg out so that the older boy tripped and went sprawling in the dirt.

Now furious, Osfrid got up and rushed at Drefan. When the latter went to try the same trick again Osfrid was ready and moved the same way, throwing his arms around Drefan and pushing him to the ground. Once on top of him, Osfrid thought it would be easy to pin Drefan's two shoulders to the ground, but the boy wriggled like a snake. Suddenly he heaved his body upwards, taking Osfrid unaware, and the boy rose into the air enough for Drefan to get his head under his opponent's chest. He head butted him, driving the air out of his lungs. Winded, Osfrid was unable to do anything for a moment or two and Drefan flipped him over and pinned his shoulders to the ground.

Osfrid looked up at the boy sitting on his heaving chest grinning down at him with his knees pinning his shoulders. Suddenly he thrust his groin in the air and the surprised boy sailed over his head to crash onto the earth. Now it was Osfrid's turn to pin his opponent and he used his additional weight to immobilise the dazed Drefan.

Osfrid got up and pulled Drefan to his feet.

'No need for another bout I think, father. It would be better to end this with honours even.'

Catinus nodded. 'Well done both of you. We might as well stop here to eat before we cross the sands to Lindisfarne.'

He and his brother smiled at one another. The wrestling bout had restored Osfrid's good humour and taken the cocky Drefan down a peg or two. Not only that, but they chatted away like friends until they reached the monastery. They might be at opposite ends of the social spectrum, but by the time that they reached the island they had discovered that they liked and respected each other.

~~~

Ecgfrith's strategy was simple. He divided his army into three columns and advanced westwards towards the main inhabited settlements at Caer Luel in the north, along the old Roman roads through the mountains to Heysham on the coast, and south west to Mamucium and thence to Wigan. Each column was to follow a scorched earth policy, driving the Britons ever westward to the coast of the Irish Sea.

The king commanded the southernmost column, mainly as it was operating in territory bordering Mercia. Ælfwine was tasked to capture Caer Luel with Octa to guide him and Beornheth, Prior Cuthbert's younger brother and Eorl of Lothian, led the centre.

'Catinus, you and your horsemen will act as scouts for Beornheth. Ruaidhrí you are to come with me with half your men and the other half are to scout for Ælfwine,' Ecgfrith told them at the war council before the three columns went their separate ways. 'Remember, I want the Britons driven out. We need to move fast before they have time to organise any resistance to us. That means we don't take slaves. Those that flee up into the hills can be rounded up later. Clear? Good, may God be with you.'

Catinus paused as he crested the saddle on the road from Isurium Brigantum near Ripon to the old Roman fort at Verbeia. They had now entered the territory of an ancient British tribe called the Brigantes. Rheged might be disunited and leaderless but the Brigantes were different. They were led by chieftains, one of whom they called their king – or brenin in their language.

The road was overgrown with weeds and many of the cobbles that had paved it had become dislodged, but it was still a much better surface to march on than tracks that were muddy when wet and dusty when dry which served as roads in most of Northumbria.

Catinus had sent twenty of his mounted warband out as a screen, half to the front and the rest to either flank. He was halfway down the hillside into the valley of the River Ribble when two of his lead scouts came riding back.

'Lord, the Brigantes are blocking the road ahead.'

'Where exactly?'

'You can't see them from here but they're just over the shoulder of the hill on the left. They're stretched right across the valley between the hills and the south bank of the river.'

'How many did you count?'

'About fourteen hundred. All are armed with spears and oval shields, a few had helmets but only one or two had a byrnie. There are a few bowmen and about a hundred boys with slings as well.'

'Go back and keep an eye on them. Come and find me if they start to move. I'll go and tell the eorl.'

Catinus thought about the situation as he cantered back to talk to Beornheth. They had some five hundred warriors plus around fifty archers and his horsemen. In total they numbered barely a third of the enemy's strength.

It had been Ecgfrith's decision not to bring the fyrd, just the war bands. The fyrd were intended to protect their homeland, not engage in an offensive operation and, besides, it was the planting season. However, they had one advantage; the Britons expected them to advance down the valley to engage them.

It had been raining off and on for the past week and, whilst it was unpleasant to wear soggy clothing most of the time, it did mean that the river would be high. Beornheth explained his plans to his commanders whilst the men set up camp in the hills south of the road.

Just before dawn they dismantled the camp and set off in two groups. Catinus led his fifty horsemen through the hills and, once they'd dropped down into the next valley, they rode as fast as they could along the valley and back over the intervening hills down towards the old Roman fort at Bremetennacum where the Britons had established a major settlement. Beornheth and he were gambling that only old men, women and children would be left there.

The settlement was surrounded by a palisade but the gates stood wide open and Catinus couldn't see any sentries. Now he and his men changed pace to a wild gallop, trying to reach the gates before the alarm was given and they were shut before they could get there.

Catinus could feel his stallion slowing down; it was blown and he swore in frustration. However, Uurad and several of his younger warriors overtook him and were only fifty yards from the gates when someone gave the alarm. Several old men, women and a few children grabbed the heavy gates and started to swing them shut. It wasn't easy. They were hung from leather hinges which had stretched over time, which meant that the bottom of the gates grazed the ground in places. Normally it took four men to shut one gate and, although there were now twice that number heaving at each gate they kept getting in each other's way and the horsemen thundering towards them made them panic.

Several abandoned the attempt just as they'd nearly managed to succeed and fled into the narrow lanes. Uurad got there first, closely followed by Leofric and half a dozen others. Seeing that the gates were secure, Catinus yelled to Eadstan and he and half a dozen men peeled off and headed around Bremetennacum to seal off the west gate.

Catinus told his men to dismount outside and enter the place on foot. To ride down the narrow lanes would be courting disaster. Although only old men, boys not yet old enough to train as warriors and a few disabled men opposed them, they were determined to sell their lives dearly in defence of their home. As they made their way cautiously towards the centre of the settlement a few of the Northumbrians were wounded and two were killed by slingshots stones and hunting arrows.

When he saw Leofric fall he lost his temper. It was his intention to round the inhabitants up and take them prisoner but he hadn't counted on losing men, especially those he was close to, such as his former body servant.

'No quarter!'

The cry was taken up and his men. Their behaviour in normal circumstances was reasonably civilised – for warriors - but now blood lust drove them on. They started to kill all those they could lay their hands on, be they unarmed greybeards, women or children. When Catinus saw the bodies of two little girls and three boys, none of whom could have been older than seven, he realised what he'd done; but by then it was too late.

The only survivors were the hundred or so who had reached the west gate, only to be faced by more of Catinus' warriors. They surrendered and even the most bloodthirsty of the Northumbrians had had enough of wanton killing by the time that they reached them. They were spared and Catinus let them flee down the valley heading towards the sea. He didn't have the resources to guard them and he was sickened by what he'd done. Releasing them was the least he could do.

Half an hour later his men had finished looting the huts and the king's hall. They rode through the settlement with blazing torches setting fire to the huts. Soon the place was a blazing inferno and black smoke rose into the still air. Satisfied that it would be seen by the Brigantian army, he led his men up the Ribble Valley towards the rear of the enemy. Most of his men were in a sombre mood on reaction to what they'd done, but Catinus was more than sombre; he was deeply depressed.

His orders were to attack the enemy formation from the rear but his heart was no longer in this campaign and he ordered Eadstan to take over whilst he rode into the hills to be by himself. Drefan watched him go, wondering whether he should follow.

'Come on, we'd better keep an eye on him,' Uurad said softly in his ear and the two rode after him at a distance, taking the two packhorses that Drefan had been leading with them.

When Catinus eventually reached the summit he turned and walked his horse slowly along the ridge above the Ribble Valley. Eventually the site of the battle came into view. It was obvious that Beornheth's tactics had worked. Whilst a few hundred of his warriors had advanced to engage the Britons, his archers had descended the hillside from the south and then proceeded to pepper the rows of Britons from the flank. Taken by surprise, the Britons didn't know what to do at first, but as more and more of his men on the right flank fell, the King of the Brigantes sent half his men up the hillside to attack the archers.

The latter merely withdrew in front of the Britons as they laboured up the hill but kept stopping to send volley after volley of arrows into the leading warriors. Some of the Britons got increasingly reluctant to continue with this folly and slowed to a crawl. Several hundred continued to pursue the archers however. When they neared the ridgeline, out of breath and exhausted, the other half of Beornheth's men appeared over the crest and charged down into them.

It was a rout. Out of the seven hundred men who had been sent up the hill only two hundred made it back down. Once they reached the bottom they kept going, back towards Bremetennacum. That was then they saw the black smoke starting to rise towards the blue sky above. They stopped, uncertain what to do. Some wanted to continue to see what had happened to their families, but others, single men in the main, fled into the hills.

Whatever they decided hadn't mattered in the end. Those who stayed in the valley encountered Eadstan and his horsemen and fled before them back towards the main fight. Most of the others who had headed for the hills were rounded up in the weeks that followed.

By the time that Catinus dismounted and sat on a rock to survey the scene below him fighting had almost stopped in the valley. It was evident from the piles of bodies that the remaining Britons had been caught between the two halves of the Northumbrian army and were increasingly squeezed into a smaller and smaller space. Completely routed, some tried to escape into the river and were swept away, others were cut down where they stood.

Catinus sat and wept. Partly because of Leofric's death, but also for the Brigantes who had effectively been wiped out as a tribe in a single day.

'Lord, you can't stay here. Night is falling and we need to go back down to the camp,' Uurad said eventually.'

Catinus nodded dumbly.

'Thank you for staying with me. Drefan, you've been a good servant but I shan't need a servant where I'm going.'

'What do you mean lord? You're not going to ..'

'Kill myself? No, that would be a sin, however much the idea appeals to me at the moment. No, I'm going to Lindisfarne to become a monk. I shall see out the rest of my days within sight of Bebbanburg across the bay whilst I try and atone for my sins.'

'What about Bebbanburg? You're the ealdorman.'

'My son ran the shire without me for seven months and he was younger then. I'm sure he'll manage very well without me. Besides, my brother will be his chaplain and he can help him until he's older.'

'Will you allow me to accompany you until you reach Lindisfarne?'

'Thank you, Uurad, but I'd rather you stay here with Eadstan for now.'

'What about me lord? You'll still need a servant until you reach Lindisfarne.'

'Very well. I suspect that Osfrid might need a servant after that.'

The boy smiled wanly. 'I'd like that but it won't be the same as serving you, lord.'

Catinus nodded but said no more.

When he told Beornheth it was plain that the eorl didn't understand or approve of his decision, but all he said was that he should ride north to Caer Luel first and see Ecgfrith.

'I'm not sure he'll make a twelve year old boy an ealdorman though. Perhaps you'd better stay in post until he's sixteen and old enough to be classed as a warrior.'

'No, my mind's made up. I'll not kill another human being and I need the peace and quiet of the monastic life to repent my sins.'

Osfrid was furious with his father when he told him he no longer had any desire to be the Ealdorman of Bebbanburg and had decided to retire to Lindisfarne as a monk. He refused to speak to him and, from then on, if he saw him around the monastery, he'd either turn away or, if he couldn't avoid him, he'd ignore him. It was as if his father had ceased to exist.

Ecgfrith had accepted Catinus' decision but he'd refused to make someone as young as Osfrid an ealdorman. Instead the shire was to be administered by Conomultus until the king decided what to do about it.

Two months later Prior Cuthbert sent for Osfrid.

'Osfrid, I'm not pleased with you. Your attitude towards Brother Catinus is upsetting all of us. An atmosphere of barely concealed hostility is not conducive to the peace and harmony we seek to cultivate here. The abbot believes that either you or he must go and your father is hardly at fault here, so it's you who should leave.'

'But where would I go,' the boy asked in dismay.

'Perhaps you should have thought of that,' Cuthbert said grimly. 'However, I have proposed another solution and Abbot Eata is prepared to give you one last chance.'

Osfrid studied his feet and didn't reply for a minute whilst he thought, then he exhaled sharply.

'I know I'm at fault and I sort of understand why my father has sought the solace of the monastic life to expiate what he sees as his sins. I can't see why it was necessary, after all they were Britons and now they've all been enslaved or expelled from what used to be called Rheged.'

After the campaign Ecgfrith had divided the former earldom of Rheged in two, appointing two of his gesith as the ealdormen of Cumbria in the north and Luncæstershire in the south.

'You seem to forget that your father was born a Briton in Mercia and you are half British yourself.'

Osfrid looked as shocked as if Cuthbert had struck him across the face. It was something he was vaguely aware of, but which he had pushed to the back of his consciousness. Now he was forced to confront it.

'Do you repent your attitude, especially the breaking of the commandment to honour your father?'

'Yes, Brother Prior. I'll go and find him now and beg his forgiveness.'

After Catinus had heard his contrite son out he didn't say anything but just pulled him into an embrace and kissed him on the cheek – a display of affection he'd never shown him before.

'I never stopped loving you, Osfrid, even though you hurt me dreadfully.'

'I always loved you too father. It's just that I'd always dreamt of being Ealdorman of Bebbanburg one day and I hated it when that was taken away from me. I can see now that I was being petulant though. I'll follow whatever path God wants me to.'

'Prior Cuthbert didn't tell you then?'

'Tell me what?'

'King Ecgfrith has written to Abbot Eata to say that he has decided what to do about Bebbanburg. Your uncle will continue as the administrator of the fortress and the shire for now and Eadstan will command the warband, but the king will confirm you as the ealdorman when you reach sixteen.'

Osfrid could hardly contain his excitement.

'Careful, you'll hug me to death!'

Osfrid let go of Catinus with a mumbled apology but his father just smiled at him.

'The other bit of news is that you are to train as a mounted warrior with Ruaidhrí when you leave here. Perhaps he might even take you with him when he pays the occasional visit to his father in law.'

It took a moment for the import of this to dawn on Osfrid, then he realised that Ruaidhrí's father in law, Benoc, was also the father of Godwyna.

Chapter Eight – The Division of the Diocese

678-9 AD

Bishop Wilfrid was furious. He had grown used to being the only bishop in the north of England and the stipends from the diocese and the three monasteries of which he abbot provided him with a large income. Now Archbishop Theodore had come up with the ridiculous idea, in Wilfrid's opinion, that his diocese was far too large and needed to be sub-divided.

It was true that he confined himself to visiting Ripon and Hexham, the other places where he was abbot in addition to the monastery at Eoforwīc, but there were priests and monks who could visit the other settlements throughout the north. He didn't see why he needed to do so as well.

As if Theodore's interference wasn't bad enough the king had also taken him to task at one of the meetings of his inner council. Whilst the Witan met infrequently, the inner council normally met weekly to advise the king on the minutiae of ruling his large kingdom.

'Bishop, I've received several complaints that members of your household are dressed far too lavishly, indeed some of them look more like nobles than servants.'

'Cyning surely it is my business how I choose to ...'

'I haven't finished, far from it,' Ecgfrith snapped.

Wilfrid looked annoyed at the interruption and at the tone the king had used.

'I'm told that you have also recruited a warband of your own, is this true?'

'Yes, Cyning. I need protection on my travels around my diocese and guards to protect the tithes due to the Church.'

'No other prelate seems to need protection. You don't see Abbot Eata with an armed escort, or Abbess Hild. They seem to manage to travel about and cover a lot more territory than you ever do.'

Wilfrid's eyes narrowed. Ecgfrith's queen, Eormenburg, had never hidden her dislike of him and Hild positively detested him. No doubt one or other, or perhaps both, had been dripping poison in the king's ear.

'You will disband your warband forthwith and in future you will dress your household in clothes more befitting their station in life. And I do mean immediately.'

'Yes, very well, if I must,' Wilfrid replied testily.

He was well aware that many of the other members of the king's inner council were trying to hide their glee at the bishop's discomfiture, and failing.

'Can we move onto more important matters, Cyning?'

'I'll decide what is important, bishop. Yet again I must ask you not to interrupt me. I haven't finished. Archbishop Theodore had written to me about the division of the Northumbrian diocese into four smaller sees.'

'Four? I'm only aware of his ridiculous proposal for three.'

'You're forgetting Lindsey. The Mercian Bishop of Lindocolina fled when Wulfhere ceded it to me. Since then it seems to have been taken under your wing but with no proper sanction for you to do so.'

'I was under the impression that the archbishop had agreed with King Ethelred that Lindsey should now come under the Lichfield diocese.'

'He had no right to do so. Lichfield is in Mercia but Lindsey is part of Northumbria.'

'But since the death of King Wulfhere recently during his war with Wessex I thought that the new king, Ethelred, had declared the treaty between you null and void.'

'He's merely playing politics. He was the one who agreed the truce. He may have done so in his brother's name but he was the one who swore to uphold it. In any case, he's in no position to challenge me over Lindsey with Wessex still contesting who controls Hwicce and the Welsh giving him problems as well.

Now back to the organisation of the Church in my kingdom, I tend to agree with Theodore that the kingdom is too much for one man. His proposal to create three sees based at Lindisfarne, Hexham and Eoforwīc seems to have merit in my eyes. Of course, you would remain as bishop here.'

'And who would these other bishops be?'

'Trumbert at Hexham and Eata at Lindisfarne.'

Trumbert was the prior at Ripon and therefore could be counted as one of Wilfrid's supporters but Eata and Wilfrid had fought as novices on Lindisfarne and they loathed each other.

'Surely as the metropolitan bishop of the north I should appoint my junior bishops?'

'You are not an archbishop, Wilfrid, and certainly not the equal of Theodore. He is the metropolitan for the whole of England.'

'But I was appointed by the Pope himself to be in charge of the Church throughout Northumbria.'

'That was in Vitalian's day, now Donus is the Pope and Archbishop Theodore has his support for his reforms.'

Wilfrid seethed with rage but he knew when he was beaten – at least for now.

'In that case, Cyning, I must travel to Rome and lay my case before Pope Donus.'

'If you must, you must. In view of the time it will take I must appoint someone to be my Bishop of Eoforwīc until we get the Pope's decision.'

'That won't be necessary, Cyning. I'll be as quick as I can.'

'No, take all the time you like. Don't return until you receive my permission to do so.'

Wilfrid knew that in effect he was being banished.

'Who will you appoint whilst I'm away?'

'Not that it's any of your concern but Abbess Hild has recommended her prior, Bosa.'

Wilfrid's heart sank. If Hild was his enemy, so was Bosa. With Eata and Bosa as bishops any influence he could exert through Trumbert whilst he was away would be negated.

~~~

Far from being away for a short time, a year later Wilfrid was still kicking his heels in Rome waiting for an audience with the Pope. Matters weren't helped by the fact that Donus had died before he'd even set out and the new Pope, Agatho, hadn't been elected until after he'd arrived. Everyone wanted an audience with Agatho but he'd been ill for a while after he took office. He'd recovered six months ago but Wilfrid still hadn't been summoned to see him.

Finally the Holy Father sent for him but, far from the private audience that Wilfrid had expected, he found himself confronted by Pope Agatho sitting amongst the priests and deacons that formed his personal entourage. Originally intended to help the Pope with his liturgical duties as Bishop of Rome, they had slowly transformed into an inner council to assist him to manage the Western Church.

It was the first time that Wilfrid had seen Agatho the Sicilian and he was struck by how old he was. Wilfrid was in his mid-forties but Agatho appeared to over twice as old.

'Welcome my son, I have read your petition to be reinstated as Bishop of All Northumbria but, for the benefit of my advisors, could you briefly summarise the main points in your submission?'

Agatho's voice was frail and quavered a little but it didn't stop him from emphasising the word briefly.

'Holy Father, I was appointed as Bishop of Northumbria by one of your predecessors, the blessed Saint Vitalian. Now Theodore of Tarsus seeks to divide my diocese into four parts and King Ecgfrith has placed another, a monk called Bosa, in my place as Bishop of Eoforwīc. Furthermore, he has appointed three others for these so called new dioceses.

'It was Pope Vitalian's intention that I should be Metropolitan of the North and I am therefore independent of the Archbishop of Cantwareburg,' he continued. 'I seek redress and your edict that I and I alone am Bishop of Northumbria.'

'Thank you Bishop Wilfrid, that was indeed commendably brief. Would you kindly retire for a moment so that I might consult my advisors?'

Wilfrid was left to pace the floor of the ante-chamber impatiently for over an hour before he was recalled to the Pope's presence.

'Bishop Wilfrid, this is too weighty a matter to be decided quickly, especially as you seem to be challenging Archbishop Theodore's position as Metropolitan of All England. 'I have therefore decided to call a synod of all available bishops to be held here in the Lateran Palace in one month's time.'

Wilfrid stood in front of the dais on which Agatho's throne sat, stunned by what the Pope had said. To his mind the matter was straightforward. The authority of a previous pope was being challenged and he had expected Agatho to uphold the original decision without having to think too hard about it. When he just stood there Pope Agatho frowned.

'That will be all for now, Wilfrid. You may withdraw.'

'Yes, Holy Father. Of course. Er, thank you,' he muttered, bowed low and fumed quietly as he left the audience chamber.

~~~

Osfrid had been surprised at how good a Master of the Novices his brother was. It is said that familiarity breeds contempt but Osfrid, who had mocked Alaric for his piety and studiousness when he was growing up, soon came to a grudging respect for him.

He never seemed to lose his patience with even the most dim-witted or obstreperous of his students and explained the gospels in a way that everyone could comprehend. He didn't teach by rote, as so many monks did, but got every boy to learn at his own pace.

Alaric never gave Osfrid any special attention or showed him any favouritism but his brother felt that he was special nevertheless. To his amazement every other novice felt the same. He would never admit it, but he actually enjoyed the two years he spent under Alaric's tutelage and learnt far more than he had expected.

Nevertheless, he couldn't wait to escape the boring life, as he saw it, on Lindisfarne and travel down to join the other boys being trained to be members of Ruaidhrí's mounted warband. At last the day dawned and he discarded the itchy brown habit he'd worn for the past two years. After a thorough wash in the sea he dressed in fine blue woollen trousers and a red tunic, knee-length yellow socks with red garters and leather shoes to replace the open toed sandals that monks wore in all weathers.

In his excitement his farewells to his brother and his father were somewhat perfunctory before he mounted the horse that Drefan had brought for him. Together they rode back to Bebbanburg. Drefan had become Conomultus' body servant when Catinus had become a monk and knew all the gossip that Osfrid had been starved of on Lindisfarne. Of course, rumours circulated but it was difficult to sift truth from fiction and little or none of it concerned things in which Osfrid was interested.

He listened eagerly to all that Drefan had to tell him as they rode across the sands and then along the dusty road that led around the bay to the fortress. It had been another dry period with no rain for over three weeks and everyone was concerned that the crops in the fields would die. Even the grass on which the livestock fed was becoming brown rather than green.

'Ethelred isn't like his brother Wulfhere was; your uncle says that he's hot-heated and seems determined to recover Linsey from us, whatever the cost.'

'We heard that King Wulfhere had been killed in battle against the West Saxons but I thought he had a son. Why's Ethelred now on the throne of Mercia?'

'Wulfhere didn't die in battle. He was wounded and it wasn't treated properly; it festered and he died of blood poisoning, or so your uncle says. He suspects that Ethelred was actually to blame for his death.'

'Did he kill his son too?'

'No, but Cenred is still far too young to rule. But all that is irrelevant, stories are beginning to circulate that Ethelred is prepared to go to war to recover Lindsey.'

Osfrid groaned. 'If only I was two years older I could go and fight them.'

Drefan laughed. 'I don't suppose that this will be your last chance to fight in a battle.'

'No, I don't suppose so, besides,' he said, brightening up, 'I want to go and see Godwyna as soon as possible and I couldn't do that if I was going to war.'

'Do you think you'll still love her when you see her again; a lot can happen in two years. Will she still be interested in you?'

Osfrid scowled at Drefan.

'Of course she will. And mind your place, boy. You are still only a servant.'

'Careful Osfrid, or your uncle might force us to wrestle again.'

Both grinned at the memory and were quiet for a few minutes.

'You uncle says that he won't need a personal servant when you return in two years' time and he becomes chaplain again.'

'Oh, what will happen to you?'

'Well, I was rather hoping I might serve you.'

'Definitely not, you're far too impudent.'

'Oh, yes. I see.'

Osfrid let Drefan ride on for a short while, his shoulders slumped in dejection, before he spoke again.

'I'm sorry. That was cruel of me. I wouldn't want anyone else to be my body servant.'

'Really? I promise I'll try to be less cheeky.'

'Don't you dare. It's one of the things I like about you. But don't ever embarrass me in public.'

'Of course not; I'm not an idiot.'

The two grinned at each other again and then dug their heels in to race the last mile up to the gates of the fortress.

~~~

The synod met in the great hall of the Lateran Palace, an impressive stone building originally built by the Plautii Laterani family who served several emperors until Nero confiscated it. The Emperor Constantine, who made Christianity the primary religion of the Roman Empire, had given it to the Bishops of Rome for their use. Now it was both the Pope's residence and the administration offices of the Roman Catholic Church.

The floor was tiled with mosaics depicting various mythical beasts. An earlier pope had planned to replace these with ones depicting the twelve apostles until someone pointed out that it would be sacrilegious to walk on them. Mosaics also lined the walls. The background colour was gold with a number of niches along each wall containing the likenesses of various popes who had been canonised.

Along the side walls six archbishops, quite a few bishops and a score of abbots sat on benches facing inwards. The Pope sat at the far end on a throne raised above everyone on a dais. Below him four monks sat at two tables ready to transcribe the proceedings.

A single stool had been placed in the centre of the floor halfway down the room. Wilfrid assumed that this was for his use but he declined to sit on it. To do so would have made him look like a criminal on trial. He would stand and walk around as he spoke in order to fix each member of the synod with his eyes.

The synod started when one of the bishops stood and introduced Wilfrid and gave a brief résumé of his background. His letter of complaint was then read out in full. He realised that he should have made it more concise when he saw a few of the older bishops starting to nod off.

The next stage came as a surprise. Two more letters were read out, one from Archbishop Theodore explaining far more succinctly why the See of Northumbria should be sub-divided and one from King Ecgfrith setting out the meeting at which Wilfrid had refused to accept the new arrangement. Both submissions portrayed Wilfrid as greedy, self-interested, lazy and a glutton.

Looking around at the sumptuous surroundings and the fine robes worn by many of those present he didn't think such complaints would find much of a sympathetic ear in this company.

'What have you to add to the letter setting out your case?' the bishop who had introduced him asked.

Wilfrid looked around the room and saw several faces he recognised included the bishop who had consecrated him and the abbots of two monasteries where he had studied in Frankia. He nodded to them and they nodded back.

'Holy Father, fellow bishops and abbots, Saint Vitalian approved my appointment as Bishop of Northumbria and he attached such importance to the post that he made me Metropolitan Bishop of the North of Britain.'

At this point the Pope held up his hand.

'Do you have proof that Pope Vitalian appointed you as a metropolitan bishop? It would be most unusual; metropolitans are normally archbishops.'

'I'm sorry Holy Father. The appointment was verbal.'

'I see. Very well, please carry on.'

'A moment please, Holy Father. Bishop Wilfrid, why was it necessary to make you the metropolitan for the north of Britain if you were the only bishop?'

'Because there were other bishops in the Land of the Picts where King Oswiu of Northumbria was Bretwalda.'

'Bretwalda?'

'Overlord or high king.'

'Thank you. And did these bishops acknowledge you as their superior?'

'It was difficult. They were appointed by the Celtic Church and didn't recognize my authority.'

'But Bishop Conomultus of Abernethy had accepted King Oswiu's decision at the Synod of Whitby had he not?'

Wilfrid cursed under his breath. Where had this man got such detailed information from? The he realised that it must be from Ecgfrith. He would know all about Conomultus as he'd appointed him as the administrator of Bebbanburg.

'Yes, but the Picts are a law unto themselves. Their king has expelled Conomultus in any case.'

'Thank you. I understand now. I think, Holy Father, that we can exclude any consideration of a separate metropolitan for Northumbria prior to today as it would seem that, whatever Saint Vitalian intended, there was only ever one Roman Catholic bishop in Northumbria until Archbishop Theodore decided to divide it into several dioceses. So I propose that we start with a clean slate when we consider whether there should be one or two metropolitans for the various kingdoms that comprise what is referred to as England.'

'Thank you, that is helpful. I agree,' the Pope said. 'Now we must turn to the question of who should be the Bishop of Eoforwīc: Wilfrid or Bosa.'

'Indeed, Your Holiness. It's a sensitive matter as it seems that Archbishop Theodore has appointed Bosa, Eata and Trumbert to the three new, smaller dioceses. I think we can discount Lindsey as that is the subject of dispute between King Ecgfrith and the King of Mercia. It means that there is no vacancy for Bishop Wilfrid, unless one of the other three is cast aside.'

'You Holiness, I must protest. I am the Bishop of Northumbria and, even if you were to accept the division that Theodore of Tarsus proposes, I would still remain as the consecrated Bishop of Eoforwīc,' Wilfrid interrupted the other bishop before he could say anything more which damaged his case.

'Yes, thank you. That is one of the matters we are here to decide,' Agatho said with some asperity. 'Unless you have anything more to add I think you may retire and leave us to our deliberations.'

It was late the next day when he was sent for again. This time he was shown into a small office where several priests and monks sat busily writing out various documents.

'Ah, Bishop Wilfrid. I have here the edict from the Holy Father which informs King Ecgfrith of the synod's ruling.'

He handed a sealed leather cylinder to the bemused man.

'But am I not to be told the contents? What did the Pope decide?'

'Have you not been told? Oh dear. Well, it's not my place to say, but you should have been informed.'

Wilfrid stormed out of the room and went in search of someone who could tell him what was going on. The first person he came across was the Pope's personal chaplain.

'I'm so sorry, bishop. It must have been an oversight not to let you know what the Holy Father has decided. I'm certain it was not his intention to keep you in the dark. Please wait here and I'll go and find someone to put this right.'

Wilfrid waited, pacing up and down the flagged floor of the corridor until the bishop who had done most of the talking in the synod came and found him. Without saying a word he led him into a bare room with scrolls and leather bound books on the shelves along one wall. The large wooden table in the centre was also covered in books and papers. It was evidently the man's office.

'Do take a seat, Bishop Wilfrid.'

He went and sat behind the table whilst Wilfrid was left to perch on a low stool the other side of the desk. He wasn't a short man but he was left looking up at the other bishop. If he was expecting an apology, he was about to be disappointed.

'Right, the main import of the Pope's decision is that you are to be restored to the Diocese of Eoforwīc and the monasteries of which you are abbot are to be returned to your control. However, the division of Northumbria into three dioceses is confirmed and, whilst you are not given metropolitan authority, His Holiness has also directed that you are to be given the right to replace any bishop in the new dioceses to whom you strongly object.

'The Pope has also decreed that your monasteries of Ripon and Hexham are to be directly supervised by His Holiness, preventing any interference in their affairs by the new diocesan bishops.'

Wilfrid felt elated. It was more than he had dared to hope for. He might not have been given full metropolitan authority but he could now get rid of both Bosa and Eata; and the king could not deprive him of either his diocese or his monasteries.

Chapter Nine – The Battle of the Trent

679 to 680 AD

'There is a messenger for you from the Eorl of Lindsey, Cyning. It's not good news.'

Octa stood dripping water from his cloak onto the straw that covered the beaten earth floor of the King's Hall at Eoforwīc. The dry summer had finally made way to incessant rain that threatened to wash away those crops which had survived so far.

The possibility of famine was a very real one and Ecgfrith was already trying to buy wheat and barley from the Continent, where the summer had been quite different; so much so that Northern Frankia and other kingdoms along the far coast of the German Ocean were enjoying a bumper harvest. Of course, Mercia, Wessex and the other Anglo-Saxon kingdoms were doing the same which pushed the price up and up.

The messenger was soaked through and, eager as he was to hear his news, Ecgfrith sent him to get changed whilst he broke the seal and took the letter from the waxed leather cylinder. He read it with growing dismay.

To Ecgfrith, King of Northumbria and of Lindsey, greetings,
I regret to have to inform you that Ethelred of Mercia has crossed the River Trent near Thorney and has invaded Lindsey. He has brought his warband and that of his eorls and

*ealdormen numbering over a thousand warriors and is
besieging me at Lindocolina.*

*I entreat you to come to my aid before it's too late. We are
short of provisions and do not believe that we can hold out for
more than three weeks, if the Mercians do not breech the
palisade before then.*

The letter concluded with the usual flowery phrases.

'How long ago did you leave Lindocolina?' Ecgfrith asked the
messenger when he returned dressed in borrowed tunic and
trousers.

'Four days ago, Cyning. I rode to the coast and travelled the
rest of the way by ship.'

'Then there is no time to lose. Octa, send messengers to
every eorl and ealdorman for them to muster with their war
bands at Selby and call out the fyrds of Deira and Elmet. Then
call a meeting of the Witan to meet there in three days' time.'

'Not every noble will be there at such short notice, Cyning.'

'It can't be helped. Enough will be present for us to decide
our strategy.'

~~~

Instead of heading for the small settlement of Selby on the
River Ouse, some twenty miles due south of Eoforwīc, Ælfwine
rode to see his brother as soon as his message arrived. He had
just turned eighteen and Ecgfrith had recently confirmed him as
Sub-king in fact as well as in name. They had remained close
whilst the boy was growing up, indeed his brother was

Ecgfrith's closest confidante and friend; consequently he was utterly confident of Ælfwine's loyalty and support.

However, that didn't mean that he was blind to his faults. Ælfwine had always been a risk-taker from the days when, as a young boy, he had climbed up into the rafters of a hall to the way that he rode his horse recklessly to win a race with his friends. One of the latter had died of a broken neck when his horse failed to make a jump over a fallen tree, but that didn't seem to deter the young King of Deira.

Of course, there were some who had reminded him of the betrayal of Oswiu by his nephew and then his son Alchfrith when they were sub-kings, but Ecgfrith was certain that there was no risk of that as far as Ælfwine was concerned.

'How are we going to relieve Lindocolina?'

Ecgfrith frowned. It was a question he had been asking himself. He didn't have the ships to land enough men at Lindsey's port of Grim's Bay, even if they were ferried there in batches. To march overland would mean crossing the River Aire a few miles south of Selby and entering Mercia before he could turn east towards the River Trent, beyond which lay Lindsey.

'I'm not happy about it, but we'll have to cross into Mercia seven miles south of Selby and then head down the west bank of the Trent until we can cross it due east of Lindocolina. It means that we will be in Mercia for several days and, if Ethelred has enough men in Mercia, we could be ambushed with our backs to the Trent.'

'Why don't you send me in advance with all the horsemen we can muster and we'll scout out the land for several miles west of the Trent?'

'Perhaps, I'll certainly put the idea to the Witan.'

Ælfwine looked a little put out but suddenly had another idea.

'We could also send a few scouts over the Trent to reconnoitre the siege of Lindocolina. We need to know how many we're dealing with and, indeed, whether the place had yet fallen to Elthelred.'

'It might be easier to do that from the east. That way our scouts won't be travelling through hostile territory.'

'Oh, yes. Good idea. Who will you send?'

'Perhaps Ruaidhrí, if you can spare him. I was going to send him with you as your senior commander but he's a good scout as well. I'll send Beornheth with you instead.'

'I'm not twelve. I don't need anyone to hold my hand!'

'Don't yell at me. Your petulance just proves that you need a wiser and older head to support you,' Ecgfrith told him quietly. 'After all, I need Octa to support me so it isn't just a reflection on your age or inexperience.'

His brother lowered his head and kicked the straw on the floor around for a minute, reminding Ecgfrith of a young boy who's just been told off.

'Very well. I suppose you're right.'

The Witan served little purpose as far as formulating plans were concerned; they merely endorsed Ecgfrith's proposals. However, at least the king knew that his nobles supported him. The only man to speak against the plan was Cuthbert. All three bishops and seven abbots were members of the Witan and Cuthbert was representing Abbot Eata, who was ill.

'Ethelred is merely reinstating the status quo, Cyning. Lindsey is south of the Humber and is physically cut off from the rest of Northumbria by the river and by part of Mercia. Would it not be better to cede Lindsey to him in return for a substantial payment?'

Ecgfrith had the feeling that Cuthbert was talking a lot of sense but he was howled down by the nobles who were after plunder as well as glory. All kings and nobles needed a steady supply of both to keep their war bands intact. Leaders who failed to keep their warriors well rewarded risked losing them to others who could offer more.

'No, Mercia is the aggressor here. They have broken the truce that King Ethelred agreed with me, albeit in Wulhere's name, and they must answer for that.'

Two days later Ruaidhrí set off with six of his best scouts and Osfrid. The boy had pleaded to go with him and, as they were only going to reconnoitre the situation, not fight, he thought the experience might be good for him. Everything was loaded onto three packhorses led by Ruaidhrí's body servant, a ferocious looking former warrior with only one eye, and a boy to look after the rest of the party. Osfrid couldn't help wishing that Drefan was coming too but he soon put the thought from his mind. He was just grateful to be included.

They arrived at Eoforwīc and boarded a knarr specially adapted to carry horses. They cast off the following morning and, blown along by a gentle westerly wind, they sailed down the Ouse to its mouth. As they entered the sea the wind backed around to the south west and the waves became increasingly choppy.

As they were making little progress tacking to and fro and Ruaidhrí was increasingly concerned for the horses, despite the tight stalls in which they were penned, they returned to the mouth of the Ouse for the night.

The next day was calmer, though the sea was still a little choppy. Thankfully the wind had veered during the night and was now coming from the north east. Their voyage down the coast was uneventful, if somewhat uncomfortable. Osfrid, in particular, found that the movement of the waves made him seasick.

He was therefore vastly relieved when they turned and ran into the harbour at Grim's Bay near the mouth of the River Humber. Grim was said to be an alternative name used by the old Anglo-Saxon deity Woden. By the time the horses were unloaded using a wooden crane and padded sling it was evening and the group camped just outside the port.

Ruaidhrí was well aware that tidings of their arrival might well be on their way to Ethelred if there was a Mercian agent in the port, so before dawn the next morning they set off along a narrow dirt track heading south west towards Lindocolina. Ruaidhrí sent out two scouts ahead but they encountered no-one except two monks on foot and several farmers going to a nearby market with carts full of produce. None of them had seen any Mercians, nor had they heard of any invasion. All of which struck Ruaidhrí as very strange. Normally such news would spread like wildfire.

By late afternoon they had reached a ruined Roman villa near which farmers had built four huts and cultivated an area of cleared forest. The inhabitants started to flee at the approach of the horsemen until Ruaidhrí called out that they were friends.

It turned out that four related families lived in the huts and farmed the land. The oldest man acted as spokesman and told them that they knew nothing of any Mercians. He'd been to the weekly market outside Lindocolina three days ago with two of the other men and they all confirmed that there was no siege.

It looked as if the message sent to Ecgfrith, supposedly from the Eorl of Lindsey, had been a forgery. The Northumbrians had been misled, but to what purpose Ruaidhrí couldn't think. It was Osfrid who solved the riddle.

'It could have only been for one purpose, to trick us into invading Mercia. That would give Ethelred the pretext to claim that we had broken the treaty so he could declare war as the wronged party.'

Ruaidhrí nodded in agreement then considered what to do next.

'We need to get back and stop Ecgfrith from attacking. The knarr won't have stayed at Grim's Bay but that doesn't matter. Osfrid, you and one of my men will retrace your steps as quickly as you can and hire a ship to take you back to Eoforwīc. If the king has left, hire horses and ride to Selby. Pray God that you are in time.'

He handed the boy a pouch of silver and turned to ride away.

'What will you do?'

'Ride to Lindocolina to check that what we've been told is correct, then head for the crossing place over the Trent near Dunham. From there we'll head north to intercept Ecgfrith if he's already crossed into Mercia. If not, we'll carry on to Selby.'

Osfrid nodded and dug his heels into his horse. He and his companion were lucky; they managed to hire a small pontos to take them north but Ecgfrith had left Eoforwīc two days previously. It took them a little while to find two horses to hire as most of those available had been taken by the army for the baggage train. The ones they hired were old and incapable of more than a sedate trot. They reached Selby just after dawn the next day to find that, yet again they were too late. The army had set out the afternoon before.

Meanwhile Ruaidhrí had ridden to Lindocolina to discover that the farmers had indeed told the truth. He briefed the eorl, then he and his men rode on west to the ferry over the Trent at Denham, arriving there at nightfall. The ferry was on the far side and the ferrymen refused to cross over at night, whatever promises and threats Ruaidhrí made.

He was left in something of a quandary. There was a road on the far side of the river, but not on the east bank. To reach the nearest crossing place, a ford usable when the water was low, as now, they would have to find their way through woods, shrubbery and boggy ground for some nine miles. It wasn't something that he'd consider attempting at night. He and his men settled down to see what the morning would bring.

~~~

Ecgfrith watched his brother lead his three hundred horsemen south towards the ford over the River Aire. It was the largest mounted force he, or any other Anglo-Saxon, had seen and it made a magnificent spectacle as the last of the servants with the packhorses disappeared into the cloud of dust kicked up by the hundreds of hooves in front of them.

The plan was for him to follow Ælfwine that afternoon. The horsemen would move faster than the slow moving warriors on foot and the baggage train, even moving at a walking pace and carefully scouting out the land ahead and five miles inland. That way he would have plenty of warning if there was an ambush awaiting him.

It took time for all two thousand men to ford the river and the baggage train took even longer. Ecgfrith was impatient to set out after his screen of mounted warriors but he knew better than to allow his army to become spread out over a long distance.

He had just started out again when he heard an unbroken boy's voice calling out his name. He turned in surprise to see Osfrid and a man he didn't know galloping along the column of marching men to catch him up.

'Osfrid? What are you doing here? I thought you were with Ealdorman Ruaidhrí.'

'He sent me to find you, Cyning,' the boy said breathlessly. 'It's a trap. Ethelred isn't besieging Lindocolina. He isn't even in Lindsey. You've been deceived.'

'What? Are you sure?'

Osfrid gave his king a pained look.

'Yes, of course you are. Otherwise you wouldn't be here. Octa!'

'Yes Cyning,' the hereræswa said as he turned his horse round and rode back to where Ecgfrith was still talking to Osfrid.

He gave the boy a puzzled look, which turned to one of alarm as the king told him the news that Osfrid had brought.

'We must turn round and get out of Mercia before it's too late, Cyning.'

'What about Ælfwine? I can't desert him.'

'Send a rider after him now and pray that he finds him in time.'

'Yes, very well. Give Osfrid your horse, Octa, it's fresher than his.' He turned back to Osfrid. 'Ride as fast as you can and warn my brother. Take two of my gesith with you.'

The boy didn't need telling twice. Before the two warriors detailed to escort him were ready he changed horses with Octa and he disappeared in a cloud of dust.

'I hope he doesn't kill my horse, it cost me a fortune,' Octa said grumpily.

'If he finds my brother in time I'll buy you a stable of the damned things.'

It took the best part of an hour to get the army turned around and heading back for the nearest crossing over the Aire and it was midday before the ford came in sight. However, it had taken too long. The road to the ford was blocked by over two thousand Mercians.

~~~

Ruaidhrí and his men had to change their plans when they awoke at dawn. A party of twenty Mercians stood on the far bank deep in conversation with the ferrymen. A few minutes later half of them boarded the ferry to cross over to their side.

With no track to follow they had attempted to stay close to the east bank of the Trent but time and time again their progress was blocked by dense shrubbery or by patches of marshy ground which they had to find a way around. Ruaidhrí assumed that the Mercians would follow him, but it would take two trips to get them all over the river and, even given the difficult terrain, travel on horseback was swifter than walking on foot.

Finally they came to the ford and a road leading south east towards Lindocolina. If only they'd followed it in the first place they could have found the Northumbrian army by now. Five minutes later they were all on the west bank. Now they had a hard packed earthen road under their hooves and they made dramatically better time.

They heard the clash of weapons and saw the dust swirling upwards in the still air before they saw the battlefield. Carrion birds were circling in the air above even now, waiting impatiently for the feast that would shortly await them.

As Ruaidhrí and his few men came around the bend he saw that he was too late to do anything. About six hundred Mercians had surrounded what was left of Ælfwine's men. They stood in a pitifully small circle with their shields locked, clearly determined to sell their lives dearly. The banner of the King of Deira still flew proudly from the middle of the circle so presumably Ælfwine was still alive.

Ruaidhrí knew that six warriors, even mounted ones, could make little difference but one look at his men told him that they were of the same mind as he was. They wouldn't be able to live with themselves if they didn't try and do something.

He sent his servant off to the west to find Ecgfrith and tell him what they'd seen. As soon as the man had ridden off, the warriors hefted their spears and rode slowly towards the back of the yelling crowd of Mercians.

When they were sixty paces away they dismounted and sent arrow after arrow into the backs of their foes. At first none of them seemed to realise that they were being attacked from the south but, after the tenth man had fallen, screaming in agony with an arrow in his shoulder, they turned and immediately realised their danger.

About fifty of them started to run towards Ruaidhrí's men. They got another two arrows away and half a dozen men fell before they mounted and rode away, to the fury of their pursuers. However, a hundred yards further on the scouts dismounted once more and sent fifteen more arrows towards the Mercians. Now there were less than thirty left of the group that had broken away to attack them.

The Northumbrians mounted once more and this time instead of fleeing they charged at their foes. Being at the rear, the Mercians weren't experienced warriors but members of the fyrd. None of them had faced a charge by men on horseback before and they turned and ran back the way they'd come.

It was like aiming at targets in practice. The Northumbrians speared man after man in the back as they fled, most of them throwing away their weapons and shields as they went. Only fifteen made it back to the main body.

The unexpected arrival of Ruaidhrí and his scouts had given the beleaguered remnant of Ælfwine's men fresh heart and they actually began to push their attackers back, killing them as they went. But it couldn't last. Ælfwine was ever rash and he was already wounded in several places. Now he got ahead of the members of his gesith on either side of him in his eagerness to kill Mercians. A man with an axe saw his opportunity and, swinging it in a circle, he took the young king's head clean off his body. It bounced away to be trampled underfoot.

A groan went up from the ranks of Northumbrians and they surged forward, determined to avenge Ælfwine's death. For a few moments they gained the upper hand but then the Mercians greater numbers began to tell and within half an hour the last warrior fell.

Ruaidhrí heard the groan and knew what it meant. He and his men charged forward, throwing their spears as they went, then drew their swords to hack down and kill as many as they could before they were pulled from their horses and stabbed to death. Ruaidhrí was the last to die and, as he felt his life ebbing away from him, his vison clouded over and everything went black. His last thought was about Lethlobar far away in Ulster. Now he would never know whether his half-brother would ever regain the throne of the Ulaidh.

~~~

Conomultus was surprised to receive a visit from Prior Cuthbert. He had dispatched the Bebbanburg warband to Selby under Eadstan's command, as instructed, and he had manned the fortress with warriors under training, men too old to fight in the shield wall and a few volunteers from the fyrd who wanted the extra pay involved.

'I need you to muster the fyrd and that of Alnwic, Jarrow, and the rest of Bernicia.'

Seeing that Conomultus was about to refuse without the proper authority to do so, Cuthbert held up his hand.

'I have had a vision sent to me by our Lord Jesus Christ. He came to me last night and warned me that King Ecgfrith is walking into a trap. It is already too late for his brother; his fate is sealed; but we can still save Ecgfrith.'

'What is this trap?'

'The Mercian invasion of Lindsey is a trick. Ethelred of Mercia intends to lure Ecgfrith and Ælfwine across the River Aire into Mercia and ambush them there. You need to muster the fyrd of Bernicia and march for Selby now. I just pray that you will be in time.'

'Why should those left in charge of the other shires do as I say?'

Conomultus no longer doubted the veracity of what Cuthbert was saying. His fame as a seer and as a holy man was too great for that.

'Because I will add my name and that of Bishop Eata to the message.'

An hour later several stable boys, grooms and others who could ride set out on the last few horses left at Bebbanburg and Conomultus sent out his own orders to the reeves of the vills in the shire for them to muster immediately.

Such was the respect in which Cuthbert was held that only a few refused to obey the summons, saying that it had not be sanctioned by the king or the Witan. By the next day over a thousand of the freemen of Bernicia were on their way to Selby. The men of Bebbanburg had the furthest to travel but they made the one hundred and forty miles in five days of hard marching. When they reached Selby they discovered that King Ecgfrith had only left two days previously.

'Have you had any further visions, Brother?' Conomultus asked Cuthbert that night, but the Prior shook his head.

In the absence of their ealdormen the leadership of each contingent of the fyrd had fallen to reeves, old men who had been warriors in their younger days and the sons of nobles who were training to be warriors. Conomultus and Cuthbert called a meeting of them that evening to discuss what they should do the next day. The discussion was going nowhere when there was a commotion outside the small church where the meeting was being held.

When Catinus walked in, still dressed as a monk but with his sword strapped to his waist, Conomultus breathed a sigh of relief.

'Good evening, Brother Prior, Conomultus,' he paused to look around the church, nodding to those he recognised. 'I have Abbot Eata's permission to join you. I thought I might be of some use.'

His brother strode forward and embraced him whilst Cuthbert smiled at him.

'For those of you who don't know Brother Catinus, he's Bishop Conomultus' brother and he used to be the Ealdorman of Bebbanburg before he became a monk.'

Conomultus had asked Cuthbert to stop calling him bishop as he no longer had a diocese, but Cuthbert had replied that once consecrated as a bishop he would always be one.

'We need to send out scouts to find out what is happening. How many horses do we have?'

It turned out that there were only eight, in addition to that of Catinus, and their riders were the stable boys, grooms and two elderly warriors who had previously acted as messengers.

'Very well, I'll take the five best riders and we'll ride down to the crossing over the River Aire to see what we find there. If necessary, we may need to press on into Mercia. I suggest that the fyrd advances to the crossing and you wait there until we return.'

No one had any better ideas so the plan was agreed.

When Catinus reached the low ridge above the ford he was startled to see the Mercian army drawn up on the near bank with the Northumbrians facing them over the other side of the river. Evidentially battle was about to commence but the ford was only wide enough to permit six men to cross at once. King Ecgfrith would lose a lot of men if he tried to force the crossing. One of the boys riding with him had brought the Wolf Banner of Bebbanburg with him and Catinus told him to wave it to and fro as hard as he could.

Half a mile away Ecgfrith was sitting on his horse sunk in grief. Ethelred had sent Ælfwine's mangled head to him in a basket at dawn. Normally messengers were inviolate but the king was so incensed by the grin on the Mercian's face that he had it struck from his body and sent it back to the King of Mercia.

The messenger entrusted with its delivery had no intention of risking his own life so he rode halfway across the ford and tossed it into the Mercians drawn up on the bank. The Mercians had archers but everyone was so stunned by the hurled head that the Northumbrian messenger was out of range before they had a chance to react.

It was Octa who noticed the waving banner and guessed its import.

'Cyning, I do believe that Catinus has ridden to our rescue.'

Ecgfrith looked up but could see little through the tears in his eyes.

'Why do you say that?'

'Because, unless I'm very much mistaken that is him sitting on a horse on the ridge over there with someone beside him waving the banner of Bebbanburg.'

Ecgfrith wiped away the tears and followed Octa's pointing finger.

'But there are only a few mounted men, and some are so small they must be boys.'

'Yes, but I'm willing to wager that the fyrd are coming up behind them. I'm sure that Catinus is trying to tell us to wait.'

'Well, although I'm itching to tear Ethelred's head from his body, just as he did to my poor brother, I'm willing to wait a little while to see if you're right.'

He was just beginning to lose patience when the first of the fyrd appeared on the ridge beside Catinus. Then more and more appeared until the skyline was full of men. Now it was Ethelred's turn to feel trapped.

Catinus was too wily to lead a thousand members of the fyrd against the Mercian army, which was both stronger and contained several hundred trained warriors. Instead he sent hunters with their bows, the few men who had proper war bows and a crowd of boys with slingshots forward to pepper the rear ranks of Ethelred's army.

The rear ranks started to take casualties and the Mercian king now faced a dilemma. If he turned to face the fyrd on the ridge his poorest quality men would be in the front rank and his best warriors wearing chainmail byrnies would be at the rear. Furthermore it would expose those same warriors to attack by Ecgfrith's men across the ford.

In the end he sent a thousand of the men in his rear ranks to attack the Northumbrians on the ridge and continued to face the main Northumbrian army across the ford. Catinus sat and watched the Mercians advance, puffing as they started up the slope. Then, when they were within range, his archers and slingers pelted them again. The unarmoured Mercians in the first rank, many without even a shield, were struck down and those behind tripped over them.

The advance began to falter until those at the rear began to push at their backs and urge them onwards. When they got close the archers and slingers withdrew and the shields of those in the Northumbrian front two ranks banged together to form a solid wall. The Mercians never had much of chance of breaking the shield wall and, when more and more of them fell, the fight went out of them and they fled, some back down the hill to the main body of Mercians but more off to the west, presumably seeking the next ford over the river and the way back into Mercia.

Even then Catinus didn't advance.

'What are we waiting for?' one of the reeves asked him.

'For the king to start his attack.'

However, a new development changed the situation again. Hundreds of Mercians, survivors of the battle in which Ælfwine and his men had been slaughtered, appeared on the ridge south of the river and behind Ecgfrith's army. Now both main bodies were caught between their foes on the opposite bank of the river and a smaller force, but one which held the high ground.

'Time to negotiate I think,' Cuthbert said to Catinus and Conomultus.

The three churchmen rode down towards the Mercians on their side of the river and, as they waited a hundred yards away, eventually there was movement amongst the opposing ranks and King Ethelred appeared with two of his gesith and a man dressed in a finely woven black woollen robe with a large gold pectoral cross around his neck. The other three churchmen assumed, correctly, that this was the Mercian Bishop of Lichfield.

'Brother Cuthbert, you are a long way from Lindisfarne,' Ethelred said with a frown. 'What are you doing here?'

'This is Northumbrian soil, Cyning. Why shouldn't I be here?'

'Who is the monk beside you who wears a sword?'

'Brother Catinus. You may be more familiar with him as the Ealdorman of Bebbanburg. My other companion is Bishop Conomultus, Catinus' brother.'

'Well, you presumably want to negotiate. What are you suggesting?'

'Both sides seem to find themselves in something of a quandary. We are both surrounded and, although we have the greater numbers, you probably have more experienced warriors,' Catinus said.

'You are stating the obvious,'

Catinus merely pursed his lips, letting the testy remark pass, before continuing.

'I suggest that both sides withdraw. You can travel to the west to the next crossing point back into Mercia and allow King Ecgfrith to lead his men back into Northumbria.'

'And Lindsey?'

'I will recommend to King Ecgfrith that he asks the archbishop to mediate between you. There is also the question of weregeld for the ambush and death of King Ælfwine.'

'Never! He was the aggressor. He died in fair fight.'

'Nearly a thousand men against three hundred from what I heard? And he and Ecgfrith were deliberately deceived into going to the aid of Lindsey. That was underhand and devious of you to put it mildly.'

Ethelred was about to explode with rage when Cuthbert stepped in.

'That is not a matter for us to debate, brother. Our concern today is to resolve the situation we find ourselves in. There can be no winners here. Leave the discussion of a treaty to the two kings in due course.'

Ethelred took a deep breath and nodded his head.

'Very well, but Ecgfrith must agree to withdraw his men if I do the same.'

'If you allow us safe passage across the ford we will inform him of our discussions.'

Ethelred gave the order for his army to part to allow the three churchmen to ride through their ranks and across the ford where they were met by a puzzled Ecgfrith.

'I'm very glad to see you; your arrival was most opportune. I've no idea how you knew to be here but you can tell me about that later. I saw you in discussion with that murdering cur, Ethelred. What does he want?'

'We were very sorry to learn of the death of your brother, Cyning. I know how dear he was to you.'

'Thank you Catinus.'

'The Mercians have agreed to withdraw and cross the Aire back into Mercia upriver if you allow them to do so. In return they will allow you to cross back in Northumbria unmolested. The matters in contention between you can then be discussed at a later date and a solution found.'

'What solution? Can he bring Ælfwine back? No. He must pay for his trickery and the blood he has shed. You, too, have lost someone dear to you due to his treachery.'

It was a moment before Catinus realised the import of what the king had just said.

'Ruaidhrí dead?'

'You didn't know? No, how could you? I was told by his servant that he died trying to save my brother. I am in his debt.'

'Now is not the time, Cyning, but we will need to discuss Alnwic. His wife is pregnant with Ruaidhrí's child. It's no time for her to be cast out of her home, nor for her to enter a monastery.'

'Yes but, as you say, there are more important things at the moment. Go back and tell that arseling, Ethelred, that I agree. We will wait for him to withdraw along the river and then I'll cross back over to Northumbria.'

~~~

'At least Ethelred had the decency to return your brother's corpse so that it could be buried with his head, Cyning,' Theodore of Tarsus pointed out. 'He even sent the rest of the bodies back in carts so that they could be given a Christian burial instead of leaving them for the carrion crows and the buzzards.'

They were sitting in the king's hall at Loidis. Ecgfrith had refused to meet Ælfwine's killer face to face and so the archbishop was having to travel to and fro between the two kings to conduct the negotiations. At least Ecgfrith had moved to Loidis which was on the north bank of the River Aire. From there Theodore could travel downstream by boat to Tanshelf, the most northern of the Mercian settlements, which was located just south of the River Aire some fourteen miles from Loidis. Helpfully, Ethelred was tiring of living in the local thegn's hall and the thegn was equally keen to see him gone. Hospitality for the king and his gesith was threatening to bankrupt him.

Ecgfrith sighed. He needed to conclude the negotiations so that he could return to Eoforwīc. Living in his late brother's hall was depressing him. The pain of his loss was fading but he would never forgive Ethelred. Both kings were therefore anxious for the treaty to be signed.

His other concern was for the future. He was coming to accept that he and Eormenburg would never have children and he had expected Ælfwine, or his son, to succeed him. Now that would never happen.

King Æthelfrith had had seven sons and four grandsons. Now the only descendants of his left alive were Ecgfrith and Oswiu's illegitimate son, Aldfrith. He couldn't see the latter ever agreeing to leave Iona and his life as a scholar to be king. In any case he was forty seven now and had never married.

Ecgfrith had even tried to have children with women other than his wife but none had become pregnant. It seemed to him that God didn't want his line to survive. He wasn't aware of the old crone's curse on his family when his grandfather had killed Ethelric of Deira and made himself King of Northumbria. If he had been he wouldn't have given it credence, but it certainly seemed as if the curse might be coming true.

In the end Ecgfrith gave up his claim to Lindsey and, in return, Ethelred paid him two chests of silver as weregeld for killing Ælfwine.

Once back at Eoforwīc he turned his attention to the many other matters that awaited him. Foremost amongst these was the appointment of a new Master of Horse and the training of new mounted warriors to replace the horsemen he'd lost. His surprising choice was Osfrid, who was now fifteen. He'd been impressed by the boy's common sense and maturity when he'd come to inform him what was happening, or rather wasn't happening, at Lindocolina, and he was an excellent horseman. He also decided to confirm him as the Ealdorman of Bebbanburg.

Eydth, Ruaidhrí's widow, had given birth to a boy, named Eochaid after his grandfather, and Ecgfrith had agreed that, in due course, he should become the Ealdorman of Alnwic. In the meantime Conomultus had moved there to help her to manage the shire. He was now fifty and he was content to end his days there. He prayed to God that he would be spared for long enough to see the boy become the ealdorman.

~~~

Eadstan had remained at Bebbanburg, as had Uurad, but many of Catinus' former gesith had sought employment elsewhere over the past two years. Osfrid's body servant, Drefan, was now fourteen and he had let him join the boys training to be warriors so he'd also need to find a new servant.

In addition to the problem of recruiting warriors to join his gesith, he now had the task of building up another mounted warband and training more men to be horsemen for the king. Furthermore he didn't have anywhere near enough horses and so he would need to buy some and establish a stud to breed his own. He sometimes wished that his uncle had stayed to help him.

Then to add to his problems, Eadstan had come to see him to say that he was too old to continue as the commander of his warband and leader of his gesith.

'You're not that old, Eadstan,' Osfrid told him, though in truth he looked ancient to the young man. 'How old are you?'

'Just over fifty, lord.'

'Oh! I see. What do you want to do?'

'Well, I know that you need to establish a stud and build up a new mounted warband. I thought I could make myself useful in doing that.'

Osfrid smiled in relief.

'That would be a great help, Eadstan. Thank you. Do you have any recommendation as to who should take your place?'

'There isn't a lot of choice at the moment as most of our warriors died with Ælfwine. Of those who are left I would suggest Uurad. He's dependable, loyal and a good fighter. No-

185

one remembers that he used to be a Pict when he was a boy. The men respect him and he's clever.'

'Thank you. Send him to see me will you?'

After Osfrid had explained that he wanted him to take over from Eadstan, Uurad thanked him but had a suggestion of his own to make.

'I need to concentrate on recruiting and training your new warband, lord. I will have Eadstan's help, of course, but I suspect that he will find himself quite busy seeking out new bloodstock and instituting the breeding programme if we are to build up our stock of suitable horses as quickly as we need to.

'I'm not sure that it's a good idea for me to lead your gesith as well. If you are to get to know your shire you will be need to be out and about quite a lot and that will interfere with what I need to be doing.'

'Yes, I can see that. Who then should command my gesith?'

'I would recommend Sigmund. He's nearly thirty now and the right age to be given more responsibility.'

'So it seems that I'm to have a Pict as the commander of my warband and a Saxon as the leader of my gesith,' Osfrid chuckled.

'Yes, lord. But it's no stranger than having an ealdorman whose blood is a mixture of Mercian Briton and Anglian.'

For a moment Uurad wondered if he'd overstepped the mark by reminding his ealdorman of his own ancestry, but then Osfrid grinned.

'A pack of mongrels to serve a mongrel; it's apt.'

Chapter Ten – Wilfrid

680 to 682 AD

Just when Ecgfrith thought that he could enjoy a period of peace and tranquillity for a change, Wilfrid returned.

He walked into the king's hall at Eoforwīc full of confidence; how could he not be? He had the Pope's personal endorsement for his re-instatement as Bishop of Eoforwīc, his unassailable title to be abbot of both Hexham and Ripon and the right to dethrone the false bishops, Eata and Bosa.

He was therefore surprised by Ecgfrith's welcome, or lack of it.

'What in God's name are you doing back here Wilfrid? I had hoped that I'd seen the last of your miserable, bloated body.'

It didn't help that Eormenburg sat on one side of her husband, smirking at him, and Bosa stood on the other glowering at him.

'I have here the Pope's edict declaring me to be the rightful ...'

He got no further.

'I didn't ask you what you were carrying. I asked you why you had returned when I'd banished you.'

'Banished me, Cyning? I left of my own accord to lay my grievances before the Pope, our Holy Father in God.'

'You obviously didn't listen to me closely enough. I told you not to return until you had my permission to do so. Do you have that permission? No. Therefore you have ignored my express instruction. You will be tried for disobedience.'

'Tried? You can't haul me before your courts. I'm the rightful Bishop of...'

He got no further before two of the king's gesith hauled him unceremoniously out of the hall. If he expected to be allowed to reside in comfort whilst awaiting his hearing before the Witan he was destined to be disappointed. He was held in a small stone built hut with an opening high up that let in a small amount of light and a stout door barred on the outside. The floor was of beaten earth covered in dirty rushes that didn't look as if they'd been changed in a year or more and rats scurried hither and thither looking for any morsel of food that the last occupants might have dropped.

There was no bed, just a straw filled paillasse with so many bugs and lice on it that it seemed to be alive. When his eyes had adjusted to the dim light he espied a leather bucket in the corner. It was stained a dark brown that was almost black with use and stank. It was obviously where he was meant to relieve himself. He sat down in the corner opposite the bucket with his bottom on the floor and his back against the wall. He drew his knees up into his rotund belly and wept. His one hope was that the archbishop would hear of his plight and rescue him but he knew it was a vain hope.

In the morning the door opened and a young boy with a face covered in grime and wearing a muck stained tunic entered carrying a bucket similar to the one in the corner. Ignoring the bishop, who was still sitting the corner, he changed it with the one already in the hut and went to leave.

'Stop! When do I break my fast?'

'You mean when do you eat?' the boy said, clearly puzzled by the question. 'Mid- afternoon.'

He said it as if that's when everyone ate and, for all Wilfrid knew, that might be true for him and his fellows.

The morning dragged on and he was glad when the door opened again. The air in the place was distinctly fetid and at least the through draft from the door to the small opening brought in some fresh air. The same boy appeared again, this time carrying a wooden bowl.

Wilfrid took it from him and looked suspiciously at the contents.

'What's this supposed to be?'

'Supposed to be nothing. It's vegetable stew. It's good, go on try it.'

'How, there's no spoon.'

The boy put out his hands and made a movement as if tipping a bowl.

'Drink from the bowl?' Wifrid asked incredulously .

The boy nodded. 'Drink the liquid and then scoop the rest out with your hands. How do you normally eat it?'

'Well, I don't eat this slop and, even if I did, I would need a spoon.'

The boy shrugged and left.

Wilfrid looked at the bowl of vegetables and barley stewed in water and tentatively tasted it. He hadn't eaten for over a day and he was famished. It didn't taste too bad and he quickly consumed it. The thought of having to wait another twenty four hours for his next meal depressed him.

The boy came in again half an hour later and took the bowl away, replacing it with a tankard of ale. Anglo-Saxons had a horror of drinking water, believing that it would make them ill and even children drank weak ale after they had got past the milk stage.

Wilfrid had little to occupy himself with so he prayed a great deal, mainly for release but also for revenge. He tried to recite passages of the Bible but surprised himself by how little he could remember.

On the fourth day he was brought a bowl of water and a towel so he could wash and a man came in to shave his face and his tonsure. He did his best to make himself look respectable but his fine robes were stained and soiled with dirt from the floor.

When he was taken outside he had never been so glad to breathe fresh air. It was raining but even that came as a relief. He felt it was washing him clean. Two warriors escorted him back to the king's hall where Ecgfrith sat with his wife on a dais at the rear of the hall. In front of them was a table at which Bishop Eata, Bishop Bosa and a man he didn't recognise sat together with a scribe. Along one wall of the hall sat twelve men who would presumably act as his adjudicators. As he was of noble blood they had to be at least thegns.

'Wilfrid, you know everyone except Ealdorman Irwyn of Loidis I think?' Bosa said, more as a statement than a question.

After his brother's death Ecgfrith had decided not to appoint anyone as Eorl of Deira. He'd continued his father's policy of creating ealdorman to look after shires. Like most kings, he found that having nobles who were too powerful reduced the king's own authority. Now, with scores of ealdormen ruling smaller areas all real power lay in his hands. The only eorls left in Northumbria now were the Eorl of Lothian and the Eorl of Elmet. They would be the last.

'You are accused of disobedience to the king in that you returned to Northumbria without his permission.' Bosa looked up from a scroll in front of him. 'Do you have anything to say?'

'I am the Bishop of Eoforwīc appointed by the Pope himself. This is not the king's appointment and so he cannot prevent my return to my diocese and he has no jurisdiction over me.'

'I think you'll find that I have jurisdiction over everyone in my kingdom, Wilfrid. You were born here and you are my subject, whatever some Sicilian Bishop of Rome may say.'

Wilfrid was surprised that Ecgfrith knew that Pope Agatho was born in Sicily and wondered if he even knew where the Island was. The king had never struck him as a particularly well educated man.

'Your father acknowledged the supremacy of Rome, Cyning. In doing so he accepted the authority of the Pope.'

'No he didn't, he accepted the Roman dating of Easter and its doctrine where it differed from that of the Celtic Church. The appointment of bishops is not a doctrinal or theological matter. Kings of Northumbria have always had the final say in the appointment of bishops and of abbots. Carry on Bosa.'

'Do you have anything to add, Wilfrid?'

'No, if you refuse to accept the Pope's edict then you are all damned to Hell.'

Bosa turned to the jury and asked if they wished for time to discuss their verdict but the senior thegn shook his head.

'Father Wilfrid wilfully disobeyed the king and he is therefore guilty.'

The description of him as a priest rather than as a bishop wasn't lost on Wilfrid. He was about to protest when he thought better of it. What good would it do him?

191

Bosa and his fellow judges conferred briefly before he turned back to the dishevelled figure standing before them.

'Wilfrid you are banished from Northumbria. If you return again you will be imprisoned for life. Do you understand?'

For a moment Wilfrid was speechless, then he grasped at one final straw of hope.

'What about my monasteries at Hexham and Ripon? They have been granted to me by the Pope.'

'Have you not been listening to a word I've said,' Ecgfrith yelled at him, finally losing his temper. 'The Pope's writ does not run in Northumbria.'

'Then you will all be damned to Hell for all eternity.'

'Get out! Get out now or I'll have you imprisoned until you starve to death.'

Wilfrid stalked out of the hall with as much dignity as he could muster. The urchin who had brought him his food and changed his soil bucket each day stood outside in the rain holding his horse by its reins. He must have been there for a little while because the water had almost washed his face clean and Wilfred saw that he had a scar running down his right cheek which made it look as if the boy was leering at him.

Wilfrid mounted and jerked the reins savagely out of the boy's hands. He rode out of Eoforwīc and headed south. Perhaps Ecgfrith had written to his fellow kings because he found no welcome in Mercia or Wessex. After a month of travelling he eventually came to the minor Kingdom of Sussex. The South Saxons were pagans in the main but their king, Æthelwealh, was willing to listen to Wilfrid's preaching.

Sussex had been experiencing a drought when Wilfrid arrived but the day he baptised the first converts it started to rain. The superstitious Saxons interpreted this as a miracle and arrived in droves to be baptised by Wilfrid. Two months later King Æthelwealh made Wilfrid Bishop of Sussex and paid for a monastery to be built for him at Selsy.

When Ecgfrith was told of this he merely grunted that at least Selsy was about as far away from him as Wilfrid could get and still be in England. Provided he stayed there, he was content.

Chapter Eleven – The Invasion of Hibernia

684 AD

The muffled sound of the downpour outside hitting the roof and the ground could be heard in the silence of the church on Lindisfarne as Bishop Eata conducted Catinus' funeral service. He had fallen ill at the end of March and had died with Alaric and Osfrid at his side. Conomultus and Eydth had set out as soon as they heard that he was ill, but the roads were like quagmires and they didn't arrive until the day before the funeral.

Osfrid stood with his brother Alaric on one side of him and his wife, Godwyna of Jarrow, on the other. They had been married the previous year and she was now showing distinct signs of the baby growing within her. Conomultus and Eydth stood on the other side of Godwyna. Eydth's son, Eochaid, had been left at Alnwic with his wet nurse.

Conomultus was only two years younger than his brother had been and he was now looking quite old. Osfrid worried that he too might die soon, which would leave Eydth without anyone to help her manage the shire. In that eventuality Ecgfrith could well go back on his promise and, instead of making Eochaid the ealdorman when he reached maturity at sixteen he might appoint someone else to take over. He needed to talk to the king at the next opportunity. He might even have to suggest that, in the event of Conomultus' death, he could combine the two shires under his rule until his nephew was old enough.

After the service they trudged through the mud to the cemetery and saw Catinus laid to rest. His grave faced east but it had a good view of Bebbanburg across the bay. Osfrid smiled briefly at the thought that his father would have liked that.

Conomultus and Eydth stayed at Bebbanburg until the weather improved and set off on a sunny day in early April to ride back to Alnwic. Life at Bebbanburg then returned to normal and, although Osfrid was blissfully happy with Godwyna and looking forward to the birth of their first child, he was only twenty and craved a little more excitement in his life. He didn't have long to wait. A month later he was summoned to a meeting of the king's war council.

Ecgfrith sat at the head of the table in his hall at Loidis. He had been on a tour of his kingdom when news arrived which made him change his plans. Osfrid was the last to arrive and was just in time to hear Octa telling the council the reason for the meeting.

'The attacks on the coast of Cumbria are increasing, Cyning, many of the Britons who fled from the region that used to be known as Rheged took service as mercenaries in Hibernia with the High King, Fínsnechta. He is now using them to raid their old homeland. They have already looted and burned three coastal settlements this year and it is only May.'

'What do we know about this Fínsnechta?'

Octa looked at Stepan, the Ealdorman of Cumbria, and nodded to indicate that he should reply.

'Fínsnechta is king of the southern branch of the Uí Néill, the most important of all the tribes in Hibernia. He became

King of Brega in 675 after killing his cousin, Cenn Fáelad, who was his predecessor. He then crushed all those who opposed him to make himself high king. He is ruthless and he's made himself very wealthy by raiding, both within Hibernia and now across the sea to the Isle of Man and Cumbria.'

'Obviously this Fínsnechta needs to be taught a lesson,' Ecgfrith said thoughtfully. 'To launch a reprisal raid we will need ships. How many do you have in Cumbria, Stepan?'

'Only five, Cyning: three birlinns and two pontos. But I also have half a dozen knarr which we use for trading; they could carry perhaps three hundred men or two hundred and, say, thirty horses.'

'Not enough. You say that this Hibernian has also been raiding Man?'

'Yes, Cyning. I know that King Alweo is very concerned about it.'

'Good. I need someone to go and see if he will join us in a joint mission against Fínsnechta.'

'My sister is Queen of Man, Cyning,' Osfrid said, trying to keep the excitement out of his voice at the prospect of being involved in the raid.

'Hmm, I need you to ready your horsemen. Scouts will play a vital role in this expedition.'

'I have a warband of thirty trained horsemen, Cyning; that's in addition to my gesith of twenty who escorted me here.'

'Very well, send for them. I want them to be at Caer Luel at the beginning of June. In the meantime you and Stepan can go to Man and see if Alweo will join us in this venture.'

~~~

It was years since Ecgfrith had been to Bebbanburg. With Osfrid away it fell to Godwyna to entertain the royal party. Thankfully the king had only brought his gesith, Bishop Bosa and a few servants with him. He only stayed one night and then continued on to Lindisfarne. He had decided to come himself because he knew that persuading Cuthbert to do as he wished wouldn't be easy. Trumbert, Bishop of Hexham, had died and he wanted to appoint Cuthbert to replace him.

He was annoyed when he got to the entrance to the route across the sands to find that the tide was still in. Godwyna had offered him a boat to take him across the bay but one look at the sea convinced him to make the longer journey by land. Ecgfrith was not a good sailor at the best of times and the choppy waves with their crests blown into sprays of spume would make for a very uncomfortable crossing, short as it was.

He therefore arrived at the monastery in a bad temper. It got worse when Cuthbert proved as obstinate as he feared.

'What do you mean, no?'

'No, Cyning, I do not wish to move to Hexham in order to become its bishop.'

'Why not?'

'Firstly, I have no desire to become a bishop or an abbot. I only became prior because Eata needed my support to introduce the Benedictine rule here. It's far stricter than the monks were used to under the Celtic regime, especially the requirement to attend services eight times a day, including the middle of the night.'

'Yes, yes, but you have done an excellent job as prior and there is no-one in Northumbria who is more devout or who is held in higher regard as a churchman; no disrespect to you Eata, but it's true.'

'I couldn't agree more, Cyning. I am well aware of my limitations,' Eata said with a smile.

'As do I, know my limitations that is,' Cuthbert stated forcefully. 'Rather than have to cope with more responsibility, I would prefer to retire to one of the Inner Farne Islands and see out my days as an anchorite.'

'Then why don't you?'

'Because God has called me to do my duty here as prior.'

'Well, now I'm telling you that your duty is to become Bishop of Hexham.'

'Cyning, if I may?' Eata intervened.

The king nodded, feeling exasperated. It was no good ordering Cuthbert to move to Hexham, he would refuse and that would put the king in an impossible position. He couldn't punish Cuthbert; the nobles and his people wouldn't stand for it. Imprisoning Wilfrid and then banishing him was different. It had proved popular in many quarters and those that supported him had the sense to keep quiet.

'Brother Cuthbert, am I correct in assuming that you would be content to stay here on Lindisfarne?'

'Yes, I may be being selfish but I like the sea. I feel closer to God here, especially on the islands.'

'Then why don't you stay here as bishop and abbot? I'll move back to Hexham if the king is happy with that solution; after all, I was prior there before I came here as abbot.'

Ecgfrith sighed with relief. It was an admirable solution.

'Thank you, Bishop Eata, I am content with the arrangement if it's acceptable to Cuthbert?'

'If I must become a bishop, then I accept.'

Ecgfrith's good humour returned. With the death of Trumbert and the appointment of Cuthbert as his replacement neither Wilfrid nor the Pope had any supporters left amongst the churchmen on the Witan of Northumbria.

When he returned to Eoforwīc he found more good news awaiting him. Pope Agatho was dead and his successor, Leo II, hadn't lasted more than a few months before he too had died. Benedict II had been elected to replace him but he was awaiting the approval of Constantine IV, the Holy Roman Emperor and for some reason that hadn't been forthcoming. Consequently there was no current pope and the papacy was in a state of turmoil. In such conditions Wilfrid's renewed petition for redress would be the least of Rome's concerns.

~~~

It had been a dozen years since Alweo had become King of Man and Osfrid scarcely remembered his sister. He'd been a small boy when Hereswith had married Alweo and now she had five children, three boys and two girls. The eldest, Æthelbald, was thirteen years old and the youngest, Thringfrith, was a boy born the previous year.

Of course, they had never met their uncle and Æthelbald, in particular, seemed intrigued by a man who, at some half a dozen years older than him, was already an ealdorman and the Master of Horse, a new concept to him. Manxmen fought on foot and, although they used horses to get from one place to another, they found the concept of fighting on horseback strange.

'Æthelbald isn't being schooled in a monastery,' Osfrid had remarked to Hereswith when they sat down to eat.

'No, he divides his time between being taught by the king's chaplain and his military training. The nearest monastery is at Heysham in Cumbria and Alweo and I worry about the raids by the Hibernians.'

'That is what I'm here to discuss, but it can wait until tomorrow.'

'I suppose you were educated at Lindisfarne?'

'Yes, by our brother Alaric. If I thought I'd get special treatment he soon disabused me of that idea. If anything he was harder on me than on the other novices, just so no one could accuse him of favouritism.'

'Of course, he was only nine and still at home when I left to marry Alweo. He was studious and devout even then.'

She looked down at the table before speaking again.

'Was father in much pain when he died?'

'No, I don't think so. He seemed to have caught some wasting sickness. He was always well built but by the time he died he was half the weight he had been. The infirmarian said that the sickness was incurable and gave him a concoction made from various herbs and plants that he grew so I don't think he knew much about it.'

'You were with him when he died?'

'Yes, he smiled at us at the end and whispered a blessing just before his soul left his poor wasted body.'

'I'm sorry we couldn't be there but, by the time the messenger reached us to say that he was seriously ill it was too late. In fact, we didn't know he was dead until after the funeral.'

'I'm sure he understood.'

'Our uncle Conomultus is well though?'

'Well enough, though he's beginning to feel his age I think.'

'My husband is of an age with him - he'll soon be fifty four - but he seems in robust good health. Well enough to sire another child last year at any rate,' she said, then blushed.

'So was father until a month or so before the end,' he replied, then cursed under his breath. It was hardly a tactful thing to say.

'You've heard that Cousin Ethelred has had a son,' she remarked, changing the subject.

At first Osfrid wasn't certain who she was talking about, then he recalled that Alweo was the King of Mercia's first cousin.

'Yes, called Cenred; slightly confusing as his cousin, Wulhere's son, is called Ceonred.'

'Both are, of course, very young,' she said in a whisper. 'We have been approached by certain Mercian nobles who have said that they will support Alweo's claim to the throne if Ethelred dies before either boy comes of age.'

'But your husband is far older than Ethelred.'

'Then, if not him, Æthelbald. He is the great-grandson of King Pybba, just as Coenred and Coiled are.'

Osfrid had forgotten that Alweo was the son of Eowa, the brother of King Penda of Mercia and that both were the sons of Pybba, the founder of the dynasty. Suddenly he realised that, just as Æthelbald was an ætheling descended from kings of Mercia, so his soon to be born child traced his or her ancestry back to Ida, the original King of Bernicia and founder of the ruling house of Northumbria. However, he wasn't clear whether that would make him an ætheling or not, presuming it was a boy.

~~~

'How many men are you taking on this raid into Hibernia?' Alweo asked when he met with Osfrid and Stepan the next day.

'Three hundred, a tenth of them mounted. All are trained warriors,' Stepan replied. Osfrid had agreed to leave the talking to him as he was the senior ealdorman and commander of the expedition.

'Our mission is to bring death and destruction to the Kingdom of Brega to teach Fínsnechta not to raid either Cumbria or Man again.'

'Well, I applaud the sentiment but you'll need a lot more than three hundred men. Even if you catch him unawares, I'm told that Fínsnechta has a permanent warband of seven hundred mercenaries, mainly Britons driven out of Rheged, in addition to his own Hibernians. At short notice he can probably call upon between a thousand and fifteen hundred men.'

'We were hoping that you might join with us to punish Fínsnechta.'

'I might, if I was certain it would succeed. At the moment it sounds as if it will fail and so make matters worse.'

'If you were to join us, how many men could you bring?'

'I can fill ten birlinns and pontos, so perhaps four or five hundred, especially if there is plunder to be had.'

'Do you have any knarrs?'

'Yes, half a dozen or so, but not the warriors to fill them. I'll not take my fyrd, they are needed here to defend Man.'

'Can you lend them to us and we'll try and fill them,' Osfrid asked. 'That way we might be able to bring another three hundred. That would give us a thousand trained warriors.'

'If we catch him unawares it might work. When do you intend to launch the raid?'

'At the end of June.'

'That gives me enough time to prepare. Some of my knarrs are away trading at the moment but they should be back in a few weeks. I'll send them up to Caer Luel by the middle of the month. We'll all meet here at Duboglassio a week later.'

~~~

Osfrid watched appalled as the monastery was set on fire. Once they had defeated Fínsnechta in battle shortly after they had landed on the shores of Dundalk Bay, they were virtually unopposed as they looted and pillaged their way through Brega. It was said that Fínsnechta had fled to the Northern Uí Néill to raise another army but he hoped that would take him time, enough for the invaders to leave before that became a problem at any rate.

Osfrid accepted that the destruction of the settlements and the enslavement of the people was necessary to stop further raids on Man and Cumbria but he drew the line at attacking monasteries and looting and then burning churches.

However, Stepan's Cumbrians and the Manxmen had no such scruples.

'They are Christians, like us. It is a mortal sin to slay priests and desecrate their churches,' he had said to the other leaders after the first church had been plundered.

'I disagree,' Stepan had replied. 'They are Celtic Christians, not true followers of our religion.'

'We only came to make ourselves rich,' one of the chieftains from Man had added. 'Where are the greatest riches to be found? In the churches and monasteries of course.'

The other Manx leaders had thumped the tables and Osfrid found himself isolated.

Whilst his men were loyal to him he realised that it would be difficult, if not impossible, to convince them not to take their share of the spoils once they saw the others doing so. However, he did forbid them from slaying priests and monks and they largely obeyed him in that, except where they were attacked by the odd churchman trying to defend Church property.

After three weeks of laying Brega waste they set off back to Dundalk Bay but they made slow progress due to the number of captives they were herding along and the carts full of booty pulled by plodding oxen.

Osfrid and his fifty men formed the rear-guard and they were still two days march from their ships when two of his men scouting at the rear of the slow moving column rode in to tell him that there was a large army some ten miles behind them.

'How large?'

'Difficult to say, lord. In these dry conditions they are kicking up a lot of dust which obscures most of them from view.'

'I need to know. How many men can you see, how much of the road do they occupy and then multiply that by the length of the dust cloud. Uurad and Drefan go with them.'

Two hours later they returned.

'Probably two thousand, lord. All on foot apart from half a dozen riders at the front,' Uurad told him.

Osfrid cantered off to find Stepan. When he told him the Cumbrian ealdorman seemed not to know what to do.

'You have a simple choice Stepan. We can't make it back to the ships, load them up and sail away in time. The Uí Néill will catch us and slaughter us like sheep if we try. So you either abandon the captives and the plunder so you can make a run for it, or else you stand and fight.'

'Yes, you're probably right.'

'There's no probably about it.'

Having felt powerless and frustrated throughout the raid now Osfrid felt that his moment had come and he took charge.

'Ecgfrith won't forgive either of us if we scuttle back to Northumbria empty handed. His instructions were to teach Fínsnechta a lesson that he won't forget. We've probably killed five hundred of his people and taken the same number captive. On top of the slaughter of his warriors when we first landed his land is effectively depopulated. That would be partly undone if we let the captives go so that's not an option.

'So, as I see it we have no alternative. We have to delay our pursuers long enough to get the plunder and the slaves away on the knarrs. They can't take all of us in any case, so they'll have to return for us. Someone will have to guard the plunder and the slaves. Let the Manxmen do it. Alweo will make sure we get our fair share later.'

'But that will leave us with less than five hundred warriors to face two thousand,' Stepan said, appalled at the odds.

'You'd be correct if we faced them in open battle but we're not going to do that. Remember our job is to delay them for a maximum of three days whilst we withdraw to the coast.'

'How do we do that?'

'We do what my father taught me. We hit them hard and then we run before they can retaliate. We start tonight but I only need my men for that. Meanwhile you can find a couple of good ambush sites.'

Unsurprisingly the Manxmen put up no argument when it was explained that their job was to run whilst the Northumbrians did the fighting. As he watched one dust cloud disappear to the east, he turned to watch the one approaching from the north. It was now about two hours before dusk and the Uí Néill were about eight miles behind the Manxmen and their straggling column.

Osfrid wondered whether they would be tempted to continue after dark but that would have been stupid. In daylight they could see where their quarry was from the column of dust; at night they risked losing them altogether.

The Uí Néill camped where the River Annalee entered a series of small lakes. When his scouts reported that they hadn't even bothered to put out sentries, Osfrid smiled grimly to himself. After tonight they wouldn't make that mistake again. Unusually for Hibernia, it hadn't rained for weeks and the undergrowth was tinder dry. By the light of the moon and the myriad of camp fires the Uí Néill had lit it was easy to see the layout of the camp.

There was a stiff breeze coming from the west, which suited Osfrid's purposes nicely. The enemy were camped between the river to the north and the shore of the lake to the east. He stationed thirty of his men to the south of the campsite and took the rest with him to the east.

Judging by the sounds emanating from the camp the Uí Néill were celebrating their victory on the morrow already. Osfrid smiled grimly; the more drunk they were the better. He waited until most sounds of revelry had died down and then he, Sigmund, Uurad and three others in his gesith crept forward to the nearest campfire. Fifteen men were fast asleep and snoring around it. It was the work of moments to slit their throats and take a number of burning brands from the fire.

Once back in the undergrowth his men ran along the bushes and piles of dead wood they'd piled up earlier and set them alight. Soon the whole of the eastern side of the campsite was ablaze and dense smoke started to blow across it. From behind the protection of the wall of fire Osfrid's men lit fire arrows and sent them high in the air to land in the middle of the camp. Two even lodged in the oiled leather tent of King Fínsnechta, setting it alight.

Men woke to find themselves breathing the acrid smoke and, coughing and spluttering, they ran about seeking a way out of the purgatory they found themselves in. In their befuddled state some even ran towards the fire before realising their error. Others took refuge in the water of the river and the lake. A few drowned when they got out of their depth but the majority stayed close to the shore, breathing the clean air close to the water's surface.

However, hundreds fled to the south, straight into the arms of Osfrid's thirty men. Of course, many got away but over a hundred were killed by the wraiths that appeared from behind trees, killed and disappeared again into the darkness.

When three blasts on a horn sounded the Northumbrians made their way silently back through the woods to where they had tethered their horses and they rode away to the east well pleased with their night's work. They had only lost one man, killed when he tried to take on four fleeing Hibernians.

As dawn broke Osfrid and Stepan rode to the top of a small hill that overlooked the Uí Néill camp. They watched as dispirited men dug graves for those killed. It looked as if many more had been asphyxiated than had been killed by his men. At a rough count about three hundred bodies were being put into the mass grave whilst the rest prepared to pursue the raiders. Osfrid imagined that the Uí Néill were now furious and determined to get to grips with their foes. It was what he wanted. Angry men are less careful.

The Uí Néill half walked half ran along the northern bank of another lake, this time a long thin one, when a hundred archers appeared out of the trees on the south bank and started to send arrows at high trajectory over the water into the packed ranks of the enemy. As few Hibernians possessed chainmail, or even a padded leather jerkin, most of the arrows caused wounds or death. Immediately the rest crouched down under their shields and stayed like that until several of their leaders rode around ordering then to make for either end of the lake so that they could attack the archers in the flank.

As the first group reached the eastern end Uurad led his mounted warband in a charge at the Uí Néill. The latter had never been charged by mounted warriors before and many turned and fled. Uurad's men threw their spears into the midst of the remainder and then retreated. Two minutes later, just as the Hibernians were forming up again to charge the archers, the horsemen reappeared and threw another volley of spears at their foes.

The same thing happened at the western end. This time it was Osfrid and his gesith who charged. When they galloped away after throwing their second spear the Uí Néill cautiously advanced on the archers again but they just melted back into the trees.

It took the Uí Néill some time to reorganise, leave a burial party to bury the dead and others to take care of the wounded before they continued their pursuit. By now they had learned caution and sent out scouts. However, the scouts were easy targets for Osfrid's horsemen.

When they were within three miles of the coast Osfrid sent Sigmund and half a dozen men to find out whether the knarrs had returned to convey them back to Man. They came back half an hour later to say that two were there and the others were expected within a few hours.

'Stepan, I'm loathe to lose my horses unless I have to but it will take a couple of hours to get them on board. I propose to send them ahead for loading with a few of my least experienced warriors whilst we delay the pursuit again. We'll have to do that in any case as the other knarrs have yet to arrive.'

'Had you suggested that you travel with your horses, leaving me and my men here on our own, I'd have said no but, as I should have expected, you are doing the honourable thing.'

Osfrid had always thought that Stepan held him in low regard. That seemed to have changed.

The approach to the beach where they'd landed lay to the north of the Creggan River with a steep hillside above it. It was an ideal spot for a few hundred men to hold off a greater number. The Northumbrians deployed between the edge of the marshy area alongside the river and the lower slopes of the hills whilst those with bows took to the higher ground and hid behind a number of rocky outcrops.

When the Uí Néill came into view they were confronted by over three hundred men blocking their way with a shield wall four men deep. The Hibernians stopped and, as was their wont, they spent some time capering about and hurling insults at their foe, before they rushed at the shield wall in a disorganised mass.

Osfrid stood near Stepan in the middle of the front rank with Uurad on one side of him and Sigmund on the other. He gripped his spear in one hand and his shield in the other. He wore his sword on his back so that it was easy to unsheathe it in the press of battle. The first man to charge at him ran onto the point of his spear and he fell with the point imbedded in his chest. It was impossible to pull it out and so he let go of it and put his hand over his shoulder and pulled his sword out just in time to thrust it into the face of the next warrior to reach him.

The man screamed and fell away clutching at his face. The third attacker had a heavy axe and he swung it over his head to strike Osfrid down. He raised his shield to block the blow and heard the wood crack as it struck, numbing his arm. He thrust his sword under his upraised shield and felt it enter the axeman's body. It wasn't until he fell away screaming that he realised he'd stabbed him in the groin.

Then the pressure eased as the enemy retreated, not because of the significant casualties they'd suffered throwing themselves at a solid shield wall, but because of the damage being inflicted on them by the archers hidden above them.

Looking at the dead and wounded between the shield wall and the Uí Néill forming up a few hundred yards away Osfrid estimated that there must have been at least three hundred dead and badly wounded. In places along the Northumbrian line the pile of bodies was high enough to provide a significant obstacle.

Stepan walked along the front of the shield wall to speak to Osfrid.

'It'll be a little while before they attack again; they need to work themselves up into a frenzy first. If we can defeat the next charge it will be dark soon and we should be able to slip away and board the knarrs.'

'Yes, but we may need to stage a fighting withdrawal. The archers won't be of any use after dark so they can reinforce us as the valley widens out near the beach. Alternatively, if we can inflict a similar number of casualties next time as we did this time our numbers will be even. In that event we may even be able to defeat them and send them back whence they came.'

'Yes, perhaps. Let's make a decision whether to go on the offensive after we see what happens during their next attack.'

At that moment the Hibernians launched their next attack and Stepan had to run to get back to his position in the line. Instead of repeating the first wild charge they sent several hundred men climbing up the hillside towards the hidden archers so that the number attacking the shield wall was no more than six or seven hundred.

However, the archers were too busy to support their comrades in the valley. Instead they whittled down the men trying to get to grips with them and then, as they got close, one group would move back to the next rocky outcrop whilst another group would continue to inflict casualties. Once the Hibernians got close the same thing would happen. The group who had retreated would send volley after volley at their pursuers whilst the second group withdrew.

The only problem was that their quivers were now nearly empty. They had perhaps halved the numbers of the enemy on the hillside and, just when the archers had run out of arrows, the Hibernians gave up and fled back down the hill.

Meanwhile the attack on the shield wall had proved no more successful this time than last. The Northumbrians had suffered some fifty casualties but the damage inflicted on the Uí Néill was many times that number.

As dark fell the Uí Néill withdrew and headed back up the valley. Stepan was tempted to charge after them and turn a retreat into a rout but Osfrid told him that they had done what they set out to do and it was now time to sail to Man and divide up the spoils. He nodded agreement and the weary Northumbrians trudged the last few miles down to the beach.

It was only then that Osfrid realised that he was bleeding from several flesh wounds to his right arm and both legs. Once they were all safely aboard the fleet of knarrs he allowed Drefan to wash his wounds with sea water to cleanse them and to slow the flow of blood so that he could sew them up with catgut.

Once he'd finished Osfrid noticed that Drefan had bound up his right bicep with a bloody cloth. He undid it to find a deep cut and, despite the youth's protests, he insisted on washing, sewing and binding his wound himself. They were already close but the simple act of treating each other's wounds had strengthened the bond between them.

Chapter Twelve – The Battle of Dùn Nectain

685 AD

Osfrid had been depressed by the looting of monasteries and churches and the slaying of priests and monks but by the time that he and his men returned to Bebbanburg in early October 684 time had numbed his memories. Besides he was returning to the love of his life and a new born son that he hadn't seen.

The news of Eadwulf's birth had reached him on Man and he and Alweo had got drunk together to celebrate. Even young Æthelbald had to be carried from the hall to his bed unconscious after imbibing too much. After that Osfrid was eager to be on his way home. He had taken his share of the spoils for distribution to his men but he had refused to take any religious artefacts and he had kept only enough for himself to defray his expenses.

Eadwulf was a month old when he returned to his fortress sitting high on its crag above an angry, grey sea. Godwyna was delighted to have her husband back but he immediately noticed that she was somewhat withdrawn and clearly unhappy about something. That night in bed, after they had made love twice, he asked her what was troubling her and she burst into tears.

'The old woman who attended me for Eadwulf's birth claimed to be something of a seer. What she told me about Eadwulf is dangerous.'

'Dangerous? How? Has our son some deformity or sickness?'

'No, nothing like that. It's what she said about his destiny. She said that he'd be King of Northumbria one day.'

'How can that be? You may have the blood of the Ida in your veins but my father was a Briton and my mother a thegn's daughter. The woman was rambling, nothing more.'

'But Ecgfrith has no children so his line may become extinct. If so my father would be one of those considered by the Witan.'

'Your father, yes, and you have a brother. We are not like the Picts who trace descent through the matriarchal line. In any case Ecgfrith is young yet, and he has a half-brother, Aldfrith. She was rambling, forget her.'

Osfrid's words reassured her but the old woman's prophesy remained at the back of her mind.

Their domestic bliss was short lived. Osfrid was summoned to a meeting of the Witan at Jarrow just a week after his return. At first he thought it was to discuss the campaign in Hibernia but he was soon to find out that, although that was part of the reason, more serious matters were afoot.

~~~

Cuthbert and the other bishops had accompanied Ecgfrith from Eoforwīc to Jarrow after the former's consecration as a bishop by Archbishop Theodore. Osfrid sensed that all was not well when he arrived at his father-in-law's hall. He was

215

accompanied by Godwyna and baby Eadwulf so that she could
visit her family and show off her son. After the initial greetings
were over her father took him to one side.

'The bishops and abbots are unhappy with Ecgfrith,
especially Cuthbert, and they are scarcely on speaking terms
now.'

'Why? What's happened?'

'Your wretched campaign in Brega is what's happened. The
churchmen are incensed by the looting of religious houses and
the slaying of priests and monks. What on earth possessed you
to do such a thing? They want you arrested and tried.'

'But I tried to stop it! It's Stepan and the Manxmen who are
to blame, not me.'

'Ecgfrith has no control over Alweo and his men and Stepan
is far away in Cumbria. You are here and it's you who will have
to answer for the crimes of sacrilege and murder.'

'I'm innocent, as Uurad and Sigmund can testify.'

'They are your men; they won't be believed.'

'Then the king must send for Stepan.'

'He has other things on his mind. Bruide and his Picts have
invaded Strathearn and Fife and driven out our people. He is
determined to recover them and teach Bruide a lesson.'

'So am I to be denied a fair hearing?'

'We shall have to wait and see. In the meantime I'm to
ensure that you remain here until the meeting of the Witan.'

Ecgfrith looked around the hall where the Witan was
meeting. He was seated in front of the altar whilst the bishops,
abbots, ealdormen and the two remaining eorls were crammed
into the nave. There was scarcely standing room for them all.

'As you know we are meeting here to discuss the breaking of the treaty with the Picts by Bruide. However, before we can do that there is one matter than I need to resolve first. Bishop Cuthbert can you please outline what happened during our recent campaign against Fínsnechta of Brega; briefly if you would.'

'Cyning, the campaign was ill conceived and recklessly executed. Churches and monasteries were looted and burnt and priests and monks were slaughtered. Such conduct is unforgivable. As the instigator of this atrocity you cannot be held entirely blameless but the main guilt lies with those who perpetrated such crimes – Stepan and Osfrid.'

'Cuthbert, you are held in high regard but you choose your words unwisely. I could not have anticipated the rapine of church property or the slaughter of churchmen. The fault lies with those who were there. Stepan step forward.'

'Cyning, Ealdorman Stepan isn't present. He has sent word that it is too far for him to come in view of the fact that he needs to muster his men to meet you in the north prior to your campaign against the Picts.'

'Then we will have to hear his testimony another time. However Ealdorman Osfrid is here. What do you have to say in your defence?'

'Thank you Cyning,' Osfrid said after he'd managed to shoulder his way through the throng to stand before the king. 'I was indeed there and I was as appalled as anyone here at the treatment meted out to the Celtic Church by the Cumbrians and the Manxmen. I protested against such behaviour and urged restraint on Stepan and the Alweo's chieftains. However, I was ignored. I ordered my men not to participate in the sacking of churches and monasteries and I was obeyed. I took no part in the division of the loot belonging to the Church after the campaign and I hold myself entirely blameless in the matter. You need to talk to Stepan, not me.'

'Do you have witnesses as to the veracity of what you claim?'

'Yes, Cyning. Uurad, the commander of my warband, and Sigmund, the leader of my gesith, or any of my men, will attest to the truth of what I have said.'

'Of course they would,' one of the other ealdormen called out. 'They are your men.'

'Nevertheless they were there and you were not!' Osfrid replied heatedly. 'Cyning I protest against this treatment of me as if I had done wrong. I have done nothing I am ashamed of. How was I to stop what was happening? I had fifty warriors; Breht was in command and had ten times my number; the Manxmen likewise.'

'Lack of numbers is no excuse for allowing sacrilege to take place,' Cuthbert said angrily.

'Really? You were once a warrior, Cuthbert. What would you have done differently?'

This time it was Conomultus who spoke. He was there as the representative of Eochaid of Alnwic. He pushed his way forward to stand beside his nephew.

'What no-one has said is how Osfrid saved the expedition from disaster. Stepan delayed too long before retreating to his ships. The Uí Néill had raised a fresh army from their tribesmen in the north which outnumbered Stepan's army two to one. It was Osfrid who took command when Stepan panicked and fought a running battle with the Hibernians so that our army could escape. Instead of castigating him you should be congratulating him. He should be rewarded, not punished.'

'You yourself said that Osfrid took command at the end. Why then did he not return the loot from the churches instead of allowing Stepan and the Maxmen to escape with it?' Bosa asked.

'Because I was too busy trying to save the lives of our army. What did you expect me to do, bishop? Halt the convoy in the face of the enemy and sort through it to take out the property of the church? In any case, I was given the task of delaying the enemy, not command; that remained with Stepan throughout. As my uncle says, it is the Ealdorman of Cumbria you need to talk to.'

Cuthbert was about to say something else but Ecgfrith held up his hand.

'Enough. We have more important things to discuss. This will have to wait until both Osfrid and Stepan can be present to answer for their actions. I will also write to King Alweo to ask for his account.

'Osfrid, you are not yet found to be at fault but you cannot continue as my Master of Horse until this is resolved. I will appoint another to take on that role for the coming war against the Picts; however, I will need your mounted warband to act as my scouts. Similarly they cannot be commanded by your man Uurad. He is to remain with you and your gesith at Bebbanburg. After the Picts have been defeated the Witan will meet again at Yeavering to hear the case against you and against Stepan.'

'Very well, Cyning. I am disappointed that you cannot trust my word but I look forward to clearing my name at Yeavering. I assume that Stepan will similarly be excluded from your army?'

The king was taken off guard. He needed the Cumbrians as they would make up a significant part of his army. The new settlers in the land from which most of the Britons had been driven were a motley bunch of Angles, Saxons, Jutes and even some Frisians and Scots from Dalriada. Loyalty to Stepan was the one thing that united them.

'That will be all, Osfrid. I need not detain you any longer.'

Judging by the king's red face he had at least managed to embarrass him. If only Ecgfrith had allowed Osfrid to command his scouts the outcome of the war might have been very different.

~~~

Ecgfrith was not feeling as confident as he might have done when he arrived with his army at Dùn Èideann, the fortress of Beornheth, Eorl of Lothian. When Stepan had joined him with his Cumbrians he had an army of three thousand men. Against that he was told that Bruide had a similar number of Picts but, as Elfin of Strathclyde and Mael Diun of Dalraida had both refused his invitation to join him he wondered about their loyalty. If they decided to join Bruide he would be significantly outnumbered.

During the years since coming to the throne after the defeat of the Picts by Ecgfrith in 671, Bruide had changed the role of the high king to that of ruler of the whole of Pictland. Now it was an established kingdom. Not only that but he'd expanded his domain, firstly to include Cait in the north, and then he'd travelled across the sea to capture the islands off the north coast known as the Orcades.

However, it wasn't his opponent that bothered him. It was Cuthbert's dire prophecy that the campaign was doomed. Thankfully no-one else had heard Cuthbert's words or the morale of the whole army might have suffered, such was the Bishop of Lindisfarne's reputation.

Towards the end of May Ecgfrith set out along the south bank of the Firth of Forth in glorious weather. Whilst the absence of rain might have been a blessing, marching all day under a hot sun was not and quite a number of men began to suffer from heat stroke. Eventually Ecgfrith had to call a halt early at Blach Ness. It took him three more days to reach Stirling where, thankfully, the weather broke and it started to rain.

All armies at the time carried only a few day's provisions with them in the baggage train. They relied on foraging to eat, but there were no livestock to be had, nor were there any vegetables or harvested crops left in the farms or the settlements. Like the people, it had all vanished.

There was an eerie silence as they approached Stirling. They found the settlement around the fortress deserted and the gates to the latter stood wide open. By now provisions were running low and the army feasted that night on stray dogs, cats and rats that they caught amongst the huts and hovels of Stirling.

They had more luck in Strathallan over the next few days as forage parties came back with deer, boar and even the odd wolf. For warriors more used to a diet of vegetables and cereal such protein rich food had a detrimental effect on their digestion and they were forever running off to squat away from the road.

The absence of any Picts was beginning to unnerve everyone. Ecgfrith and his commanders couldn't understand why Bruide didn't try and defend his kingdom. All they saw of the Picts was the odd warrior on a small pony on the skyline. Then the forage parties started to disappear and Ecgfrith had to send them out in increasing strength.

His scouts also started to vanish. After a week there were only half of Osfrid's original warband of fifty left and they were increasingly nervous of going too far from the main body.

Eventually they came to the head of the Firth of Tay and they crossed the rivers that fed into it one by one until they came to the River Tay. There were no fords across it this far downriver, but there was a wooden bridge just north of the confluence with the River Isla. Now the Northumbrians saw their first Picts; a force of about a thousand was holding the far side of the bridge.

The Picts were in no sort of formation. They danced to and fro yelling insults at the Northumbrians and brandishing their weapons and small round shields. Ecgfrith smiled to himself. This was too easy. He sent his archers forward and they sent volley after volley into the packed ranks of their foes. With no armour, their shields did little to protect them and several scores fell dead or wounded. The Picts took a little while to realise what was happening and then they hurried to get out of range.

As soon as they withdrew from the other side of the bridge Ecgfrith sent his warriors across. They spread out on the other side to form a shield wall just as the Picts launched an attack.

There was no formation to it. They ran at the Northumbrians screaming insults in a disorganised mass. A few even managed to leap in the air and land several rows deep into the Northumbrians. They were quickly killed, but not before they had taken several men with them.

A hundred Picts died trying to break through the shield wall but far fewer of Ecgfrith's men were killed. When the horsemen clattered over the bridge and swept around to take the Picts in the flank they broke and ran. Had Osfrid been there to restrain them they might not have chased after the fleeing Picts. As it was they managed to cut down a score or so before a large group of the Picts turned and faced them.

Against several hundred the fifty horsemen didn't stand much of a chance. Their horses were speared and the riders were killed as they lay on the ground or else they were pulled from their mounts and then stabbed to death. Less than thirty made it safely back to the main body.

Ecgfrith continued his march down Strath Mor, fording the smaller river that ran down part of the glen where it turned up into the hills to the north. They camped that night on the other side of the ford and the king set double sentries, fearing a night attack. It didn't come but Ecgfrith awoke the next day to find that it had started raining in the night and it was still coming down hard.

He sent his scouts out but they couldn't see far in the gloom and the rain so they stuck close to the column.

'Are we wise to stray so far into Pictland,' Octa asked him at one stage.

'They flee before us; they fear us, and rightly so. I'm determined to bring them to battle so that I can convince them once and for all who is Bretwalda of the North. '

His hereræswa looked far from convinced.

'Cyning, bretwalda was title that the Caledonian kings bestowed on Oswiu because they respected him and they acknowledged him as their leader. It's not something you can impose on them.'

'Are you saying that they don't respect me? Didn't Bruide make himself King of the Picts through force? '

'Yes but he was born a Pict. He is one of them. Your father used diplomacy, bribery and threats and only resorted to force when he had to.'

Ecgfrith looked at the rain streaming down Octa's face for a minute, then shrugged.

'Well, it's a little late for diplomacy now. Besides, it wouldn't have worked on Bruide; he only understands force.'

They camped that night beside a small lake. Beyond the lake were wetlands – a whole series of small lakes and ponds connected by small streams. The ground was boggy and Ecgfrith was pleased by this; it protected his flank.

When he awoke in the morning it was to a bright, sunny day. The rain of yesterday was merely an unpleasant memory. Now he could see further. To the south there was a range of low hills. On the top of the highest sat a small fortress, a circular palisade with a watchtower in the middle.

Octa sent half a dozen horsemen to see if the fortress was occupied and another small group to scout the glen to the east. When neither party had reappeared after an hour he began to get worried. He had just warned the camp to arm themselves when the Picts appeared.

~~~

Bruide had watched the Northumbrian camp from the watchtower inside the fortress of Dùn Nectain since dawn. Now he had Ecgfrith and his wretched Northumbrians just where he wanted them. His policy of stripping the land of people, livestock and stored crops had worked. The enemy were frustrated and hungry. The skirmish at the bridge had merely been a ploy to make sure that they walked into the trap he'd prepared. He hadn't like losing a few hundred men, but it had been worth it.

Dùn Nectain was the Mormaer of Angus' principal stronghold and it was larger than it looked from below. He watched a boy on a hill pony canter up the valley to the south of the hills on which the fortress stood, out of sight from Ecgfrith's men. He rode in through the gates and gave a message to the mormaer. The man mounted the watchtower and handed it to Bruide who broke the seal and scanned the contents. He smiled and was about to give it to the mormaer when he remembered that he couldn't read.

'Beli and Mael Duin are five miles away. They'll be here well before noon.'

Beli was Elfin of Strathclyde's son. Elfin was elderly now and Beli was the power behind the throne. Unlike his father, he didn't like the Northumbrians and was keen to rule without interference from anyone, least of all Ecgfrith. Mael Diun had agreed to Bruide's plan for fear of isolation otherwise.

'In that case the trap is sprung. Give the signal.'

The mormaer waved down at the boy with the pony who mounted and was about to ride out of the gates when Bruide yelled down for him to stay where he was. He'd spotted the two groups of riders leaving the camp below.

'Tell the boy to ride to warn the warband to the east about the scouts coming their way. None are to return to warn Ecgfrith. Then take a dozen of your best men and lie in wait for the horsemen coming towards us. As soon as they cross the ridge to approach the gates they are to be killed. Make sure they are out of sight first though. Now go!'

The boy, who was called Taran and was Bruide's son, lay under a gorse bush with the Mormaer of Atholl, who commanded the warband blocking the route to the east. When the six riders appeared, the mormaer nodded and Taran put his fingers in his mouth. A split second later a piercing whistle gave the signal to spring the ambush. Fifty men shot to their feet and ran at the horsemen, whilst fifty more ran to cut off their line of retreat. It was the work of seconds to pull the riders from their horses and kill them.

One of the horses bolted and ran straight at the blocking group, who jumped out of its way. Luckily one with more courage than the rest stood his ground and aimed his spear at the animal's chest. It ran straight onto the point, knocking the man to the ground, but then it fell to its knees, collapsed sideways and lay still.

Those scouting the fortress met a similar fate and, once Taran returned to tell his father that the other party of horsemen were no more, he left again to take the message to those manning a beacon on the next hill.

'Light the fire, quickly now,' he yelled excitedly in his treble voice.

Five minutes later the pile of wood caught from the kindling and ten minutes after that the fire was alight well enough for the men to throw wet straw onto it to produce white smoke that was visible for some distance.

~~~

Octa was the first to notice the smoke and he went to find Ecgfrith.

'That bodes ill for us, I'll be bound,' he muttered.

'Yes, it's a signal to the Picts, but to do what?'

He had his answer half an hour later when over two thousand of them appeared blocking the valley to the east. At the same moment two thousand more lined the hills either side of Dùn Nectain.

'That must be every warrior that Bruide could find.' Octa said, looking worried. 'I suggest the time has come for us to retreat, Cyning.'

'Yes, you're right. They'll press us hard if we do, but a fighting withdrawal seems like our only choice or else we'll be hemmed in by Picts on two sides with the marsh on the other.'

The tactic was working. The Northumbrians formed an L shaped shield wall to hold off the sporadic attacks by the frenzied Picts and they'd gone about a mile to where the marsh petered out so that they could form a proper long shield wall when they saw another army advancing up Strath Mor towards them.

'Who in the Name of God are they?' Ecgfrith asked Octa.

As they came closer they could distinguish the banners of Strathclyde and Dalriada.

'I suppose it's too much to hope that they have come to support us,' Octa muttered.

~~~

Crows and buzzards flew over the battleground seeking their next tasty morsel. Even the wolves ventured down from the hills to eat as much as their bellies could contain. Over two thousand – nearly every Northumbrian warrior worthy of the name – lay scattered over the valley floor. Only a handful had escaped. Amongst the dead lay Ecgfrith, Octa, Stepan of Cumbria and Beornheth of Lothian, Bishop Cuthbert's brother. Northumbria was left with no eorls, only a few ealdormen – all of them elderly and infirm, except for Osfrid, and a score of thegns after that fateful day. The kingdom would take a long time to recover from the slaughter of the twenty first of May in 685, if it ever did.

PART TWO – ALDFRITH

Chapter Thirteen – Two Funerals

685 to 687 AD

Three days before the fateful battle Bishop Cuthbert arrived at Bebbanburg to see Osfrid. He had sailed over in one of the monastery's small fishing boats and brought the faint whiff of yesterday's catch with him into the hall. Osfrid and Godwyna were sitting at a table talking to Sigmund, Uurad and Morcar the reeve.

The matter which concerned them all was Ecgfrith's obvious intention to hold Osfrid to account for the oppression of the Hibernian Church. Osfrid's main concern was to preserve Eadwulf's inheritance. They were debating how best to achieve this when a servant came and diffidently whispered in his master's ear that the bishop had just landed on the beach below the fortress. Osfrid was puzzled and slightly alarmed. Cuthbert hadn't come to see him before and he suspected that he wouldn't be the bearer of glad tidings. Biting his lip, he and his companions made their way down to the beach.

'Bishop Cuthbert, welcome to Bebbanburg. To what do we owe the pleasure?'

Osfrid was being polite; it wasn't how he felt towards the man who had publicly castigated him for what had happened in Brega.

'I owe you an apology, Osfrid. I know now that you tried your best to rein in the excesses of Stepan's Cumbrians and the Manxmen.'

'What caused you to change your mind?' Osfrid asked in surprise.

'Can we go up to your hall? It is the least of what I have come to say.'

'Yes, of course.'

As they walked in through the sea gate and up to the hall Osfrid felt as if he was walking on air; a great weight had just been lifted off his shoulders. Then, as they approached the hall the feeling of relief changed to one of resentment that he should ever have been blamed in the first place. However, what Cuthbert had to say when they sat down drove that from his mind.

'Last night Christ himself came to me in a vision. He told me that I was wrong to blame you for what happened in Hibernia. It was the fault of the king for choosing the wrong man to command the campaign and of Stepan for intentionally looting Church property. What Our Lord went on to say was like a cold dagger in my heart. He said that both Ecgfrith and Stepan would be punished. They and all the army of Northumbria would be wiped out by the Picts at a place called Dùn Nectain in three days' time.'

There was a stunned silence after Cuthbert had finished speaking. It was Osfrid who broke it.

'Are you certain, Cuthbert?'

'My visions have never proved false in the past.'

There was a hint of reproof in the statement.

'Where is this Dùn Nectain?' Sigmund asked, looking at Uurad, who'd been born a Pict.

'I've never heard of it, but then I had never been anywhere more than a few miles from our settlement until I became Catinus' servant.'

'My uncle might know,' Osfrid said suddenly. 'After all he was the Bishop of Abernethy, the diocese of the Picts.'

Osfrid's birlinns were kept on the beach in the shelter of Budle Bay. Several were escorting his knarrs who were away on trading missions but two were still there. One was on its side being repaired and re-caulked but the other was ready for sea. Unfortunately the tide was out so it was three hours before Sigmund and the gesith managed to get her launched. They would crew her with Uurad as the helmsman.

'Take care husband, I need you home again safely,' Godwyna said as she kissed Osfrith goodbye.

'Don't worry, I'll be back soon.'

He scooped up Eadwulf from where he stood uncertainly on his little legs, clutching his mother's skirts and kissed his baby son before lifting his tunic and blowing a raspberry on his belly. The little boy screamed with delight and clutched at his father's hair. Osfrid kissed both of them again and handed the boy to his wife before scrambling aboard.

The wind was from the east and it took them barely four hours to reach the bay at the mouth of the River Aln. There were no horses available so they had to walk from there to the hall at Alnwic, a distance of five miles. Cuthbert was fit for his age but slow and it took another two hours to get there. As they approached the sun was setting and a warm sunny day turned into a cool evening.

Conomultus came out of the hall with Eydth and five year old Eochaid to greet them.

'Cuthbert, Osfrid,' he said smiling at them. 'This is an unexpected pleasure.'

'You might not think it quite so pleasurable when you've heard what Bishop Cuthbert has to say, uncle.'

'Dùn Nectain? I've heard of it but never been there,' he replied when he was asked if he knew of it.

'What do you know about it?'

'It's the main stronghold of the Mormaer of Angus. I think it's about fourteen miles north-west of the monastery at Arbroath on the east coast.'

'We need to go there and there is no time to lose.'

'Why?'

So Cuthbert told him of his vision.

The next morning they set out again, not in the birlinn, which now acted as their escort, but in one of Conomultus' knarrs which could carry six horses. Eochaid had asked to go with his guardian and sulked when he was told that he was too young. Conomultus laughed and said there would be plenty of time for adventures when he was older. The boy didn't stop scowling but he nodded in understanding.

It was a hundred and twenty miles by sea from Amble – the nearest harbour to Alnwic – to Arbroath and it took twenty four hours to sail there. However, it was dangerous to try and navigate in unfamiliar waters after dark and so they spent the night in the small harbour below the palisaded fortress at Dùn Barra.

Although Dùn Èideann was the principle fortress of the Eorl of Lothian, Cuthbert's brother preferred the smaller stronghold on the rock jutting out into the German Ocean. They were welcomed by his wife and her son, Behrt, a youth of fifteen who was halfway through his training to be a warrior.

Although Cuthbert was his uncle, Behrt hardly knew him and seemed to be somewhat in awe of him. When he was told of Cuthbert's vision he was visibly shocked.

'Does that mean that father is dead too?'

'We don't know, Behrt. That's why we need to get there as soon as possible and find out what the situation is.'

'When is this battle supposed to take place?'

'On the twenty first,'

'But that's tomorrow!'

'I'm well aware of that!' his uncle replied brusquely. 'I'm sorry, I didn't mean to snap. I think we're all a little on edge. Tonight we'll all pray in the church for the safety of Ecgfrith, his army, and especially for your father.'

It was mid-afternoon when they arrived at Arbroath and it took time to unload the horses. Nevertheless, they still had a few hours of daylight left and they set out heading north-west. The abbot from the monastery had offered to guide them as soon as he found out who the two bishops were. Osfrid, Sigmund and a member of his gesith made up the other members of the group of riders. The rest were left with the knarr and the birlinn.

The abbot wasn't a proficient rider and his mount was a sturdy but docile hill pony. The fastest the pair would go was a sedate trot, which frustrated the rest. Even the two elderly bishops were capable of riding at a gentle canter. It took them nearly four hours to travel the dozen miles to Dùn Nectain and the sun was setting over the hills to the west by the time the fortress came in sight.

The gates were closed but as they approached the abbot called out who he was and they creaked open to admit him and his companions.

'What brings you here, Father Abbot, and who's that with you?'

In the dusk it wasn't easy to see who had spoken, nor could the speaker make out who the other six riders were, other than one was clearly a boy, presumably a servant.

'Come in to the hall,' the voice continued without giving the abbot the chance to reply. 'You will have to forgive me if I stink; I haven't had a chance to wash the blood and filth off me as yet.'

By the light of the fire and the torches in the hall the visitors could see the torn and bloodstained tunic their host was wearing. His face was streaked with dirt and dried blood and, as he sank down into a chair at the head of the table, clearly exhausted, a man dressed as a Celtic priest with a tonsured forehead came to clean and sew up two cuts on the man's right arm.

'Bishop Conomultus! I never expected to see you again after I drove you out of Abernethy,' the man exclaimed, clearly puzzled by his presence.

'I'm here at the invitation of Bishop Cuthbert, Cyning,' he replied in English, knowing that the man seated in front of them, King Bruide, spoke both English and his own tongue equally fluently.

'Cuthbert! Well, well, we are indeed honoured. Were you hoping to join your ill-fated king? If so I fear you are in for a disappointment.'

'No, Brenin,' he replied in the Brythonic language, 'I was visited by the Lord Jesus three nights ago who told me of fate of Ecgfrith's campaign in advance.'

'A vision? Do you expect me to believe that,' he scoffed.

'How else would we know where to come to, and when, Brenin?'

'What was the message in this vision if not to warn Ecgfrith he was walking into a trap?' Bruide asked, now a little less sure of himself.

Suddenly he winced as the priest finished sewing his wounds up and bit off the end of the length of catgut. He jerked his arm away from the priest and curtly told him to leave.

'To recover his body and take it to Iona for burial.'

'Iona? Why there?'

'I know not. But that was what Our Lord told me to do.'

'How strange. Well, I have no objection but, to do that you'll have to find his corpse first. There are well over two thousand of them out there. We will recover those of our own men in the morning, but the buzzards can have the wretched Northumbrians.'

'You cannot do that,' Cuthbert protested. 'They are Christians, just as you and I are Christians. They deserve a proper burial in consecrated ground.'

'Why should I?'

'Because, if you don't, just as I prophesied the death of Ecgfrith so I will tell you of your end. Do you want to know the day and manner of your demise, Bruide? Will such knowledge haunt you every day from now until then? It would me and I'm looking forward to meeting my maker.'

Bruide was now looking extremely agitated.

'No, you old wizard, I don't want to know, nor do I even want to think about it. Curse you, Cuthbert. Very well, I'll get my men to bury the invaders in a common grave and you can consecrate the barrow we'll put over it. Now get out of my sight, and don't expect me to provide you with food and lodging tonight. You can sleep in the stables for all I care.'

'Thank you, Brenin. Once more thing, if, as I suspect, the body of my younger brother is also lying out there, I would like to take him back to Dùn Barra for burial alongside my family.'

'Yes, yes. Now get out.'

'How do you know when Bruide will die?' Osfrid asked curiously as they went towards the stables.

Cuthbert replied without looking at him.

'I don't. How could I? '

~~~

It took them three hours to find the two bodies they were looking for the next morning. They started soon after dawn and made for the place where the standard of Northumbria was stuck in the ground, leaning drunkenly at forty five degrees. They wept openly as they made their way through mutilated bodies with thousands of flies buzzing around them.

The Picts had already started to remove their own dead whilst the Strathclyde Britons and the Dalriadan Scots were busy looting the bodies of both sides of their valuables,

236

helmets, byrnies and weapons. All this was done in sombre silence. It seems all were stunned by the carnage of the previous day.

Ecgfrith's body was located fairly quickly as it was only twenty yards from the standard. The Eorl of Lothian took longer to find. Eventually Cuthbert recognised two of the dead as members of his gesith. After that it didn't take long to find Beornheth. His right arm lay separated from his torso and his face had a cut all down his right cheek which exposed the bone. Evidently he had lost his helmet by that stage and there was no sign of it nearby. Perhaps it had already been looted.

Having found the two corpses the problem was one of transport. True to his word, Bruide had ordered several mass graves to be dug for the Northumbrian dead. There were no wounded; any such had long since had their throats cut. However, there was no sign of the King of the Picts and no-one else seemed inclined to help the two bishops. The abbot had already returned to his monastery, his job as guide done.

Eventually Conomultus spotted Mael Duin, the King of Dalriada, supervising the burial of his own dead further down the valley and he walked down to meet him. After a quarter of an hour he returned.

'The Dalriadans are returning home tomorrow and King Mael has offered to let us travel with him to Dùn Add. He'll also give us space on a cart for the king's body. We'll need to sew it up in a leather tent and put it in a coffin packed with herbs to make sure it doesn't stink on the way. From there we can get a ship to take us across the sea to Iona.'

'I'll come with you,' Cuthbert said. 'I was going anyway as I hope to find Aldfrith there. If he is, we need to persuade him to return with us. He's the last of the line of Æthelfrith and so is the only candidate to be the next king. However, I know that my brother will want to be buried with our mother and father at Dùn Barra.'

'I'll take him with me and stop there on the way back to Bebbanburg,' Osfrid offered. 'We've no cart and so it'll mean carrying your brother's body slung over a horse until we get to Arbroath, I fear.'

'He won't be aware of the indignity and the important thing is that he is buried with his family. Would you please warn those nobles and thegns who are left that the Witan will need to meet and confirm Aldfrith's election? I'll send a message letting you know what day we hope to arrive. You'll need to tell Bosa, Eata and the abbots too. I suggest the Witan meets at Hexham as that's fairly central,' Cuthbert said and Osfrid nodded.

After Cuthbert had said a blessing over Beornheth's remains the two groups parted.

~~~

Aldfrith was discussing some finer points of theology, particularly the differences in doctrine between the Celtic and Roman churches, with Adamnan, the Abbot of Iona, when Cuthbert and Conomultus arrived with Ecgfrith's body. At first the two men ignored the arrival of the ship; it wasn't an unusual occurrence. It wasn't until the prior knocked on the door and told them that Bishop Cuthbert had arrived that the two men broke off their debate and made their way unhurriedly down to the beach.

238

'Bishop, this is an unexpected pleasure.' The mild rebuke at not giving the abbot advance notice of his arrival was diplomatically phrased.

'Yes, forgive us for not warning you that we were on our way, Father Abbot, but we had no time to lose. I'm not sure whether news of the Battle of Dùn Nectain had reached you yet?'

'No, we knew, of course, that King Ecgfrith had invaded Pictland but not that a battle had taken place.'

'The Northumbrians were caught in an ambush by King Bruide, abetted by the kings of Strathclyde and Dalriada. Their army was wiped out and Ecgfrith was killed.'

The faces of both Adamnan and Aldfrith paled and neither said anything for a moment.

'We have brought the king's body with us in the hope that you might agree to bury it here, in this holy place.'

'Ecgfrith's corpse is with you? Then I suppose I can't refuse your request but only the bodies of Caledonian kings have been buried here before.'

'Ecgfrith was Bretwalda of Caledonia before Bruide defeated him.'

'Yes, I suppose you're right.'

'Father Abbot, I would regard it as a favour if you would allow my brother's body to be laid to rest here,' Aldfrith said.

Up until that moment Adamnan had forgotten that Aldfrith was Ecgfrith's half-brother.

'Of course, but we must hold the funeral without delay. The corpse will be decaying already, I'm sure.'

'It is tightly sewn in leather and packed in a simple coffin with herbs but, yes, the sweet smell of decay is becoming more and more obvious,' Cuthbert replied with a smile.

The whole time Conomultus had stood silently behind Cuthbert but then Aldfrith recognised him.

'Bishop Conomultus isn't it? We met at Abernethy several years ago when I came to consult some books at the monastery.'

'Yes, lord, I remember it well. Those were happier days.'

'You call me lord? Why?'

'Because you are the last of the line of Æthelfrith and, if you are willing and the Witan confirms it, your brother's successor as king.'

Aldfrith looked as if he had been struck in the face. The thought had evidently never occurred to him.

'But, although Oswiu was my father he was never married to my mother.'

'As there are no legitimate heirs, that doesn't matter, lord,' Cuthbert explained.

'I need to think about this, please excuse me.'

Aldfrith almost ran from the beach in the direction of his hut.

'What happens if he says no?' the abbot asked quietly.

Cuthbert shrugged. 'There are other Idings, sons of younger sons of Ida the first King of Bernicia, but I suspect it would mean a period of disruption and perhaps even the end of Northumbria as one kingdom. Besides so many died at Dùn Nectain the other Idings are either men too old to fight or young boys. What Northumbria needs now is a king who is neither too elderly nor too young and who has an undoubted right to the throne. That man is Aldfrith.'

'Let's leave him to get used to the idea for a while. I'll speak to him this evening as I know him better than anyone. Come, we must get Ecgfrith's corpse unloaded and make arrangement for the funeral tomorrow. The coffin will lie in the church tonight. Will you both keep a vigil with it?'

'I will, much as my poor old knees will pain me,' Cuthbert said with a grimace.

'I'll join you, of course; then you won't be alone as far as suffering from the infirmities of old age is concerned,' Conomultus offered.

Conomultus at fifty five was four years older than Cuthbert but he seemed in better health, though both were suffering the agonies of old age. In truth the long journey seemed to have worn out the Bishop of Lindisfarne. Anyone not knowing the two men would have said that Conomultus was the younger.

No one knew what Adamnan had said to Aldfrith the previous evening but when he joined Cuthbert and Conomultus for their vigil that night he told that that he knew where his duty lay; he would return to Northumbria with them.

Iona lay off the south-western tip of the Isle of Mull and was exposed to winds coming across the sea from the west; unfortunately that was the prevailing direction. On the day of Ecgfrith's funeral it was blowing a gale and the wind tore into the monks as they struggled to carry the simple wooden coffin, making them stagger. At times it was so strong that they came to a standstill. Their habits and those of the two bishops flapped vigorously and they had to be helped across to the church.

Once inside they were, of course, protected from the wind but it howled around the building making it difficult for the congregation to hear the prayers and the homily delivered by Cuthbert.

When they emerged again the wind had died down a little, but now it carried horizontal rain into the faces of the mourners and pall bearers as they struggled the short distance to the cemetery. Once the coffin had been lowered into the grave and both Cuthbert and Adamnan had said a few final prayers, everyone was only too thankful to get in out of the wind and rain. Only Aldfrith remained, kneeling by his brother's grave lost in meditation, ignoring the water dripping from the end of his nose.

His mind was in a turmoil. When he was a boy his one desire was to be a great warrior like his father, Oswiu, but the king showed little interest in his eldest son. For a time Aldfrith wondered whether it was because he was a bastard; certainly Oswiu seemed eager enough to forget his mother once he became betrothed to the daughter of the King of Rheged. But he seemed to pay as little attention to her son, Alchfrith, or his daughter as he did to Aldfrith. It wasn't until Oswiu married Eanflæd that he took any interest in his children. Perhaps he had only really loved her and that was why he took a delight in her offspring.

Aldfrith sighed as the wind whipped his robes around his torso as he knelt by the grave. He hadn't really known Ecgfrith so he didn't hate him, but he resented the problems he had left behind. It had taken Aldfrith a long time to discover where his true passion in life lay, and it wasn't in exercising power or being a warrior.

242

He took delight in scholarship, especially discovering what had happened in the past and why. He was also a theologian. So much of what was written in the Bible puzzled him so he'd spent a long time trying to unearth the truth. Because he questioned some of what the priests and monks accepted as fact, he had never taken the final step and become one of them. Now he wondered whether that had been wise. Had he been in Holy Orders he wouldn't be eligible to be King of Northumbria. It was not a role he desired, not now at any rate, nor did he think he was capable of being a good king.

He had an orderly mind, he was a good administrator and he had earned the respect of his peers, but he felt that was as far as his qualities went. Nevertheless, he felt obliged to accept what fate evidently had in store for him. Northumbria needed him as its ruler and so he would meet his obligations. Sighing he got to his feet and, with a last look at Ecgfrith's grave, he made his way to the church, now thankfully with the wind at his back, to pray for God's help in the days and years to come.

~~~

The Witan which met in the monastery church at Hexham was a sorry affair. Apart from the three bishops and the abbots of Melrose, Ripon and Jarrow, only six of the eighteen ealdorman who had been appointed by Ecgfrith were present. A dozen had died at Dùn Nectain and of those left behind only Osfrid was under the age of fifty. Conomultus was also there as the representative of the boy Eochaid.

There had been nearly three hundred thegns too. Most had been with Ecgfrith's army, only those from the three shires that bordered Mercia had remained at home. However, thegns no longer attended the Witan, and hadn't since the creation of ealdormen.

The church itself was as mean as the attendance. Unlike the stone-built churches of Whitby, Ripon, Eoforwīc and Lindisfarne, that at Hexham was built of wood with a roof of timber covered in sods. The grass was long and the earth retained the rainwater meaning it was unkempt in appearance and really too heavy for the supporting rafters. Consequently it creaked occasionally, making those below fear that it might collapse on top of them.

The only stone building at Hexham was the abbot's lodging, built when Wilfrid was abbot. Osfrid thought it was typical of the man to have concentrated on his creature comforts when visiting in preference to the house of God.

The interior of the church was as primitive as the exterior. Apart from the altar with its gold cross and candlesticks, there was no ornamentation. The floor was of beaten earth covered in rushes and the only seating was benches either side of the chancel and a chair and prie dieu for the officiating priest. The benches were occupied by the members of the Witan and the chair by John of Beverley.

Bishop Eata had died earlier in the year and the new bishop was formerly the Abbot of Beverley in Deira. Although junior to the two other bishops present, he presided as the host.

Bishop John asked for those æthelings who wished to be considered for the vacant throne to stand up. To Osfrid's amazement the first man on his feet was Benoc, Godwyna's father.

He knew that the man was sixty one and suffered from acute stiffness in his joints. The thirty mile journey to Hexham must have been agony for him. When Osfrid had spoken to him to commiserate on the death of his son at the fateful battle he had said nothing about a bid for the throne.

'I am Benoc, son of Hering, son of Hussa, son of Ida and cousin of Æthelfrith, who was, as you all know, the father of Oswald and Oswiu and grandfather of Ecgfrith. Hussa was King of Bernicia and my father, Hering, should have succeeded him but the Witan decided otherwise and made Æthelfrith king instead. He drove me and my father into exile and I was only able to return when Oswiu came to the throne. Later he made me Ealdorman of Jarrow. I therefore claim that I have a prior claim to the throne over Aldfrith who was born out of wedlock.'

Having delivered his thunderbolt, Benoc sat down and Aldfrith slowly got to his feet.

'My lords, spiritual and temporal, I am here because Bishop Cuthert came to Iona and asked me to come. He, like me, no doubt thought that, as I was the only surviving grandson of Æthelfrith, the first King of Northumbria, I would be the only candidate. I have no great desire to rule and I would be content to return to my studies on Iona, but one thing prevents me. I am convinced now that ruling this kingdom is God's purpose for me.

'Benoc says that, by the rules of primogeniture, his father had a better right to be King of Bernicia when Hussa died than my grandfather did. This is true. However, it is not the practice of Anglo-Saxons to use primogeniture to determine the succession? That is determined by the Witan who choose from amongst the æthelings. My understanding of the meaning of ætheling is a male member of the royal dynasty. Whilst Benoc may be entitled to regard himself as an ætheling of the Kingdom of Bernicia, he is not an ætheling of the Kingdom of Northumbria. That term is restricted to the male descendants of Æthelfrith who, by marrying into the royal house of Deira, created a new dynasty to rule the Kingdom of Northumbria.

'If that is not the case, then any male descendants of Ida and any surviving members of the Royal House of Deira should be eligible for election here today.'

With that Aldfrith sat down and an excited hubbub ensued. It was a little while before John of Beverley could re-establish order but, when he did, Cuthbert got to his feet.

'I suggest we need to make a ruling on the admissibility of candidates for the throne in view of what Prince Aldfrith has said. Personally I don't think that bastardy should be a factor. There are other kings who have been born illegitimate, in Wessex and Mercia for example. There is, however, a practical point I think we need to consider. Whether or not Ealdorman Benoc should be considered as an ætheling of Northumbria, there is his age to consider and the fact that, tragically, his son was slain at Dùn Nectain. If your choice fell on him who would be king when he dies? If the answer is Aldfrith, better he is elected now, rather than later.'

Benoc laboriously rose to his feet again.

'I may have lost my son but I have two grandsons, Eochaid of Alnwic and Eadwulf of Bebbanburg.'

The statement made Osfrid sit up with a jolt. Was Benoc saying that his son was an ætheling? How his father would have loved that: from shepherd boy to prince in two generations. He looked across the chancel at Conomultus who raised his eyebrow quizzically and smiled grimly. If Benoc was chosen it would make the two cousins rivals for the throne in due course. It didn't seem possible and it was time someone introduced a cold dose of reality to the proceedings. Conomultus stood as soon as Benoc had been helped to sit down again.

'Speaking as the guardian of one of Benoc's grandsons and uncle of the other I would like to point out that one boy is five and the other one and a half. It will be well over a decade before either are old enough to be candidates to succeed Benoc, were he to be elected. I'm a churchman not a warrior but I believe that in the dire situation we find ourselves in we need a man of vigour and ability to lead us. Like me, Benoc is hampered by his advancing years. I mean no disrespect, ealdorman, but your day has passed.'

John cleared his throat noisily.

'Very well, does anyone else wish to speak before we vote on whether Benoc should be considered a candidate for the vacant throne?'

Osfrid stood and turned to address the Witan.

'As the father of Eadwulf, and hopefully more grandsons for Benoc,' he began and then waited for the laughter to die away, 'I believe that he and Eochaid should be recognised as æthelings. However, my uncle is correct when he says we need a man who has a long reign ahead of him so that he can restore Northumbria's fortunes. That man is Aldfrith.'

~~~

247

Cuthbert felt exhausted after Aldfrith's coronation was over and was dreading the journey back to Lindisfarne. He was now fifty one which, although it was a good age, many churchmen had lived decades longer. The previous Pope, Leo II, had been seventy two when he died and the Pope when Ecgfrith came to the throne, Vitalian, had lived until he was ninety two. Cuthbert was under no illusion that he would live as long as they had.

It was only seventy miles from Hexham to Lindisfarne but it took Cuthbert a week to get there. Osfrid insisted on accompanying him all the way and Conomultus joined them as far as Alnwic. Cuthbert needed frequent rest stops and uncle and nephew took advantage of these to go hunting. They bagged pheasants and the smaller breeds of deer in the main but couldn't eat them there and then as they needed to hang for a while. Some were added to the larder at Alnwic and the rest taken on to Bebbanburg. Cuthbert declined the offer of some for his monastery saying that he didn't want his monks to get used to eating meat or they'd want it all the time.

It was the evening on the last day of September by the time Cuthbert arrived at Lindisfarne, having departed from Osfrid just after midday. His monks were overjoyed at his return but Cuthbert retired to his hut as soon as he could and collapsed onto the straw paillasse that served as his bed. He slept for twenty seven hours, to the consternation of everyone except the prior, a monk from Iona named EadBehrt, who realised how gruelling travelling so far, and under such great mental strain, must have been.

Two days later Cuthbert seemed to have recovered and he resumed his duties; however, he confided in EadBehrt that he continued to feel weary and drained. From the time of his return EadBehrt began to assume more and more of Cuthbert's duties as abbot.

As soon as he rode into Bebbanburg Osfrid jumped from his horse and watched as his wife ran to him, all dignity forgotten. He only had eyes for her face as he pulled Godwyna into a hug, then he became aware that her belly was distended.

'Are you?'

'Yes, I'm pregnant again. The baby's expected early in the new year.'

Osfrid kissed his wife tenderly and took her off to their chamber to celebrate their reunion in private.

The baby turned out to be a girl who they christened Guthild. From the first Eadwulf was jealous of the new arrival and the attention she took away from him. It was not a trait that endeared him to his father, though Godwyna always made excuses for him.

Shortly after the birth Aldfrith arrived and quickly made it clear that he was on more than just as tour of Bernicia.

'I find myself in something of a quandary, Osfrid,' he said that evening after they'd eaten and Godwyna had gone to bed. 'Northumbria is without leaders and I'm not such a stranger to the realities of the world to think that our enemies - that is the Picts and the Mercians - won't be tempted to take advantage of that. Even Elfin of Strathclyde may be drawn to invade Cumbria.'

'How can I help, Cyning?'

'I know that my brother held you partly responsible for what happened in Hibernia but I have taken the trouble to talk to those few who were there and are still alive. I know you opposed that fool Stepan. I therefore believe that you are both trustworthy and loyal. Is that true?'

'Yes, Cyning. Absolutely.'

'Good. I need to create an inner council of people I can rely on. Unfortunately Cuthbert says he is too old to travel anymore and Bishop Bosa and I; well, let's just say that there is little that we agree on.'

'And John of Beverley?'

'Yes, a good man I think. I intend to ask him to join my council, and your uncle, Conomultus, too.'

'I'm pleased, he's like my father was: loyal and very capable. He claims he's too old and just wants a peaceful life, but the years have not sat as heavily on him as they have on Bishop Cuthbert.'

'Just so. My first problem is to appoint new ealdormen and thanes. There are so many who died at the hands of the Caledonians that it is difficult to know where to start.'

'Might I suggest that you need someone reliable on your northern border as the first priority?'

'Are you suggesting yourself?' Aldfrith said, not without a hint of suspicion in his voice.

'No, I have no desire to leave Bebbanburg. Besides it's the most important fortress in Bernicia. No, I was thinking of Cuthbert's nephew, Behrt. He's just about to turn sixteen. Although that is very young to be burdened with responsibility, you are not blessed with a wide choice from amongst the nobles. If he was made Ealdorman of Dùn Èideann he could also be given the responsibility of warden of the borderlands.'

'But wouldn't he want to be Ealdorman of Dùn Barra, like his father?'

'He has a younger brother who will soon be fourteen. He might become ealdorman when he's older. In the meantime his mother could manage the shire.'

'Good. I'm grateful to you for your suggestions. I'll go to Dùn Barra next and make a decision then. Will you accompany me?'

Osfrid groaned inwardly. He had wanted to stay with his family a little longer but he could hardly say no to the king.

'Of course, Cyning.'

'Whilst we are on our own I think we can dispense with the title.'

'Thank you, Aldfrith. Is there anything else I can help with at the moment?'

'The Mercians aren't far from my mind either, but Ethelred seems fully occupied by his struggle with Wessex at the moment. Long may that continue. Cumbria remains a problem, of course. Stepan had no children, nor are there any other close relatives still alive. I need a good commander in charge to hold the border against Strathclyde.'

'There are many new settlers there who Ecgfrith brought in after he drove out most of the Britons. They are not all Angles, of course, but there may be some amongst the Saxons or even the Frisians or Jutes who would make good leaders. I do know that Stepan was not fond of them and wouldn't have them in his warband. Therefore they didn't die with him.'

'Thank you. That's helpful. Perhaps after Lothian we should go onto Cumbria.'

Osfrid's heart sank further when he heard the 'we'. Evidently he was going to be away from Bebbanburg for some time. With winter only a few months away he hoped that he would be able to return before travel became impossible.

~~~

In the event Osfrid was away even longer than he'd feared. Having sorted out the situation in Lothian and Cumbria, Aldfrith decided that he needed to secure his northern border. He had sailed back to Iona and asked Abbot Adamnan to accompany him to see the kings of Dalriada and Strathclyde.

It was early December before they braved the winter storms to sail between the Isles of Luing and Shuna into Loch Melfort. The sea had been choppy but, apart from the odd brief squall, the weather had been kind to them. Grey clouds scudded overhead as the rowers bent their backs to propel the birlinn that the King of Islay – one of the sub-kings of Dalriada - had loaned them up the loch. Half an hour later the helmsman brought the ship skilfully alongside the jetty with a gentle bump. Boys waiting on the shore caught the ropes thrown to them and they tied them off securely to posts on the jetty.

As Osfrid followed Aldfrith and Adamnan ashore he looked up at Dùn Add, the fortress of King of Dalriada. It looked impregnable and he recalled his father telling him how Oswiu had captured it through trickery to put the present king, Mael Duin, on the throne.

Mael himself came down to meet the visitors accompanied by a score of warriors. Evidently he wasn't taking any chances.

'Abbot, King Aldfrith, what brings you to Dalriada?'

His tone wasn't hostile but neither was it overly friendly.

'Can we go up to your hall, Mael, and I'll explain,' Aldfrith replied with a smile.

The King of Dalriada shrugged and proceeded to lead the way through the settlement clustered around the hill on which the fortress sat. The day had started out grey but dry, now the clouds turned darker and a mixture of rain and sleet stung their faces, blown in on an easterly wind.

As they ascended the path to the gates Osfrid turned and saw the rowers backing water as they took the borrowed birlinn away from the jetty before heading back down the loch and out to sea. Being stranded here in a strange land gave him a distinctly uncomfortable feeling. They were now dependent on Mael Duin's goodwill.

Once in the warmth of the hall they sat around a large rough-hewn table and servants brought ale, bread and cheese for them to eat. Mael waited a while, talking about nothing important, before he suddenly changed the subject.

'Why would you risk venturing into Caledonia where your brother and most of his nobles and warriors perished? Don't you realise that there is nothing Bruide would like more than to kill the last member of the House of Æthelfrith, leaving Northumbria leaderless. If that happened it wouldn't take him long to push his frontier down to the Twaid.'

'Why the Twaid? There are no Picts who live in Lothian,' Aldfrith asked, clearly puzzled by the idea.

'No, but we still call it Goddodin and the Picts are kin to the Britons who live there.'

'Only so far as both were inhabitants of Britain before the Romans came centuries ago.'

'Our language is similar; the main difference is that Caledonia was never conquered by Rome; but that's not important. Bruide will seize on any excuse to expand his kingdom. It isn't in the interest of either Dalriada or Strathclyde for him to become too powerful.'

'You believe that he has an obsessive desire for power for power's sake?' Adamnan asked.

'I do, as does Elfin. We joined him to defeat Ecgfrith when he invaded because we were frightened of your brother, Aldfrith. We see now that it was Bruide we should have feared. Perhaps we picked the wrong side, but it's too late now.'

'He's putting pressure on you?'

'To acknowledge him as our overlord, what you Anglo-Saxons term Bretwalda, yes. Oswiu was our Bretwalda but he was only interested in keeping the north peaceful. Bruide isn't.'

'When I was in Rome I read about a great king a thousand years ago called Alexander,' Aldfrith exclaimed. 'He united lots of small nations in a country called Greece so that they could attack their habitual foe - a mighty empire in the east called Persia. He defeated it and became its monarch but, not satisfied with securing peace for Greece, he carried on conquering kingdom after kingdom. It seems that Bruide suffers from the same compunction to subjugate others just for his own satisfaction.'

'Yes, I think you're right,' Adamnan agreed. 'I too have heard of this Alexander the Great. He also suffered from paranoia, distrusted his own commanders, several of whom he killed. Eventually he died whilst still a young man, poisoned by his own men according to some accounts.'

'Bruide may not be an Alexander but I think you are right to be wary of him,' Aldfrith said. 'Have you talked to Elfin about this?'

Mael nodded. 'We have agreed to come to the defence of the other if Bruide attacks us, or anyone else for that matter.'

'Well, you needn't fear Northumbria in that regard. My only interest is in preserving my present northern border against attack. My kingdom needs time to recover. My aims include making it more prosperous, encouraging scholarship and developing our culture and the arts. I have no desire, or the ability, to be a warrior king.'

'Well then,' Mael said with a smile. 'Let's drink a toast to our alliance and the frustration of Bruide's overweening ambition.'

The next day Aldfrith and Mael swore a binding oath to defend each other in front of Adamnan and, whilst Mael and the abbot went on to persuade Elfin to do the same, Aldfrith and Osfrid returned to Caer Luel in one of Mael's birlinns.

~~~

Cuthbert knew that his time on earth was fast coming to an end. He felt increasingly weary of the world and decided to spend what time he had left in meditation and prayer as an anchorite. He therefore wrote to Aldfrith informing him of his decision and recommending the prior, EadBehrt, who had been elected by the monks, as his replacement.

Aldfrith was at Loidis trying to decide on who should be ealdormen and thegns in Elmet when the letter arrived. He was tempted to drop what he was doing and ride north to see Cuthbert. However, upon reflection, he realised that Cuthbert would already have handed over to EadBehrt and taken up residence on whichever island he'd selected as his home for the rest of his life.

It wasn't until Bishop Bosa came to see him that he realised how much he was going to miss Cuthbert. The Bishop of Eoforwīc and the king did not get on. Bosa believed in every line of the Bible whereas Aldfrith enjoyed debating possible interpretations of what was meant in each gospel. He had serious reservations about much of the Old Testament in particular. Bosa was horrified that anyone, even the king, could question anything in Holy Scripture.

Aldfrith had enjoyed theological discussions with Adamnan and, in the brief time he'd known him, with Cuthbert. Such intellectual exercises were now denied him and he missed them. He was therefore delighted when Bishop Wilfrid arrived during the summer. Here was a scholar who was highly regarded throughout the Roman Church and Aldfrith took a malicious pleasure in seeing how discomfited Bosa was by his nemesis' return.

Bosa handled the situation badly. He demanded that Wilfrid be banished again, as he had been by Ecgfrith.

'Are you telling me what to do, Bosa?' the king asked, his eyes narrowing dangerously.

'No, of course not Cyning. But Bishop Wilfrid was banished on pain of imprisonment and, as far as I'm aware, his banishment is still in force.'

'Is it? And who can lift the ban?'

'Only the king...' His voice trailed away.

'Precisely. The king. So all I have to do is lift the order is it not?'

'Yes, Cyning,' Bosa said dejectedly.

'Consider it lifted. Will you please inform Bishop Wilfrid accordingly?'

'Me, Cyning?'

'Yes, are you incapable of carrying a message for your king?'

'No, of course not. I'll let him know,' he replied stiffly.

'Thank you for lifting my banishment, Cyning,' Wilfrid said when they were alone together a few weeks later. 'The conversion of the South Saxons to Christianity was rewarding, of course, but I missed the land in which I was born.'

Wilfrid had the sense to get to know Aldfrith better before he raised the first of the matters which he wanted resolved.

'Cyning, you know that I used to be Bishop of Northumbria?'

'Northumbria? I thought your diocese used to be Eoforwīc. There are two other bishops in Northumbria are there not? John of Beverley at Hexham and EadBehrt at Lindisfarne.'

'Yes, Cyning. But the Pope gave me the authority to approve or reject their appointments and I believe it would be more satisfactory to combine them into one diocese again.'

'With yourself as bishop?'

Wilfrid nodded.

'Yes, the Pope himself appointed me.'

257

'But to the see of Eoforwīc, not Northumbria, I think?'

'That's true,' Wilfrid confessed. 'But that was because he didn't wish to oppose Archbishop Theodore's misinformed policy of dividing my diocese into three. By giving me control over their appointment he effectively made them subservient to me.'

'Subservient? I think not. I suspect the desire of the synod who advised the then pope was to avoid disunity amongst the bishops of Northumbria as it was one kingdom.'

'Are you then opposed to my re-instatement? Surely you wouldn't wish to go against a papal edict?'

'The Pope who made that decision is now dead. John the Fifth is now the Pope. In any case the decision is mine. The Pope is our guide in spiritual matters but he shouldn't interfere in matters outside that.'

Wilfrid had heard this before from Ecgfrith and he was too astute to pursue an argument he evidently wasn't going to win.

'Very well, Cyning. I'll leave you to ponder all that I have said and I look forward to hearing your decision.'

Aldfrith had enjoyed debating with Wilfrid and he respected his reputation as a scholar. He was so unlike the rigid Bosa and he found himself tempted to replace him with Wilfrid.

A week later Aldfrith had another argument with Bosa, this time over the introduction of a much more formal liturgy to replace the more impromptu form of service that Aldfrith was used to. That decided him and he sent for both Wilfrid and Bosa.

'Bishop Wilfrid I have listened to your argument that the Pope appointed you to the see of Eoforwīc and I think that my brother was wrong to ignore that. I have therefore decided that you should be restored in accordance with the Pope's decree. Bosa I am sorry that this means that there is no diocese for you in Northumbria. It is not your fault that King Ecgfrith went against the Pope's wishes and installed you as bishop. You are not being banished but you must find somewhere else where your ministry is needed.'

Bosa was seemingly struck dumb by the king's announcement; not so Wilfrid who smiled triumphantly at his unfortunate fellow bishop.

'Thank you Cyning. I will serve you and God to the best of my ability. May I ask if my other appointments – that is as Abbot of Ripon and Hexham are also to be restored to me?'

Aldfrith was completely taken aback by this. He had expected Wilfrid to be grateful. He hadn't anticipated that he would be so acquisitive and opportunistic as to ask for his former monasteries as well.

'You may ask, though this is hardly the time nor the place to do so. The answer is no. Be satisfied with what you have been granted, bishop.'

Wilfrid's discomfiture at such a public rebuke brought Bosa a little comfort, but he left the king's presence without saying a word and set off within the hour to return to Whitby, where he had been a monk before being consecrated as a bishop.

~~~

The twentieth of March 687 was cold but fine. There was a slight swell but the sunlight glistened on the sea making it look as if it was blue dappled with blobs of shimmering white as a man and a boy, both wearing monks' habits, pushed a small

259

boat off the beach below the monastery of Lindisfarne and climbed aboard.

Alaric was accompanied by one of his novices, a thirteen year old called Edward who was the senior amongst the current crop of his students. In May he'd be fourteen and would return to Alnwic to start training as a warrior. The small fishing boat was loaded with food and water for the week for Cuthbert. Whilst Alaric rowed Edward steered. They smiled at each other, enjoying the break in routine. Alaric was fond of Edward and would miss him when he was gone.

Edward called out to Cuthbert as they neared the small islet but the anchorite didn't answer his hail. They brought the small craft alongside the jutting shelf of rock that served as a landing stage and Alaric jumped ashore whilst Edward tied the small boat to a rock. The novice then started to unload the supplies.

He looked in through the tiny doorway into the beehive shaped hut built of loose stone but the interior was so dark compared to the bright day outside that at first he couldn't see anything. As his eyes adjusted to the gloom he could just make out Cuthbert kneeling in prayer and so he waited for him to finish. When Edward joined him the monk still hadn't moved so Alaric went inside the hut and tapped the anchorite gently on the shoulder.

There was no response and, when Alaric touched his cheek to confirm his suspicions, he found his flesh was deathly cold. He stumbled outside, pushing Edward away so that he couldn't go inside, and sobbed with grief. Like all the monks of Lindisfarne, he'd revered Cuthbert as a Holy man and a prophet. His death came as a great shock and for some time he was paralysed by his misery. Edward guessed what had happened and came to put a comforting hand on his master's shoulder whilst they both wept. Eventually Alaric pulled himself together and, telling Edward to get in and untie the boat, he took the tiller whilst the boy rowed them back to the monastery. Leaving the novice to secure the boat on the beach and unload it again, he went to inform EadBehrt.

Cuthbert had left instructions that he was to be buried on the islet where he died. However that was impractical. It was bare rock. He was therefore taken back to the monastery and a grave was dug in the floor of the church beside the altar, near that of Saint Aidan, the first Bishop and Abbot of Lindisfarne. He was regarded as a saint whilst he was still alive and as soon as he died they started to call him Saint Cuthbert long before the Pope officially canonised him.

Cuthbert had been dead for a little while before Alaric had found him and rigor mortis had set in. They had therefore been forced to break his knee and hip joints to get him in his coffin but EadBehrt had sworn those involved to secrecy. If people knew that his body had been abused in that way it would have detracted from the awe in which the dead Cuthbert was held. EadBehrt was no fool. He realised the potential of a shrine where two renowned saints were buried. It would make Lindisfarne as famous as Iona and, as a pilgrimage destination, the monastery would become wealthy.

The shock of finding Cuthbert's body had a profound effect on Alaric. He gave up his role as Master of the Novices and became an anchorite himself, but living on a different islet to the one that Saint Cuthbert had inhabited. There he could suffer the repeated nightmares engendered by his discovery of Cuthbert's corpse without disturbing his fellow monks.

Chapter Fourteen – Wilfrid's Rise and Fall

688 to 691 AD

Theodore of Tarsus was making a tour of all the dioceses in England. He was now eighty six and found travelling distressingly tedious. He had resorted to a carriage but, despite the padded seats, the rigid axles made it just as uncomfortable as a farmer's cart. By the time he reached Eoforwīc he was exhausted and suffering from considerable pain in his arthritic joints. He was therefore not in the best of moods.

When he entered the king's hall he discovered that Adamnan, the de factor head of the Celtic Church, was also paying a visit to Eoforwīc and his moroseness changed to anger.

'What is the Abbot of Iona doing here, Cyning? I was under the impression that you, like your father and brother, had embraced Rome and put the foolishness of the Celtic Church behind you.'

'Perhaps you would like to go and take your rest after your long and arduous journey, archbishop? When you return you may be in a better mood and be prepared to conduct yourself in a more courteous manner.'

Aldfrith's voice was icily polite but he might just as well have told the archbishop to get out and come back when he'd recovered his manners.

In fact Adamnan was there as the emissary of Fínsnechta, the High King of Hibernia, as Aldfrith explained to Theodore when he joined them for the evening meal.

'You jumped to the wrong conclusion earlier, Theodore. Adamnan isn't here as Abbot of Iona but to negotiate the return of the church property that was looted and the captives that were taken during Stepan of Cumbria's raid four years ago.'

'Oh, I see. I owe both of you an apology in that case.'

'It's already forgotten,' Adamnan told him, smiling. However, Aldfrith said nothing.

'Are you visiting every diocese, Theodore, or is there a special reason for coming to Northumbria?' Wilfrid asked.

His tone was friendly but the archbishop sensed a wariness behind the question.

'No, I'm making one last visit to all my bishops before I get too old to do so. However, I've come to the conclusion that I may already have left it too late. My body isn't coping very well with being jostled and bumped around for hours at a time. But I do want to meet your new bishop, EadBehrt.'

He noticed Adamnan glance at Aldfrith when he said that and Wilfrid frowned.

'Is there something I should know about him?'

'He was the monks' universal choice,' Aldfrith replied, 'and I knew him well years ago when we were on Iona together. He is a devout man and he'll make a good abbot.'

'On Iona? Is he a member of the Celtic Church then?'

'He accepts the doctrine of Rome,' Wilfrid said smoothly, 'well most of it at any rate.'

Aldfrith shifted uneasily in his ornately carved chair.

'What Bishop Wilfrid means to say is that he is a devoted servant of God who is an aesthete, as Cuthbert was. He has little time for the trappings of wealth and the ostentation that some of our colleagues seem to be so fond of,' Aldfrith said, trying not to glance at the richly decorated robe that Wilfrid was wearing.

This was in stark contrast to the plain coarse woollen habit worn by Adamnan. The only thing which distinguished him from the humblest of his monks was the silver cross which hung from a leather thong around his neck. A monk would have worn a plain wooden one. Although Wilfrid and the king got on well together most of the time, Aldfrith deplored the bishop's love of rich clothes, fine jewellery and what he regarded as an extravagant life style.

Theodore was also dressed in a fine woollen robe but it lacked the silver wire embroidery of Wilfrid's and the archbishop only wore one jewelled ring, not several on each hand like Wilfrid. Although Aldfrith's tunic and trousers were made of finely woven wool, they were unembellished and the only jewellery he wore was the signet ring that he used to seal documents.

'So will you be going on to Lindisfarne tomorrow, archbishop?' Wilfrid asked to break the uncomfortable silence.

'No, I need time to recover. I was hoping that Bishop EadBehrt could come here.'

'I'm not sure that he would be willing to stray into the diocese of another bishop,' Wilfrid said in a tone which indicated his displeasure at the idea.

'He will if I command it,' Theodore said, losing patience. 'I'm too old to travel so far north. Cyning, would you mind sending him a letter from me?'

'No, of course not, Theodore. It would be my pleasure.'

'Thank you. Then we can enjoy each other's company for a few days until he arrives.'

'Sadly I fear not. I am expected at Whitby for a service in remembrance of my father who, as you know, is buried there. I have invited Adamnan to accompany me as he would like to see their magnificent church. I would also like to meet my half-sister, Ælfflæd, who is now the abbess there. However, Bishop Wilfrid will stay to entertain you until my return.'

'He won't be accompanying you?'

'No, he and the former abbess, Hild, disliked each other and I understand that my sister is cast very much in the same mould as she was.'

Wilfrid and Theodore stood on the steps of the king's hall in the rain as it swept across the compound in gusts. They waited until the king and his party rode out of the gates before rushing back inside to dry off in front of the central hearth.

'Well, I for one am glad to forego the pleasure of see this magnificent new church at Whitby. Have you seen it?' the archbishop asked Wilfrid.

Before he could reply Theodore added, 'of course you have, at the Synod in 664.'

'Yes, but it was only partially completed then,' Wilfrid replied. 'The chancel had been roofed and that's where we met. The foundations for the north and south transept were in place and the walls of the nave had been built but were open to the sky. Work had yet to start on the west front or the central tower so it's difficult for me to envisage what it looks like now.'

'Isn't it a little odd that you haven't visited one of the most important monasteries in your diocese in the past twenty years?'

'You forget that I spent a fair number of those years in exile and was even imprisoned at one stage,' he replied somewhat tersely.

'No, I haven't forgotten. You are evidently in dispute with the abbess and, from what I hear, your fellow bishops in the north as well.'

'They sided with Bosa so it's hardly surprising that I don't have their support.'

'Perhaps, but schisms in the Church in England, of which I am the head, are anathema to me. I would like to see you reconciled with your fellow bishops and abbots.'

'I fear that is hardly likely to happen. I may be abbot of the monastery here at Eoforwīc but Aldfrith has denied me Hexham and Ripon, which the Pope granted me.'

'The trouble with the papacy is that we keep electing men who die within months of their appointment. So far this century there have been eighteen. One pope countermands the decisions of his predecessor and consequently no one pays much regard to papal edicts anymore.'

'Eighteen? I thought that there had been sixteen?'

'Pope John died a year ago. Presumably the news hasn't reached you here yet? Unfortunately his successor only lasted a few months. Now a Greek called Sergius has been elected.

He's in his mid-thirties and hopefully his reign will last for decades.

'However, his accession hasn't been without its problems. Two other contenders for the papacy conspired against him and the Byzantine emperor tried to imprison him.

'All that is in the past now, but it does serve to illustrate that the power of the Pope is a transient thing. I don't think you can rely on it to achieve your objects.'

'You mean that the Pope's grant of Hexham and Ripon monasteries to me is worthless?'

'I fear so.'

Wilfrid looked glum for a moment before speaking again.

'In that case I shall just have to persuade Aldfrith to grant them to me.'

~~~

Aldfrith and the half-sister he'd never met, Ælfflaed, had got on well from the start. Both were scholars and liked debating the finer points of theology, and they and Adamnan did so far into the night.

He was impressed by the church; only that at Ripon came close to it for size. That on Lindisfarne could have fitted into the nave at Whitby with room to spare, whereas most other monasteries were constructed completely of timber.

One thing put a slight damper on his good mood though. He had forgotten that Bosa was now the prior at Whitby and meeting him again was a trifle awkward, though Bosa hid any resentment he might have felt. It was the only matter that he and his sister disagreed about during his stay. She maintained that not only was his treatment of Bosa shabby but she also questioned Wilfrid's fitness to be Bishop of Eoforwīc. Although Aldfrith defended his decision to replace Bosa, he was beginning to wonder whether he'd made the right choice after all.

Ælfflaed had the sense not to pursue the matter once she had made her feelings clear and left the king to ponder the situation. Bosa went out of his way to be pleasant to him, which added to his doubts over his wisdom in dismissing him.

Adamnan had been particularly captivated by the splendour of the magnificent church with its windows of stained glass. He had never seen a building so fine. However, he was even more enthralled by the library at Whitby. He had brought a book about the Holy Land as a present for Aldfrith from the library on Iona and he was proud of the collection of books and scrolls that he and his predecessors had amassed there. However it paled into insignificance compared to that of Whitby.

When the king and his friend left Whitby they travelled north to visit the monastery at Jarrow on the River Tyne. This was an unusual establishment in that it consisted of two separate monasteries, one on the north bank of the River Tyne and one on the south bank. Adamnan had particularly asked to go there in order to meet the monk in charge of the scriptorium.

At seventeen Bede was young to be given such responsibility but, as Adamnan soon realised, he was clever, knowledgeable and passionately interested in history. He had just started to write a history which he proposed to call *historia ecclesiastica gentis Anglorum* - the History of the English Church and People. Adamnan had been fascinated by the project when he'd been told about it and he spent several days helping Bede to carry out some of his research whilst, at the same time, consulting books and scrolls not available to him on Iona about matters he was interested in.

Aldfrith was not keen on spending any longer than necessary at Jarrow. He hadn't forgotten Benoc and his insults during the meeting of the Witan when he was elected king. He had no desire to see the old man again and he was on the point of returning to Eoforwīc, leaving Adamnan to follow on when he was ready, when a messenger arrived.

The news he brought was ominous. Bruide had married at long last and his bride was the daughter of Elfin of Strathclyde. Not only that, Mael Duin of Dalriada had just died and his successor was a cousin of Bruide's. It looked as if the King of the Picts was about to unite all of Caledonia under his leadership.

~~~

Osfrid was celebrating the birth of his second son, Swefred, when a message arrived to warn him that the king was on his way north. The last few years had been good for Osfrid and Godwyna. Aldfrith's peaceful reign had brought prosperity in its wake. The vill below Bebbanburg had expanded with several more craftsmen establishing workshops there. Not only did this benefit Osfrid directly through the licences they were obliged to purchase from him, but the gold, silver, leather and iron goods that they produced were carried on his knarrs to markets in Frankia, Fresia and the Anglo-Saxon homelands of

Saxony, Anglia and Jutland. Naturally he charged for their transportation and also took a cut of the profits they made.

Eadwulf was now four and his daughter, Guthild, two. His son's jealously of Guthild hadn't lessened and he refused to have anything to do with her. When Swefred was born Eadwulf had thrown a tantrum and Osfrid had lost his temper with him, smacking him hard to stop the boy screaming and pounding his little fists on the floor. He'd been shocked at the smack; his father had never hit him before and he retreated into a sulk which he kept up for three days before finally going to see his parents and apologising.

Osfrid smiled and gave the boy a hug to show he was forgiven but Godwyna saw the expression in Eadwulf's face as he returned his father's embrace. It disturbed her. Instead of the pleasure at being forgiven that she had expected to see, his face was contorted into a grimace that conveyed both hatred and vindictiveness. She knew then that she had to keep Eadwulf from being alone with the baby.

What neither parent knew was that Benoc had told his grandson about his lineage when they had last visited Jarrow. Eadwulf had been too young to fully understand all that Benoc had said, but he's grasped the fact that he was descended from the kings of Bernicia and that he had more right to the throne than the bastard Aldfrith had.

This was why he hated Swefred, not so much because his parents' affection was now divided amongst three children, though that was also true, but because his brother would grow up to be his rival for the throne. He might have only a hazy idea what being king meant at four, but he knew that he was important and powerful and that appealed to him.

271

Osfrid and Godwyna had no idea about the poison that her father had dripped into Eadwulf's ear; poison that would fester and grow with the passing years and inevitably lead to tragedy.

'I've just come from Jarrow and I'm on my way to see Behrt,' Aldfrith told Osfrid as they sat alone in front of the central hearth in the hall at Bebbanburg, enjoying a goblet of mead together after everyone else had retired for the night.

The old hall was mean and primitive compared to others Osfrid had seen. It had been built nearly two hundred years ago and had been patched and repaired ever since. Now the roof leaked in places during heavy rain and it stank of smoke and the faeces and urine that had soaked into the rush covered earthen floor over the years. Even Aldfrith, who was no lover of luxury having endured primitive living conditions on Iona and elsewhere for most of his life, had wrinkled his nose in distaste when he'd entered.

Godwyna had been nagging Osfrid to have a new hall built for ages and now, having seen the king's reaction to his home, he determined to do something about it. His thoughts were dragged back to the present at the king's next statement.

'I'm worried that Bruide is becoming too powerful and may try and extend his territory southwards, either into Lothian or into Cumbria.'

'Is there any evidence of this, Cyning?'

'No hard evidence, no. But Elfin is growing feebler and his son, Beli, is the real power in Strathclyde now. He was friends with Bruide before but, now that his sister is the Pictish queen, the two are even closer. In the past Rheged used to stretch into Galloway on the far side of the Solway Firth before

Strathclyde seized the area. Now I hear rumours that Beli is using the expulsion of the Britons from Rheged to incite his own people, who are also Britons, to exact revenge by invading Cumbria. I have no doubt that Bruide is egging him on.'

Aldfrith stopped speaking and gazed into the dying embers of the fire. Osfrid said nothing, sensing that the king hadn't finished.

'My real fear is that they will launch a concerted attack and that Bruide will invade Lothian at the same time. I'm confident that we could defeat either an attack on Lothian or on Cumbria, but not on both simultaneously.'

'How can I help, Cyning?'

'I want you to go and see your brother-in-law, Alweo of Man. Get him to promise to launch raids on the coast of Strathclyde if Beli invades Cumbria. That should force him to abandon his invasion and return to defend his homeland.'

'I see. And Behrt?'

'I want him to intensify his preparations to defend Lothian. If Bruide sees that we are ready to give him a bloody nose if he crosses into the land south of the Firth of Forth he might think twice about it.'

'Very well, I'll get ready to leave as soon as possible.'

'Thank you. It would be quickest if you travelled west to Caer Luel where I've arranged for a birlinn to take you across to Duboglassio on Man.'

~~~

Because this was going to be a peaceful mission, Osfrid decided to take Eadwulf with him. Godwyna had been against the idea, saying that her son was too young at not quite five to undertake such a long journey but Osfrid convinced her that it would be a good opportunity for him to strengthen the bonds with his eldest child. He placated her by agreeing that it was time to build a new hall and he left her to start drawing up the plans; a proposal she embraced with considerable enthusiasm.

The journey to Caer Luel was uneventful. Osfrid had decided to take ten of his gesith with him as escort and a few servants leading packhorses to travel as swiftly as possible. Eadwulf had started out riding his small pony but, despite his excitement – or possibly because of it - he got tired quite quickly and Osfrid lifted him up to sit in front of him on his own horse whilst Drefan rode forward to grab the reins of the pony. The boy dropped off to sleep after a while cradled in his father's arms and Osfrid felt supremely contented by the close contact with his son's small body.

By the time they arrived at Caer Luel Eadwulf had completely forgotten his animosity towards Osfrid and the two were as close as any father and son, and a lot closer than most. The birlinn was waiting, as promised, and they set sail early the next morning.

The sea was a dull grey, reflecting the brooding clouds above, and the waves had the kind of swell associated with the aftermath of a storm. The north-westerly wind had died down though and the birlinn carved its way forward under sail alone. The experience was exhilarating, especially for Eadwulf, as they slowly climbed up to the crest of one forty foot high wave, and then slid with increasing speed down the other side into the trough.

Eadwulf squealed with pleasure every time it happened and, although the ship's boys laughed at him, they enjoyed the experience just as much as he did, all except one.

The boy sent up the mast as lookout wasn't enjoying the ride nearly as much. His perch whipped about with the motion of the ship and he clung on for dear life every time the birlinn crashed down into the bottom of a trough. He had never been seasick in his life but the violent motion of the slender top of the mast was making him distinctly queasy.

He was so absorbed in his own misery that he was late in spotting another sail. It appeared only when both ships were on top of a wave and disappeared when one or other were in a trough. It was therefore difficult to make out what she was at first, especially as she was heading in the opposite direction under oar power so he couldn't see the device on her sail.

'Ship in sight,' he yelled down when she appeared on the crest of a wave for the second time and he was certain that his eyes weren't playing tricks.

'Where away?' Osfrid called back.

'To the west, about a mile from us and heading north east.'

Osfrid was about to ask why the lookout hadn't seen the other craft earlier but that could wait.

'What sort of ship is she? Birlinn or knarr?'

'Birlinn; a big one, perhaps eighteen oars a side.'

That would mean a crew of perhaps fifty. Osfrid's ship had twelve oars a side and, even with his gesith, a crew of only thirty six, excluding the four ships boys.

'She's changing course,' the lookout called down.

'What to?'

'I can't tell yet, she's disappeared again; ah, there she is. She's heading to intercept us and she's raising her sail.'

Osfrid thought rapidly. The other birlinn would be heavier but she had a bigger sail and a longer waterline so she'd be faster if she had a clean bottom. They were a mile away and the Cumbrian coast was at least twenty miles to the east of them. They would never make it before they were overhauled. On the other hand Rumsaa, the nearest port on Man, was slightly nearer at about fifteen miles. Not that it made much difference; the other ship would intercept them long before they could get there.

~~~

Godwyna would have built their new hall of stone if she had her way but Osfrid had been opposed to the idea.

'The few stone built churches I've been in are cold, even on hot days. The stone walls seem to suck the heat out of you,' he'd told her. 'No, stick to timber, but you can make the foundations and sub-wall out of stone if you wish. It'll keep the bottom of the timber planks from rotting, as they do if they're in contact with the earth.'

She remembered seeing the ruins of a Roman villa when she was a child and the foundations, which were all that was left, had stayed in her mind. The stubby brick pillars that were laid out in a grid pattern were, her father had told her, to support the stone floor. What he didn't know was that the purpose of the hypocaust, as it was known, was to enable hot air to circulate under the floor, keeping the villa warm in winter.

However, she had liked the idea of a suspended floor to keep the damp from rising into your feet and she was determined to do something similar in her new hall. She had discussed the idea with Morcar, the reeve, but at first they came up against an obstacle. Brick making was unknown in Anglo-Saxon England. Instead they would have to use stone but those used for the top level would have to be cut so that every small pillar was level and at the same height. As there were no masons nearer than Jarrow, where the Abbot of St. Paul's Monastery on the south bank was replacing the timber monastery church with a small stone one, she decided that she would have to go there. It would also give her the opportunity to visit her father.

Leaving Swefred and Guthild in the charge of the baby's wet nurse, she set off on a miserably wet day in June 689 with those members of her husband's gesith who hadn't accompanied him. She stayed with Conomultus on the first night and he, horrified at the thought of her travelling with just a maid and a dozen warriors, decided to accompany her the rest of the way.

She was looking forward to seeing her father again. She realised that, at his age, this might be her last opportunity to do so. Little did she realise how right she was. When she arrived at Jarrow she found her father ill in bed.

'I fear it's not good news,' Conomultus told her after he'd examined him. 'He's contracted the plague.'

It transpired that he wasn't alone, it ripped through the population of Jarrow and the two monasteries with more than half the inhabitants falling victim to it. Godwyna abandoned all idea of recruiting a mason and devoted herself to nursing her father. Conomultus joined the monks and nuns from the monastery in treating the sick and at first it seemed that he was lucky, but then he became feverish and complained of a severe headache and feeling weak. The next day he was shivering and took to his bed. Then swollen, painful black pustules appeared in his armpits and groin.

The next day Benoc died in agony. Godwyna sobbed at his bedside until they came to take his body away. The monks were going to cast his body into the common grave with the rest of the victims before covering his body in quicklime, but she stopped them and ordered them to dig a grave in the family plot. They did as she asked but Benoc was buried there like the rest, in a winding sheet and covered in quicklime, rather than in a coffin.

It would have been easy for her to allow herself to sink in misery but Godwyna was made of sterner stuff and, as soon as she heard about Conomultus, she went to nurse her husband's uncle. He'd been taken to the infirmary in the Monastery of St. Peter on the north bank of the Tyne near a vill called Wearmouth. It was a little older than its twin monastery dedicated to St. Paul on the south bank near Jarrow, though both had only been established fairly recently.

Conomultus was now fifty nine and she never thought that he'd survive. Over the past decade he'd lost weight and appeared frail but, despite his bouts of vomiting which weakened him further, there was a wiry strength to him. Her intention was to make his passing as comfortable as possible and she kept putting a sponge soaked in mead to his lips in the hope that the alcohol would deaden the pain. However, to her amazement, the pustules didn't burst – the usual sign of imminent death – and on the fourth day they started to go down.

His slow recovery coincided with a waning in the number of new cases and by early September two weeks had passed without any further victims. By then Conomultus was well enough to travel and he escorted Godwyna as far as Alnwic. She had wanted to stay at Jarrow to find out what would happen to the shire following her father's death but felt that she had to return to Bebbanburg once she had managed to recruit a mason.

Like the rest of the population, the workmen constructing the refectory at Jarrow had lost several of their number to the plague and the master mason was extremely unwilling to lose one more of his men. However, he had an apprentice who was always arguing with him and he eventually decided that he would be better off without him.

His name was Thierry and he was eighteen. On the way back she learned that he'd been apprenticed to his uncle since the age of twelve. He should have completed his indenture a year ago but his uncle was unwilling to register him as a mason because he would then have to pay him more.

'He died of the plague so officially I'm still an apprentice, but I know more about building in stone than that oaf of a master mason,' he told Godwyna as they rode north.

He'd shown her some of his carving and a few designs he'd been working on privately and she was impressed. She had raised Osfrid's comments about stone buildings being cold but he explained that stone walls took time to warm up, but once they did they retained the heat, unlike timber walls. She decided to ignore her husband's instructions and build the hall in stone after all.

She had heard nothing about Osfrid's mission to Alweo of Man whilst she was away but expected that there would be news of him and their son when she reached home. They had been gone for nearly four months now but Morcar shook his head when she had asked him and she began to worry.

~~~

Osfrid woke to another miserably wet day in the hut he shared with Eadwulf, Uurad, Sigmund and Drefan. He poked his head out of the door and contemplated the lush green countryside surrounding the hill fort of Béal Feirste, meaning river mouth of the sandbanks. It was where he and his crew had been taken after they had surrendered to the Hibernian birlinn.

Once he could distinguish the sail he had realised that the warship belonged to the Ulaidh, one of the two major nations that inhabited Ulster. The Ulaidh were the enemies of the Uí Néill, the other nation who fought for supremacy in Ulster. As he had fought the Uí Néill in the past he calculated that the Ulaidh would be friendly and he told his helmsman to heave to and wait for the other birlinn to come within hailing distance.

'Who are you and why is a Northumbrian warship sailing in these waters?'

'I'm Osfrid, Ealdorman of Bebbanburg. I'm on my way to see my sister's husband Alweo of Man.'

'Alweo is no friend of ours.'

'Why? His men helped me to defeat Fínsnechta of the Uí Néill five years ago.'

'His men raided Béal Feirste a year ago whilst we were away fighting the wretched Uí Néill and enslaved many of our women and children.'

'I'm sorry to hear that but that was nothing to do with me. Who am I speaking to?'

'Bécc Bairrche mac Blathmaic.'

'I've heard of you. You are married to the daughter of Lethlobar mac Echach, a good friend of my father's.'

'I too know of you and your reputation. You are welcome to come with us to Béal Feirste where we will show you what Ulaidh hospitality is like.'

'Thank you but, I need to continue on my way to Man.'

'I told you, Man is our enemy. I insist you accompany us back to Ulster.'

Three months later Osfrid and his men were still there. He had asked, even begged, to be allowed to leave many times but his request had always been politely declined by Bécc. He was beginning to give up hope of ever escaping when he heard that Lethlobar was on his way to visit the hill fort. His one chance of leaving lay with him.

'Why are you here?' Lethlobar asked him as they sat eating side by side in Bécc's hall the following evening.

'I was on my way to see Alweo and his wife, my sister Hereswith, when Bécc intercepted my birlinn. He insisted that we accompany him back to Béal Feirste and we've been here all summer.'

Lethlobar looked past his daughter, who was sitting on his other side, to check that Bécc wasn't listening but he was laughing uproariously at some joke that the man beside him had told.

'We may have a gripe with Alweo but your father was ever my friend and we owe you a debt of gratitude for weakening the Uí Néill so much that they haven't troubled us for years now.'

'Can you help us?'

'It's difficult. Bécc is the local king and I'm merely his wife's father. I have my own people, of course, but I have to tread a wary path. My father may have been King of the Ulaidh but I am not powerful enough to seize the throne – and I'm getting old. Bécc is likely to be the next King of the Ulaidh and I can't afford to cross him.'

'Is there no hope then?'

'Leave it with me. He's in love with my daughter. Perhaps she can persuade him. I suspect that you'll have to promise not to go near Man though.'

'Very probably the reason for my visit there has come to an end by now in any case.'

'Very well. We'll speak again tomorrow. Now tell me of my brother, Ruaidhrí. There was a time when I saw him as a rival, but I was never destined to succeed Eochaid.'

'He's dead. You didn't know?'

Lethlobar shook his head. 'No, how? He was young.'

'At the battle of the River Trent. He died in a futile attempt to save Ecgfrith's brother, Ælfwine, when he was ambushed by the Mercians. He has a son though, called Eochaid. My uncle is his guardian.'

'Named after our father. Well, well. One day I'd like to meet him.'

282

~~~

Godwyna had almost given up hope of ever seeing Osfrid and their eldest child again. Aldfrith had warned her that he would have to presume that his ship had sunk and appoint another ealdorman. He had already given Jarrow to someone unrelated to her and, as he'd pointed out to her, he already had one shire – Alnwic – without a proper ealdorman. He couldn't afford to have two like that on the east coast of Bernicia.

Eochaid was now ten and so it would only be another half a dozen years before he could be confirmed as ealdorman. She just prayed that Conomultus would live that long. If he did he'd be sixty five, far older than most of his contemporaries.

Swefred had just started to toddle and had become a great favourite of Theirry and his workmen who were building the new hall. She and the children had moved into a hut in the meantime as the footprint for the new building would be the same as the old. However, Theirry had proposed a radical design whereby he would put a second floor above the hall divided into three separate chambers – one for her and Osfrid, one for the children and their servants, and a guest room.

The structure had just reached the top of the first storey when a lone horseman had been spotted riding as if the devil was on his heels down the last incline before the stronghold. Morcar told one of the sentries to sound the alarm and the garrison came piling out of the warriors' hall and various huts occupied by those who were married, pulling on armour as they ran to their posts.

'It's Drefan,' one of the youngsters with better eyesight than most called out as the galloping figure came closer.

'Drefan!' Godwyna exclaimed, her mind in a turmoil. Now at last she would have tidings of Osfrid and Eadwulf, but she didn't know whether the news would be good or bad.

'There's a party of horsemen just on the skyline,' the same youth called out as a dozen or so riders appeared behind Drefan.

'We're back!' Drefan shouted out as he pulled his lathered horse to a halt in front of Godwyna. 'Did you miss us?' he asked with a huge grin on his face as he jumped down to land in front of her.

She didn't know whether to hug him in relief or hit him, though both would have been beneath her dignity.

'You're all safe?'

'Yes, we're all fine. We had a little sojourn in Ulster; never did reach Man,' he explained. 'But I'm sure Lord Osfrid will want to tell you all about it himself.'

~~~

Aldfrith wasn't at all pleased when he found out that Osfrid's mission to see Alweo had been a failure, but the northern frontier seemed quiet for now so he soon forgot about it. He had other problems to worry him. His elderly nobles kept dying and, as it was only five years since the disaster at Dùn Nectain, most of the younger generation who would take over from them were still too young. Even those who had reached sixteen, and were therefore counted as adults, lacked any experience.

It wasn't his only concern though.

'It's time you married, Cyning,' Wilfrid kept saying. 'You're now fifty seven and, even if you had a son soon, he would need time to grow to maturity before he could succeed you.'

Reminding Aldfrith of his mortality did little to endear Wilfrid to him. He was already trying the king's patience with his continual importunity about Ripon and Hexham. He didn't seem to be able to take no for an answer and one day, when yet again he referred to the Pope's letter reinstating him as abbot of both monasteries, Aldfrith's patience snapped.

'You do nothing but nag me, Wilfrid. You are far too grand for a humble priest; the way you dress and conduct yourself and the wealth you ostentatiously display, anyone would think you were the king, not I.'

'Cyning, have I not served you faithfully?'

'You serve no one but you own grasping self, Wilfrid, and I'm sick of it and sick of you. I thought that you were a scholar, someone on the same intellectual plane as me, but that sole virtue pales into insignificance when compared to your multitude of faults.'

'Aldfrith, I must protest...'

'Protest all you like, just not here. Get out. I've had enough of you to last me the rest of my lifetime, even one as short as mine is likely to be, as you so kindly pointed out. You have a week to put your affairs in order, after that you had better be beyond the borders of Northumbria or you will find yourself in the most unpleasant cell I can find. Now go, go.'

Wilfrid looked as if someone had slapped him in the face with a wet fish, but one look at the king's face convinced him that Aldfrith meant every word. Six days later he entered

Mercia with as much of his wealth as he could carry in two carts, which were all Aldfrith would allow him. A week after that Bosa returned as Bishop of Eoforwīc.

Chapter Fifteen – The Battle for Cumbria

693 – 696

No one in Northumbria was sorry to hear of the death of Bruide in 693 after a short illness. The King of the Picts had been a thorn in the side of Northumbria ever since he was sixteen. His infant son was far too young to be a contender for the vacant throne, which was seized by Taran, the Mormaer of Angus and a distant cousin of Bruide's.   His queen entered a monastery and his son disappeared in mysterious circumstances shortly after Taran's enthronement.

Aldfrith was relieved at the news, though Bosa and Behrt of Lothian both warned him that Taran was likely to be just as much of a problem as Bruide had been. He was glad to see the back of Wilfrid but one thing he'd said kept nagging at him – the need to marry and beget an heir. The problem was that he was now nearly sixty and he would have to find a wife who was much younger if she was to give him children. Not many women would want to marry an old man.

Meanwhile Osfrid was wrestling with problems of his own. He had hoped that his bond with Eadwulf would have improved during the time that they were away in the summer of 689. Initially they had grown closer but the enforced stay in Ulster had put their relationship under strain. The little boy was bored and he blamed his father. Osfrid came to the conclusion that his elder son was not only petulant and self-interested but that he had a cruel and ruthless streak in his nature.

The hill fort at Béal Feirste was full of animals, not only the usual dogs, rats and other vermin, but also sheep, cows and horses. Osfrid heard stories that someone was maltreating the sheep; a few were hamstrung and then one was found with its throat cut. Later on two calves were found which had been stabbed.

Osfrid had no reason to suspect that his son was to blame but one evening when Eadwulf was asleep he examined the small knife he had been given before they left Bebbanburg. It was hardly a formidable weapon, but it had a sharp blade some three inches long. He found that it had been cleaned but not well. There was encrusted blood under the hilt and spots of it on the blade.

He set Drefan to watch his son surreptitiously and two days later, when a dog had been found with a wounded leg, he confirmed what Osfrid had feared. Eadwulf was the culprit.

'But I need to practice if I'm to become a warrior, father,' the small boy had bleated when confronted.

'You will learn to be a warrior when you're much older, and it won't be by attacking defenceless animals. These people depend on their livestock for their living. I shall have to pay them for the damage for which you are responsible. But that is unimportant when compared to the flaws in your character it reveals. You are thoughtless and cruel. Unless you mend your ways you won't succeed me as ealdorman, Swefred will. Do you understand what I'm saying?'

Unfortunately Eadwulf did, but not in the way that his father had intended. It was the wrong threat to make if he wanted the boy to change. Now Eadwulf not only saw his brother as a rival for his parents' affection but also to his right to inherit Bebbanburg and the shire.

As if the boy wasn't resentful enough, Osfrid's next action made his son hate him. He put Eadwulf across his knee in front of Uurad and Drefan, lifted up his tunic and pulled down his trousers before spanking his bare bottom until it glowed a bright pink.

After that the attacks on the animals ceased but the boy refused to speak to Osfrid and kept it up until they returned to Bebbanburg again. After that he would only speak to his mother. He was as obstinate as he was cruel and he could bear a grudge for a long time.

In 693, when Eadwulf was nine Osfrid packed him off to Lindisfarne to be educated. He was young to become a novice but by that time his father couldn't stand the sight of him. Five year old Swefred, on the other hand, was the apple of his eye.

Godwyna didn't share her husband's despair of the boy. She tended to see the good in her children and closed her eyes to their faults. The gulf between her eldest child and her husband upset her and she tried to reconcile them, which made her failure to do so even more frustrating. She and Osfrid still loved each other, but their different attitudes to Eadwulf had definitely weakened their bond.

The week before the Bishop of Lindisfarne had written to Osfrid saying that his Master of Novices, Turstan, was having trouble with Eadwulf. He'd had to discipline the boy recently and he'd taken the punishment, which was cleaning out the stables, badly. At first he'd refused to do it but, when told that the alternative was a beating in front of the other novices, he'd relented. However, he'd started to spread malicious rumours about Turstan and had ended up being beaten anyway.

The bishop went on to say that Eadwulf was having a disruptive effect on his fellow novices and on the whole monastery and, unless his behaviour improved, he would have to ask Osfrid to remove him.

At least the incident had made Godwyna realise that Eadwulf was something of a brat and they ceased to argue about him. Now they only disagreed about what could be done about his behaviour. The invitation to the marriage of Aldfrith and Cuthburh, the twenty five year old sister of the King of Wessex, therefore came as something of a relief. They could at least forget about him for a while and enjoy the royal wedding.

Aldfrith had been invited to Wintan-ceastre, the capital of Wessex, for the ceremony and, rather than travel through Mercia to get there, he decided to go by sea and asked Osfrid to organise the necessary ships. After his last voyage Osfrid decided to take no chances this time and put together a fleet of three large knarrs to carry the king, the nobles and their ladies who would be attending and took all six of his birlinns as escort.

Sea travel was a rare experience for Godwyna and she was looking forward to the adventure as well as spending time with her husband away from Bebbanburg. Not only had they argued about Eadwulf but Osfrid hadn't been best pleased when he found out his instructions about the new hall had been ignored by his wife and she had gone ahead and built a hall of stone anyway. The extra cost had also been something of a bone of contention. She hoped that, once away from the place, all that could be forgotten, at least for a while.

They had invited Conomultus, Godwyna's sister, Edyth and her fourteen year old son, Eochaid, to join them. However, Conomultus had replied that the journey would be too much for him. He was still managing the shire whilst Eochaid underwent his training as a warrior, but these days he often had to hold court from his bed.

Both Guthild, now seven, and five year old Swefred had been allowed to come and the young boy spent most of the time following Eochaid around the ship. It was obvious that the boy hero worshipped his older cousin.

The journey down the east coast and through the sea between England and Frankia was uneventful apart from three days spent stormbound in a harbour on the Kent coast. They did see several other ships, some of them warships, from time to time but they gave such a large fleet a wide birth and they arrived at the port six miles south of Wintan-ceastre safely.

They had to wait for three hours whilst a messenger was sent to Wintan-ceastre but King Ine of Wessex came in person to welcome his sister's future husband. If he was dismayed by the stooped greybeard with wispy hair barely covering his bald head he hid it well. Whether Cuthburh could remain equally stoical when she met her bridegroom for the first time remained to be seen.

On the day of the wedding Ine appeared wearing a long blue robe with embroidered ribbon trim at the neck and end of his three-quarter length sleeves. Under that he wore a scarlet undershirt. A dagger with a gold hilt in a scarlet leather scabbard hung from his gold studded belt.

Aldfrith was positively dowdy by comparison. He looked more like a priest, except he wore no chasuble. He too had chosen a long robe instead of the tunic and trousers worn by Osfrid and most of the younger nobles, but his was light grey. The only ornamentation was the dagger with a ruby inset into the pommel and the small gold crucifix suspended from a gold chain around his neck.

Cuthburh echoed the style of her husband-to-be. Her green mid-calf woollen overdress covered a cream linen under tunic which reached the ground. Even her girdle was plain: a white silken rope. Her thick, long hair, which Aldfrith later discovered was a rich golden colour, was hidden under a plain white linen headrail held in place by a simple silver circlet.

She had met Aldfrith the previous evening so she at least had had a chance to get used to his aged appearance.

'There is only one way that I'm going through with this marriage,' she had told Ine as soon as they were alone later that evening. 'I'll do my duty and give Aldfrith an heir, provided he's capable at his age,' she said with a sniff, 'but I want your promise that you'll support my desire to become a nun when he dies, which he must do soon by the look of him.'

Ine had resisted her repeated entreaties to be allowed to enter a monastery for a decade. As his only sister he was aware of her political value to him and now, with Northumbria as an ally, Ethelred of Mercia would be faced with potential foes on two of his borders; three if you counted his continuing problems with the Welsh to the west.

'One boy isn't enough, three would be better. And don't forget you may well have some daughters.'

'Three!' she said, aghast at the prospect. Quite apart from the sex that would be necessary to conceive, the thought of which made her shudder, there was the pain of childbirth itself.

The prospect of going through it all more than once, and with the elderly Aldfrith at that, filled her with dismay.

'No! I'm sorry but no.'

'I'm your king as well as your brother, you will do this because Wessex needs you to.'

She thought for a long moment.

'Two,' she said eventually. 'I draw the line at two boys. And I'll pray every night that I have no daughters.'

Now she put on a brave face as she walked down through the press of guests to join Aldfrith at the altar rail. He smiled at her gently and she felt some relief at the kindness she saw there. She smiled back, albeit briefly, before turning to face the bishop who was conducting the service.

At last the interminable day drew to a close and the unwilling bride was led upstairs by the ladies of the court to be undressed by them and bathed in rose water oil by her maid ready for her husband.

Aldfrith came in, followed by a rowdy bunch of men, who he ushered back out of the door before slamming it firmly in their faces. Instead of rushing to undress, as she had expected, he came and sat on the bed beside her and gently stroked her hair.

'I too am a virgin,' he admitted. 'We will have to guide each other through this.'

Cuthburh smiled up at him. It seemed that he was as nervous as she was. She was naturally a kind-hearted woman and what he'd said made her take pity on him.

'Get undressed and get in beside me. My mother has told me what to expect so I have some idea what is involved.'

'Then that is more than I have. It's not something a man, especially one as old as I am, can ask another man for guidance about. I recall that when we were young my friends and I used to speculate about lying with a girl, but I don't think any of them knew exactly what to do. In any case, it's so long ago that I have long since forgotten that part of my life.'

She giggled.

'Girls talk about it too, you know. Perhaps we can manage to work out what to do together.'

Afterwards they lay side by side. He had never felt so alive, or so sated. He had shown little interest in sex, even as a young man, so obeying the Lord's strictures about carnal relations outside marriage had been no hardship for him. Only now did he realise what he'd been missing all those years.

His wife, on the other hand, was grateful that she had married a kind, gentle and loving man. It was so different to what her mother had led her to expect. It seemed from what she had been told that her father was something of a brute when it came to fornication. If so, he was the opposite of Aldfrith. His age seemed to matter less now, though she'd been disappointed that he'd had enough after the first time. Having sampled the fulfilment that making love had brought her, she wanted to experience it again, and again. Perhaps they'd make love again in the morning she thought as she drifted off to sleep.

~~~

The tranquil life of the newly married couple continued for another six months after they had returned to Northumbria.

Then, just after Cuthburh had made him even happier by informing him that she was pregnant, came the news that Beli of Strathclyde had invaded Cumbria.

He hadn't thought about it until then, but he recalled that Osfrid had never reached Man to conclude a treaty with Alweo. That afternoon three messengers set out; one to Osfrid with instructions to sail to Man to see his brother in law. Another rode to Berhrt with two letters, one appointing him as the Hereræswa of Northumbria; the second instructed him to take what forces he could raise in a short time and go to the aid of Cumbria. The third went to the Ealdorman of Luncæstershire with orders for him to join Behrt.

This time Osfrid was taking no chances. There were three birlinns currently at Bebbanburg and he took all of them. Once again Eadwulf, now ten, had begged to go with him. In truth he would rather have taken Swefred. His younger son might only be six but he was mature for his age in body as well as in mind. In contrast, Eadwulf had grown less likeable as time went on. He was beginning to wish in earnest that his younger son could inherit Bebbanburg instead of the elder.

Thankfully Godwyna had put her foot down and told Eadwulf that, after what had happened the last time, he would be staying at home. The boy went into another of his lengthy sulks and didn't even come to see his father off.

When they landed after a swift and uneventful passage Osfrid had been greeted by a young man he hardly recognised. Æthelbald was now twenty five and, as Osfrid learned later, the de facto ruler of the island.

He explained that his father was now crippled with pain in his joints and couldn't move without help. Even after this warning Osfrid was dismayed to see the change in Alweo. The King of Man was now fifty five and, although Osfrid was only fourteen years younger, his brother-in-law looked nearer twice his age.

He was pleased to see his sister, Hereswith, again and his other two nephews, Heartbehrt and the thirteen year old Thringfrith. Her daughters had long since married, both to Mercian ealdormen, and left the island. He was a little surprised to see that HeartBehrt was still living in his father's hall. The man was now twenty two and he'd expected him to either be married or serving in Ethelred of Mercia's gesith.

It was Thringfrith who explained the situation. The boy was apparently given to gossip and, sitting next to Osfrid at the evening meal, he chatted away being so indiscreet Osfrid wondered if he had been put up to it for some reason.

'My brother's in disgrace,' he confided in Osfrid.

'Heartbehrt?' the latter asked in surprise.

'No,' the boy looked at him as if he was dense. 'I can't imagine him doing anything to horrify mother. No, Æthelbald; he prefers to plough the whole field, not just one furrow.'

At first Osfrid wasn't sure what his nephew meant, then it dawned on him. Presumably his eldest brother was a womaniser.

'Is that why he hasn't married yet?'

'Yes, unfortunately one of those he seduced was Heartbehrt's betrothed. It was all very exciting at the time. You can gather from that that nothing much ever happens here, apart from the very occasional raid by the Hibernians, that is.'

'When was this?'

'Six months ago. Father wasn't as crippled then and he was still in charge. Heartbehrt was going to become a thegn when he got married as the girl was an heiress, but the scandal put an end to that. She was sent off to the mainland to become a nun and her estate was seized by father. It was shortly after that that he became crippled. It's ironic really; it means that her estate will become Æthelbald's in due course, instead of Heartbehrt's.'

Thringfrith had said all this with just a little too much relish at his brother's misfortune and he gathered that he didn't much care for Heartbehrt.

'What happens to him now? He must be very bitter at the turn of events.'

'Yes, obviously Æthelbald wants him gone. His presence is a constant reminder of his fall from grace and the two didn't get on long before this. I think Æthelbald might be hoping that you'll offer Heartbehrt a place in your gesith.'

'I'm not sure that's a good idea,' Osfrid said quickly, concerned by the prospect of becoming involved in the family squabble. Whatever he might think of Æthelbald's morals, he would be King of Man eventually, and perhaps quite soon. Northumbria needed to keep him as an ally.

'Well, you may find that it's necessary if you want Æthelbald's co-operation in whatever you've come here to discuss.'

Osfrid looked at him is surprise, wondering if the boy was a mind-reader. It seemed that, far from resenting his interference, Æthelbald would welcome it.

Three days later Osfrid left accompanied by a disgruntled Heartbehrt whilst Æthelbald prepared his fleet to raid the coast of Strathclyde. He said farewell to Alweo knowing that he wouldn't see him again. As he kissed his sister on the cheek before he boarded his ship she asked him to take care of Heartbehrt.

'He's the innocent party in all of this,' she murmured. 'It's just his bad luck not be born the eldest.'

It was obvious that Æthelbald was hardly her favourite. She must know too that she would be expected to retreat to a monastery when the time came. At least she would be spared witnessing the new King of Man giving unbridled vent to his lust.

His small fleet left the harbour and turned into the open sea. As the prow of his birlinn rose and fell as it met the short chop of the open sea, Osfrid wondered how Thringfrith would turn out. Despite his addiction to gossip, Osfrid had rather liked him. He prayed that he would grow up to be a man of honour like his father.

~~~

When he returned to Bebbanburg he had planned to ride with his warband to join Berhrt but the news that greeted him changed his plans. The day before he returned a messenger had arrived from Edyth with the sad tidings that Conomultus had died. He was sixty six and had gone peacefully in his sleep. Osfrid was sad but it wasn't unexpected, given his uncle's age. At least Eochaid was now sixteen and had completed his training as a warrior. There was no reason why the king couldn't confirm him as the Ealdorman of Alnwic.

He therefore sent Uurad ahead with the warband to join Behrt whilst he set off for Alnwic on a dismal grey day in early July; a day which matched his mood. He rode beside the ten year old Swefred on his pony on one side and Sigmund, the captain of his gesith, on the other. Godwyna and Guthild travelled in a carriage made from a small cart with a hooped roof, which slowed their progress to a crawl. Osfrid was relieved that Eadwulf was still on Lindisfarne, though he would be returning next month to commence his training as a warrior.

He had only visited his eldest son once during his time at the monastery and he felt guilty about it. The boy had seemed meek and submissive but once Osfrid had seen him dart a look his way when he thought his father wasn't looking. It conveyed resentment and even hatred. Osfrid couldn't understand why he should feel that way; granted they had never been close, but he didn't think he had done anything to cause the boy to be so antagonistic towards him.

Suddenly an idea struck him. He'd send him down to Alnwic to be trained. Perhaps he'd strike up a rapport with Eochaid as they were close in age. When he mentioned the idea to Godwyna she had supported the idea. Perhaps she was dreading the return of the surly Eadwulf as much as he was.

As they neared Alnwic towards evening the clouds broke and blue sky began to appear. The welcome from Edyth and Eochaid was warm but muted, given the circumstances of their visit. The meal that evening was a subdued affair and, out of respect for Conomultus' memory, no one got drunk.

On the next day the sky was cloudless and it grew warm quite quickly. Osfrid had expected Eochaid to invite Bishop

Eadbehrt of Lindisfarne to conduct the ceremony but he was apparently too ill to travel. Instead the local priest presided.

Osfrid was somewhat ashamed that he hadn't known of Eadbehrt's ill health. It had been some time since he had visited Lindisfarne and he resolved to go and visit him on his return. It would be good to see his brother, Alaric as well. He could tell Eadwulf about his military training at the same time. He was ruefully aware that one of the reasons for not visiting the monastery as often as he should have was his unwillingness to confront his son.

After the service Eochaid said a few words in praise of his mentor and guardian and then Osfrid asked to speak.

'My father was a great man; born a Briton in Mercia he rose to be Ealdorman of Bebbanburg, the former stronghold of the kings of Bernicia. His younger brother Conomultus had no less an exalted career in the Church. From a poor monk he became a priest and then chaplain to King Oswiu of blessed memory. As such he was one of the king's closest advisors and much of Oswiu's success was due to my uncle's advice and diplomacy. When his conscience wouldn't allow him to support Oswiu's actions during the invasion of Dalriada, he chose to retreat to Iona and become a simple monk again.

'But it wasn't his destiny to remain in obscurity. He was chosen to be the Bishop of Abernethy and became the spiritual leader of the Picts. No doubt he would have ended his days there if Bruide hadn't expelled him during his ruthless campaign to establish himself as King of the Picts. As it was, he spent his final years administering first Bebbanburg and then Alnwic.

'He was a strong character and both our family, and here I include Edyth and Eochaid, and the kingdom owe him a great deal. He may be in heaven now but let us keep him alive in our hearts.'

As he went to sit down again first Edyth and then Eochaid came up to him and threw their arms around him. Words were unnecessary.

After Conomultus was lowered into the ground in his simple wooden box Osfrid went to speak to Eochaid.

'You know that your cousin Eadwulf and I don't get on. He is due to leave Lindisfarne in a month or so and begin his training as a warrior. Godwyna and I think it best if he doesn't do that at home.'

'And you want me to train him with my young men?' Eochaid cut in as Osfrid plainly struggled to find the right way to phrase his request.

Osfrid smiled in relief.

'Yes.'

'Of course, I'd be pleased to help. However, that's on the understanding that he behaves himself and doesn't cause problems. I hear that his time at Lindisfarne hasn't been exactly trouble free.'

'I'll make it clear to him that, if he doesn't, then I'll disown him and make Swefred my heir.'

'I have a feeling that you'd like to do that anyway.'

'Perhaps, but I can't unless I have a good reason to do so; one that the king will accept.'

'Very well, send Eadwulf to me and we'll see what we can do with him.'

Osfrid was kneeling at Bishop Eadbehrt's bedside with the prior beside him when his brother Alaric came in, ushering Eadwulf into the small hut ahead of him. The bishop was frail and could no longer walk unaided but his mind was as sharp as ever. Osfrid looked up and, as he'd expected, he saw the hostility in the glance his son gave him before he nodded perfunctorily to the bishop and then the prior. Osfrid got to his feet.

'It's good to see you again brother,' he greeted Alaric. 'How are you, Eadwulf?'

'Fine, as if you'd care.'

'Watch your tongue boy; the Bible commands us to honour our father and mother.'

Eadwulf stiffened before looking down at the ground in response to the bishop's reprimand.

'You'll be leaving here in six weeks' time when you turn fourteen, unless of course you wish to remain here as a monk?'

Eadwulf looked at Osfrid as if he was mad.

'Why would I want to become a snivelling monk?'

Alaric cuffed him around the ear.

'Show some respect in the presence of the bishop.'

'I see that you haven't learned humility whilst you've been here. You're still insufferably arrogant,' his father told him, not trying to hide his dislike.

'What good is humility to a warrior? As I'll be the next Ealdorman of Bebbanburg I have every right to be proud.'

'I'm not dead yet, boy.'

Eadwulf looked down at the bedridden bishop before replying.

'You're no longer young either. Many men die in their thirties.'

Osfrid pursed his lips. His son was making no secret of the fact that he was looking forward to his father's demise.

'This squabbling is getting us nowhere. I've decided that you cannot be trained to be a warrior.'

He paused and took pleasure in the look of alarm that crossed his son's face before he continued.

'Not at Bebbanburg, at least. Your cousin Eochaid has kindly offered to take you in. However, he has warned me that if you give him any trouble he'll send you back to me.'

'Thank you, father,' the boy replied with an ironic grin. 'I'll be sure to be on my best behaviour.'

~~~

At long last Osfrid was free to ride to join Behrt outside Caer Luel. The latter had driven the Strathclyde Britons out of most of Cumbria but they continued to hold the town. It was a strongly fortified place; the stone built walls around the old Roman town had fallen into disrepair in places but the Anglo-Saxons, not having the local skills to repair them, had filled the gaps with a tall palisade.

The Britons had been able to capture it with ease. The sentries had grown lax and hadn't spotted the assault ladders that the invaders had placed against the walls until it was too late. Unfortunately the new masters of the place kept a much better watch.

However, the topic of conversation when the senior commanders met in Behrt's tent that evening wasn't about the siege. News had just reached them that the queen had been safely delivered of a baby son who Aldfrith had named Osred. The succession had been a concern for Northumbria's nobles for some time now.

'The question now is will Aldfrith live long enough to allow the boy to grow to manhood?' Behrt said quietly to Osfrid whilst the others were busy getting drunk in honour of the new ætheling.

'He's sixty one; I doubt he will make it until he's into his late seventies,' Osfrid replied gloomily.

'No, I agree. He's already lived longer than his father did. But Osred is the only descendent of the house of Æthelfrith. Better to have him as king, even if he's still a boy, than the alternative.'

'Which is?' Osfrid asked, puzzled.

'For the various descendants of Ida through his other sons to squabble over the throne. Northumbria would descend into chaos and we'd be very vulnerable to attacks from the Picts, the Strathclyde Britons and the Mercians.'

Osfrid sucked his teeth. He knew that Behrt was right but he couldn't see a solution.

'What do you suggest?'

'We need to form a council of regency to rule the kingdom until Osred is old enough to rule unaided.'

'Council of regency? Wouldn't rule by several people with conflicting interests be too unwieldy?'

'No, I'm not talking about some sort of Witan. I'm proposing three regents – a triumvirate if you like.'

'And who would these three be?'

'Myself, Bishop Bosa and yourself perhaps, if you are willing?'

'I don't know, Behrt. I'll have to think about it. I agree with you that we need peace and stability - something that King Aldfrith has brought the kingdom after decades of warfare – but I'm not sure how acceptable this proposal would be to the Witan.'

'Very well. Give it some thought. I'm sure I don't need to add that you mustn't discuss this with anyone, not even with Godwyna.'

'You have my word.'

~~~

In the end the siege of Caer Luel came to an end rather more quickly than Behrt had anticipated. Beli had escaped back into Strathclyde after being defeated by Behrt leaving half of his raiders to fend for themselves in Caer Luel. He had raised a larger army as soon as he'd returned to Strathclyde and now he was marching to the relief of the Britons trapped inside Caer Luel. The first that Behrt knew of its advance was when a group of Osfrid's scouts saw the vanguard crossing an area of open country called Solway Moss.

'It was close to nightfall when we first saw them so the main body are likely to camp on the far side of the River Esk and cross it tomorrow morning,' the chief scout told him.

'Sketch me the land between the Esk and here,'

The scout drew his sword and drew several lines in the dirt floor of Behrt's tent.

'This is the Esk,' he said pointing with the tip. 'It's possible to ford it here but then they'll have to cross the Lyne three miles further on, here. Then they'll only be about five miles from Caer Luel.'

'Thank you; summon the commanders. Then you and your men better get ready to guide us into position during the night.'

That night Behrt's men, all but five hundred members of the fyrd who were left to maintain the siege of Caer Luel, moved into position ready for dawn.

As the sun rose behind its blanket of cloud the following morning, Beli's army rose to find that it had rained hard during the night. Most had slept rolled into their cloaks and, although the weather had now improved somewhat, they were wet, cold and miserable. Some tried to light a fire with damp wood to cook up a mixture of oats and water but most made do with bread and cheese. At this point the alarm was sounded. The enemy had appeared on the south bank of the Lyne, defending the ford.

Beli wasn't too concerned. He'd expected the Northumbrians to become aware of his advance sooner or later and there didn't appear to be more than hundred or two guarding the far bank. Then one of his men came running up to tell him that the ford across the Esk was similarly guarded.

'What's that bloody man Behrt up to?' he asked of no one in particular. 'I'm marching into Cumbria, not back the way we came.'

He had just ordered his men to form up when a man came running to tell him that an army had suddenly appeared from the east. Now Beli was concerned. It seemed that he was trapped in the triangle of land formed by the Esk and the Lyne.

~~~

Osfrid had been given command of the detachment with the furthest to go. His task was to prevent the Britons from retreating back into Strathclyde. Behrt fully intended to make sure that Beli would be in no position to trouble Northumbria again for years to come. He didn't seek to merely defeat Beli's army, he wanted to annihilate them, like the Picts had done to Ecgfrith's army eleven years before.

Behrt was outnumbered, possibly by as much as two to one, but half his men were trained warriors who were better protected and better armed than the Britons. The other half were drawn from the Cumbrian fyrd who were equipped similarly to the majority of the Britons. He had left five hundred of the fyrd behind to keep the enemy bottled up in Caer Luel so he had no more than fifteen hundred men against Beli's three thousand. He just hoped that would be sufficient.

The Britons charged towards the Northumbrian shield wall in a disorganised mass. However, Behrt had chosen his position well and the onrushing Britons found themselves floundering in an area of bog. As they struggled to wade through it flight after flight of arrows descended on them, shot from behind the shield wall. This enraged the Britons and they struggled even harder to force their way through the morass so that they could get to grips with their foes.

Behrt was standing in the middle of the shield wall and he watched as the first few men struggled clear of the marsh. The man who rushed at him was clearly exhausted and struggled to raise his axe above his head. As he did so Behrt thrust his sword forward into the man's exposed chest and he fell back. Unfortunately the sword was trapped between the man's ribs and, in an effort to keep his hands on it, Behrt was pulled forward out of the line.

Another axeman seized the opportunity to swing his weapon at Behrt's head and he was forced to block it with his shield. This left his chest exposed and a Briton with a pitchfork stabbed him in the chest. Fortunately the prongs were made of wood and made no impression on his chain mail clad torso. The spearman standing to Behrt's right stabbed the man with the pitchfork and the latter joined the mounting number of dead in front of the shield wall.

A horn sounded repeatedly and gradually the frenzied attack on the Northumbrians petered out. Only a few were foolish enough to withdraw back through the bog and most of them were struck down by arrows. The rest found an easier path to the north and south of the bog.

Behrt, though shaken by his close shave, quickly assessed the situation. The Britons had lost nearly three hundred men – a tenth of their total number - in the mad attack, whilst his casualties numbered no more than forty, and many of those only had flesh wounds.

Beli was in a quandary. He was trapped with only enough food to last his men for a day or two at most. A frontal assault on the main Northumbrian army hadn't worked and, even had it been more organised, the bog in the centre ground meant he could only attack on two narrow fronts. He therefore decided to cut his losses and retreat back into Strathclyde.

Osfrid saw the enemy massing on the opposite bank and readied his men to hold the ford. It was only wide enough for four men or two horses to cross abreast and, after the recent rain, the water was nearly waist deep and quite fast flowing. He placed his twenty archers in front of the shield wall so that they could pick their targets and do as much damage as possible.

The first two rows went down peppered with arrows, creating an obstacle for those behind until their bodies were pushed away to float downstream. Osfrid saw that his men were wasting their arrows and so he ordered the head bowman to detail off individual archers and give them their targets. This time another eight men went down but with only one arrow in each. The row behind were hit in similar fashion and, having lost twenty men with no result, Beli changed tactics and sent forward his own archers.

These were huntsmen and their bows were less powerful than the war bows of the Northumbrians. Nevertheless they started to inflict casualties and as there were over a hundred of them, Osfrid was going to lose a war of attrition. After he'd lost five of his men to fourteen of the enemy bowmen, he withdrew them behind the shield wall.

Immediately Beli sent another wave of his men across the ford. This time, firing at high trajectory, the arrows did little damage to the enemy. Several were caught on the small shields they lifted above their heads and only two men were hit, one in the shoulder and one in the face. The second volley had more luck and this time two men were killed and another three wounded, but the attack didn't falter and now the Britons were only five yards from the bank.

Osfrid had packed the exit point with slippery, well-watered, mud and sunk pointed stakes horizontally every foot or so in three staggered rows, making it exceedingly difficult to clamber up to where the Northumbrians waited.

Naturally the Britons in the lead tried to avoid the sharp stakes but the pressure of those behind them, eager to get at the enemy, forced several on them onto them. Others kept slipping back into the water and the Northumbrians stabbed downwards at those who were trying to scramble up the bank.

For a moment it looked as if this attack would also fail, then a few managed to use the bodies of the dead to claw their way up onto level ground. At first these were easily dispatched by the waiting warriors but, as the pile of bodies mounted, the shield wall was forced back until the Britons had established a narrow bridgehead on the far bank.

Osfrid had been wounded on his left arm and was finding wielding his sword increasingly difficult when suddenly the pressure eased and the Britons started to retreat. At first Osfrid was at a loss to understand why Beli should halt his attack just when he was about to overwhelm Osfrid's defences but then he saw the reason.

Behrt had brought his forces forward into the area where the Britons had camped last night and had attacked the enemy in the rear whilst they were concentrating on capturing the ford. The two armies faced each other across less than a hundred yards of open land. Although Beli had lost perhaps a quarter of his numbers, he still had the numerical advantage, but his men were dispirited and unwilling to launch yet another attack on a shield wall.

As Osfrid watched, one of his men sewed up his wound and bandaged it. By the time he was finished both leaders had met in the middle between the two armies and, when they shook hands, Osfrid breathed a sigh of relief. A truce had evidently been agreed.

An hour later he stood with his men along either side of the track that led north from the ford as the men of Strathclyde walked between them on their way home. They received a few dark looks and more than a little invective but most shambled past, looking defeated. The garrison from Caer Luel brought up the rear, Beli having agreed to surrender the town as part of the deal.

The army of the Strathclyde Britons may not have been annihilated, as Behrt had planned, but they had been significantly weakened. It was unlikely that they would give Northumbria any trouble for some time to come.

Chapter Sixteen – Disaster in the North

698 AD

'Have you heard the news, Osfrid?' Godwyna asked excitedly as she entered the hall after returning from visiting her husband's cousin, the Thegn of Bebbanburg Vill.

'What news, have the Picts invaded?'

'No, it's good news. Queen Cuthburh had given birth to another son, this one is to be called Otta.'

'Yes, we should rejoice I suppose, but it doesn't help the succession. Aldfrith is obviously still virile enough to beget children but he's an old man now. How old will Osred and Otta be when he dies, that's the important question?'

'Well Eadbehrt was seventy six. If the king lives as long as that, Osred would be thirteen.'

'That's still too young to rule a kingdom as vast as Northumbria. In any case, few men live as long as Eadbehrt.'

Eadbehrt had succeeded Saint Cuthbert as Bishop and Abbot of Lindisfarne and had done much to promote the cult of the saint, turning Lindisfarne into an important pilgrimage destination. This had brought wealth to the monastery which Eadbehrt had used to extend the small church and construct other stone buildings, such as a refectory so that the monks could all eat together instead of in the huts they shared with one or two others.

Eadfrith was a scholar of some repute who had already written a book entitled *the Life of St. Cuthbert* and who had now embarked on producing an illuminated version of the four gospels. Osfrid had been shown the opening page of the Gospel according to Saint Luke by his brother during his last visit to Lindisfarne and he'd been awed by the richness of the decoration of each letter. Not only did the care taken over the calligraphy and the illustration show great dedication on the part of the new bishop, but it was evident that he was a skilled artist as well.

'What will happen when Aldfrith dies then?'

Osfrid was tempted to tell his wife of Behrt's proposal but he remembered his oath not to do so just in time.

'It will be up the Witan to choose a successor.'

'But if Osred and Otta are too young, who then will be the æthelings considered?'

Osfrid shrugged. 'All descendants of Ida I suppose.'

'Including our sons and my sister's son, Eochaid?'

'Unlikely. Æthelings are descended through the male line only as far as I'm aware.'

'I'm glad. Being King of Northumbria is a thankless task, especially as there will be many others who think they have a better right to the throne.'

'I agree, Eadwulf and Swefred are well out of it.'

~~~

Their daughter, Guthild, was now twelve and Osfrid and Godwyna had started to think of possible husbands for her. They hadn't reached any conclusions, and she was still a little too young to marry, when Eadwulf returned during his training to be a warrior at Alnwic. To everyone's surprise he brought Eochaid with him. It was evident that the two young men were close friends and, to his parents delight, he seemed to have lost his truculent attitude. Not that he showed any signs of affection, but at least he was no longer openly hostile.

The other surprise was that the eighteen year old Eochaid showed an obvious interest in Guthild whilst she seemed equally enamoured of her cousin. Osfrid and Godwyna smiled at each other, remembering their attraction to each other at similar ages.

The one person who wasn't delighted by the burgeoning love between the two cousins was Eadwulf. He had brought Eochaid with him to go hunting, get drunk and generally enjoy himself with his friend. Now, deprived of his company whilst he went riding with Guthild and spent time talking to her, Eadwulf became surly once more. If Eochaid was aware of the change in his friend he said nothing, but he was so wrapped up with Guthild that he probably didn't even notice.

When he returned to Alnwic he was betrothed to Guthild with a wedding date set for the following year when the bride would be thirteen. To his parents' surprise, Eadwulf announced his intention of sailing on the next Knarr to travel abroad. His plan was, apparently, to become a mercenary in Frisia.

He reasoned that this would give him experience as a warrior, something he was unlikely to get in peaceful Northumbria. Osfrid thought that it was more likely that he was just plain bored and craved adventure. Whatever the reason, no-one was sorry to see him go.

Swefred had observed the relationship between his sister and his cousin develop and had been secretly pleased by her betrothal. They got on well together and, although he would hate it when she left Bebbanburg, he couldn't think of anyone else he'd rather she married. He liked Eochaid, even hero worshipped him, though he kept that very much to himself. On the other hand he hated his brother with a passion; something else he kept well hidden.

He was a quiet boy but still waters run deep. He gave everything he did and said a great deal of thought and, for ten, he was clever beyond his years. He admired his father and modelled himself very much on him.

The thing that upset him most was the thought that one day that ungrateful swine Eadwulf would inherit Bebbanburg and become the ealdorman whilst he would be lucky if he secured a place in the king's gesith. More likely he would end up serving another ealdorman, certainly not Eadwulf. He swore that the day his brother became master of the grim fortress overlooking the German Ocean would be the last day he would set foot in the place.

What made it even harder to contemplate was the knowledge that his father would far rather he inherited than his elder brother. He even thought about becoming a monk, like his uncle, Alaric, but he knew the quiet contemplative life in a monastery would bore him to tears.

Intuitively Osfrid understood his younger son better than he let on. He knew how he felt about Eadwulf and the thought that he would take over from him when Swefred deserved it so much more saddened him. It was two years yet before he would send the boy to Lindisfarne to be educated and six years before he would have completed his training as a warrior. Nevertheless he began to think about his future. Perhaps he could ask Aldfrith to grant him a vill so that he could at least become a thegn.

Over the past two years he hadn't thought much about Caledonia. Beli had been behaving himself since his defeat near Caer Luel but there had been developments in both Dalriada and in the Land of the Picts.

Shortly after he'd returned from Cumbria he heard that Domnall Don had died and Ferchard ua Dúnchado had taken the throne of Dalriada. However, his reign didn't last long before Ferchard was killed by his cousin Béc ua Dúnchado.

Taran of the Picts had also died a year previously. He had been succeeded by Bridei against some opposition from a minority of the mormaers; opposition which Bridei had dealt with decisively by killing his opponents and murdering their families. They had been replaced by men he was certain he could trust but it had made him very unpopular in some parts of his new kingdom.

Such turbulence was good news as far as Osfrid was concerned. For a start Beli of Strathclyde would be too wary of what was happening on his other borders to be plotting revenge against Northumbria for his defeat in Cumbria.

It was late August before the summons came. Bridei had evidently decided that his grip on the Picts was strong enough to flex his muscles by invading Lothian. Behrt hadn't waited for Aldfrith's permission, but had called out his own fyrd and begged Osfrid, Eochaid and the other Bernician ealdormen to do the same. Because Bridei had already taken most of the area immediately south of the Firth of Forth, the muster point chosen was Dùn Barra, Behrt's stronghold at the north eastern tip of Lothian.

When Osfrid arrived with his gesith and warband he was met by Behrtfrith, Behrt's younger brother, a boy of fifteen who was still training to be a warrior. He directed them to a place where they could camp and explained that his brother had gone with his gesith to reconnoitre the Pictish invaders.

'They've reached Ecclesbrith,' Behrt said that evening to those ealdormen who had arrived. 'They appear to be in some strength – perhaps one and a half thousand on foot and about fifty on those mountain ponies of theirs.'

A quick tally around the room revealed that the gesith and warriors who had accompanied their lords totalled some four hundred; another thousand members of the fyrd would arrive in the next day or so. There were eight shires in Bernicia plus another three in Lothian. Of the eight only four had arrived so far though all three of Behrt's ealdormen were present. Osfrid was surprised to see that Eochaid had yet to arrive. If he'd set off when Osfrid had he should have been there several hours ago.

He didn't arrive until noon the next day. Apparently he had travelled via Bebbanburg and stayed the night there. Osfrid was annoyed at his tardiness but he supposed he couldn't blame him for wanting to spend a few hours with his betrothed. He would have done the same.

When the war bands and the fyrds were all present Behrt sent Osfrid out with his scouts to locate the Picts. He found a forage party first. They were six miles east of Ecclesbrith and were in the process of looting a farmstead. The farmer, his wife and six children ranging in age between eleven and three lay scattered around the three huts that served as their barns and living accommodation. It was obvious that all the women, even a girl of five had been raped before they were killed.

Osfrid saw red, and without thinking that saving one of them for questioning might have been a good idea, he led his sixty men in a charge into the dozen Picts. It took less than four minutes to kill them all. He had slain the last one himself. He had tried to run but Osfrid had ridden him down, chopping his head from his body with one blow of his sword. It was only then that he saw that his quarry had been a boy of about twelve or thirteen. It didn't matter, he was equally as guilty as the men.

Time was of the essence so there was no time for a Christian burial. They carried the farmer and his family into their hut and set fire to it to cremate their poor abused bodies. They left the Picts where they lay for the wolves and the carrion birds to feed on.

Osfrid crested a small ridge to see the main body of the Pictish army a mile away near the coast. He agreed with Behrt's estimate of fifteen hundred but he was puzzled by it. It was too small a force to capture Lothian and establish the border on the River Twaid, if that was their intention, and too large and unwieldy to be merely a raiding party.

The other thing that puzzled him was the slow progress they appeared to be making. It had been over two weeks since they had reportedly crossed the border near Stirling yet they had only advanced fifteen miles into Lothian in all that time. It was almost as if they didn't want to stray too far from their homeland.

By noon the next day Behrt had drawn up his small army across the coastal strip with his right flank by the start of the beach and his left secured by his horsemen, all of whom were under Osfrid's command with Eochaid as his deputy.

The Picts spent some time running about, whooping and hurling insults at the Northumbrians in a language which few understood. The meaning was clear though. Behrt's army stood stoically waiting. Some, especially those in the fyrd, were frightened by the Picts intimidating tactics but most were merely amused. They'd seen it all before and knew that the enemy were trying to work up enough courage to charge a shield wall.

Finally, with a roar several of the Picts broke away and started to run towards the Northumbrian line. The rest streamed after them. There was no formation, just a mass of half-naked bodies wielding a small shield and either a sword, spear or axe. Few, except some of the chieftains, wore chain mail though many had helmets of various descriptions – mainly round pots with no protection for the face, ears or neck.

In contrast the Northumbrian warriors wore either a chain mail byrnie or armour made from boiled leather and their helmets had either a nasal or metal masks with eyeholes that covered the upper part of the face. Some even had a chainmail avantail to protect the neck. Their shields were much larger too. All were circular, made from lime wood and reinforced by a metal boss and banding around the rim. They were much heavier than the targes carried by the Picts but they offered protection from throat to knee when held in front of a man.

The warriors stood close together, shoulders almost touching, so that the shields overlapped. The most vulnerable parts of the body in the shield wall were the lower leg and the feet. Most warriors wore leather shoes but Osfrid had his cobbler make him a pair of stout leather boots with a steel toecap and metal strips sewn into the upright part of the boot to protect his shins.

The Picts hurled themselves at the front rank of Northumbrians, trying to pull their shields down so that they could stab at the faces and torsos behind them. Osfrid allowed his shield to drop as a Pict grabbed it so that the man behind him could thrust his spear at Osfrid's neck but, before he could do so the Ealdorman of Bebbanburg stabbed the man holding his shield in the neck and brought it back up just in time to deflect the spear point. The man behind Osfrid grabbed the Pict's spear and yanked it so that the man wielding it was pulled forward onto Osfrid's sword.

He placed his foot on the Pict's body and pulled his sword free with a sucking sound ready to deal with the next assailant, but there wasn't one. The Picts were in full retreat. The next charge was dealt with as easily as the first one and then, to Osfrid's amazement the Picts fled.

They had certainly suffered casualties – perhaps a hundred or so dead and as many wounded who were later killed by the victors – but not enough to cause them to flee quite so readily. It seemed to Osfrid as if it was deliberate, but he was too busy getting the horses brought forward so that he and his warband could chase the routed Picts to give it much thought.

They pursued them until dusk, killing at least another hundred, before returning to the battlefield. Behrt had set up camp half a mile away, clear of the stench of blood, urine and faeces and the birds and animals who were already feasting on the Pictish dead. The Northumbrians had only suffered thirty killed and forty wounded, most of those flesh wounds. The dead had been laid out ready for a Christian burial in ground that the priests were busy consecrating.

'I smell a trap, Behrt. Picts don't normally give up so easily. It was almost as if they want us to chase after them,' Osfrid said at the war council in the eorl's tent later.

'Rubbish,' Behrt snarled. 'We beat them and now they are fleeing back to Pictland with their tail between their legs. We need to go after them and make sure that they understand that raiding Lothian isn't worth the cost.'

'How far will you chase them, lord?' Eochaid asked.

'As far as necessary. For every settlement and farmstead of mine they have burned and pillaged I'll do the same to three of theirs.'

'You intend to enter the Land of the Picts? Has the king authorised this?' another ealdorman asked.

'He has charged me with the defence of our border with Pictland. That is sufficient authority.'

There was a general murmuring amongst the ealdormen before Eochaid spoke again.

'The fyrd can only be used to defend Northumbria without the king's specific agreement to do otherwise,' he pointed out. 'If you cross the border you cannot take the fyrd with you, which would leave you with too few men. We'd be vulnerable and in a land that our foes know and we don't.'

He didn't mention the disaster when King Ecgfrith's army had been annihilated but it was at the forefront of everyone's mind.

'Are you a coward, boy?' Behrt sneered. 'It was obviously a mistake to allow you to become an ealdorman before you're ready for the responsibility.'

'I'm no coward. I would have thought I'd proved that today, but I'm not an idiot either. Pity I can't say the same about you.'

'Stop it both of you!' Osfrid barked, then continued in a quieter voice. 'The Picts are our enemies, not each other. Now let's all calm down and discuss matters rationally. I see no problem in venturing a little way into Pictland to wreak what havoc we may, but we need to be able to retreat quickly if we run into too much in the way of opposition. I agree with Ealdorman Eochaid that we mustn't risk walking into a trap.'

'Since when have you been appointed commander of the army of Bernicia?' Behrt demanded. 'May I remind you that you are an ealdorman whereas I am an eorl?'

'I'm here at your request, lord, not on the orders of the king. Bebbanburg is not in Lothian, in case you'd forgotten, and I answer only to Aldfrith. My presence is therefore voluntary. We set out to expel the invading Picts; we've done that. I'm willing to make sure that they don't come back in a hurry, but I won't risk my men's lives unnecessarily.'

There was a general murmur of agreement from the others, except for the three ealdormen of shires in Lothian. They kept quiet but their demeanour indicated that they weren't too happy about their eorl's plan.

Behrt looked around the tent and then spat on the ground.

'Very well. I am disappointed in your lack of courage. You are letting a golden opportunity to teach the Picts a serious lesson pass you by and I shall make my views clear to the king when I report to him. Perhaps he'll be able to find a fresh set of nobles who know their duty better.'

The threat impressed no-one. Northumbrian nobility had only just recovered from the losses suffered amongst its ranks thirteen years before.

The fyrd was disbanded and a disgruntled Behrt led six hundred and fifty warriors over the bridge across the River Forth under the noses of the Picts in Stirling. Evidently the man in charge of the fortress didn't feel strong enough to contest the crossing and the remnants of the Pictish raiders had continued their retreat northwards along Allan Water rather than join up with the garrison to confront the Northumbrians.

If the undefended bridge had increased Osfrid's misgivings, the continuing lack of any opposition made him almost certain that they were courting disaster. The actions of the Picts made no tactical sense unless, as he suspected, they were deliberately leading the Northumbrians on, but Behrt wouldn't listen.

At least Behrt hadn't continued his headlong pursuit of the Picts but had sent out parties to loot and burn the local farmsteads and slaughter the people. He succeeded in the former but the locals had vanished with their livestock. Even the grain stores had been emptied and the contents carted away. This frustrated the Northumbrians' desire for retribution but, more seriously, food was now in short supply.

When one of the foraging parties discovered a small settlement which was still inhabited it did them no good. The Picts and their livestock had taken refuge in a large roundhouse built of stone. There were no windows, though it was presumably open to the air at the top, and the small entrance was barred by a stout wooden door to which a number of overlapping iron reinforcing plates had been nailed.

The hungry warriors were driven mad by the sound of bleating sheep, lowing cattle and squealing pigs coming from inside the stone building but, when they tried to batter the door down using a tree trunk, the Picts threw rocks, spears and oil down from the top. This was followed by a couple of flaming torches which set light to the oil. Six men were set on fire and those that survived begged to be killed so as to end their agony. No-one had any heart for a further assault on what they later found out was called a broch.

The incident dented everyone's enthusiasm for continuing the incursion; even the eorl agreed that the time had come to withdraw. However, when they came to the bridge over the River Forth near Stirling they found the way across was blocked by a force of two thousand Picts.

~~~

Aldfrith had become a father for the second time toward the end of 697 and now his wife had just told him that she was pregnant once again and the baby was expected in the autumn. He was delighted; his queen less so. Otta's birth had been long and difficult. Indeed the wise woman who had supervised the birth had told her that she had been lucky to survive. She had lost a lot of blood and had needed significant stitching.

She had explained this to Aldfrith, but he seemed to think that it wouldn't happen again and insisted on sleeping with her as soon as she had healed up. Cuthburh's initial liking for Aldfrith – she wouldn't call it love – had changed over the years. Initially he had been gentle with her but, as time went on, he had become rougher and more demanding. Evidently he was making up for all those years of celibacy. Now she was frightened of giving birth again. There was nothing she could do about it now but, as soon as the baby was born, she would tell Aldfrith that she wanted to become a nun.

'Where are you going now?' she asked her husband as she saw his body servant packing.

'I'm going to visit Bede at Yarrow for a few days.'

'Again? You spent a week with him last month.'

In fact she wasn't displeased by the thought that she wouldn't have to spend the next few nights sharing a bed with him.

'I want to see how his research into his *Ecclesiastical History of the English People* is progressing. The monks have also just started work on the *Codex Amiatinus*, the bible in Latin that I intend to send as a gift to the Pope, and I need to discuss the details with Abbot Coelfrid. Besides, the mint at Wearmouth has just started to produce the new sceattas and I want to make sure they've got the design correct.'

Coins up to that point had only been produced by the money lenders, most of whom were based in Lundenwic. These were gold thrymas in the main, which were impractical for everyday usage and really only suited to large scale transactions. For the first time the new lower denomination coins were to be produced with the king's name inscribed on them, together with Aldfrith's symbol, a lion with an upraised tail.

'I won't be back for some time though as I want to travel north to Lindisfarne after that to see how Eadfrith's gospels are

325

progressing and to look at a new work that his calligrapher had just started, the *Echternach Gospels*. I'm told that they won't rival Eadfrith's own gospels in terms of artistry and richness of illumination but I'd like to see them for myself all the same.'

Not for the first time Cuthburh thought that Aldfrith would have been much happier had he stayed a scholar, rather than being forced to assume the throne. She didn't suppose for one minute that he'd given any thought to the conflict with the Picts on his northern border. Any of his predecessors would have been there commanding the army, but Aldfrith was content to leave such matters to Behrt.

Two days after he'd left an exhausted messenger arrived with tidings of the war. What he had to say caused her to send another messenger racing after Aldfrith.

~~~

Behrt hastily summoned his ealdormen to his side and, still sitting astride their horses, they hotly debated what to do. One or two blamed the eorl for walking into the trap but Osfrid, who had been the loudest to voice his concerns, shouted above the hubbub that recriminations could wait. The important thing now was how to get back across the River Forth.

'Suggestions?' Behrt asked.

His confidence had been visibly shaken by the turn of events. Never before had he asked for proposals; his form of consultation was to put his plan forward and dare anyone to contradict him. As Osfrid and Eochaid seemed to him to be the ones most likely to have good ideas, he looked at them first.

The two cousins had been conferring quietly and now Eochaid nodded at Osfrid, indicating that he should speak for them both.

'If we send the archers forward to provoke the Picts and inflict what damage they can on them, eventually their patience will be exhausted and they'll launch the usual disorganised charge.'

He went on to explain what the Northumbrians should do as soon as that occurred and, as no one had any better ideas, Osfrid's plan was adopted.

The Picts got more irate and unsettled the longer the storm of arrows lasted. Their own bowmen and slingers were out of range as the longer and more powerful Northumbrian composite bows could send an arrow half as far again as the Picts' hunting bows. They did deploy their bowmen in front of them at first but, as they suffered numerous casualties without harming a single one of their foes, they were quickly withdrawn.

At last the younger and more hot blooded of the Picts could take no more and they started to run towards the Northumbrian shield wall a hundred yards from them, yelling at the tops of their voices. The archers each fired one last arrow and ran back through the lines of infantry.

Suddenly, when the leading Picts were no more than fifty yards away, the shield wall split in to two and Osfrid led seventy horsemen through the gap in the line. They fanned out into wedge formation and kicked their horses into a canter and then a gallop. The wedge sliced its way through the mass of Picts like an axe splitting firewood. The Northumbrians didn't even try to spear their enemies on the way, the tightly packed formation knocked them aside like chaff in the wind. Several were trampled under the horses' hooves, but that wasn't important. Osfrid's task was to create a breach in the Pictish army so that the warriors on foot who followed on could reach the bridge.

The horsemen were, by necessity, funnelled into a formation three abreast by the narrowness of the bridge and several of those in the rear of the wedge had to slow down to wait their turn. The Picts hauled them from their saddles and were in the process of killing them when the men on foot arrived.

They were running in a column with shields facing outwards, those on right flank carrying them unusually on their right arm. This made it difficult for the Picts to stab them as they rushed past. The Romans would have recognised the formation as similar to their testudo, though these warriors had never heard of it. The idea had been Eochaid's.

As Osfrid reached the far side of the bridge he felt something thud into his back. There was no pain initially but he seemed to lose control of his limbs immediately afterwards. He fell from his horse and, as he hit the ground, his helmet rolled clear and the hoof of one of the following horses struck his temple. Blackness enveloped him and he died before he was even aware that his spine had been broken.

Behrt had insisted on being in the centre at the rear of the horsemen and it was now apparent why he wanted this. When he approached the bridge he and six members of his mounted gesith turned and charged into the mass of Picts assaulting the men on foot. Their charge rode down the Picts trying to pull the shields away and allowed the majority of the warriors to reach the bridge. It cost him and his men their lives though.

Once over the bridge no one seemed to know what to do as the Picts massed ready to charge across it, so Eochaid took charge.

'Form a shield wall at the exit from the bridge; archers aim into the flanks of the Picts as they try to cross.'

Time and time again the Picts tried to force their way over the bridge and time and time again the Northumbrians repulsed them, causing them heavy casualties. They themselves lost men too, of course, and those in the front two ranks soon got weary, but Eochaid rotated them until at last dusk descended over the battlefield.

By that time there were so many of their dead that the Picts were having to climb over a rampart of bodies to get at the Northumbrians. Then Eochaid had an idea and he sent axemen down the bank to hack at the nearest bridge supports. The Picts kept up their attack even as darkness enveloped the scene but, finally, the combination of the weight of the Picts, both dead and alive, and the weakened supports, caused the bridge to collapse at the southern end. Hundreds of Picts were dumped into the fast flowing waters of the Forth and at last the Northumbrians, or what remained of them, were safe.

Eochaid was so weary that he collapsed where he stood and it wasn't until Drefan came to find him that he was aware that both Osfrid and Behrt had been killed. The Northumbrians retreated a little way until the stench of the battlefield was less obnoxious and camped. Of the six hundred and fifty men that Behrt had led into Pictland a mere three hundred and twenty had escaped, and half of them were wounded.

It was no consolation to him, but Eochaid estimated that the Picts must have lost well over a thousand men over the course of the past week, and for little or no gain. It would not endear Bridei to his mormaers or their men. At least he was unlikely to make any more raids into Lothian for some time to come, but it was a heavy price to pay for peace.

Chapter Seventeen – The Return of the Exiles

698 to 703 AD

It was with a heavy heart that Eochaid rode up to the gates of Bebbanburg. He had decided not to send a messenger ahead with the news but to tell his aunt and his betrothed himself. The survivors of the Bebbanburg warband and of both his gesith and Osfrid's rode with him. Of the sixty men who had ridden to war, only twenty two had returned and a third of them sported bandages. His own warband wasn't mounted and they were making their own way back to Alnwic.

The borrowed cart that accompanied them contained Osfrid's body and four men too badly wounded to ride. It was three days since he was killed and the corpse was beginning to stink. Eochaid had been tempted to stop and get a coffin made at the first settlement they came to but he wanted to make sure that Bebbanburg didn't hear about Osfrid's death before he got there.

When he was still two hundred yards from the gates Godwyna and Guthild walked out to meet them. It was evident from their faces that they knew what had happened. He supposed it was obvious from the absence of Osfrid on his horse and the dejected mien of the cavalcade.

'Is he… is he badly wounded?' Godwyna asked looking towards the cart.

Eochaid dismounted and walked towards them.

'I'm afraid that it's worse than that. I've brought his body back so that he can rest in peace at the place he loved.'

Godwyna broke down and knelt in the dirt, tears running down her face. Guthild ran to her and, kneeling beside her, cradled her mother in her arms as if she was the child and she the comforting parent.

Eochaid stood there feeling helpless when Swefred appeared on his small mare accompanied by three other boys of a similar age. They had several game birds tied to their saddles and it was obvious that they had been hunting.

'What happened? What's wrong?'

The boy looked helplessly from his mother and sister to Eochaid.

'It's your father, Swefred. He was killed during the last battle with the Picts. He died heroically saving the rest of the army,' he added as if that would make his loss more bearable.

'What? Where were you? Why didn't you save him?'

It was no good saying that he had been so busy fighting his own way over the bridge that he hadn't even seen Osfrid fall. There would be a suitable occasion to relate all that had happened but this was neither the time nor the place.

'I'll explain later. Now I need you to do something for me. You father's body is in the cart but we had no coffins. Can you get one brought here and help me put your father in it. Will you do that for me?'

The boy nodded dumbly and, ignoring his friends, he mounted the mare again and rode down to the settlement to see one of the carpenters. It wasn't until his father had been laid in the coffin and he had helped place it in front of the altar in the small church inside the fortress that the implications of his father's death struck him.

The detested Eadwulf was the elder and would now become the ealdorman. Even if he wasn't the younger brother, at not quite eleven Swefred was far too young to inherit. He tried to hold back the tears but he couldn't stop crying. Not only had he lost his beloved father but his hated brother would now return.

~~~

In fact it wasn't until the following spring that Eadwulf put in an appearance. He and his band of Frisian mercenaries had been fighting in some petty squabble over land in Amorica and it had taken several months for the news of his father's death to reach him.

'I need to return to Northumbria,' he told his captain that evening.

'You're going nowhere, lad. You signed a contract with me and I've signed a contract to help this lord to expel his uncle from the land he's seized from him, so that's that.'

Eadwulf hadn't been wasting his time since he joined the warband in Frisia. Most of the other warriors had fallen on hard times and bore a grudge against someone. They were an embittered lot and were only interested in gold and silver. Few were Christians and even those that professed to be had no conscience to speak of. So it was an easy matter to suborn enough of them by promises of wealth and women when he became an ealdorman.

A week later he challenged the captain for the leadership of the band. At first the man didn't take the challenge seriously and told him to do something anatomically impossible. However, he realised that the situation was serious when over a third of his men started to chant Eadwulf's name.

He was a seasoned warrior with biceps most men couldn't get both their hands around and had twenty years' experience of killing, both in combat and quietly in the dead of night. In contrast, Eadwulf was not yet sixteen, skinny and, as yet, beardless. As far as the captain knew he hadn't even killed his first man.

He drew his sword and waited, refusing the offer of a shield. Eadwulf welcomed the man's contempt for his abilities. He was in for a rude shock. He might have few admirable qualities but he had learned his trade well with Eochaid's trainers. One had told him that he had never had a more dedicated student, or a more ruthless one.

The two circled each other, each sizing up his opponent and looking for an opening. Eadwulf hadn't followed his leader's example and discarded his shield and held it close to his body with his eyes just showing above its rim as they danced around each other.

Suddenly the captain made his first move. He was surprisingly fast for a man of his size and weight. He feinted towards Eadwulf's head then, when the latter raised his shield to protect it, he stabbed at his feet. But Eadwulf had expected it. The man had betrayed his intentions with his eyes. The captain's sword slid harmlessly off his young opponent's shield.

The older man was momentarily off balance and Eadwulf sized the opportunity. He brought his own sword round and the blade sliced into the older man's right forearm. The cut was deep but it was only a flesh wound. Nevertheless it would slow him down and so he tossed the sword in the air.

Eadwulf was caught off guard by the unexpected move and he missed his opportunity to strike whilst the man was fleetingly unarmed. He caught the weapon deftly in his left hand and proceeded to demonstrate that he was equally adept at using it in either hand. Eadwulf was now the one at a disadvantage. A shield on the left side is useful at blocking cuts and thrusts from a right handed man but it is of little use at blocking them from the other side.

Realising that it was now more of an encumbrance than useful, Eadwulf surprised the captain by throwing it at him. The brass-bound rim caught the other man on the bridge of his nose. Not only did it hurt but it temporarily blinded him. Eadwulf leaped to the left to evade a wild sword thrust at where he'd stood a split second before. As he did so he brought his own blade round horizontally. It connected with the man's torso with a jar that almost caused him to drop his sword but it had achieved its purpose.

Neither were wearing mail or leather coats and the sharp edge cut through the woollen tunic as if it was made of paper. It connected with the side of his ribs, breaking two of them. One of the jagged ends punctured a lung and from then onwards it was only a matter of time.

The captain was struggling now, both to breathe and to defend himself against Eadwulf's increasingly aggressive attacks. Several of the men called for Eadwulf to show mercy but he had no intention of doing so. He wanted to take over the captaincy of the band and make them his men. To do that the old captain had to die.

Shortly afterwards Eadwulf knocked his opponents sword aside and thrust the point of his own sword up into the soft flesh under his chin and into his brain. The captain was dead before he hit the ground.

~~~

'Where do you expect us to go?' Godwyna asked, trying to keep her temper in check.

'I don't really care, mother. I just want you, your brood and my father's men out of here by nightfall.'

Eadwulf had arrived on two hired knarrs that morning. He had brought fifty five Frisian and Frankish mercenaries with him who would form his gesith and his warband. Drefan and the remainder of Osfrid's warriors weren't needed. Even Morcar the Reeve was told to leave.

'What are we going to do, mother?' an angry Swefred asked, fingering the dagger at his waist. 'I'd like to kill him.'

He recalled that he'd promised himself he'd leave Bebbanburg if his brother became the ealdorman, but now it had come to it he found that he was loathe to do so. It was his home.

'That's empty bluster and you know it,' she replied tersely. 'We're all angry at the way that Eadwulf is treating us but he is the ealdorman now and he has the law on his side. As far as you're concerned you can start your education early, that is if Bishop Eadfrith will take you. Your sister and I have no option but to seek refuge with Eochaid at Alnwic.'

At this Guthild's eyes lit up. Perhaps her brother's return wasn't such a bad thing after all.

That afternoon Swefred set off for Lindisfarne escorted by Drefan and carrying two letters, one addressed to Eadfrith and the other to Alaric asking him to act as his nephew's guardian. She explained that, once Guthild was safely married to Eochaid, she proposed to enter the monastery at Coldingham. She therefore needed someone to take charge of her youngest child for the next five years.

Alaric studied Swefred when he reported to him after seeing Eadfrith and being accepted as a novice.

'Do you want to become a monk, nephew?'

'No!' Swefred almost spat at him. 'I want to become a warrior and Ealdorman of Bebbanburg, like my father.'

'You know very well that's not possible. Eadwulf is the ealdorman and, as he's sixteen, the chances of his dying in the near future aren't high. Besides he'll doubtless marry soon and have children of his own. His son will inherit even if something did happen to him.'

'Then I'll have to pray that he dies childless, won't I?'

'Don't be flippant, especially where religion is concerned. We pray for the good of others, not for ill to befall them.'

Swefred merely grunted in reply and Alaric sighed. He couldn't blame him for being angry at the hand that fate had dealt him.

'If you don't want to become a monk then, what do you want to do when you reach fourteen?'

'Become a warrior, of course.'

Alaric ignored the boy's rudeness.

'Who would you serve? Eochaid as he's marrying your sister?'

'No! He's friends with Eadwulf.'

'He might not be after the way he's treated Guthild. Love is much more powerful than friendship.'

'Perhaps. In any case I've got to wait for another three years before I need to make any decisions. A lot can happen in that time.'

~~~

Swefred wasn't the only one angry at events after the battle near Stirling. Aldfrith had taken the opportunity presented by Behrt's death to reorganise Lothian. The king was dismayed at the eorl's incursion into the Land of the Picts. He realised now that leaving him as the virtual ruler of the North had been a mistake. Consequently he'd divided Lothian into four shires instead of three and had made Behrtfrith an ealdorman, not an eorl.

He remained as lord of Dùn Barra but the other fortress, Dùn Èideann, was given to the new ealdorman. This was another grievance which Behrtfrith nursed. He vowed to be avenged for the perceived insults the king had heaped upon him and so, when he was invited to Bebbanburg to go hunting with Eadwulf, it didn't take much for the latter to recruit Behrtfrith as an ally.

Eadwulf was busy forging alliances elsewhere too. Bishop Wilfrid was surprised to receive a letter from the new Ealdorman of Bebbanburg.

My lord bishop, it began.

I grieve for the wrongs that have been done to you and it is my most fervent desire that you should be restored to the Bishopric of Northumbria, not just of Eoforwīc, but of the whole kingdom, as used to be the case.

If that is also your desire please let me know and perhaps we can work together to achieve this most noble of objectives.

You will appreciate the sensitivity of the matter so I'd be much obliged if you would burn this letter as soon as you've read it. My messenger can be trusted absolutely, so please send your reply with him.

Your servant,

The letter was unsigned and bore no seal.

Wilfrid sat contemplating the contents for a while before he threw it on the fire burning in the central hearth of the modest hall he occupied as the Bishop of Leicester. His most earnest desire was to return to Northumbria and claim the bishopric as well as recover his monasteries of Ripon and Hexham. However, he didn't see how a mere ealdorman, and one who was still beardless, could help him achieve that.

He tried to forget the tempting offer that Eadwulf had made but he couldn't get it out of his head and two days later he sat down to write a reply.

Greetings, he began,

I was intrigued by your letter but I fail to see what influence you could bring to bear to get me reinstated. However, it may be helpful if we could meet to discuss matters further. It will need to be somewhere discreet where we wouldn't attract

unwanted attention. With that in mind, it is time that I visited a
vill called Flichesburg which I have recently acquired on the
River Trent in Lindsey. It is near the junction with the Humber. I
suggest you could sail there in a small boat, perhaps disguised
as a fisherman?

I will be there for the first few days in September. Perhaps
we will meet then?

Your servant in God,

Eadwulf grimaced at the thought of masquerading as a fisherman and he certainly wasn't about to spend however long it took to sail from Bebbanburg to Flichesburg being buffeted about on the open sea in a small boat. In the end he decided to travel on a knarr carrying a cargo to Lundenwic.

After four days of battling adverse winds the knarr entered the estuary of the River Humber and beached for the night on a sand spit between the mouth of the River Trent and Read's Island. At dawn the next day Eadwulf and one of his men disembarked their horses and headed off to the south. An hour later they came in sight of Flichesburg, a small settlement sitting on a low ridge rising out the flat land bordering the river.

Evidently it was good farming land, the soil below the settlement being enriched by alluvial deposits every time the Trent flooded. Eadwulf left his horse with his escort in a small copse half a mile from the settlement and walked from there.

As the sun got higher in the blue sky the cold, damp autumnal morning began to warm up a little. The dew disappeared and Eadwulf's initial sombre mood began to lighten. By the time he arrived at the outlying huts he was positively cheerful. As he entered the place the grassy track turned to alleys of churned up mud mixed in with detritus, animal and human faeces and the body of the odd rat. The sweet smell of plants and grass was replaced by a stench that he found worse even than that of a battlefield after the conflict was over. He was amazed that the fastidious bishop could stomach it.

It turned out that Wilfrid was even more appalled at the state of his latest acquisition than Eadwulf was.

'The place is even worse than a dung heap, if that's possible. I really must apologise. I'd no idea it was like this. I've told the reeve that the filth is to be removed and put at least a mile downwind from the village. The elders can pay for a man and a boy to collect the night soil every morning. I'm really sorry that you had to wade through it. Er, would you mind taking your shoes off before you enter the hall?'

Eadwulf looked at the clean rushes on the earth floor and nodded. A servant knelt and removed the soiled shoes, taking them away to be cleaned. Eadwulf didn't know why the man bothered; he'd have to walk back though the stinking settlement as soon as his business with the bishop was concluded.

'Now, you said you had a plan to get me re-instated as Bishop of Northumbria, I think?' Wilfrid said once they were seated on chairs in one corner of the hall.

Despite the increasingly warm day outside a fire blazed in the centre of the room on which two of the cook's boys were erecting a cauldron suspended from a tripod. The cook and another boy were busy chopping up vegetables and meat at a table nearby ready to put into the cauldron to make pottage for the midday meal. Eadwulf suspected that the meat would be spooned out later and set aside for Wilfrid; few apart from nobles ate meat very often.

'Aldfrith is getting old. Oh, he may have a few years left in him, but not that many I suspect,' Eadwulf began. 'You must have heard that Queen Cuthburh is to retire to a monastery in Wessex. I gather that the birth of their third son, Osric, was another difficult one and she has refused to allow the king to sleep with her again. Although he'd had warnings of her intention, her rejection of him has hit him hard.'

Wilfrid smiled inwardly at the assumption that Aldfrith must be near death because of his age. Evidently the young noble with him didn't realise that Wilfrid had been born in the same year as the king.

'What has this to do with my return to Northumbria?'

'Aldfrith has invited me to become a member of his inner council. Previously Eorl Behrt had represented Bernicia but the family has fallen out of favour since the fiasco near Stirling. I could play on the king's impending entry into Heaven to convince him that he needs to heed the Pope's instructions and make peace with you or risk the fires of Hell.'

Wilfrid looked at the young man, barely out of boyhood, sharply. The sneer which accompanied this statement had shocked him. Whatever else Wilfrid was, he was devout and he believed absolutely in God and his Son, Jesus Christ. He suspected that the cynical young ealdorman was a non-believer; an apostate who used the faith of others cynically to his own advantage. For a moment he considered sending Eadwulf packing.

However, he desired above all else to be re-instated and, despite his disgust at what Eadwulf had said, he decided to pursue the conversation a little further.

'And what would you want from me in return?'

'Who said I wanted anything?'

'Don't play games with me boy, I'm not a fool. The Ealdorman of Bebbanburg doesn't travel all this way at some discomfort and risk to himself to help an old bishop he hardly knows.'

'Well, since you ask, there is something you can do for me.'

'Come on, spit it out.'

'Who do you think the next king should be when Aldfrith dies?'

The question took Wilfrid by surprise. The succession wasn't something he thought Eadwulf would be that concerned about. Then he remembered who his mother's father had been.

'Aldfrith has three sons so they are the obvious candidates.'

'Boys of four, two and a baby? No-one will follow them unless their father lives long enough for them to grow to manhood. I don't think that's likely, do you?'

'You may be correct, but then there are other Idings.'

Ida, the first king of Bernicia, had many sons; the exact number was disputed but amongst them were Eadwulf's great grandfather and another called Ocga. The latter's son, Leowald, had two sons one of whom was dead but Cuthwin was very much alive and, at forty, he could well be an attractive candidate to the Witan. The fact that he already had two sons, Cenred, who was thirteen, and five year old Ceolwulf enhanced his prospects.

'You mean Cuthwin?'

'He is the most obvious one, yes.'

But his grandfather, Ocga, was a bastard. My great grandfather was the son of Ida and his queen, Beornoch.'

'Being a bastard didn't stop Aldfrith from becoming king, and your claim is through your mother. Strictly speaking you are not an ætheling.'

'You don't seem to be on my side. Perhaps I made a mistake in coming here.'

'Perhaps, but I'm only pointing out what everyone will be saying if you put yourself forward to succeed Aldfrith.'

'Then I need to build up support in the interim. Will you support me when the time comes?'

'If I'm Bishop of Northumbria, yes.'

'That ship sailed a long time ago, Wilfrid and you know it. The most you can hope for is to replace Bosa as Bishop of Eoforwīc, or perhaps Lindisfarne or Hexham.'

'Not Lindisfarne, the aesthetic lifestyle wouldn't suit me; and I want my monasteries of Ripon and Hexham back.'

'That may have to wait until I'm the king.'

'Very well, arrange to have me reinstated as bishop with a promise to return my monasteries and you'll have my support when the time comes.'

~~~

'Gerrit, I have a sensitive task for you.'

The Frisian mercenary who had waited with the horses whilst Eadwulf walked to Flishesburg grinned in anticipation.

However, the scar which ran down his right cheek from close to his eye to his chin turned the grin into more of a leer.

'Yes, lord. Does it involve killing?'

Gerrit was only in his early twenties but he'd been killing since he was eleven and had developed a taste for it. He was quite without a conscience; he'd kill anyone from old men to young children and take pleasure in it.

'Yes, the man I want dead is a thegn called Cuthwin. His vill is near Hexham, but you'll need to be discreet. It must look like an accident.'

'Does he have family?'

'A wife and two sons, one thirteen and one five. If you can kill them as well and can still make it look accidental, then do so. But they're not important so let them live if you can't make their deaths look natural.'

'Perhaps I could cut their throats and burn down their hall so it looked as if they died in the fire?'

'I leave the details to you. Here's a pouch of silver for your expenses. Don't go throwing it around and drawing attention to yourself.'

'You don't have to tell me how to fart and piss, lord. I'm a big boy now.'

'Umm, don't let me down. I'll see you back at Bebbanburg.'

Gerrit might think he knew how to remain unnoticed but Eadwulf's experience of Frisians was that they liked to whore and get drunk as soon as they had any money to spend. Once in their cups they were prone to boast. He would just have to hope that the man had enough sense to stay in the background until the job was done.

~~~

Cuthwin glared at his eldest son.

'Why did you run away from Jarrow?'

'It was boring,' the boy replied defiantly. 'Bede had me copying out all his research notes. That's all I ever seemed to do.'

'You're still thirteen, you've another seven months before you'll be old enough to train as a warrior.'

'Why?'

'Because no-one will accept you until you're fourteen, and then only if you're big and strong enough.'

He looked at Cenred. His size wouldn't be a problem; he was already as big as most boys of fourteen and even some fifteen year olds. He was broad shouldered and his biceps were developing well. He already looked like a warrior; well, except for his face. It was nearly pretty enough to belong to a girl. Framed by his long brown hair, it now scowled at him and his piercing grey eyes narrowed in speculation.

'What if I could find a noble to accept me for training?'

'Who do you have in mind?' his father asked in surprise.

'Eochaid, the Ealdorman of Alnwic.'

'How do you know him?'

'He came to visit Bede at Jarrow a few months ago and I was told to show him around the monastery. We got on pretty well.'

'Very well. I'll write to him but, if he doesn't accept you, you'll return to Jarrow until you're fourteen.'

'Thank you father.'

Whilst they were waiting to hear back from Eochaid, Cenred started to train with his father's small warband. As a thegn, he could only afford to keep five warriors. They were men who were too old to serve in a noble's warband but that didn't matter. Their duties were mainly to collect taxes, escort the odd criminal who was being taken to stand trial in the ealdorman's court and to guard the gate to the hall compound during daylight. This was mainly to keep out animals and small boys up to mischief rather than a serious attempt at defence.

One of them also trained the coerls, freemen who were members of the shire fyrd, how to fight. He was now given the task of training young Cenred. They had been working at his swordsmanship on a mild spring day in 700 AD on the open ground in front of the hall when a stranger rode up to the gate. Cenred and his instructor took a break and the latter walked towards him, sheathing his sword as he went.

The sentry on the gate had asked him his business but the man looked towards Cenred when he replied.

'Is your father home boy? I have an urgent message for him.'

The man spoke English with a strange accent and the scar on his face made both of the warriors suspicious.

'Who is the message from?' the instructor asked.

'That's none of your business; go and fetch Thegn Cuthwin,' he told Cenred.

The boy stared at him but didn't move.

'You heard the question,' he said. 'Who is the message from?'

The messenger was evidently getting impatient at the impasse and was about to display his anger when the door to the hall opened and Cuthwin emerged with his wife and Coelwulf.

'What's going on?' he demanded, but before anyone could say anything the messenger sprang into action.

He drew his sword and killed the sentry with a thrust into his neck. He dug his heels into his horse and it sprang forward. As Cenred's instructor went to draw his sword he too was cut down. The rider yanked on the reins to bring the horse to a sudden halt, his forelegs pawing at the air. Cuthwin was so surprised he just stood there whilst his wife cowered behind him, her body shielding her young son.

Gerrit leapt from his horse and stabbed Cuthwin in the chest. The thegn fell to his knees, his hands ineffectually clawing at the wound as he tried to stem the blood gushing from it. By the time he was dead Gerrit had hacked at the head of the thegn's wife and she had fallen on top of the boy badly wounded. Gerrit was about to pull her off to stab down at Coelwulf when he felt an agonising pain in his back.

He lurched around to see Cenred standing there holding a seax dripping blood. He cursed himself for forgetting about the other whelp and went to rectify his error when the boy beat him to it, thrusting the seax upwards into his mouth and on into his brain. The Frisian registered a look of surprise before he toppled sideways and lay still. Cenred stabbed him several more times to make sure that he was dead then ran sobbing to his father.

He knew immediately that he was dead and, wiping away the tears, he went to his mother. The two had never got on and ever since Coelwulf had been born she had lavished all her affection on her younger son. Cenred didn't blame his brother but he hated his mother for her neglect of him. She hadn't even bothered to say goodbye to him when he left for Jarrow eighteen months previously and for that he could never forgive her. Now, when he found that she had died of the grievous wound the stranger had dealt her, he found that he felt nothing. He was as indifferent to her in death as she had been to him in life.

Unlike ealdormen, who were officers appointed by the king, the land owned by thegns passed down from father to eldest son. Cenred was therefore now the thegn. It wasn't until after the funerals of those who had been killed by the mysterious stranger had taken place that he turned his thoughts to the future. He still needed training as a warrior. The reeve could look after the vill whilst he was away but care of his little brother was more problematical. He sent a messenger to report what had happened to the ealdorman and then sat down to write to Eochaid once more.

~~~

Eadwulf was alarmed when he heard about the murder of Cuthwin. He cursed the dead Gerrit; he had a funny idea of what being discreet meant. Perhaps he'd intended to kill everyone in the hall and burn it down, as he had said, but had been killed before he could do so. He sighed. There was nothing to trace the man back to him. Although many knew he employed Frisians as his warband, there were plenty of others in Northumbria.

A few months later he received an invitation to celebrate Christmas at the king's new hall at Driffield in southern Deira. It wasn't something he could ignore; besides it would give him an opportunity to meet other ealdormen whose support he'd need when Aldfrith died.

Driffield lay some twenty-five miles to the east of Eoforwīc and ten miles inland from the coast. Overland it would mean a journey of over a hundred and fifty miles, which would take a week or so. The obvious way to travel south was by sea and this time he could travel openly. He went aboard his largest birlinn and, accompanied by two knarrs to transport his horse, those of his escort and the packhorses he set sail on an overcast day in early December.

Few travelled by sea this late in the season. Storms were commonplace and the biting easterly wind cut through clothing to chill one's bones. However, dressed in a wolf skin cloak and a woollen hat Eadwulf could ignore the cold as he stood at the prow of his ship. Birlinns were broad in the beam, though not as broad as the wallowing knars, and had a high prow and stern. The waist, where the rowers sat, was closer to the water and, to add to their misery, sea spray washed over them as their oars powered the ship forward into the rolling waves.

Once clear of the land, the sailors lowered the mainsail from the yardarm and the birlinn turned and headed south propelled by the wind. The rowers shipped their oars and dried themselves off before donning dry tunics and cloaks. Now they huddled in whatever shelter they could find whilst the ship rolled back and forth as each successive wave struck it beam on before passing under it.

Few fancied staggering to the lee side to be sick but there were too few leather buckets for all those who became queasy. Eadwulf had enjoyed standing at the prow with the wind in his face but he was no sailor and soon he too was emptying his breakfast into a bucket. Perhaps the long journey on horseback would have been preferable after all, he thought after being sick for the fourth time. After a while the wind veered and strengthened and the motion became a little easier; by then Eadwulf was past caring.

At noon on the second day the captain saw a black cloud on the horizon making its way swiftly towards them.

'Squall,' he bellowed. 'Take in the sail and make sure everything is secure. Rowers to your posts; bring her round head on into the wind and keep her like that.'

The ships boys and the younger sailors scrambled up to the yardarm so swiftly that one would think that someone was holding a flame to their posteriors. Hauling the billowing canvas up and lashing it to the yardarm was no easy task but the sailors had secured the sail and were back on deck before the squall hit.

The rowers struggled against the waves and the wind to bring the ship's head around. They had nearly made it when a ferocious gust pushed the bows back the other way and torrential rain lashed the ship from stem to stern.

The rowers, chilled to the bone, fought resolutely to bring the bows around again so that they were facing into the waves. For a horrific moment Eadwulf thought that they were going to fail and that the birlinn was about to broach and capsize. However, one last pull by those on one side, matched by the oarsmen backing their blades on the other, brought the birlinn back on course. Eadwulf breathed a sigh of relief; all they had to do now was to keep the bows facing into the foam-streaked waves.

However, unlike the later longships, the sides of a birlinn didn't curve up until they were vertical. Such a design made the former more seaworthy but birlinns were built so that the top strake was angled at forty five degrees. In a heavy sea waves could easily wash over the sides of the ship and collect in the bilges. Although he couldn't hear it above the howling wind, he could see a significant amount of water sloshing about and he realised that it would sink the birlinn if it was allowed to get much deeper. He grabbed a leather bucket, emptied the vomit out of it, and started to bale. The men and boys who weren't rowing followed his example and grabbed other buckets, helmets and anything else capable of holding water and began to throw the water back over the sides. They weren't emptying the bilges, but at least it wasn't getting any deeper.

Just when they were nearing exhaustion the squall vanished as suddenly as it had appeared. Everyone was cold and exhausted and the bilges still had to be emptied, but at least that could be done at a sustainable pace now. A quick check established that one ship's boy had been swept overboard and two men had broken bones, otherwise the only other damage was minor. A thoroughly chastened Eadwulf gave the order to resume their original course, vowing silently to himself that he would return overland, however long it took.

~~~

Eochaid scowled as Eadwulf approached him. The latter had waited until Swefred had left his cousin's side before doing so and tried to smile engagingly as he offered the other man a goblet of mead. Eochaid took it with a grunt but said nothing.

'I'm sorry you have had to take in my brother, but I'm afraid that he and I never got on, probably because he was our father's favourite,' he began.

'I heard that your parents had no problems with either Swefred or Guthild. You were the only one who gave them grief.'

'Only because Osfrid made no secret of the fact that he would have preferred Swefred to succeed him instead of me,' he replied a little more heatedly than he had intended.

'If you seek to make amends then it is to your sister and brother you should apologise, not to me. I will always support my wife.'

Eadwulf sighed. 'We used to be good friends, Eochaid. I would rather have you as my ally than my enemy.'

'Why should I be either? We may be family but I think it best if you keep your distance and I keep mine.'

'Very well. You may live to regret this.'

'I can't think why. Are you threatening me?'

Eadwulf said nothing further but went off in search of Berthfrith. At least he knew he could count on him.

'How many ealdormen would support me as king when the time comes,' he asked Berthfrith later when they were alone.

'Probably my three fellow ealdormen in Lothian for a start. They won't commit themselves but they can see the sense in having a proven warrior as king instead of a young boy.'

'Eochaid is my enemy I fear, but I believe that I can count on the votes of the ealdormen of Hexham, Durham and Catterick.'

'Bishop John of Hexham might join us and, if he does, his brother, the Ealdorman of Beverley, may well follow suit. However, we really need Wilfrid's vote. His support would persuade many. He still carries a lot of weight in Northumbria, even if the king can't stand him. Will Bishop Eadfrith vote for you? After all Lindisfarne is in your shire.'

'I think that the most I can hope for is for him to abstain when the Witan comes to vote.'

'So, at the moment there are twenty seven members of the Witan, including yourself, and we have ten who will probably vote for you. We have to engineer Wilfrid's reinstatement as Bishop of Eoforwīc. Some will follow his lead, especially the abbots, who are an unknown quantity at the moment.'

'I agree, but how do we bring that about?'

'Aldfrith has taken the loss of his wife to the Church badly. Perhaps we can encourage him to blame Bosa for that. Wilfrid has appealed to the Pope once more. Perhaps this time Aldfrith will listen to him. After all, his own approaching death must be weighing on his mind and he won't want to anger God's representative on Earth, will he?'

~~~

Wilfrid arrived in Rome to find that Pope Sergius had just died. He kicked his heels impatiently until Pope John VI was elected at the end of October 701. This time he was more successful in obtaining an audience and by February 702 he was on his way back to England with an edict from Pope John appointing him as Bishop of Eoforwīc in place of Bosa. He also said that Wilfred's monasteries of Ripon and Hexham should be restored to him.

This time Wilfrid was accompanied by a Papal envoy called Eddius who would negotiate Wilfrid's return with Aldfrith. Wilfrid was now sixty-nine and finding travelling long distances tiring. By the time that they reached Meaux in Frankia Wilfrid was feeling distinctly unwell. During the service of compline Eddius noticed that Wilfrid's face looked peculiar and he was having difficulty in singing the responses. The left side of his face looked as if it had collapsed and one eye was lower than the other. Wilfrid tried to use his arms to stand but he had evidently lost the use of them.

He slowly recovered in the infirmary but his seizure had given him a shock. One night he had a dream in which the Archangel Michael came to him and warned him that Osred would succeed his father and that the boy would need Wilfrid's spiritual guidance.

Thoroughly chastened, Wilfred resumed his journey, travelling in easy stages. He finally arrived back in Kent in April 703 and stayed with Brihtwald, the Archbishop of Cantwareburg who had succeeded Theodore ten years previously, whilst Eddius went ahead to present the Papal edict to Aldfrith.

~~~

Eddius was surprised at the primitiveness of the king's hall at Eoforwīc. Whereas the church was built of stone, albeit on a smaller scale and plainer than he was accustomed to seeing on the Continent, the hall was built of timber and reeked of a mixture of smoke, stale urine and sweat. He tried not to wrinkle his nose in disgust as he approached the two thrones at the end of the hall, but didn't entirely succeed. On one sat an old man and beside him on a small one sat a boy of about seven. Aldfrith hadn't missed the contempt in the Papal envoy's demeanour. In consequence his cause was lost before he even began speaking.

'Domine,' he began in Latin. 'I bring you greetings from the Holy Father and his wishes for a long life.'

'Not something that seems to be granted to most popes,' Aldfrith replied with a wry smile. 'God seems extraordinarily eager to gather each one to his bosom almost as soon as they are enthroned. Do you even know if Pope John is still alive?'

'As far as I'm aware. Why? Have you heard anything?'

'News takes a long time to reach us here in the North.'

'Pope John is still in his forties so I'm sure he'll be with us for a long time yet.'

He looked at the grey bearded, balding man with the grey wrinkled face and thought that Pope John was likely to outlive this king at any rate.

'Let us pray so. Now, to what do we owe the honour of a visit from a Papal envoy?'

'I bring an edict regarding the scandalous treatment of Bishop Wilfrid and the refusal of previous kings to restore him to his rightful place. The Pope insists that you reinstate him as Bishop of Eoforwīc and as Abbot of Hexham and Ripon.'

As he spoke he stepped forward to hand the king the Pope's edict but the warrior standing to the left of the two thrones pointed his spear at him, preventing him from getting any closer. The boy sitting beside the king got up and, with a sly smirk on his face, took the parchment from Eddius and handed it to his father. Aldfrith didn't bother to break the seal before handing it to the cleric standing behind his throne.

Bosa opened the letter and quickly scanned the contents before whispering in the king's ear.

'It seems that nothing has changed. This Pope, like others before him, seeks to usurp my prerogative as king to appoint my own bishops. Please go back to Rome and tell him that he need not concern himself with Northumbria. We are well served by the bishops we have and have no intention of changing them.'

'Be very afraid, Aldfrith; you may be a king but you are mortal, like all men. Your time to enter heaven is not far off and your high and mighty defiance of the Pope will serve you ill when it comes time for you to be judged before God.'

Without waiting for a reply or the king's leave to depart Eddius, spun around and marched out of the hall. An hour later he was mounted and, accompanied by his escort, he was on the road back to Cantwareburg.

He left a worried Aldfrith behind him. Eddius' words haunted him and, despite the scorn of his eldest son and the opposition of all three bishops in Northumbria, he sent word to Cantwareburg that Wilfrid might return and present his case to him in person.

Chapter Eighteen – The Usurper

704 to 705 AD

Wilfrid travelled north eagerly, if not quickly. As he sat on the cushioned bench inside a small covered cart he wondered about the reception he would receive. Aldfrith was worried about his immortal soul, which was encouraging. On the other hand he wasn't confident that the king would be prepared to dispossess Bosa once more in order to restore him to the diocese of Eoforwīc.

He also thought about Aldfrith's successor. Osred, Otta and Osric were all far too young to rule Northumbria if he died in the next few years. Perhaps he should support Eadwulf after all, although that young man had done little to fulfil the promise he had made at Flishesberg.

As the cart trundled through the green countryside of late autumn - the fields bare of harvested crops and ready for the spring sowing and the russet leaves already falling from the trees - another idea began to form in Wilfrid's mind. Perhaps there was a third option.

For the first part of the journey he passed through the rolling countryside of Kent and Mercia. The sun shone much of the time and what rain there was came in brief showers. That changed when he crossed the Humber and entered Northumbria. The province of Deira was similar to the shires in the south, unlike the bleak moorland and the hills of much of Bernicia, but now the weather turned.

Rain lashed down, beating on the oiled leather roof of the cart, and the temperature dropped considerably. Gusts of strong wind drove the rain through the open sides of his wagon, despite the leather curtains that served as doors, and chilled him to the bone. Gone were the days when Wilfrid had been corpulent. As he'd aged he'd grown leaner, his once fat jowls now hung like empty purses on his face and the skin under his rich woollen robes was similarly baggy and wrinkled.

His joints ached, especially in damp weather, and he walked with a pronounced stoop, leaning on his bishop's crook for support. He no longer cut an impressive figure but his eyes were still bright and intelligent and his brain worked as well as it ever did.

Eventually the covered cart with its escort of three bored horsemen on loan from the archbishop, followed by Eddius on a docile mare and two servants sitting on a larger cart laden with Wilfrid's possessions, pulled into the settlement of Driffield. This was now Aldfrith's favourite abode and the place was overflowing with nobles, churchmen, servants and thegns seeking an audience with the king.

'I'm Bishop Wilfrid here to see the king,' he said after he had managed to clamber with some difficulty and Eddius' aid from his conveyance.

'Is he expecting you?' asked an indifferent official to whom Wilfrid had been directed by a servant boy who had come to see what they wanted.

'Yes, he invited me. Now go and tell him that I'm here,' Wilfrid said with a touch of his old imperiousness.

The man turned to leave.

'Wait! At least have the courtesy to show me to my lodgings first.'

'Lodgings? The place is full to overflowing; even the tavern is sleeping three to a bed. You'd do best to pitch your tent down by the river. I'll send someone to fetch you if and when the king wants to see you.'

A disgruntled Wilfrid climbed back into his cart and set off to find a space amongst the others camping alongside the headwaters of the River Hull, a tributary of the Humber.

After two days sitting doing nothing he clambered back into his cart and, accompanied by Eddius on foot and a servant leading the horse pulling the cart, he made his way back up to the hall. This was another timber building like the one at Eoforwīc and just as primitive, but at least it had the advantage that it was of recent construction so that it didn't smell too badly of smoke inside and the roof was still watertight.

He'd heard nothing but he was fed up with waiting. With Eddius clearing a path for him through the throng, he slowly made his way to the far end where Aldfrith sat on one throne and Osred, now eight, sat on a smaller one by his side looking bored.

As the bishop tapped his way past people with his crook he heard a few who recognised him whisper his name. The whispers grew into a loud murmur and the king, who was now slightly deaf, turned to Osred.

'What are they babbling about?' he asked querulously.

'The priest Wilfrid is here, father.'

'Wilfrid? Ah good. I need to make my peace with him.'

'Domine,' Eddius began in Latin. 'As you have requested, Bishop Wilfrid has come to see you.'

Wilfrid would have fallen to his knees but he wasn't confident of being able to rise again in a dignified manner, even with help. Instead he bowed low.

'Cyning, thank you for seeing me. I'm here to resolve the issues of my diocese and my monasteries at Ripon and Hexham.'

Aldfrith contemplated the man standing before him. Despite his diplomatic phrasing the king detected an underlying arrogance; an assumption that all three posts would now be restored to him. Well, he was in for a disappointment.

'Wilfrid, you have ever been a thorn in my side, but now that we are both of an age when our entry into Heaven or Hell cannot be long delayed, I am ready to reach a compromise with you.'

At the mention of Hell Wilfrid's eyes opened wide. He had never even considered the possibility that he was headed for anywhere except God's kingdom. He had no doubts that the scholarly Aldfrith was similarly bound.

'Compromise Cyning?'

'Yes, I have no intention of removing Bosa from his bishopric and it would also be wrong to deprive John of Beverley of either his diocese or monastery of Hexham. However, I am prepared to offer you Ripon. The abbot had recently died and so your appointment there would cause no upset.'

'I see, and are you therefore proposing to create a fourth diocese in Northumbria?'

'What? No, of course not. You would become the abbot, nothing more.'

'And if I don't accept this compromise, as you call it, what then? After all, you will still be in conflict with His Holiness to the peril of your immortal soul.'

Aldfrith shifted uncomfortably on his throne but it was Osred who replied.

'Have a care, priest. Remember to whom you speak.'

The high treble voice with which this was said didn't detract from the authority radiating from the boy. Evidently Osred was mature beyond his years. Wilfrid quickly re-appraised his opinion of the young ætheling. Perhaps he would be worth cultivating after all. Any intention he might have had of supporting Eadwulf when Aldfrith died ceased at that moment.

'I meant no disrespect but it is difficult to hide my disappointment. May I suggest another option?'

'Go on,' Aldfrith said, with a warning hand on his son's arm for him to remain silent.

'So as not to upset Bishop Bosa, may I have your oath that, when he dies and if I am still alive, I will be allowed to replace him.'

Aldfrith thought about this for a moment whilst Osred whispered in his ear.

'If Bosa does indeed die first I would want John of Beverley to replace him. That would leave Hexham free for you, in addition to Ripon. Does that satisfy you?'

Wilfrid realised that, even if he hadn't got all that he wanted, it was as good a deal as he was likely to get.

'Thank you Cyning. I accept.'

~~~

Swefred woke up feeling extremely ill. The previous evening he'd celebrated his sixteenth birthday and the end of his training. Now he could consider himself a warrior. He had only the haziest recollection of the previous night when he'd drunk far too much mead and ale – a lethal combination - before falling into a stupor. He wondered who had put him to bed. Then all other thoughts fled as he reached for the piss bucket and was violently sick.

After he'd washed his mouth out and jumped into the River Aln to bathe he felt a little better. Once dressed in thick woollen trousers, tunic and cloak to ward off the biting December wind, he went in search of his friend Cenred to see if he could throw any light on what he'd got up to.

Cenred was a year older than him and was now a member of Eochaid's gesith, but the two had liked each other when they had first met two years previously. By then Cenred was already an accomplished swordsman and he'd volunteered to teach Swefred. The difference in their status didn't seem to matter; Cenred was a thegn, although he seemed content to let his reeve run his vill, whereas Swefred was a landless younger son.

Swefred found his friend busy packing.

'Where are you going?' he asked in surprise.

'My reeve has died leaving my nine year old brother in charge.'

'Are you worried that he'll try and usurp your position as the elder?'

'No,' Cenred laughed. 'He wouldn't dare, but he's too young to manage the vill on his own. To tell you the truth, I should have returned when I finished my training but the life of a carefree warrior in Eochaid's gesith was more attractive than dealing with the petty concerns and problems of my vill.'

'I'll be sorry to see you go. You've been a good friend to me.'

'Yes, I'll miss you and the camaraderie here. My little brother and the old men who form my little warband won't be the same. Perhaps I'll return after I've found a new reeve?'

'I hope so. Well, good luck.'

Once Cenred and his servant had left Swefred went to find Eochaid. As he walked towards the ealdorman's hall he felt something wet land on his cheek. Lost in thought he hadn't realised that it had started snowing. He shivered, despite his thick cloak and hurried into the warmth of the hall.

'Ah, Swefred,' Eochaid called out as he brushed the snow off his shoulders on the threshold. 'Come in and shut that bloody door. How are you feeling after last night?'

Swefred grinned. 'I've felt better, lord.'

'Ha, you'll have to learn to pace yourself my boy. And stick to either ale or mead, don't mix them. Now come and sit beside me. You and I need to talk.'

Swefred did so and waved away the proffered leather tankard of ale.

'For God's sake,' he said to the boy standing at his elbow. 'Do you want me to puke all over your lord? Go and fetch me a goblet of milk if you want to do something useful.'

As the servant rushed away to do as he was bid Eochaid gave the young man an appraising glance.

'What do you propose to do now that your training is over?'

'Well, I had hoped that I might fill the vacancy left by Cenred's departure.'

'News travels fast, it seems. I might have expected you of all people to know that he's gone. You always were as thick as thieves. If I didn't know Cenred's sexual tastes better I might have thought that you were bedfellows.'

Swefred bristled at what he perceived to be a slur on his manhood.

'Don't worry. I know that's not true, but you need to be careful. There's others around here who have been whispering about you two.'

'Who's been insulting me? I'll tear out his guts and wear them as a torc.'

'Calm down. I don't allow fighting amongst my men. I know neither of you is a virgin. There's scarcely a girl under twenty in Alnwic that Cenred hasn't tried to bed, and you're not much better. Just take what I've said as a warning not to get too close to one man to the exclusion of the others. Leadership is all about uniting a disparate group of men to act together for the good of all.'

When the time came, Swefred would remember Eochaid's advice and make it his guiding principle.

'Now, about your future. I can't take you into my gesith; there are others with a prior claim to that favour. However, I can offer you a place in my mounted warband.'

'Thank you, lord. I accept, of course. For now,' he added.

'For now?'

'Yes, if anything happens to my brother then I wish to be free to return to claim my birth right as Ealdorman of Bebbanburg.'

'Hmmm, very well. It seems unlikely to me, but naturally I would release you from your oath to me if you inherited Bebbanburg.'

~~~

The onset of the winter weather persuaded all those camping in leather tents outside Driffield to seek the warmth and shelter of their own halls, even though the Christmas season was about to start. In the middle of December Osred celebrated his ninth birthday but the feast was cut short as his father was taken ill halfway through the meal.

The next day he recovered sufficiently to send for Bosa and Edmond, Ealdorman of Eoforwīc. However, Bosa himself was unwell and so his prior accompanied the ealdorman, arriving the day before Christmas. His sixty year old half-sister, Ælfflæd, Abbess of Whitby, also struggled through the snow to be with the king in what everyone thought might be his last days.

He rallied sufficiently to take mass on Christmas Day but then he had a relapse and fell into a coma from which he never awoke, dying on the first day of the new year, 705 AD.

'What do we do?' Edmond paced up and down the small room off the king's hall, wringing his hands in agitation whilst the servants prepared the body for burial.

'Don't be so pathetic,' Ælfflæd said briskly. 'The gravediggers will need to start work now; the ground is rock hard and it will take them time to dig a deep enough hole.'

'What here? At Driffield? Not Eoforwīc?'

'Yes, here. It is my brother's wish. You need to send messengers to all members of the Witan to meet at Eoforwīc as soon as possible. It will take time for everybody to assemble in this weather; let's say in three weeks' time.'

'But who will succeed? Osred's too young and you are the only adult member of the House of Æthelfrith who is still alive.'

'Who says I'm too young?'

Osred had entered the room whilst they were talking and, barely giving his father's corpse a glance, he strode belligerently towards Edmond.

'Everyone will. Kings have to be trained warriors.'

'The Witan has considered younger candidates in their time.'

'Perhaps, and no doubt they will formally consider you and your brothers, but they won't elect you.'

Ælfflæd could see that an argument was likely to develop and stepped in before things were said that couldn't be retracted.

'Stop it both of you. Show my brother some respect. The Witan will decide, not either of you.'

'Very well, aunt, but I'm the only legitimate choice. Who else is there?'

'Cenred for a start.'

'Cenred? What, you mean the thegn?'

'Yes, the Witan will have to consider all descendants of King Ida now.'

That gave Osred pause of thought. He'd forgotten about the other branches of the Idings – those who could trace their descent back to Ida.

'I think that would be unwise. If we go outside the House of Æthelfrith there will be hundreds of claimants. After all, Æthelfrith was the first King of Northumbria. Ida was only King of Bernicia and he had so many sons, both legitimate and illegitimate, no-one is quite sure how many there were. You mentioned Cenred, for example; he's descended from one of Ida's bastards. How many more are there?'

'Hundreds is something of an exaggeration, Edmond. A dozen perhaps. Those who consider themselves to be æthelings can present their case so everyone can see that the election is fair and can then unite behind the Witan's choice. Otherwise we'll have nothing but dissention and strife.'

~~~

Eochaid was puzzled.

'I've received summonses to attend the Witan from two different people,' he told Heartbehrt, who was now the captain of his gesith and leader of his warband.

'Really? Who has the right to summon the Witan?'

'Normally it would be the person appointed to do so by the king but that person was Bishop Bosa, who is ill and apparently likely to die. One summons has come from the Ealdorman of Eoforwīc for the nobles and senior churchmen to meet there on the fifteenth of February and one from Behrtfrith, the senior ealdorman of Lothian, for us to meet at Yeavering on the last day of January.'

'Yeavering? In the middle of the Cheviot Hills? It seems a strange place to meet in winter. I thought it was the old summer palace of the kings of Bernicia.'

'It is. I can only think that it was chosen to make it difficult for the Deiran members to get there in time.'

'This stinks like rotten fish. What will you do?'

Eochaid shrugged. 'Go to both I suppose. But you had better prepare the gesith and the mounted warband to accompany us.'

'By the way, have you heard about Ethelred?'

'The King of Mercia? No, why?'

'He had abdicated, or been forced to, and has left England to travel to Rome.'

'Really? Who is king now? His son Coelred?'

'No, his nephew, Coenred, Wulfhere's son.'

'What? The one who has a reputation of acting like a pagan, even though he professes to be a Christian?'

Heartbehrt nodded. 'Yes, I can't imagine what possessed the Mercian Witan to elect him. He's as unpredictable as he is dissolute.'

'All we need is for him to decide that now is a good time to invade Northumbria whilst we are without a leader.'

'Hopefully he will be too busy consolidating his own position. There are plenty of Mercians who'd have preferred Coelred, even if he is only sixteen.'

A fortnight later the weather had improved considerably. The snow had given way to rain, but for the last few days it had been dry and the roads were at least passable. Despite this it was still January and the ground was covered in frost each morning and the east wind was bitterly cold.

When Eochaid and his men approached Yeavering along the valley of the River Glen he saw from the few banners fluttering in the light breeze that they were only the seventh contingent to arrive. Five belonged to the four Lothian shires and that of

Bebbanburg and the sixth to the Bishop of Hexham, John of Beverley.

As he got closer he was surprised by the number of armed men present. The place was more like the camp of an army on campaign than a peaceful gathering of the Witan. He had a nasty feeling about this assembly and he was glad that he had brought his sixty mounted warriors with him.

They camped beside the stream that ran down from the valley to the east of the hill called Yeavering Bell, well away from the main camp by the river. When he rode up to the king's hall accompanied by Heartbehrt and three of his men, Eadwulf and Behrtfrith came out to meet him.

'Welcome Eochaid. You are one of the first to arrive. I'm surprised that more aren't here already.'

'The notice was short and it is the middle of winter; and the place is almost inaccessible. Why choose a summer residence to meet?'

Both men ignored the question and the implied criticism.

'Well, if they don't arrive tomorrow we'll start the day after without them,' Eadwulf said, almost with glee.

'I suggest we give them a little longer. What does the bishop say?'

'Oh, he'd wait until doomsday. However, we need to get on with it. The kingdom is vulnerable until we have a strong leader on the throne.'

'But surely you'll wait for Osred? After all he is Aldfrith's heir.'

'Why he's a boy. As I said we need a strong leader.'

With that Eadwulf turned away and Behrtfrith followed him back into the hall.

~~~

'All those who claim to be æthelings of Northumbria should stand,' John of Beverley, who was presiding, said after he'd managed to establish some sort of silence in the hall.

Only Eadwulf got to his feet.

'What are you doing, cousin? You are no more an ætheling than I am,' Eochaid called out in shock.

'You can also claim Benoc of Jarrow as your grandfather, so you too are an ætheling.'

'But that's through our respective mothers. I thought æthelings had to be descended through the male line.'

'These are unusual times, Eochaid. Now do you wish to stand or not?'

'No, but I wish to nominate Osred, son of Aldfrith, and I will stand proxy for him.'

'This is most unusual,' Bishop John said, obviously unhappy at the way things were going.

'If I may help, bishop,' Eadfrith of Lindisfarne said as he got to his feet.

'The Witan, once properly convened, may elect anyone they deem suitable to be the king. It is only convention that restricts contenders to æthelings. The clue is in the title – ætheling means throne worthy. The only true æthelings of the line of Æthelfrith are Osred, Otta and Osric. In view of their youth the Witan may decide that another, not of the direct royal line, is more suitable.'

'Thank you Eadfrith, that is most helpful.'

'Pardon, bishop, but I hadn't quite finished. Whether this Witan has been properly convened is another matter entirely. Even if it was, I suggest that the proper course of action is for you to adjourn it – possibly to a more suitable location – until more nobles and the three æthelings I mentioned can be present.'

'No,' Eadwulf thundered, hitting the table in front of Bishop John with his first. 'This matter will be decided today, before we have the Picts swarming over our border to the north and Coenred and his Mercians plundering Deira.'

'I'll not be part of this farce,' Eochaid said angrily and made for the door but several of Eadwulf's men stepped in front of him to bar his way out.

Seeing this, Heartbehrt, who had accompanied his lord to the meeting, gave a piercing whistle and Swefred and several other members of the Alnwic warband stepped through the doorway and held the points of their swords against the necks of Eadwulf's Frisians.

'Stand aside. I don't want bloodshed to mar a Witan, even if it is an illegal one like this is,' Eochaid ordered.

Unwillingly the Frisians did as they were told and Eochaid left, followed by his men. However, Swefred couldn't resist a Parthian shot – so called because they were famed for firing one last arrow at their foes as they rode away.

'Father always said you'd come to a bad end, brother. It looks as if you're just about to prove him correct.'

~~~

'Give me fifty men and I'll take Bebbanburg for you,' Swefred said breathlessly to Eochaid as the Alnwic contingent cantered away from Yeavering.

Eochaid couldn't see the point of pursuit; after all, without his opposition he was certain that Eadwulf would be elected king. Nevertheless, he didn't trust the man and he wanted to put as much distance between them as possible.

'I thought it was impregnable?'

'It is normally, but my brother has foolishly taken all his Frisians and most of the rest of the garrison to Yeavering. Few will be left to man the fortress. I should be able to trick my way in, and even if I can't I know a secret entrance that I found as a small boy.'

'Why do you need my men then?'

'To keep my brother out once he discovers he's lost his precious fortress. That should give you time to raise an army to deal with him and the Lothians.'

'How will you trick your way in?'

Swefred pulled a cloth from the bag hanging from his saddle.

'Using this.'

At dawn the next day a contingent of men rode towards Bebbanburg under the wolf's head banner that had been adopted by Catinus when he'd been appointed as the first Ealdorman. Without wondering too much why their master had returned so quickly the sentries swung the main gates open and Swefred and his borrowed men rode in.

He held his breath until they had passed the second gate and rode onto the grassy knoll where the lord's hall stood.

'My lord, we didn't expect you back ....'

The reeve's words faded away as Swefred pulled off his helmet which, like his brother's and many Anglo-Saxons who could afford one, had a visor fixed in place which protected the eyes and nose.

Unlike Morcar, the reeve in his father's day, this man was fat and balding. He had a goblet of mead in one hand and, judging from the grease in his beard, he had been in the process of tucking into a hearty meal.

'Who are you?'

'Your new lord. Where is the captain of the garrison?'

'New lord?'

'My name is Swefred, Eadwulf's younger brother. Now where is the ...'

At that moment a red faced man came running up followed by a score of armed men, mostly old men and boys – presumably those under training.

'Disarm them,' Swefred ordered calmly.

His men surrounded the new arrivals and the elderly warriors – the ones with sense – lowered their weapons but some of the boys decided to try their luck. One lunged at Heartbehrt who batted his spear aside with his shield. Before the youth had time to recover Heartbehrt punched him in the chest with the boss of his shield. The assailant fell onto his bottom, dropping his spear, much to the amusement of Heartbehrt's men.

Only one boy, more obstinate than the rest, was wounded in the brief encounter and ten minutes later the former garrison were expelled from the fortress, together with the reeve and those servants who professed a loyalty to Eadwulf. Swefred then took Heartbehrt and two of his senior warriors on a tour of the fortress, explaining how the second gate, which turned the entrance into a death trap, worked.

He also showed them the chute down which rubbish was thrown to end up on the beach. From there the high tide would carry it away. The inner end was only protected by a wooden trap door, so Heartbehrt suggested that the blacksmith should make a metal grille with a lock in order to prevent an enemy from using the chute as a means of entry.

'Would you really have climbed up that filthy chute if you hadn't managed to trick your way in?'

'Why not? It was a trick my grandfather used to good effect,' Swefred replied.

'Not here?'

'No, to capture Dùn Breatainn in Strathclyde.'

'Really? I was told it's impregnable.'

'Well, it's fallen twice to my certain knowledge.'

Once they had distributed barrels of arrows around the walls and prepared a deadly welcome along the stretch of enclosed roadway behind the main gate, Swefred and his men waited for the inevitable attack.

Three days later Eadwulf's army appeared from the west. Swefred and Heartbehrt climbed to the top of the watchtower to join the sentry who had sounded the alarm.

'There's hundreds of them,' the man said in awe.

'Don't worry. The Ætheling Alchfrith brought hundreds against Bebbanburg thirty five years ago,' Swefred told him.

'What happened?'

'Most of them are still here.'

'What? Where?' the sentry asked, crossing himself as if he expected them to suddenly appear.

'Under the ground over there.'

'How many do you think there are?' Swefred asked Heartbehrt.

'His eyes are better than mine,' he replied, gesturing towards the sentry.

'Well, I can see eight banners, lord. There's about a hundred horsemen in the lead and then a mass of infantry but it's difficult to estimate how many.'

'How long is the column?'

'Perhaps five or six hundred yards, that is before the baggage train starts.'

'And how many warriors can you see in the front rank?'

'Perhaps six abreast, but they're milling about a bit.'

'Well done lad. That gives me a rough idea.'

The sentry blushed with pleasure at the praise.

'I think my dear brother has managed to amass an army up to three thousand strong. Not bad in three days.'

'He must have been preparing for this to have mustered so many so quickly; not necessarily for the siege of Bebbanburg, but the need to fight for the throne he's usurped.'

As the enemy drew closer, Swefred could make out the banners.

'It seems that Eadwulf has enlisted the support of Cumbria, Otterburn and Hexham in addition to the four shires in Lothian and his own men.'

'That's only eight shires, including this one. There are another ten in the kingdom, most of them more densely populated than the ones in the north.'

'Yes, but they are wide spread and it will take some time to muster their fyrds and then march here. We must expect a long siege,' Swefred said gloomily. 'Thank goodness Eadwulf laid in supplies to last him and his men through the winter.'

~~~

Eochaid was wondering if sending his captain with Swefred had been such a good idea. Only now, when he was faced with raising an army to support Osred, did he realise how much he had come to depend on his quiet efficiency and common sense.

He started by sending messengers to the leading churchmen to enlist their support – not only the three bishops but the abbots as well, including Wilfrid at Ripon. Another man took a letter to Cenred. He might only be a thane but even he had a better claim to the throne than Eadwulf had. He was certain that he wouldn't want to see a usurper prevail. For one thing they tended to get rid of all their potential rivals to stifle potential opposition.

Cenred's vill lay in the shire of Durham and Eochaid hoped that he could persuade his ealdorman to side with Osred. Messengers were sent to Jarrow and Catterick and to four of the five shires in Deira, but he decided to travel to Eoforwīc himself.

Having sent his warband and a few of his gesith with Swefred he could only afford to take five men with him after leaving enough to guard his hall and his family. Being so few and travelling light they covered over forty miles each day, setting out at dawn and stopping just before dusk. On two nights they managed to stay at a monastery but on the other they had to camp.

Without tents, they were lucky enough to find an overhanging rock which gave them some protection from the rain that started at midnight. However, when they set off again they soon got soaked in the downpour. The rain made them miserable and they kept their heads down inside their hoods as they plodded on. Suddenly half a dozen horsemen materialised in front of them and the same number rode out of the trees behind them. Being winter, they would have seen them amongst the denuded trees had they been alert.

'Who are you and where are you headed?' a man in a helmet with a nasal barked at them.

'Edmond, don't you recognise me?' Eochaid asked as he pushed back his hood.

'Eochaid? What are you doing so far south?'

'You've heard about Eadwulf?'

'Usurping the throne? Yes, that's why I'm on my way to Catterick.' He paused as a thought crossed his mind. 'Do you support Osred as the true king?'

'Once he's properly elected by the full Witan, and not that stunted version that Eadwulf got to accept him, yes.'

'Good. The Deiran ealdormen are mustering there.'

'Where are your men then? This can only be your gesith.'

'It's taking time to mobilise the fyrd so they and my warband are following on. Do you know how many men Eadwulf has?'

Eochaid nodded. 'I can't be specific because the messenger left before the siege started but Swefred thought he had about three thousand or so.'

'That's more than we thought. Perhaps Luncæstershire have joined him as well.'

Eochaid shook his head.

'I don't think so. The message listed the banners Swefred had seen. That of Cumbria was there but not Luncæstershire.'

'Then I don't know how he has raised so many men so quickly.'

'Perhaps he's enlisted the aid of the Picts or maybe Beli of Strathclyde is supporting him?'

'Possibly. In which case I wonder what he's promised them in return.'

~~~

Swefred stood on the battlements of Bebbanburg looking down at the enemy camp on the west side of the fortress. They had taken over the thegn's hall and the huts of the local people and put up numerous tents as well. Now that he could study the besiegers more closely he realised that Eadwulf had brought over more Frisian mercenaries to bolster the war bands and the fyrd of the shires loyal to him.

He and Heartbehrt had counted numbers independently and had come up with around two thousand six hundred. Of these three hundred were mercenaries, another five hundred were trained warriors serving the various ealdormen and the rest were members of the fyrd. Many of the latter wore their normal clothes and carried and axe, spear or farming implement as a weapon. About a hundred were hunters and the like who were good archers but their bows didn't have the range to trouble the defenders on top of the palisade which itself stood on top of a cliff nearly a hundred feet high.

Eadwulf had made one attempt to capture the sea gate on the second day of the siege but had been repulsed with the loss of thirty of his men. He knew the fortress even better that Swefred did and he was well aware of the folly of attacking the main gate.

As Swefred watched a battering ram started to make its slow, lumbering way towards the sea gate. It was now two weeks since the siege had started and the ram had obviously been made over that period. It was carried on eight stout wheels and consisted of a frame from which a tree trunk was suspended. The ram had a pointed end to which iron plates had been nailed. The frame itself was covered by a pitched roof to which hides had been nailed to protect the men pushing the ram from arrows and anything else the defenders might hurl down on them. Swefred had to admire his brother's ingenuity.

In fact it wasn't Eadwulf who had come up with the design but one of his Frisians who had read about siege warfare as conducted by the Romans. The ram lumbered to the foot of the path that lead up to the sea gate and there it halted. Swefred smiled to himself. Pushing the ram up that slope wouldn't be easy.

As he watched his brother rode forward accompanied by his banner bearer. The banner was the same as that flying from the watchtower inside the fortress – a wolf's head in black on a yellow ground.

Swefred descended the tower and walked leisurely to the palisade beside the Sea Gate.

'What do you want, brother?'

'I'm not your brother, damn you, I'm your king. Now stop this foolishness and open the gates to my fortress.'

'So you can kill us all? I don't think so.'

'You have my word that, provided you restore Bebbanburg to me by noon today, you may march out unarmed and go where ever you wish, provided its outside Northumbria.'

'And you expect me to trust your word? Why should I? You've always hated me and wanted me dead.'

'True. Very well then. You will become my prisoner but your men may go free. You owe it to them to save their lives.'

'What do you say to that, Heartbehrt?'

The big Mercian had joined him on the parapet and he grinned down at Eadwulf.

'Good morning, cousin. I wouldn't advise you to try and push that ram up this slope at the moment, or hadn't you realised that it's covered in ice?'

It was true. The evening before the defenders had poured water down the slope which had frozen overnight.

'Cousin? Do I know you?'

'I'm your Aunt Hereswith's son, Heartbehrt. I would have liked to get to know you but, alas, that's not to be. After all you'll be dead as soon as the true king, Osred, gets here with his army.'

'That's a lie! No one is going to follow a nine year old boy.'

'Yes, you're right. It was a lie. I have no desire to get to know a traitorous devil like you, cousin or not.'

Eadwulf was getting more and more angry. This was getting him nowhere. He knew that the other ealdormen were mustering in Osred's name at Catterick and would soon move against him. He had perhaps a week after his spies let him know that they were on the march, which wouldn't be long now. The only good news as far as Eadwulf was concerned was that those arriving at the muster had slowed to a trickle, according to his spy who had left there two days ago.

The day had started bitterly cold, but as it wore on, the weak sun slowly thawed the ice on the path and two hours after noon the ram recommenced its ponderous progress towards the gates.

'Where's the snow when you need it?' Heartbehrt complained.

'Still, when they eventually batter down the gates they'll be in for a nice surprise,' Swefred said with a grin.

'Of course, we could delay them even further.'

'How?'

'Open the gates and send the archers out for some target practice.'

Fifteen minutes later, whilst the ram was still some eighty yards from the gates, they swung open and a dozen archers and a few boys with slingshots darted through them. The Frisians pushing the ram were protected from above but exposed to the front and sides. The first volley of arrows and lead shot brought down five men at the front and another volley took out four more.

There had been thirty men pushing the ram and seeing what had happened to their comrades enraged them. Forgetting about the ram they charged towards their tormentors. The archers and slingers sent one more volley their way, bringing down seven more men, then they ran back through the gates. It was a close run thing but the gate slammed shut after the last man, just as the Frisians reached it.

Now they were exposed and spears and rocks rained down on them as the archers rushed up the steps to the parapet. Realising that it was futile to stay where they were, the Frisians retreated whilst arrows brought down a few more. All in all Eadwulf had lost nearly a tenth of his mercenaries for no gain. Even the ram which had taken so long to build was useless. When the men pushing it had abandoned it, it had rolled back down the slope, hit a rock and had toppled onto its side, splitting part of the frame. It would take several days to repair.

When Eadwulf launched his next assault with the ram he sent a screen of men with shields in front of it with his own bowmen backing them up. This time the ram reached the gates without the loss of more than a handful of his men.

The gates were stout but they weren't going to resist the battering they were getting for ever. The defenders did their best; hurling rocks and even jars of oil followed by flaming torches down onto it. The fire blazed brightly for a while but the hides had been soaked in water and little damage was done.

Finally the timbers bracing the gates in place gave in and the remnants of the gates collapsed. Yelling in triumph Eadwulf's warriors stormed through the entrance, clambering over the shattered timbers. Only when they were inside the fortress did the leading wave of men realise that they had walked into a trap.

Instead of seeing the interior of the fortress open and vulnerable, they gazed in amazement at yet another section of tall palisade. Even worse, this one had just one small postern gate in it. This was so small as to allow just one man at a time, stooping low, through it.

Swefred's archers and slingers launched a barrage of missiles at the men crowding into the small area between the outer palisade and the new one. At first those at the rear, eager to get into the place and start looting, raping and pillaging, didn't realise what the problem was and kept pushing at those already inside, frustrating their efforts to retreat.

Slowly the message got through that it was a trap and the attackers withdrew leaving behind them well over two hundred dead and badly wounded. Not all had been killed by the defenders; many had been crushed to death or trampled underfoot.

Morale in Eadwulf's camp was at a low ebb that evening. Those ealdormen who had voted for him had done so in the belief that he was a strong leader who was experienced in the art of war. Now his younger brother, who had only just completed his training as a warrior, was making a fool of him. To make matters worse, they knew that Osred's army could only be a few days' march away.

PART THREE – THE LAST OF THEIR HOUSE

Chapter Nineteen – The Boy King

705 AD

Behrtfrith was beginning to wonder whether he'd made the right choice in backing Eadwulf to succeed Aldfrith. His recent conversation with him had left him feeling frustrated and apprehensive.

'You need to forget about Bebbanburg, Cyning. It's virtually impregnable, you're bogged down here losing men to no good purpose and their morale is suffering. Meanwhile those who support Osred are gaining strength every day and when they get here they'll pin you against the fortress and destroy you.'

'Nonsense. My scouts keep me informed of their movements. They have only reached the crossing over the River Tyne, still at least a week away from here. Once I have captured Bebbanburg it is Osred and the Deirans who'll be trapped between my army and the fortress.'

'And how will you do that? You haven't managed to do it in three weeks. What makes you think one more week will make any difference?'

Eadwulf's eyes narrowed in anger.

'Don't argue with me! I'm your king. Besides, I know a secret way into the place.'

'Then why haven't you told me that before?'

'Because there are risks attached.'

'Where is this secret entrance?'

'Up the rubbish chute from the beach. The access inside the fortress is by the east wall and not far from the sea gate. If we can send in a small group of men at the dead of night, they should be able to capture the gate and open it to let us in.'

'It sounds risky to me. The sentries might see them on the beach or they might be intercepted before they manage to open the gates; and they'll get suspicious if they see men massing below the gates.'

'Which is why we need a dark night. There is a new moon tomorrow night and the recent fine weather is coming to an end. Cloud cover will make it too dark to see anything at any distance.'

'They'll still hear the assault force beyond the gates. However quiet you tell them to be a large group of men will be heard on a still night.'

'Which is why I'll use my Frisians as the first wave to hold the gate once it's been opened. They are the best trained warriors there are anywhere and they know how to make a stealthy attack.'

'You haven't heard then?'

'Heard what?'

'They've had enough. They have lost a quarter of their men and their captains blame you for that. It doesn't matter what you promise to pay them, they've had enough. They are leaving tomorrow.'

'What? They can't desert me now. How would they return to the Continent anyway?'

'They're not. The Picts you recruited are going with them; together they plan to depose Bridei and put their leader, Nectan, on the throne.'

'Nectan? He's plotting to become King of the Picts?'

'Yes, he's Bridei's younger brother. Didn't you know?'

'Beware of younger brothers,' he said with some fervour and spat onto the ground. 'They should be killed at birth.'

'A bit late for that.'

Behrtfrith watched Eadwulf carefully. He'd expected him to send for Nectan and the Frisian captains and offer them something that would persuade them to stay, but he just sat on his camp stool brooding. He left him to it and walked down towards the beach well out of arrow shot from the fortress.

After an hour he reached a decision and went to find the captain of his warband.

~~~

Shortly after dawn Swefred was making his usual rounds of the defences with Heartbehrt when one of his men came looking for him.

'Lord, something is happening in the enemy camp.'

Swefred ran to the watchtower and a minute later he looked down at his brother's camp and tried to make sense of what he saw. At first it looked as if many hundreds of the besieging army were going off to confront Osred's relieving force but, instead of heading to the south or west they headed north. Whichever way Osred's army came it wouldn't be from that direction.

There seemed to be some sort of quarrel going on in front of Eadwulf's tent. The man he thought might be his brother struck the man he was arguing with and swords were drawn. The dispute was getting ugly and Swefred began to laugh; something he hadn't done in earnest for some time. It looked as if his brother's army was falling apart.

Behrtfrith had been astounded when Eadwulf had struck him. He'd been half expecting a fierce reaction when he'd told the erstwhile king that his attempt to establish himself on the throne was over, but a verbal not a physical one.

'I advise you to take what few mercenaries are left to you and flee back to Frisia before it's too late; I'm heading south to make my peace with Osred, if I can.'

'Traitor!' Eadwulf yelled at him.

Behrtfrith was expecting a tirade of verbal abuse but what he hadn't anticipated was Eadwulf punching him in the face and then trying to draw his sword to kill him. Fortunately Eadwulf's own men held him back. Behrtfrith's gesith had drawn their swords when their ealdorman was struck but he managed to calm them down.

'You're a fool, Eadwulf. God alone knows why I thought you'd make a good king. You're nothing more than a spoilt brat who lashes out like a petulant child when he doesn't get his own way. Good luck when Osred gets here.'

After Behrtfrith had left, taking his three hundred men with him, Eadwulf had ignored the remaining ealdormen and withdrew into his tent, telling the sentries not to let anyone in.

It didn't take long for the other three Lothian ealdormen to decide to follow Behrtfrith's example but, instead of following him, they decided to head home and disband the fyrd, trusting

Behrtfrith to represent them. They reasoned that, had they also headed south, it might have looked as if they were intent on blocking Osred's advance.

When Eadwulf had calmed down he realised with dismay that he was now left with a five hundred men to confront probably around three thousand, and the loyalty of the remaining ealdormen was dubious to say the least. They had probably stayed because they didn't know what to do.

Later that day Swefred watched with glee as the last of the besiegers marched off to the west. Now only Eadwulf and his gesith were left and, being mercenaries, he doubted that they would be bound by their oath to defend their lord to their last breath in the same way as Anglo-Saxons would.

His suspicion was well founded and later that day the Frisians brought Eadwulf - king for less than two months – up to the main gates of Bebbanburg and left him there, bound hand and foot, before taking two of the birlinns anchored in Budle Bay and setting off back across the German Ocean to find new employment back on the Continent.

Swefred was left in something of a quandary. He knew that his brother would have killed him, probably slowly and painfully, had he managed to capture Bebbanburg, but Swefred had a deep belief in the ties and obligations of family. He couldn't just hand Eadwulf over to the Witan for trial and certain execution. When the riders he'd sent out as scouts returned to say that Osred's army was only two days away he knew that he had to make a decision, and make it quickly.

~~~

'You're a traitor, in league with your brother,' Osred accused Swefred when the Witan had gathered in the hall at Bebbanburg.

'Calm down Osred. If Swefred is at fault the Witan will determine that and decide what punishment, if any is due,' Edmond of Eoforwīc told him firmly.

Osred sat down beside his brothers, Otta and Osric, still fuming that Eadwulf had been allowed to escape. Otta had looked fearful when Osred had lost his temper; he knew only too well how dangerous he could be when in a rage. The five year old Osric just looked bemused and leaned against Otta's shoulder for comfort.

'We are here to decide first and foremost who should be elected king,' Bishop Eadfrith began. 'We can move onto the recent revolt and its consequences later.'

As the Witan was meeting in his diocese he had been chosen to chair the meeting. However, as he had also been involved in what had happened to Eadwulf, he was anxious that the Witan didn't focus on that first.

'The three sons of the late king are present and are eligible to be considered. Is there anyone else with a claim to the throne?'

Eyes swivelled to look at Swefred, Eochaid and Cenred, all of whom might have put themselves forward. Cenred looked as if he might be about to stand, but then subsided back onto the bench he was sitting on.

'Very well. I ask each of the three æthelings present to stand and present their case.'

Osred leaped to his feet and began speaking in an excited treble voice.

'My father was king and had three sons, of whom I am the eldest. Some have doubts that I can rule as I'm still young and not yet a warrior but my father trained me to succeed him and I am certain that I will make a good king. Neither of my brothers should be considered; they are even younger than me. I'm the obvious choice.'

The boy had spoken well, though no doubt he had been coached by Bishop Wilfred who had become his mentor in the past few weeks.

'Thank you Osred. Otta?'

'I have no wish to be king.'

'Osric?'

The boy just shook his head.

'Very well. It seems that we have no contest. Does anyone wish to say anything?'

Wilfrid rose to his feet with difficulty and cleared his throat.

'I am very pleased that the right person has been chosen to be king but, as he himself said, he is barely nine years old. He will therefore need guidance and advice until he's of an age when he can rule on his own. I propose that regents be appointed to assist him to rule until he is of age.'

Osred's eyes narrowed at this. He didn't believe that he needed help to rule and he suspected that what the bishop had said was disingenuous. The word regent meant someone who ruled on behalf of a king.

'That seems sensible, thank you Wilfrid,' Eadfrith said, smiling at the Abbot of Ripon. 'Who should form the regency? I suggest that it would give too much power to one man but too many regents would prove unwieldy.'

'Then I suggest two,' one of the ealdormen called out.

'Do we have any proposals?'

'Wilfrid is a scholar of some repute and a man wise in the ways of the world,' Edmond suggested.

'Good. Anyone else?'

'A churchman should be balanced by a warrior. One of the ealdormen should assist him.'

This time it was John of Beverley who had spoken.

'Who then?'

'Behrtfrith is our most experienced warrior,' one of the Lothian ealdormen tentatively suggested.

'Behrtfrith! But he was Eadwulf's most ardent supporter!' Eochaid exclaimed.

'I believe that the idea has some merit,' Edmond said quietly but was drowned out by the hubbub of those arguing for and against the idea amongst themselves.

Bishop Eadfrith looked on in dismay then called one of the sentries over. A moment later the rhythmic banging of swords against shields by the four sentries in the hall gradually restored order.

'Thank you. Unless we can behave properly and observe the rules of the Witan I shall have no option but to adjourn the meeting. Now, Edmond I believe you were saying something?'

'We were divided over the succession and that nearly led to civil war. Had it not been for Swefred's stout defence of Bebbanburg we might well have so weakened the kingdom that the Picts and the Mercians could have walked into Northumbria and we would have been unable to oppose them. What we need now is unity under King Osred's rule. To achieve that we must put the past behind us and move on. I say that there is merit in having a representative of each side as our two regents.'

At mention of Swefred's name Osred's grey eyes sought out the Ealdorman of Bebbanburg and glared at him. Evidently the former's loyal service counted as nothing in the new king's eyes because of what had befallen his brother.

After another hour's discussion Wilfrid and Behrtfrith were elected as regents until Osred turned sixteen. The Witan then moved onto the replacement of the late Bosa as Bishop of Eoforwīc. This time it was Osred who asserted his authority.

'My father had already chosen Bosa's successor before he died. Of course, Bosa outlived my father for a short time and so he wasn't able to implement his choice, but I do so now. The man chosen is John of Beverley; congratulations bishop.'

John bowed and smiled his thanks whilst Wilfrid fumed. The boy king had neatly outwitted him.

'And who should take Bishop John's place at Hexham, Cyning?' Eadfrith asked.

'I know that Wilfrid has long coveted the See of Eoforwīc. I believe that he should be compensated for losing that struggle by becoming both Bishop and Abbot of Hexham.'

Wilfrid was surprised initially but quickly thanked the king before anyone could object. At least he was a bishop in Northumbria if not Bishop of Northumbria; and he'd regained Hexham. It was only later that he realised how clever Osred had been. By rewarding Wilfrid he'd ensured the regent's loyalty and had consequently gained some power over him.

'Before we come to the customary swearing of fealty to the new king, there remains the matter of Eadwulf,' Eadfrith said a little hesitantly.

'Finally we come to it,' Osred broke in. 'I say that his brother Swefred is a traitor for letting him escape and should be punished accordingly.'

'I didn't let him escape, Cyning. He was my prisoner and I gave him a choice. Either he stood trial or he became a monk so that he could never again become a candidate for the crown. He chose the latter.'

'Knowing that he would have been found guilty by the Witan and executed had you not given him that choice,' Osred said heatedly. 'You usurped my prerogative to deal with him and by so doing you are as much a traitor as he is.'

'I think you are forgetting, Osred, who saved your throne. You should be congratulating Swefred, not chastising him.' Eochaid said firmly.

'You will address me as Cyning,' Osred almost screamed.

Several of the ealdormen looked at each other in alarm at this display of rage and some wondered whether they had made a mistake in choosing Osred as king.'

'My apologies Cyning,' Eochaid said smoothly. 'Nevertheless, the fact remains that you owe your throne to the man who you now name as a traitor.'

'Be careful or you will lose your shire too, Eochaid.'

Swefred stiffened at the use of the word *too*. It implied that he was about to lose Bebbanburg.

'Cyning, I see little purpose in pursuing this further. You, and the kingdom as a whole, owe a great debt to Ealdorman Swefred for almost singlehandedly defeating the usurper Eadwulf. He is now a monk and, as I understand it, is currently on his way to Iona exiled from Northumbria forever,' Wilfrid said calmly. 'He can no longer challenge you for the throne and this solution enables us to unite your kingdom under your rule.

'Had you been forced to execute him there would have been those who would have blamed you for his death and perhaps you would have stored up trouble for the future. This solution is the one I would have recommended in any case.'

'Well, it's not one I would have accepted. Be very careful bishop. You owe me for Hexham. I can easily undo what I have done.'

'I think not, Osred. You are still a child and you have the status of king but not the power.'

The man who had spoken was the Ealdorman of Luncæster, the one noble who had not taken part in the recent campaign on either side.

Osred glared at him with his piercing grey eyes.

'Perhaps not yet, but I will have that power in a few short years and then I shall be able to right the slights and insults I'm suffering now.'

'If you live that long,' the ealdorman replied impassively. 'Given the way you're behaving now, I wouldn't put money on it. Kings need the loyalty and support of their nobles, however old they are. A throne is never a secure seat. Try and remember that.'

'Are you threatening me?' Osred almost squeaked.

'No, merely pointing out the harsh realities of life, Cyning.'

Eadfrith let the uneasy silence last for a few moments and was about to dismiss the Witan when he realised that the nobles still had to swear fealty to Osred. At first the ceremony went smoothly but when Swefred knelt to give his oath and raised his hands to clasp those of the king, Osred whipped his hands away.

'I don't accept your oath and as far as I'm concerned you are no longer welcome in my presence.'

'Very well, Cyning. Nevertheless I swear to be your loyal servant and to exercise my duties as the Ealdorman of the Shire of Bebbanburg to the best of my abilities and in your best interests.'

Osred also refused to accept the oath of the Ealdorman of Luncæster. However, he reacted differently.

'Then you are a fool as well as a spoilt little brat, Osred. If you won't accept my oath, I'm sure that Coenred of Mercia will be only too happy to.'

'Stop, this is madness,' Behrtfrith broke in. 'As regent I won't allow your stupidity to cost Northumbria one of its largest shires. The loss of Luncæstershire would make Deira and Elmet almost impossible to defend. Hold out your hands Osred of I'll do so by force. Good, now give your oath.'

'You'll regret this, Behrtfrith,' the boy hissed after the oath had been given.

'I'm already regretting it, Cyning,' the man replied.

But it wasn't forcing Osred to accept the oath that he was regretting. It was deserting Eadwulf for this brat.

Chapter Twenty – Border Warfare

712 AD

When Wilfrid died at Ripon in 710 Osred still had a few months to go before his fourteenth birthday. However, the bishop had ceased to be an effective regent some two years previously after he suffered another seizure. When he recovered he retired to Ripon and never left again before his death. His death left Behrtfrith as the only regent so he called another meeting of the Witan, this time at Ripon following Wilfrid's rather lavish funeral.

The latter had expressed a desire just before his death for his chaplain, Acca, to take his place as Bishop and Abbot at Hexham. As the man had effectively been running the diocese and looking after the two abbeys during the last two years of Wilfrid's life, it seemed a logical choice and the Witan approved his appointment on behalf of the king, who seemingly lacked any interest in the matter.

However, that still left the matter of the regency. Behrtfrith had become increasingly powerful during the latter stages of Wilfrid's life and the other nobles were anxious to find someone who could stand up to him. The Deiran ealdormen would have liked to nominate one of their number but no-one was willing to take on the responsibility, or else they were considered too weak to be able to cope with both the headstrong and unpredictable king and the equally difficult Ealdorman of Dùn Barra.

Their eventual choice was Ælfflæd, Abbess of Whitby. She was the sister of King Oswiu and thus Osred's aunt. Ælfflæd was a devout Christian and blessed with sound common sense; two qualities that could never be attributed to her nephew.

As Osred grew up he became more stubborn and, lacking the ability to get his own way as a ruler, he started to behave badly. At first this amounted to a lack of courtesy towards his nobles and cruelty to his servants. When he reached puberty at around the time that Wilfrid died his interests became sexual. No girl was safe from his predatory desires. Matters came to a head when he visited his aunt at Whitby.

He was particularly taken with a young novice who was a year older than he was. Despite Ælfflæd's warning that her nuns were sacrosanct, Osred made his way to the nun's hall when they had settled down to sleep after Matins. He quietly searched until he found the girl asleep on a simple platform with the other novices. Putting his hand over her mouth he pricked her neck with a dagger and whispered in her ear that she would come to no harm if she came with him quietly.

He led her by one hand and held the dagger with the other until they reached his room in the guest hall. There he gagged her, ripped off her habit and raped her three times before he let her go.

The poor girl was too frightened to tell anyone what had happened but six months later it was all too evident that she was pregnant. When she was sent to see the abbess she knew what would happen, but she was still too afraid to say that the king had raped her.

'You cannot remain here, of course,' Ælfflæd told her, 'but I would like to know how you got in this condition. Was it one of the monks, or perhaps one of the boys being educated here?'

The girl shook her head but said nothing.

'If not one of them, then it must have been a visitor.'

Ælfflæd noted the alarm on the girl's face and, thinking back to her guests at that time, she suspected she knew who the culprit was.

'I suppose it was Osred?'

The look she received in return confirmed her suspicions. She sighed. Her nephew was getting a reputation as a letch and a rapist but this was the first time, to her knowledge, that he had abused a nun to satisfy his desires.

'Did you go to his bed willingly or did he force you?'

'He put a knife to my neck and threatened to kill me,' she stammered, weeping.

'Pull yourself together. It wasn't your fault. My nephew will have to learn that he can't get away with this sort of behaviour.'

When the girl continued to sob the abbess invited her to sit down.

'As you are the innocent party in all this, I'm going to make an exception in your case. I'm going to send you away to have the baby. Afterwards you can continue your training at the monastery at Coldingham.'

'What will happen to the baby,' the girl asked tentatively.

'I'll arrange for him or her to be brought up at the place I'm sending you to.'

'Where's that?'

'Bebbanburg.'

~~~

Swefred read the letter from Ælfflæd with a grim smile. He had stayed well clear of any contact with Osred since the Witan in 705, only attending further meetings of it when he had to, and then staying in the background and not drawing attention to himself.

However, rumours about the king's dissolute behaviour were rife throughout Northumbria. Hearing that he had managed to get a novice nun pregnant came as no surprise to him. That evening he told his wife about the letter and the request that they house the girl until her baby was born.

He had married Kendra, the daughter of Behrtfrith, the previous year. It was far from the love match that his father and grandfather had enjoyed; it was a marriage of convenience. Knowing how much Osred hated him Swefred was apprehensive about the day that the king came of age. He had therefore deliberately sought out allies and Behrtfrith, being the most powerful noble in Bernicia, was an obvious man to cultivate.

The girl had been fourteen when they wed, eight years his junior. However, she looked like her father and he was one of the ugliest men Swefred knew. Nevertheless, he found that they had much in common and the marriage had been a success. Now she was expecting their first baby.

'What do you think, Kendra?'

There was little romance in their lives and neither used words of endearment when talking to the other. Indeed the mere fact that his wife was pregnant came as something of a surprise to both of them, given how few times they had actually made love.

'The abbess is one of the regents so it would be difficult to refuse her request, I suppose. In any case the child can be brought up as our son's companion, if it's a boy that is.'

'And if the nun's baby is male too.'

'Yes, of course. But I have a feeling about this. I think it was meant to be. Of course, if I'm wrong and the two are of different sexes, then her baby can go to either Lindisfarne or Coldingham and be dedicated to the service of Christ.'

And so the matter was settled. Kendra's baby was born first – a boy they named Ulfric and a month later another boy was born. The mother was sent to Coldingham as soon as she was fit to travel and her son – who they named Æthelwald - was brought up with Ulfric.

'You do realise that, as the king's bastard, he's really an ætheling,' Kendra said to her husband one night.

'I suppose so, after all his grandfather was illegitimate. However, no one must know. Not only would it embarrass Abbess Ælfflæd but it might put his life in danger.'

'It would embarrass Osred more.'

Swefred snorted. 'Nothing would embarrass that reprobate.'

'He's deeply unpopular you know.'

'I'm not surprised. It will be interesting to see what happens when he gets to rule on his own.'

That day was meant to be in December that year but the Witan, most of whose members dreaded the day that Osred was given power over them, decided to accept the recommendation of the two regents that the king should have to wait another two years, until he was eighteen. It didn't come as a shock to the youth. His aunt had already berated him for raping her novice and warned him that he had to prove himself fit to be king before she and Behrtfrith would hand over power to him. However, her warning didn't alter his behaviour, it just made him even more frustrated.

~~~

In August 712, just after the birth of Æthelwald and the departure of his mother to Coldingham, Behrtfrith called for a muster of the Lothian and Bernician ealdormen and their forces to repel yet another incursion by the Picts over the River Forth. This time they had come in some strength and shortly afterwards it seemed that the Britons of Strathclyde had also invaded Cumbria. It looked like a concerted effort to move the border south. Behrtfrith extended the call to arms to the rest of Northumbria and moved the muster point to Bebbanburg.

'Do we know what their strength is?' Swefred asked the regent as soon as he arrived.

'Reports are vague and contradictory but they seem to be moving in three columns, each consisting of roughly two thousand warriors.'

'Isn't that rather stupid of them? We can defeat each in turn.'

'That's probably true, but they are moving quickly and we'll be pressed to assemble enough men and tackle each of them before they've made serious inroads into Lothian. The other problem is the harvest. The men who make up the fyrd are mostly farmers and those whose homes are threatened will be loath to leave their fields until the crops are in.'

'They will have to be told to leave it to the women, children and their bondsmen then. We are going to need every man we've got to send this lot back where they came from. Oh, and another thing, Behrtfrith. We need to trap them here and kill them on our land. We've learned the folly of chasing them back into Caledonia twice now.'

'You don't need to lecture me on that point, Swefred,' he replied with some vehemence. 'You may have lost a father but I lost a brother at Stirling Bridge and my father at Dùn Nectain.'

'Yes, I'm sorry. Just so we are clear that we need to do as much damage as possible to the invaders whilst they are on this side of the Forth.'

'I agree.'

Behrtfrith relaxed slightly before continuing.

'The question is, how do we prevent them from fleeing back to safety?'

'By getting behind them so that we attack each column from the north?' suggested Swefred.

A grin slowly spread over the other man's face.

'Brilliant! It won't be easy to get behind them but cutting of their retreat will panic them too.'

~~~

Eochaid said farewell to Heartbehrt with a heavy heart. They had become close friends in the time he'd been the former's captain and Eochaid had come to depend on him. However, with the death of Coelred, Æthelbald had been elected as King of Mercia and his younger brother had been summoned home to become King of Man.

Fortunately the summons to the muster at Bebbanburg had come the day before he left and he'd promised Eochaid that he would raid Strathclyde in force as soon as he was able to.

'That should sent Beli scuttling back home,' he'd said with a grin.

'Won't you have to get Æthelbald's permission?'

'Why? What will he do? Try to unseat me? Don't forget the Mercian Witan could just as easily have chosen me or Thringfrith to be king. He's not a direct descendent of Penda; we're the grandsons of his brother Eowa who is still regarded as a traitor by many Mercians. No, he won't feel secure on his throne yet awhile and I suspect that he'll be anxious to mend his fences with me.'

The news that he could expect raids to commence on the west coast of Strathclyde in a few weeks' time came as something of a relief to Behrtfrith. He'd managed to assemble four thousand men at Bebbanburg, a thousand trained warriors and the rest from the fryd, and another four hundred from Luncæstershire had gone directly to the aid of Cumbria.

'With any luck Beli will turn tail and head back to Strathclyde once the Manxmen start their raids. The men of Luncæstershire and Cumbria will harry them all the way with the aim of weakening them so much that they will be concerned about further raids and possible attacks from Dalriada to consider bothering us again,' he told his commanders once they were all assembled in Swefred's hall.

Osred sat beside Behrtfrith, who had been appointed as the Hereræswa of Northumbria by the Witan. The king had refused to acknowledge Swefred when he'd arrived and had only nodded a greeting to Kendra when Behrtfrith had whispered in his ear that he would take it amiss if he snubbed his daughter.

'The northern column is presently moving along the coast towards Dùn Èideann,' he said pointing at a rough layout that his chief scout had sketched in charcoal on the wooden floor in front of the king.

'It's not clear whether they intend to try and capture the fortress or bypass it and continue towards my own stronghold at Dùn Barra. Either way we need to trap them between our army and the coast. The other column of Picts was last reported in the hills to the south of Dùn Èideann and I can only presume that they are headed for the valley of the River Twaid. Some of Swefred's mounted warband are shadowing them so we'll know more in due course. At any event I suggest that we forget about them for now.'

'How will you trap the Picts in the north?' Eochaid asked.

'By blocking the road along the coast with half our force and then bringing the other half up behind them to prevent them retreating. My aim is to annihilate them, just as they did with Ecgfrith's army twenty seven years ago.'

'Who will command which force?'

'I will command the blocking force with the king. Swefred will command the army which will attack them from the west.'

At the mention of Swefred's name the king rose to his feet; his face dark with anger.

'No, I forbid it! That traitor let his brother escape on the pretext that he would become a monk. Well, he's betrayed you all. Eadwulf didn't stay a monk for long did he? Now he has a son who could challenge me for the throne. The whole family should be executed!'

'Including my daughter and grandson, Cyning?' Behrtfrith asked coldly.

'You should never have allowed her to marry a man I intend to arrest as soon as I'm allowed to rule as a king should.'

A deathly hush descended on the hall as the two stared at one another, the elder calm but coldly furious, the younger beside himself anger.

'I suggest that we need to consider what's in the best interests of the kingdom,' Eochaid said quietly. 'I agree that Swefred is the most able military commander, after our hereræswa, that is,' he added hastily, 'and it is logical for him to command the other army, especially as it has such a difficult mission. He will have to get behind the enemy's line of advance without being detected and then appear at exactly the right moment. It's not a task I'd want.'

There was a general murmur of agreement with the last point.

'Cyning, your obvious hatred of Ealdorman Swefred is unwarranted. It was he who captured this very stronghold in order to deny it to Eadwulf and he was the person who defeated him with a mere handful of men and caused his army to disperse. With all due respect, that is not the action of a traitor.'

'But he allowed him to escape and to breed to produce more pretenders to my throne!'

'They are not a threat to you, Cyning; no more than Eochaid, Swefred or their sons are. You are born of the House of Æthelfrith, the first King of Northumbria. They are not his descendants.'

Everyone turned to look at the man who'd spoken.

'Bishop Eadfrith, I'd not realised that you were present at this war council,'

'I'm here, Cyning, because I and some of my priests and monks intend to travel with the army to give you our blessing and the Holy Sacrament, especially just before you fight.'

'I'm sure that will give our men heart, bishop, thank you,' Behrtfrith said quickly, before the king could make some snide comment.

If Osred wasn't an atheist, he was something very close to it, and made no effort to hide the fact that he thought that the clergy were deluded fools.

Later that evening Behrtfrith sought Swefred out and took him outside where they could talk privately.

'That idiot will become our ruler in two and a half years' time and there is nothing we can do to delay it further. We were lucky the Witan didn't decide to allow him to rule from this coming December when he turns sixteen.'

'I'm even more concerned than you are, but there is nothing we can do about it.'

'Isn't there? Of course, one or more of us may die in battle this year, but assuming we all survive, we need to start planning for the day he's let loose.'

'What do you have in mind?'

'I don't know yet. Of course, there are some kings like Ethelred who were persuaded to abdicate and become monks.'

'That didn't seem to work too well with my brother.'

'No, but he can never claim the throne again after breaking his vows as a monk.'

Eadwulf had left Iona a year after arriving there and had married the daughter of some minor kinglet in Hibernia. He was now serving the High King as captain of his bodyguard. Swefred had heard that he had a daughter and a son called Earnwine but that was two years ago and he'd heard nothing since.

'I can't see Osred as a monk somehow.'

Both men looked at each other and burst out laughing at the thought. After that they became downcast again.

'It seems that there is only one solution.'

'I fear so.'

Both knew that they were talking about assassination.

'Well there's time enough yet, let's see how things develop,' Swefred said as they parted.

~~~

As he led his small army through the series of hills that ran fifteen miles or so inland from the coast of the Firth of Forth, Swefred was only too well aware that they were a mere ten miles from the valley of the Twaid where the second half of the Pictish army were reportedly pillaging their way eastwards.

When his scouts came to report that the second army of Picts were now well to the south east of them he breathed a sigh of relief. By now he calculated that he must be near the point where he had to turn and head north. If he'd judged it correctly, it would bring him and his men out fifteen miles to the west of Dùn Èideann and at least five miles behind the Picts.

Behrtfrith had told him that he planned to be in position to the south of the stronghold and the settlement that surrounded it on the sixth of September. As it was now the fifth Swefred believed that he had judged it perfectly, but he couldn't be certain until he made contact with the rear of the enemy army. He and his men marched along the coast for another three miles before camping for the night.

Apart from several showers of rain and leaden skies which threatened more, the weather had been typical for late summer. They had passed burned out farmsteads and settlements as they moved eastwards, which angered the men and made them eager to get at their foes. Detachments stayed to bury the dead and then raced to catch up with the main body. By the time they set up camp revenge was the only thing on everyone's mind.

Swefred gathered everyone around him and he stood on one of the baggage carts so everyone could see him. Of course, not everyone one could hear him - there were too many for that – but those who could relayed his message to those who couldn't.

'Vengeance is a meal best served cold,' he began. 'I know that you are thirsting to get at the men who have slain our women, children, old men and bondsmen and ravaged the countryside many of you call home. However, tomorrow we must set about our work with cold determination, discipline and purpose. It's no good rushing at the bastards piecemeal, eager to kill as many of them as you can. Too many will slip through our fingers that way. We need to be methodical and stay in formation. We have them in a trap. Don't let any escape. Be a ring of steel around them and tighten the noose until they are all dead.'

The cheering that greeted his little homily was so loud that Swefred feared the enemy might hear it. Of course, they were still probably five or six miles away – two or three hours march on the morrow. Allowing for moving into formation, he considered that they should be in position by a little before noon if they left at dawn. Noon was when Behrtfrith had asked him to attack the Picts' rear.

Swefred rode forward with the captain of his gesith, a man called Uurad, the same name that his father had borne. The fact that he was half-Pict and he was about to slay a lot of his father's people didn't seem to bother him particularly. He'd served Osfrid before he'd joined Swefred; that was after Eadwulf had kicked him and his fellow warriors out of Bebbanburg. He was totally loyal to Swefred, as were all his gesith. He was the sort of leader who men followed because they wanted to do so above all else; not just because he paid, fed and clothed them.

As they cautiously crested a low ridge nine miles from Dùn Èideann they saw a large encampment about a mile ahead of them. They quickly withdrew and Swefred and Uurad crept forward on their bellies until they were partly hidden by a bush on the skyline. The Picts were busy getting ready to move out, men were forming up, tents were being packed onto carts and a forage party headed out to the south.

It was a fine day, but chilly – the sort of day where the air was clear and you could see a long way. Swefred could just make out the stronghold of Dùn Èideann on top of its rock some seven miles away. Suddenly he spotted movement between the Dùn and the encampment. Several riders were approaching from the east at a gallop. Almost certainly they had come to report that they had found their way blocked by Behrtfrith's army.

Swefred had almost expected the Picts to race off to engage the Northumbrians but evidently their leader had more control over his men than some of his predecessors. The work of striking camp continued whilst a party of some forty horsemen, some mounted on ponies but many on steeds similar to the one he was riding rode off to investigate. He assumed that it was their leader, his nobles and his bodyguard.

He wondered idly whether the man in charge might be King Nechtan himself. He hoped so. His death should restore peace to the border for some time to come. He'd seen enough and he and Uurad slithered back down to where the rest were waiting.

~~~

Behrtfrith sat beside King Osred to the rear of their army. He had similar numbers to the Picts but he'd drawn them up in a formation designed to inflict maximum casualties on them. The archers and boys with slings were in front, ready to withdraw through the spearmen behind them as soon as the Picts got close. Then came the warriors from the various warbands together with the ealdormen and the thegns. They formed the front rank some six hundred strong.

Behind them stood fifteen hundred members of the fyrd in three ranks. Their job was to push at the backs of the warriors

411

and prevent them from being forced backwards. If a warrior fell, then one of the fyrd from the second rank would take his place. Like the warriors they were equipped with spear and shield but not all had the helmet, sword or seax possessed by the warriors. None had the protection of a byrnie or a thick leather jerkin like those in the front rank.

The formation was bowed like a shallow bowl. The numbers of the fyrd in the centre were denser than on the flanks so as to prevent the centre of the bowl from giving way. As the battle progressed and more and more Picts became engaged, the flanks would move forwards and inwards to confine the Picts and eventually encircle them on three sides. It was a formation called the bull's horns which Aldfrith had read of and told Behrtfrith about; but he'd never seen it used and he didn't know how well it would work.

At first all went as planned. The Picts charged en masse and the first few rows were killed or wounded by the archers and slingers before they retreated through the shield wall. The furious onslaught by the Picts drove the centre in and, instead of closing the horns, the ring of steel was in danger of breaking asunder.

Seeing this Behrtfrith dismounted and, followed by his gesith, he forced his way through the fyrd until he reached the front rank in the centre, or what was left of it. At that moment a man in the front rank was killed by an axe-wielding Pict. Before the man could pull the axe clear of the corpse Behrtfrith thrust his sword into the belly of the axeman and, pulling it out, he barged the Pict behind him out of the way with his shield and cut the man next to him down.

He had created a momentary breach in the enemy line and, followed closely by his gesith, they started to widen it, cutting and hacking furiously until they had cleared an area around them. Now the Northumbrian centre advanced until their line was restored. The wings of the horn also pushed forward, cramming the Picts into a smaller and smaller area.

It was at that moment that disaster struck. One of Picts, a boy of twelve, had crawled forward with the broken half of a spear he'd picked up until he was in front of Behrtfrith, who was fighting off two men with his sword and shield. The boy looked up and saw the ealdorman in his byrnie nearly on top of him. He edged forward another foot just as one of Behrtfrith's assailants fell dead on top of him. Nevertheless the boy had an arm free and he stabbed upwards under the hem of the byrnie and into the Northumbrian's groin.

The wound wasn't immediately fatal itself, but Behrtfrith dropped his guard in reaction to the sudden agonising pain and a Pict managed to grab the rim of his shield, pulling it downwards. Another man saw the opening and thrust his spear through it and into Behrtfrith's neck. He dropped to his knees, his sword and his shield dropping from his hands, and a Pict with an axe swung it, taking his head clean off.

His gesith fought on but the heart had gone out of them and word of the hereræswa's death swept through the Northumbrian ranks. Once more the Picts pushed hard to break through the shield wall and all might have been lost if it wasn't for the king.

Osred had watched the progress of the battle closely from his horse and when he saw the centre of the line buckling for the second time, he rode his horse through the ranks, pushing men aside, until he reached the front. Stabbing down with his spear he skewered three men before his horse was killed by a spear thrust into its chest.

The king leaped clear as it collapsed under him and landed on the spearman who'd slain his horse. With a cry of rage he hacked at the man's neck with his seax and then, pulling his sword from its scabbard, he started to lay about him like a man possessed. The Picts drew back out of range of his flashing blades and he pressed home his advantage, his men following him with cries of Osred, Osred. The enemy centre broke and started to pull back.

It was at that moment that Swefred joined the fray. His men had charged through the Picts' baggage train, setting fire to it as they went, and continued into the rear ranks of the Picts. Right at the rear were the horsemen. They tried to escape but they were quickly surrounded, pulled from their mounts and killed.

The Picts now started to panic. They were leaderless and surrounded. Swefred halted his men and re-formed them, warriors in the shield wall and the fyrd behind. Slowly they advanced driving the Picts before them. It wasn't much of a fight. The ones at the back were always the least experienced, the cowards and those who were wounded but who could still fight. They were no match for Swefred's warriors. Slowly the net around the Picts tightened as more and more fell.

The Northumbrians didn't escape unharmed. They had lost a couple of hundred in the first part of the battle and they continued to suffer casualties, but they were in the tens, not the hundreds. Finally the encircled Picts had had enough and they surrendered.

Swefred called for his men to stop the slaughter but Osred wasn't finished.

'No quarter, no quarter,' he yelled as he continued to hack and thrust at the Picts before him.

At first his men did as he told them but then more and more were sickened by the unnecessary killing and they gradually stopped. Eventually even Osred ended his onslaught, too exhausted to continue.

When they counted the bodies the next day the Northumbrians had lost just over three hundred dead and those likely to die of their wounds, but there were fifteen hundred dead Picts. There were no wounded; the king had ordered them killed where they lay. A couple of hundred had escaped and there were three hundred prisoners who would be sent to the slave markets.

Behrtfrith had achieved his aim of destroying the invaders; it was just a pity he didn't live to see the scale of his victory.

~~~

'You played your part well, Swefred,' Osred told him, somewhat grudgingly, the next day when he called his commanders together to plan his strategy for dealing with the second column. 'It's just a pity that you allowed Nectan to escape.'

Swefred shook his head. 'He wasn't the commander of this column, Cyning. We killed all the leaders; not one escaped. The man in charge was the Mormaer of Angus. He died together with two more mormaers. King Nectan must be with the other column.'

'Are you contradicting me, Swefred?'

'No, just telling you the facts.'

'And I'm telling you that you failed to capture Nectan and for that you must be punished.'

'Just a moment, Osred. You do not have the power to punish anyone; least of all Swefred who carried out a difficult mission with great success yesterday. As he says, there is no evidence that Nectan was with this column.' Eochaid was incensed at the injustice of what Osred had just said.

'Don't argue with me, Eochaid, or you too will be dealt with. In case it's escaped your notice, one of my regents is dead and my aunt is ill and in no position to rule. I'm taking full control of my kingdom.'

'That is not what the Witan decided,' Edmund of Eoforwīc stated firmly. 'You are still fifteen and you are not to rule without regents until you're eighteen. The Witan will just have to appoint new regents.'

'He is quite correct, Cyning,' Bishop Eadfrith said with a certain amount of glee.

He detested Osred as an apostate and a rapist of nuns.

'Who won the battle yesterday? You'd probably all be dead of it wasn't for me. I will rule and you will all obey me or I'll find ealdormen and bishops who will.'

'We all owe you a great debt of gratitude for your valour yesterday, Cyning. Perhaps I can suggest a compromise? That you come into your kingdom this December when you are sixteen.'

The speaker was the Ealdorman of Catterick, one of Osred's few close friends. To the disgust of Swefred, Eochaid and a few others, the rest supported the compromise and Osred reluctantly accepted it.

As Swefred later told his wife, 'it seems that your father was wrong; we don't have two and half years to prepare for hell; just three short months.'

Chapter Twenty One – Swefred the Heræswa

712 AD

With one Pictish army dealt with, the Northumbrians turned their attention to the one in the south making for the River Twaid. Osred tried to take command of the army but he was voted down and, much to his anger, Swefred was elected as the new heræswa. He immediately sent out scouts to locate the Picts and, in the meantime, moved the army to Penecuik.

When he received news that the Picts were in the range of hills known as the Monadh Pentland and heading south east towards the junction between the Twaid and a small river called Leither Water he called a war council and outlined his plan for dealing with them.

The Northumbrians outnumbered their enemy by almost two to one and presumably they were not yet aware of the fate that had overtaken their fellow Picts. Only Osred spoke against the plan, but he was ignored, which only increased his resentment.

Swefred needed a Pict from among the captives to unwittingly decieve the enemy leader. His would be a vital role in his plan and he needed to be young enough to be gullible, but old enough to be credible. In the end he chose a thirteen year old boy who was the son of a minor chieftain.

The boy was hauled into Swefred's presence and told that he was to be the heræswa's new body slave. Swefred didn't speak his language but Uurad, who acted as interpreter, had been brought up bilingual by his parents. As might have been expected, the boy spat at Swefred and declared defiantly that he'd rather die. He was punched in the head for his insolence and then taken outside and shown a noose hanging from a tree. When it was put around his neck he quickly changed his mind.

The main problem was that, as the boy didn't speak English, he couldn't very well overhear the misinformation that Swefred wanted passed on to Nectan. He got around that by using a warrior in one of the Lothian warbands who also spoke the language. He was told to pretend to be a renegade Pict who was helping the Northumbrians and he fulfilled the role admirably.

The boy was allowed to overhear the three men talking with Uurad translating for the supposed benefit of the pretend Pict. Later that night the man who had acted as a Pict came and took the boy into the woods where a horse waited.

'Ride and tell King Nectan what the Northumbrian turds intend. They would know I'd betrayed them if I disappeared, but hopefully they'll think that you just ran away. You'll find our army camped at the old hill fort at Dunslair. Follow the direction the sun rises until you come across a small river then follow it south for about twelve miles until you see the old fort on the east bank. Clear? Good. Now get going.'

~~~

Swefred sat on his horse beside Uurad as they watched the retreating Pictish army below them as it snaked along the valley floor. The day had started overcast and had deteriorated. Now

419

it was drizzling and if the rain got much heavier it would be difficult to make out the enemy at this distance. Not that it mattered.

Swefred's whole objective had been to get the Picts to leave the hill fort. Like many similar constructions of the Britons who'd inhabited the region before the coming of the Romans, the defences consisted of a series of concentric ditches and earthen ramparts culminating is a palisade which ran all the way around the top of the hill. If the Northumbrians had been forced to assault it they would undoubtedly have won, given their superior numbers, but at some cost. This way Swefred hoped that he could keep casualties to a minimum.

Osred had peevishly refused to accompany an army commanded by Swefred and had ridden back to Eoforwīc with his gesith and a few companions, including the Ealdorman of Catterick. The latter's departure had robbed the army of forty warriors and two hundred and fifty member of the fyrd but Swefred reckoned that was a price worth paying to rid himself of the malevolent stares the king kept giving him.

He left behind a niggling worry in the back of Swefred's mind about the future, though. It was only three months before Osred would be old enough to rule on his own and he knew it would soon pass. Then the king would be free to take his revenge on Swefred and his family. He had to do something before that happened but, rack his brains as he might, he couldn't come up with any ideas except flight into exile. He banished such thoughts and tried to concentrate on the immediate problem.

The river valley the Picts were following would take them to an area known as Auchencorth Moss, a boggy area which they would have to skirt. If, as he hoped, they skirted it to the north, they would have to cross two minor tributaries before coming to the river known as the North Esk. That was where he planned to bring them to battle. Unfortunately, this time his plans went wrong.

The first he knew that the enemy had done the unexpected was when his scouts came in to report that the Picts had opted for the southern route around Auchencorth Moss. Not only had Swefred been outwitted, his army was on the wrong side of the North Esk now. By the time that they had crossed the river and headed up into the high hills to the south west of Dùn Èideann they would be at least half a day's march behind the Picts. He had to think of some way to delay them.

Numerous streams and small rivers ran down the steep sided valleys in the Monadh Pentland. The enemy's line of retreat lay over two high ridges and, from what the Ealdorman of Dùn Èideann had told him, the enemy were likely to head across the open moorland before crossing one ridge and then the other, higher one that lay two miles apart. They could then descend onto the broad coastal plain and choose any of a number of routes back to Stirling.

Unwillingly the ealdormen agreed to send the mounted warriors in their gesiths and warbands with Eochaid. That would give him some one hundred and eighty men with which to hold the further pass. It was a tall order as the col between the hills was a mile wide. As they were about to set off Behrtfrith's son, Beorhtmund, made a sensible suggestion.

Although he was only fourteen, he had been allowed to succeed as Ealdorman of Dùn Barra without opposition. Kendra's brother was as unlike his father as it was possible to be. He was quiet, thoughtful and diffident. He was also a lot better looking; something which didn't endear him to his ugly sister.

Now he hesitantly approached Swefred and asked if he could speak to him.

'Of course, Beorhtmund, you don't have to ask permission. You are an ealdorman as well as my brother through marriage,' Swefred replied with a smile to put the boy at ease.

'Well, why don't you get archers to ride double with the warriors? I know it will slow them down but they'll still be able to move twice as fast as the Picts on foot. That way we'd have a much better chance of delaying the Picts until our army can come up behind them.'

His voice trailed away.

'I'm sorry if it's a stupid idea...'

'No, it's a brilliant idea! Well done. Would you like to go with them in charge of the archers?'

'May I?'

The boy beamed at him, his grey eyes shining with pleasure. Swefred had been Behrtfrith's ally but the older man had been the dominant one in their relationship. He had a feeling that he had made a friend for life of his son and this time it would be Swefred who led. That could be useful when the inevitable clash with Osred came.

~~~

Nectan cursed the day that he'd decided to try and move his border south to the Twaid. He'd convinced himself that a boy king on the throne of Northumbria made the kingdom weak, especially one as dissolute and unpopular as Osred. Now he was the one whose throne was under threat. He lost three of his mormaers when the first column was annihilated and now he had a feeling that the two accompanying him were plotting his removal one way or the other. Fortunately he ruled the most powerful of the sub-kingdoms and he was fairly certain he could recover from the fiasco, provided that he could extricate the rest of his army safely.

At first he had believed the boy who'd escaped from the Northumbrians. In any case he didn't want to be trapped in a hill fort with dwindling supplies. However, when his scouts reported his foes waiting for him across the North Esk, he became suspicious.

He hung the boy over a fire so that his feet slowly cooked. The pain was unbearable but the lad had told the truth. Torture didn't elicit any more information from him than he'd already divulged on arrival at the hill fort. Nectan eventually tired of his screams and thrust a spear through his heart. He was cut down and his body was left to burn as a warning to others. If his mormaers had been plotting against him, the fate of an innocent boy convinced them to tread extremely carefully. Nectan was safe for now.

'Brenin, the Northumbrians are holding the pass head of us,' the scouts reported as Nectan crested the first of the two cols.

'In what strength?'

'We could only see a couple of hundred but many more could be waiting on the reverse slope.'

Nectan cursed. How had they got ahead of him? Unless the men waiting at the crossing over the North Esk had been a ruse to make him take the southern route.

'Ride around to the south and see how many are waiting there.'

'Is that wise, Brenin?' one of the mormaers asked. 'If they are merely a deception to delay us you are giving their main force time to catch us up.'

'Do you think I'm a fool? Do you not think that I don't know that? Unless you have something useful to say, shut up.'

When he saw the scouts looking at him, their mouths agape at hearing one of the mormaers scolded, he turned his anger on them.

'What in the name of Hell are you still doing here? Go! I want you back within the hour.'

Eochaid wasn't an apprentice in the art of war. It had occurred to him that Nectan might send out scouts to determine his strength before they attacked. However, he had expected them to climb to the top of the hill to the south of the pass to see how many men he had in the dead ground behind the col. He had therefore sent half a dozen mounted warriors and the same number of archers to secure the peak. He had placed them under Beorhtmund's command in the mistaken belief that this would keep the boy out of harm's way. He was under no illusion that he and his two hundred odd men would survive defending the pass against a couple of thousand Picts.

When Beorhtmund saw the fifteen Picts mounted on their sturdy mountain ponies heading away from the main body he thought that they were heading his way, but they veered off towards another pass immediately to the south of his position. He was wondering what to do when one of his men scrambled up to where he was crouching between two rocks, screened from below.

The man spat out a globule of phlegm before speaking, presumably to indicate what he thought of the Picts.

'They'll soon be in trouble. See that light green area, lord? It looks like grass but it's sphagnum. It floats on top of water in a peat bog. Watch.'

The horsemen below soon realised their mistake when three of their ponies sank up to their knees in the morass. It took them nearly an hour to extricate them and then they sat there debating what to do.

'I've no idea where they live, but it's evident that they haven't come across that type of bog before,' the warrior said as he spat once more in the Picts' direction.

Suddenly both men stiffened as the Picts started urging their ponies up the slope towards their position.

'Go down and bring the archers up here, tell the others to mount, keep out of sight, and wait for my orders.'

The archers quickly took up positions behind the various rocks that were scattered over the summit of the hill. There was a crag some fifty feet tall immediately below them so the enemy wouldn't be able to make a direct assault on their position, but would have to go around to the west where the slope was covered in grass with few rocks.

The first flight of arrows killed two men and a pony as well as wounding one of each. The wounded pony reared up, depositing its rider on the ground. He cracked his head on a rock and was killed instantly. The dead pony collapsed onto its side, trapping its rider's leg beneath its body. In a few seconds the number of their foes had been reduced by a third.

Buoyed up by their success, the archers gained confidence and took more careful aim at the remaining Picts as they quickly dismounted and started to charge up the hill. The archers' next volley killed three more men and wounded two; one in the leg and one in the shoulder. The remaining five realised that they would never reach their foes alive and headed back to their ponies.

They had just mounted when a third volley disposed of three more. The remaining two took to their heels but suddenly six horsemen appeared over the side of the hill to their right and slammed into them. A minute later it was all over. The wounded were killed and Beorhtmund was slapped on the back in congratulation by his delighted men. Fifteen dead Picts and none of them had even so much as a scratch.

Meanwhile Nectan had got tired of waiting. The site of the skirmish had been hidden from view by the shoulder of the hill and so he had no idea what had befallen his men. He came to the reasonable conclusion that they had run into the rest of the Northumbrian army waiting on the reverse slope of the col and decided not to attack. Two thousand against perhaps double that number when the enemy held the high ground was not a recipe for success.

Instead he turned and led his army north east along the line of hills heading towards the low lying area between the end of the hills and the Firth of Forth. Eochaid shadowed him, riding along the tops of the hills. He had sent Beorhtmund and his gesith off to find Swefred and appraise him of the situation. Now all he could do was to hope that the main body could reach the end of the Monadh Pentland before Nectan did. They both had the same distance to travel, each having roughly one side of an equilateral triangle to cover, so it would be a close run thing.

~~~

Now fully recovered, Ælfflaed was furious when she heard what had happened. She blamed the Witan for being weak without Behrtfrith to dominate it, but there was no way that she was going to hand over power as regent to her nephew when he reached sixteen. She was would soon be sixty but she hoped to live long enough to see out her role until Osred reached eighteen. However, she needed another regent to help her. The obvious choice was Swefred, the new hereræswa. The problem was the king's antipathy towards the whole family.

Eventually she decided that to appoint anyone other than the Hereræswa as regent would be foolhardy, given the power he wielded. Her nephew would just have to get on with it. She prayed long and hard for his survival during the current war with the Picts and sat down to write to him and to the three bishops. She would need their support in the Witan to overturn the decision to allow Osred to rule alone from this December. It was now October so time was short.

~~~

Beorhtmund had suffered under his domineering father all his life. He was constantly criticised and told he would never be a strong enough character to succeed him when the time came. It was no surprise that the boy lacked self-confidence and was afraid of his own shadow.

However, he was clever and had qualities that his father had lacked. One of these was charm. His diffidence and warm

427

personality won him friends and those nobles who had derided him before now praised him for wiping out the Pictish scouts and consequently saving the lives of Eochaid and his men.

If he didn't manage to overcome his shyness and lack of self-assurance straight away, it went someway to changing his opinion of himself. From now on he took Swefred and Eochaid as his role models and tried not to think about what his father would have said every time he had to make a decision.

Swefred saw in the boy some of the strategic ability he knew that he himself possessed. He left him in command of the archers but he also brought him into the small group who he used as a sounding board before he put his plans to the war council. Once or twice Beorhtmund found solutions to problems that Swefred had failed to solve himself. One of these was how to recover from the fact that the Northumbrians had arrived at the northern tip of the Monadh Pentland two hours after the Picts had.

The only silver lining to that particular cloud was the fact that they had managed to capture the Picts baggage train and recover the spoils from their looting, together with some of the livestock they'd stolen. There wasn't a great number of sheep and cattle left as the Picts had been unable to forage much recently and feeding two thousand men and all their camp followers had reduced the animals they'd collected to a handful. Nevertheless it would feed the Northumbrians for a few days whilst the Picts went hungry.

'All we can do now is to harry their retreat back to their homeland,' Swefred said dejectedly to his half a dozen close companions.

'Not necessarily,' Beorhtmund said quietly.

'What do you mean?'

'Well, my idea may be nonsense, but how many ships are there at Dùn Èideann?'

'I've no idea, but there are usually a few trading knarrs and some birlinns...' Swefred's voice trailed away. 'You mean use them to transport part of the army along the Firth and land them ahead of the Picts?'

Beorhtmund nodded. 'Do you think it could work?'

'I've no idea, but it's worth a try. At best an army on foot can travel at two miles an hour, including necessary stops; a ship can sail at five or six knots if the wind is in the right direction, as it is at the moment.'

'How far is it to the head of the Firth?' Eochaid asked.

'About twenty five miles by sea from Dùn Èideann and some thirty miles by land from where the Picts must be now.' Swefred mused. 'Five hours by sea plus allow another five for the men to get there and embark; twelve hours allowing for disembarkation and getting into position. It'll take the Picts fifteen hours or more to get there, and it gets dark soon so they'll have to stop for the night.

'Right. Let's get the men embarked tonight and we'll set sail at dawn. I'll take the blocking party by sea; Beorhtmund, it was your idea so you can come with me. Eochaid, will you chase the Picts but don't hurry them too much?'

In the end Swefred managed to load all the archers and three hundred of the professional warriors onto the various craft he commandeered from the harbour below Dùn Èideann. It was fewer than he'd hoped but it would have to do.

When Nectan's scouts came back to report that the Northumbrians were holding the bridge across the River Forth he was incredulous. He knew that the main body was nipping at his heels, killing stragglers and barely being delayed by his rear guard. Now it seemed that he was trapped between them and another force who had somehow captured the bridge that led to safety. He rode forward to see for himself, half hoping that his scouts were mistaken.

They weren't. Not only were the men holding the far bank seasoned fighters wearing byrnies and helmets but the banks to either side of them were lined by archers who would inflict terrible damage on his men if they tried to contest the bridge.

'Brenin, the rear guard have broken. The Northumbrian horsemen are now riding along our column cutting our men down. Every time we stop to fight them off they ride away and come back again as soon as we move again. What should we do?'

The King of the Picts looked at the chieftain who'd spoken and shook his head. The women and children who'd been with the baggage train had already been captured and would be no doubt sold into slavery. The whole campaign had been a disaster.

'I'll try and negotiate a truce,' he said wearily.

A short while later he rode alone, except for his standard bearer, to the south side of the bridge.

'I am Nechtan mac Dargarto. Where is your king? I wish to negotiate.'

'King Osred isn't here, Brenin, our commander is the Ealdorman Swefred. If you advance alone and unarmed to the centre of the bridge he will meet you there. I will accompany him as interpreter.'

'No need. I speak English, probably better than you do. Tell him he too must come unarmed.'

When Swefred met him in the middle of the bridge Nectan nodded his head in greeting before speaking.

'Before we discuss anything, I would be grateful if you would send a messenger to your army to halt the carnage at the rear of my column.'

'If you grant my messenger safe conduct, I will do so, but only for two hours. If I haven't send another messenger by then my men will continue to take their revenge on yours for the plundering of our land and the slaughter of our people.'

'Agreed.'

After Beorhtmund had ridden off to find Eochaid with one of Nectan's mormaers to ensure his safety, Swefred told Nectan his conditions for allowing the rest of his army to return to their homeland unmolested.

'You will provide a thousand sheep and five hundred head of cattle to make restitution for the losses suffered by us.'

'I have little option but to accept the terms, though you may have to wait a while for me to gather so many animals.'

'Two weeks, no longer. You will bring them here. You will also give your oath on holy relics not to invade Northumbria again whilst you are king, and you will surrender your two sons to me as hostages. The elder will be returned to you once the livestock are handed over, but your younger son will remain as my guest until he is sixteen. If you fail to keep your word, and that includes preventing other Picts from raiding across the border, your son will die and die painfully.'

Nectan chewed his lip in agitation. Both his sons were dear to him but the younger, a boy of nine called Óengus, was his favourite. To lose him for seven years was unthinkable, but what option did he have, he asked himself. Eventually he nodded.

'My eldest son is with me but Óengus is with his mother. It will take time for him to get here.'

'Don't play games with me, Nectan. I sent an emissary to the fortress of Stirling as soon as we landed here. I know your wife is up there.'

'You landed...'

Now it was clear how Swefred had got ahead of him. He had to admire the man's ingenuity, little thinking that the idea was that of a fourteen year old boy.

'I see,' he continued, 'very well I'll send a man to tell my son to join me. Is that all?'

'Yes, I will let you know when I'm ready for you to make your pledge. Bishop Eadfrith will administer the oath but he will have to obtain a suitable relic. I'll send a birlinn to Lindisfarne. The arm of Saint Oswald should suffice, don't you think?'

Nectan might be many things but Swefred knew he had a reputation for being a devout Christian. He would never break a vow sworn on such a holy object.

Chapter Twenty Two – Death of a Tyrant

714 - 716 AD

'It's not entirely Osred's fault you know, both he and Otta were spoilt by their elderly father.'

'You're just making excuses for him. Whatever your brother's errors in bringing up his sons, we are faced with the consequences. Osred is immoral, self-indulgent, unpredictable and irresponsible. And now it looks as if Otta is travelling down the same path, no doubt led astray by his elder brother. The only one of the three who seems normal is Osric, but he's fourteen and has only just started his training as a warrior with Eochaid.'

Thankfully the Witan had baulked at allowing Osred to rule at sixteen and, much to the latter's rage, had deferred in once more; this time to eighteen.

Swefred had travelled down to Whitby to see Ælfflaed to discuss urgent matters with her. As she got older and less able to travel he found that more and more of the running of the kingdom fell onto his shoulders. However, he didn't feel comfortable about making important decisions on his own.

'I know that you're right,' she sighed. 'I know that my time left in this world is limited and I haven't been able to give you the support you need. I think it's time I handed over to another, perhaps to Bishop John?'

433

'He is a Holy and devout man and a scholar who has seen something of the world. He'd be a good choice I think.'

Swefred didn't try and comfort Ælfflaed by telling her that she'd get better. She would know a lie for what it was, however well intentioned. She had spent her whole life at Whitby from the time she was a baby and seemed quite ready to die there. She had expressed a desire to be buried near her predecessor, the blessed Saint Hild, and her parents, Oswiu and Eormenburg.

Swefred had placed Osric with Eochaid after he finished his education at Lindisfarne deliberately to keep him away from the influence of his two brothers.

When Ælfflaed died two months later Osred tried once again to persuade the Witan to allow him to rule alone as he was now nearly eighteen, but Swefred and John of Beverley managed to get the Witan to delay the inevitable until the king's birthday in the middle of December.

With his cousin on the throne of Mercia and both Strathclyde and Pictland still recovering from their disastrous invasion two years previously, Northumbria was peaceful and prosperous. At home Swefred enjoyed playing with his two year old son, Ulfric and his foster son, Æthelwald, who had acquired the nickname Moll. Eochaid and his family were frequent visitors and life seemed idyllic.

In early November he could no longer ignore the storm clouds gathering on the horizon. If five weeks' time the Witan would gather at Eoforwīc to formally recognise Osred as king in his own right and to swear fealty to him. Swefred was not so stupid as to consider attending. He might as well put his head in a noose. He considered laying in supplies for a long siege and defying Osred to try and take Bebbanburg but that would be the act of a traitor and a rebel. He was neither of those things.

He therefore made preparations to leave. Two weeks later he set sail with his family, little Æthelwald Moll and his gesith in two knarrs and three berlins to brave the winter storms around the north of Caledonia with the intention of offering his sword to his cousin Heartbehrt, King of Man.

However, when they eventually reached Man after surviving two storms it was only to find that Heartbehrt had been killed in a hunting accident the previous September. The present King of Man was Thringfrith, Alweo's youngest son.

~~~

Osred sat on his throne positively gloating as the Witan congratulated him on becoming the absolute ruler of Northumbria. As the nobles trooped forward one by one to swear to be loyal and faithful to him, his demeanour can best be described as bored distain. When Eochaid knelt and took the kings hands in his Osred leaned forward and whispered in his ear.

'Your relationship to the traitor Swefred has not been forgotten, Eochaid. I will be watching you very closely. You can start to earn my favour by sending Osric to me.'

'Why, Cyning, he has only just started his training to be a warrior.'

'I don't trust him. I trust Otta but Osric and I have never been friends. I need to keep him close to me.'

'Osred is taking steps to eliminate his enemies, or those he perceives as enemies,' Eochaid told Beorhtmund three months later when the latter came down to visit Alnwic. 'He's ordered me to send Osric to him.'

'What are you going to do?'

'Well, I won't let Osred get his hands on Osric, that's for certain. I have a nasty feeling that the boy would suffer some sort of accident.'

'You mean Osred would kill him?'

'Otta's no threat to him - he's completely under his thumb – but Osric could well be if he's allowed to grow up. I gather that he has sent men to arrest Cenred and his brother too.'

'Because some might consider them æthelings? What happened?'

'They were held up in a snow storm and someone managed to get a warning to them. They got away safely.'

'Where to?'

'They've joined Swefred on Man, or so rumour has it.'

'How long will it be before he sends men to arrest us I wonder?'

'He won't take Dùn Barra in a hurry and the whole of Lothian will rise up if he tries.'

Eochaid smiled, remembering the unsure little boy, almost scared of his own shadow, just two and a half years ago. Now Beorhtmund reminded him more of Swefred than he did his former self. He was self-confident and a strong leader, but he was still quiet and thoughtful.

'Have you seen anything of that sycophantic little rat that Osred gave Bebbanburg to?'

'No, he's hardly ever there. He hangs around Osred most of the time, no doubt hoping for more scraps from his table.'

'What are we going to do? There are more and more complaints about what is laughingly called the king's justice. Anything that comes before him is decided in favour of who can pay most.'

'There is only one solution as far as I can see.'

'Revolt? Depose Osred?'

'I wouldn't trust him not to try and recover his throne even then. No, death is the answer.'

~~~

At first Thringfrith was unwilling to offer sanctuary to Swefred, saying that he didn't need more warriors or mouths to feed, but then the Hibernians from Béal Feirste raided several villages on the west coast of Man and enslaved the inhabitants. He and Swefred combined their ships and forces to launch a retaliatory raid, burned part of their town and carried off seventy women and children as slaves. Eventually negotiations resulted in the release of both sets of captives and a truce was signed.

After that Thringfrith reluctantly agreed that having his cousin around might be useful and he gave him a vill in the north-west of the island. His warriors turned into farmers and for a time Swefred thought that his destiny might be to remain a Mercian thegn.

When Cenred and Ceolwulf joined him, shortly followed by Osric, Swefred began to realise how bad things had become in Northumbria. It was the autumn of 714 before he heard news about Eochaid and his family. He'd been deprived of Alnwic and they had sought refuge with Beorhtmund in the fortress of Dùn Barra. Standing on an outcrop of rock separated from the mainland by a narrow strip of sea and accessible only via a wooden bridge which could be raised and lowered as needed, the stronghold was even more impregnable than Bebbanburg. Besides, it lay in the far north east corner of Lothian, all of whose ealdormen detested Osred.

The new Ealdorman of Alnwic, who Osred had appointed to replace Eochaid, made the mistake of raping the daughter of a local reeve. Even worse, he allowed his gesith to bed whosoever took their fancy, even married women and young girls. The reaction of the local people was predictable. One night someone opened the gates of the palisade around the lord's hall to the Alnwicshire fyrd and they slaughtered the ealdorman and his gesith as they lay in a drunken stupor.

When the king sent men to punish them they found the hall, the vill and all the surrounding vills in the shire deserted. The people had taken to the hills.

Alnwic wasn't an isolated incident. Other vills where the people had been abused and treated dishonourably revolted against the rule by Osred's favourites and outlaws became a problem throughout the kingdom.

It was against this background that Swefred returned with Cenred in the spring of 716. Leaving his family, Osric and Coelwulf on Man, he landed near Dùn Barra. Whilst his gesith made camp and he set off on foot with just Cenred and Uurad as his companions to talk to Beorhtmund.

~~~

'He's made Otta his hereræswa,' Beorhtmund said glumly.

'An eighteen year old boy with absolutely no military experience? The Picts must be quaking in their shoes,' Swefred replied with a snigger.

'He has to go before he ruins the kingdom. Beorhtmund and I have discussed this and the only real solution is to kill him.' Eochaid stated.

Silence greeted this statement whilst everyone thought about what Eochaid had said.

'It seems that we're all in agreement, but how do we go about achieving that,' Cenred asked eventually. 'And who will succeed him once we do get rid of him. Not Otta. Osric?'

'We've had enough of boy kings, no. It has to be someone who is experienced enough and someone we can rely on to rule fairly and wisely,' Swefred said.

'You? After all your brother was on the throne briefly. You are descended from Ida and you would make a great king,' Beorhtmund suggested.

'No!' Swefred said vehemently. 'Whatever my qualities, or lack of them, I'm not an ætheling. Descent through the mother's side doesn't count. That rules Eochaid out as well I fear.'

'I agree.' Eochaid looked thoughtful for a moment. 'But you're descended from Ida through the male line, Cenred.'

The latter tried not to look pleased at the suggestion and failed.

'Would you all support me?'

'It looks like a choice of you or your brother, and he's still a boy. Of course, there are other families descended from Ida on

439

the male side, but they are unknown quantities; so yes. You have my vote,' Swefred grinned.

Having settled on the objective, the execution of their plan remained a problem. They discussed open revolt, assassination and calling the Witan to depose Osred. The latter option was soon dismissed. It was too fraught with difficulty. Who would call the meeting? Bishop John? Would he be prepared to do it? Probably not; all three bishops had gone remarkable quiet since Osred had turned eighteen.

No one was in favour of assassination. It was the coward's tool and could be counter-productive in bringing the kingdom back together afterwards. The last thing they wanted was for Osred to be regarded as some sort of martyr.

'Open revolt it is then,' Swefred said.

'I know that the four shires of Lothian will be with us,' Beorhtmund said, 'but there are fourteen other shires.'

'We can forget about Cumbria and Luncæstershire. They are the other side of the mountains and, if we launch our revolt in late winter the passes will still be blocked by snow.'

'Bebbanburg, Alnwic, Catterick, Jarrow and Loidis are in the hands of Osred's toadies. That leaves the other four shires in Deira and four in Bernicia.'

'We don't want to leave anything to chance. We can't be certain that all eight shires who still have their original ealdormen in place would join us. After all they swore fealty to Osred.'

'We can't rule out the possibility that he could do something stupid like calling on Æthelbald of Mercia for support too.'

The southern border had been quiet for a long time, mainly because the Mercians were locked in a power struggle with Wessex for domination of southern England. However, Æthelbald might see helping Osred as a way of gaining an ally in his struggle with King Ine of Wessex.

'We don't seem to be getting very far,' Cenred said, pointing out the obvious.

'Perhaps we need to draw him north so we can fight him on our ground,' Swefred said thoughtfully.

'How do we do that?'

'By taking back Bebbanburg.'

~~~

Bebbanburg wasn't going to be easy to take. Swefred now regretted fitting the locked grille over the entrance to the rubbish chute; that would have been the easy way in. He only hoped that the sentries weren't over-vigilant.

He'd waited until the new moon but it was a night overcast by dark clouds in any case. Fortunately it was dry, though rain seemed possible, given the state of the sky. He crept forward accompanied by his best two climbers. He reasoned that there would be fewer sentries on the eastern side facing the sea, especially as it was only just after high tide and there was very little beach exposed.

On the western side the rock face was vertical but it was more of a steep incline on the eastern side. Above it the palisade loomed some fifteen feet tall. The two young men and Swefred watched but in over half an hour they saw no-one look over the palisade. Swefred tapped the two climbers on the shoulder and they scrambled up the rock towards the base of the timber wall until it was too dark to see them.

He retraced his steps to a point where the beach widened out and then turned left to find where he'd left Beorhtmund, Eochaid and their three gesiths crouched in the bushes not far from the sea gate. All told they numbered seventy – mostly experienced warriors with a handful of youths who had yet to experience battle. The latter were excited at the thought of going into action and some might have thought them a liability on a clandestine operation like this, but the three ealdormen had allocated an older mentor to keep an eye on each the youngsters.

Each man had wrapped everything that might have clanked or rattled in cloth and now they moved silently towards the gates, which were somewhere ahead of them hidden by the blackness of the night. The success of the venture all depended on the two climbers managing to get into the fortress unseen and then noiselessly killing the sentries on the sea gate. They waited impatiently for what seemed ages with the gates in sight, illuminated by a brazier whose flames lit up the inside of the palisade and cast a dim red glow visible from the outside.

Suddenly they heard a muffled cry and everybody tensed. Shortly afterwards one of the gates swung open and Swefred and his men ran forwards. He could see that one of his climbers was lying on the ground with two other men, presumably defenders. A third man was clashing swords with the other climber. Swefred cursed. The din would wake the garrison, whose strength he didn't know. All possibility of being able to kill or capture them whilst they were asleep was now at an end. He just prayed that they could reach the inner palisade with its small postern gate, built at the time of the siege by Eadwulf, before the enemy.

He thrust his sword into the man fighting his remaining climber as he ran past, dragging his sword out of his body as he went. One of the younger warriors beat him to the little gate in the inner wall and shoulder charged it. Thankfully it was unlocked and the youth stumbled through it as it flew open, clutching at his dislocated shoulder and crying out in agony.

Swefred ignored him, leaving someone else to push the joint back into place. Now he was inside the fortress proper and made for where he knew the warriors' hall to be, Beorhtmund and Cenred at his side. As they had agreed, Eochaid and a few of his gesith had remained behind to secure the two gates.

A warrior dressed in just a tunic loomed out of the darkness and Swefred thrust his sword at his neck. The man raised his shield just in time but that exposed his groin and Cenred thrust his spear into him. He man screamed and went down. Another of the garrison appeared from his right and he felt an axe strike his shield, nearly ripping it from his arm. This time it was Beorhtmund who killed the assailant.

A man carrying a torch came out of the hall twenty paces in front of him and now he could see that there were about twenty men forming up as a shield wall in front of him. Several more were spilling out of the hall behind them, but not too many. Only a few had managed to put on a byrnie or leather armour and a helmet but they all had a weapon of some sort and a shield.

Leaving Beorhtmund and their warriors to deal with the garrison, Swefred, Cenred and Uurad ran to their right and made for the ealdorman's hall. This had a torch blazing in a sconce by the door. He could see two sentries guarding the entrance and, as he ran to tackle them, the door burst open and a man wearing a byrnie and an ornate helmet with a faceguard, topped by a crest of crouching lion, burst out of the hall. Behind him a woman and two children peered fearfully round the side of the open door.

Leaving his two companions to tackle the sentries, Swefred made a cut at the man who was evidently the new lord of Bebbanburg.

'Who are you,' the man grunted as he tried to parry Swefred's assault.

'Swefred,' he replied, making a thrust towards the man's leading leg.

His opponent dropped his shield to absorb the blow and Swefred smashed the boss of his own shield into the over-elaborate faceguard. It did little to protect the man's nose and he saw blood, black in the light of the torch, running down his neck.

The new lord took a step back and Swefred pressed his attack home. Feinting with his shield towards the man's face again and then stabbing him in the stomach when he raised his shield to protect his head. The chain mail links were strong, but only strong enough to deaden the blow. A few of them split asunder and the tip of the sword cut into flesh by several inches.

The man cried out and dropped his shield. It was far too late and Swefred calmly took advantage of his folly by stabbing him in the neck. The man dropped to the ground and his wife ran to him, sobbing. Swefred relaxed after checking that his two companions had also killed their opponents. It was a mistake. The lord's elder son, a boy of ten, screamed in rage and flew at him clutching a seax in his right hand.

He dropped to one knee and thrust it up under the hem of Swefred's byrnie, intending to stab him in the groin. The seax dropped from his grasp just in time as Cenred stabbed his spear into the boy's back. He was wounded but not dead. As he shrieked in pain and fell onto his back, Cenred thrust his spear down again into the centre of his chest, breaking through his ribcage into his heart.

Seeing her son killed as well as her husband, the woman tried to grab the fallen seax but Beorhtmund clubbed her over the head with the pommel of his sword and she dropped unconscious. Cenred quickly bound her arms and feet with her own girdle and a belt taken from one of the sentries and left her. The three walked into the hall - the stone hall built by Swefred's mother – and found several terrified servants cowering in a corner, one of them hugging the other boy, a lad of perhaps five or six, to her.

With a smile he recognised several of the servants as ones who had been here when he was the ealdorman. He pulled off his helmet and told them not to be afraid. No harm would come to them, or the dead lord's son.

The three of them went back outside to be met by a grinning Uurad walking towards them with his helmet in one hand and a sword dripping blood in the other.

'It's all over, Swefred. The men are rounding up the sentries and the rest of the people living here now. Do you want to speak to them?'

'Yes, those who were here when I left can stay with their families, of course. The rest are to be stripped of weapons, armour and anything of value and expelled at dawn. They can fend for themselves. I hope they have treated the inhabitants well whilst they've been here or they may experience some rough justice.'

Cenred nodded.

'It'll probably take a week or so before the news reaches Eoforwīc and the fat hits the fire. Then we'll see what happens.'

~~~

Bishop Eadfrith read Swefred's letter with mixed feelings. He'd been asked to call a Witan to meet at Bebbanburg in one month's time to depose Osred and elect a new king. He deplored Osred's morals and the injustice he perpetrated but he feared that the kingdom now faced civil war. He opposed all forms of killing and hoped that there could be a bloodless solution to the present situation. He decided to travel the short distance to Bebbanburg and see what could be done.

As he travelled over the sea towards the fortress he could plainly see that the stronghold was surrounded by an armed camp. At first he thought that the place was under siege and nearly turned around to head back to Lindisfarne, but then he realised that the gates were open and people were going to and fro.

As he landed Swefred and his wife, Kendra, came down to meet him with their son Ulfric and their foster child, Æthelwald Moll. Both boys were now four and evidently close as they stood together holding hands. Eadfrith smiled at them but then frowned as he looked at the large encampment.

'It seems that you are preparing for war, rather than a Witan, Swefred.'

'Why don't you come up to my hall, bishop, where we can talk in more comfort?'

'Comfort has never been one of my priorities, but lead on.'

'I agree that Osred is a bad king and a worse Christian but you have sworn fealty to him,' the bishop said as soon as they were seated in the hall with the four ealdormen of Lothian and Cenred.

'Not me; he refused to accept my oath initially, if you recall, and I had fled to Man before the second oath.'

'Perhaps, but the others will be foresworn.'

'He lost our loyalty when he capriciously deprived ealdormen of their shires with no good reason so that he could reward his toadies,' Beorhtmund said angrily.

The bishop thought for a moment.

'Would it help if I formally absolved you of your fealty to Osred?'

One of the other ealdormen shrugged. 'We are already in revolt against his rule, but if it would sit better with our fellow ealdormen and the priests, then why not? Thank you bishop.' He added hastily, realising that he'd been a bit churlish.

'Where is Eochaid, by the way? I had expected him to be with you, Beorhtmund.'

'He's gone to retrieve his shire.'

'Ah, of course. I assume that the camp outside contains the warbands and the fyrd of Lothian. There must be at least a thousand men there?'

'So far,' he confirmed. 'We expect the ealdormen of four of the other Bernician shires to join us soon.'

The bishop nodded.

'And Deira, Cumbria and Luncæstershire – will they support you?'

'That remains to be seen. All we desire is to depose Osred and elect a new king. We suspect we won't be able to do that without a show of force but we hope to avoid war if possible.'

'I'm relieved to hear it. Who will succeed Osred if you succeed? Not Otta, I assume, and Osric is too young. So it will have to be another ætheling. You Swefred? After all your brother was king briefly.'

'No,' he replied flatly. 'Cenred.'

'Ah, of course. Son of Cuthwin, son of Leoldwald, son of Egwald, son of Aldhelm, son of Ocga, illegitimate son of Ida.'

'You know your genealogy, bishop.'

'I'm a scholar. You tend to remember these things. Of course, Ida had twelve sons.'

'Yes, but few of them had sons of their own and only the Houses of Æthelfrith and Leoldwald have descendants alive today,' Cenred said quickly.

'Possibly, others may disagree.'

'They may claim it but cannot prove it, as I can,' Cenred said a little heatedly.

Swefred put a calming hand on his forearm.

'If there are others, then presumably they can state their claim to the Witan.'

'That is true. Very well then, I will write to John of Beverley and Acca of Hexham to appraise them of the situation. If they agree, I will then summons them, the abbots and the ealdormen to a Witan to be held here. But when? Shall we say six weeks from now?'

'I would rather it was sooner, Eadfrith,' Swefred said. 'I want to prevent a war, as you do. If we delay it may be too late to avoid it.'

He didn't add that the fyrd would not want to be away from their homes and their fields for too long with the sowing season approaching.

~~~

Osred rode north with his army intent on putting down the uprising before it got too serious. Knowing his temper no one dared tell him that Swefred had now mustered over two thousand men and so he was convinced that the thousand he was taking with him would suffice.

He was disabused of that notion when he crested the last ridge to the south west and saw the extent of the encampment below the fortress.

'It may only be those who have answered the call to attend the Witan, brother,' Otta told him placatingly, though he didn't really believe it himself.

'What, and they've brought their warbands and their fyrds to a meeting have they? You're a fool Otta.'

'What will you do?'

'Do? Why demand that they disperse or lose their shires and probably their lives - and those of their families - if they disobey me. After all, I'm their king and they've sworn an oath to be loyal to me. You'll soon see, most of them are cowards and they'll back down when I confront them.'

As they approached the camp men started to arm themselves and form up ready for battle. Osred halted two hundred yards from the rebels' front rank and rode forward another fifty yards until he was confident that all were in range of his powerful voice.

'Men of Northumbria, what is this? You all know me I'm your lawfully elected and anointed king.'

At that moment a horseman burst out of the trees to the right of where the king was sitting on his horse and galloped towards him. It took everyone by surprise and, before anyone could react, the man threw his spear with unerring accuracy at the king before racing back into the trees. No one else knew who the assassin was but, despite the full face helmet that had once belonged to the previous lord of Bebbanburg, Swefred recognised the markings on the assassin's horse. It belonged to Cenred.

Otta cried 'No' as he saw his brother fall. He threw himself off his horse and ran to his side. He cradled him in his arms but he knew that the heavy weight he held could only belong to a corpse.

'No,' he shrieked. 'It cannot be. Who has done this? A chest of gold to the man who brings me the murderer's head.'

Several men rode off into the trees at this but Cenred was long gone.

Swefred rode out of the stronghold and halted his horse just in front of his army.

'I bitterly regret this Otta. It was none of my doing. Oh, I'd have happily killed your brother, but in fair fight. This was the coward's way.'

Otta stood up and glared at Swefred.

'This is your fault, traitor. If you hadn't returned my brother would still be alive. I'll have your head for this!'

'It is your brother who was the traitor; he betrayed the nobles and the good people of Northumbria with his whoring, sacrilege, injustice and cruelty. I'm glad that he's dead, but I regret the manner of his going. I suggest that you take him to Lindisfarne to be given a Christian burial. The Witan will have to decide what becomes of you.'

'He never believed in your God and the last place he would want to be buried is on Lindisfarne. I'll bury him at Driffield, near where our father is buried.'

'Then you will have to wait until the Witan is over.'

'Who says? You? You are an outlaw.'

'You don't seem to realise the realities of the situation, Otta. You are outnumbered two to one and, by the look of it, few of your men seem very keen to fight for you.'

'But, with my brother dead, I am his heir. Who else is there? Osric? He's a child.'

'So are you. Besides, your behaviour has mirrored Osred's and that has endeared you to no one. There are other æthelings as well.'

'Such as? You, I suppose?' he sneered. 'Or do you intend to invite Eadwulf back?'

'Why does everyone assume I want the throne? I'm not an ætheling, neither is my brother. No, I refer to the Leoldwaldings, Cenred and Ceolwulf.'

'They are not of the House of Æthelfrith.'

'No, but they can prove their descent from Ida through the male line.'

Otta looked around him and his shoulders slumped.

'It seems you have won after all, Swefred. Very well, I'll tell my ealdormen to stay for the Witan and ask them to send the army home now. What do you intend to do with me?'

'Provided you are not elected, which seems likely, I will recommend that you are allowed to go into exile.'

'Exile? Where?'

'I don't really care. Hibernia, Frankia, Frisia. You choose.'

'How do you know I won't come back and claim the throne?'

'Because everyone will remember that you are a sacrilegious wastrel like your brother and no one would support you.'

It was a pity for his sake that Otta didn't remember Swefred's advice.

Chapter Twenty Three - Cenred

716 – 718 AD

After his election Cenred set about dispossessing the men who Osred had favoured and restoring the original ealdormen to their shires. The dispossessed joined Otta in exile; a decision that worried Swefred as it gave him a power base of resentful nobles in Neustria, where he had been welcomed as the guest of King Chilperic II.

A few months after his arrival Chilperic joined the Frisians in attacking Austrasia and Cenred joined his army with his small group of supporters. It was to provide Otta with a good training in the art of war and some useful allies, all of which boded ill for Northumbria in the future.

Cenred sent for Osric soon after he had begun his reign and was much taken with the boy. He was as dissimilar to his elder siblings as it was possible to be. At fourteen he had already decided that he wished to be a scholar like his father but, also like him, not to enter Holy Orders. Unlike Aldfrith, though, he was witty as well as bright and Cenred found him a congenial companion. When Coelwulf, now sixteen, joined his brother at Eoforwīc, the two boys soon became friends; a friendship that would last throughout Osric's lifetime.

Meanwhile Swefred settled back down to the life of an ealdorman, dispensing justice, collecting taxes and managing his estates. Cenred had appointed him as hereræswa again, which took him away from Bebbanburg from time to time but he left the northern border to Beorhtmund. Mercia was still engaged in a power struggle with Wessex so the southern border wasn't a concern either.

The one area where there was some conflict was Cumbria. When Beli had retreated back into Strathclyde five years previously, the Cumbrians had followed them across the Esk into Galloway and had seized the coastal strip along the north shore of the Solway Firth. Now Beli was plotting to take it back. It was a useful buffer zone and Cenred had told Swefred that he wanted him to make sure that it remained part of Northumbria.

After he had become a hostage Óengus, Nectan's younger son, had remained at Dùn Barra as a guest of Beorhtmund. When he was eleven he had been sent to Lindisfarne to be educated and, now that he was fourteen, he was ready to start his training as a warrior. He had just arrived at Bebbanburg to join the other trainees when Swefred sent for him.

'Do you miss your parents, Óengus?'

The question took the boy off guard. It was the last thing he had expected to be asked and he thought for some time before he replied.

'It is five years since I last saw them. At first I missed them quite dreadfully, especially my father. I was in a strange land with people whose customs and language I didn't understand and all I wanted to do was to go home. Then I realised that I could spend the next few years being miserable until I was a man and was allowed to return home, or I could make the best of it. I chose the latter course.

'Since then I have learned to speak English, made some good friends, learned a great deal and I've been happy. Now you ask if I miss my parents. To tell you the truth I rarely think about them anymore. If I was allowed to return home now I honestly don't know how I'd feel. Home is here. I get on well with the other boys who're learning to be warriors and I'm happy. If I went back to the Land of the Picts I would feel like a stranger, just as I did when I first came to live here.

'I suppose I'd get used to it again but, to be truthful, you are more civilised and there are aspects of life as a Pict that I found unpleasant. Does that answer your question?'

Swefred laughed. 'Rather more fully than I had expected. Thank you. If I asked you to go back to see your father for me on the understanding that you'd then return here, would you do that?'

'I suppose so. I think my parents would like to see me again; my brother less so.'

'I'm sure they would. You parents might be loathe to allow you to go when it came time for you to leave, though.'

'I'm sure, but you have my word. My father wouldn't expect me to break an oath.'

Swefred looked at Óengus speculatively for a moment and then made his mind up.

'I want you to take a message to him for me.'

'I see. Am I allowed to know what's in this message?'

'Yes, I don't see why not – provided you swear to keep it to yourself.'

'I swear. Do you want me to do so on a Bible?'

'No, your word is good enough for me. Strathclyde is plotting to attack the Cumbrians who have settled along the north shore of the Solway Firth. I want to enter into an alliance with your father so that he will move against Strathclyde if Beli attacks us.'

'Why should he do that?'

'Because I won't interfere if he keeps some of the territory he captures. And I will give you a free choice about whether you stay there or return here to complete your warrior training.'

'I suspect it would suit my father to reduce the power of Strathclyde but he will want more than your neutrality.'

'How do you know what he wants until you've spoken to him?'

'Because I know what I would want if I was him.'

'And what's that?'

'Your active help.'

'Why?'

'Because, with Northumbria as an ally, he can try to unite all of Alba, which I'm told is what the Picts are now calling Caledonia, under his rule.'

'I doubt that is in Northumbria's best interest.'

'It'll happen sooner or later, just as either Mercia or Wessex will eventually dominate all of England south of the Humber.'

'Who has taught you to think like this? You sound more like a great scholar than a fourteen year old boy.'

'When I was at Lindisfarne I was sent to Jarrow to learn from a monk they call the Venerable Bede.'

'Bede is an astute man but for him to have taught you to think strategically like that you must have a clever mind. I hope you're never King of the Picts, or even worse, of a united Caledonia, er, Alba.'

'Why?'

'Because I think you would give Northumbria problems.'

Óengus laughed.

'Don't worry, I'm more of a thinker than a doer.'

'You'll go to see your father for me then?'

'Yes, but only to arrange a meeting between you. There are too many details that need to be sorted out for me to act as your emissary.'

'Very well. I'll meet him at the bridge near Stirling in two weeks' time.'

~~~

Otta was on the run. Chilperic had conducted a victorious campaign and been crowned king of the united kingdom of Frankia, Austrasia and Neustria. Then, just when everybody thought that the war was over, Chilperic's army had been attacked and defeated by Charles Martel, Duke of the Franks. Now Martel was the virtual ruler of the three kingdoms and Chilperic was his prisoner, though he was still the titular king.

Otta had had enough of the complex politics of the Continent and decided to return to England incognito with a handful of friends.

'It's time I dealt with Cenred and with that damned man, Swefred.'

'How,' one of his companions asked. 'Will you try and raise an army?'

'Not at first. I'll kill Cenred by stealth and then invite the Witan to elect me as king. Don't you know? I'm a reformed character!'

His friends burst out laughing. If anything Otta was more of a rake that Osred ever was.

They thought he was joking about killing Cenred, but he was in deadly earnest.

~~~

'I'm sure that we can both get what we want by diplomacy backed up by the threat of force, rather than outright war,' Swefred suggested.

He had walked onto the middle of the bridge over the River Forth below the brooding mass of the fortress at Stirling on a blustery day, the wind whipping at his cloak. He was unarmed but, in any case he needed both his hands free; one to clutch at the handrail on the creaking bridge and the other to keep his cloak wrapped around him to keep off the squally showers that kept driving at him horizontally. He was beginning to think that he should withdraw and try again on a less blustery day when Nectan rode up to the other side of the bridge accompanied by Óengus.

The boy translated for his father, which puzzled Swefred because he knew that Nectan spoke English well.

'Why do we need you to translate? The last time the two of us met on this very spot your father told me himself that he spoke English well.'

Óengus grinned whilst Nectan kept his expression blank.

'It gives him time to think how best to reply,' the boy replied in Latin, a language his father didn't speak.

Swefred smiled at Nectan who looked at his son curiously but said nothing. The conversation continued through Óengus.

'Why are you against war?'

'Why waste useful lives? Besides war can have unpredictable outcomes.'

'What is your proposal?'

'That we advance from here towards Dùn Breatainn and, when we have surrounded his stronghold, we offer to negotiate.'

'What do you hope to gain from these negotiations?'

'Recognition that Southern Galloway is now part of Northumbria and a cessation of his attacks on it. And you? What do you want Nectan?'

'To move my border west to include the land from the Campsie Fells to Loch Venachar, where it was forty years ago.'

'Very well. If we are agreed, let's get out of this wind and meet here again in two weeks' time with our armies.'

In the end it went better than Swefred had dared hope. The sudden invasion by the Picts from the north-east and the Northumbrians from the south-west had caught Beli completely by surprise. He only had supplies inside Dùn Breatainn to last him a couple of weeks and ten days after the siege started he agreed to negotiate. He had little to bargain with and eventually agreed to the demands made by Nectan and Swefred.

Swefred was in for one surprise though. Óengus opted to return with him to Bebbanburg, much against his father's wishes.

~~~

The winter of 705/706 was a fierce one. The snow came early at the start of November and blizzards prevented travelling any distance until the thaw started in late March. Starving wolves came down out of the hills and attacked anyone who ventured far from their homes. When Cenred heard that a pack was even prowling around the outskirts of Eoforwīc he decided to organise a hunt to eradicate the menace.

The man who slipped into a tavern in the poorer part of the town wore a dirty brown cloak over his good quality woollen tunic. The two men he sought were sitting in their usual place in a corner away from the hearth in the middle of the taproom. Everyone else in the place was huddled around the only source of warmth.

Even though they were out of earshot of the rest of the customers the man kept his voice low.

'Cenred is leading a wolf hunt the day after tomorrow,' the new arrival told them. 'The wolves are reportedly living in the wood to the south of here so that's where he'll be headed.'

'How many will go with him?' one of the other men asked.

'The pack is said to be quite large – perhaps six or seven strong – so the king will take maybe fifteen mounted men with him in addition to a few huntsmen with dogs to flush the wolves out of their den.'

'Thank you. Here is what we promised you,' the first man said handing the informer a pouch of silver under the table.

Tucking the pouch out of sight, he took his leave of the other two and left the tavern. As he made his way back through the mixture of mud and slush to the king's hall, another man slipped out of the shadows and followed him. The informer was so intent on not losing his footing in the slippery conditions that he never heard the other man come up behind him.

The latter put his hand over the informer's mouth and yanked his head back, exposing his throat. He slit his throat expertly and pulled the body into a side alley. Checking he hadn't been seen, the killer retrieved the pouch of silver and made his way back to the tavern just as the other two left.

'Well done,' Otta said as he took the proffered pouch. 'It's a pity we'll have to freeze our bollocks off waiting for Cenred tomorrow but the prize is worth it.'

~~~

Otta and his men did their best to keep warm whilst they waited. They had entered the wood just before dawn and, keeping a wary eye out for the wolves, scouted the tracks that the hunt was likely to follow. Once satisfied that they knew the wood sufficiently well they settled down to wait.

The air was clear, the sky was blue and the temperature was well below freezing. Despite wearing every stitch of clothing they possessed, the icy cold soon started to penetrate through to their skin. Reluctantly Otta let his men move to and fro in an effort to keep warm. Then the one sent to keep watch at the edge of the trees came running back.

'They're coming,' he yelled excitedly.

'Keep your voice down, damn you,' Otta said in a fierce whisper. 'Right, you all know what to do. Get going.'

A pair of mounted men took up position at the side of each track, keeping well back into the leafless trees. As luck would have it Cenred also split his men up to follow the dogs along the three main tracks in the hope of locating the wolves. Otta was certain that they weren't in the wood that morning but, of course, Cenred wasn't to know that.

As Cenred and three companions trotted past, Otta and one of his men joined the group. Everyone was so intent on watching for the wolves that no one noticed the two new arrivals at first. However, the ealdorman riding beside the king looked curiously at the horseman who rode up to join them on Cenred's other side. By the time he had realised with a shock that it was Otta it was too late.

Otta drew back his spear and thrust it into the king's side. Cenred fell from his horse with a cry and the man behind him stabbed his spear down into his eye socket and thence into his brain. The ealdorman recovered quickly from his shock and thrust his own spear into the man who had killed the king. One of the other nobles completed the job of killing the third assassin whilst the captain of Cenred's gesith took off after Otta mouthing curses.

Suddenly the latter pulled his horse to a stop, turned it back to face the way it'd come and threw his spear at his pursuer. He missed the man but hit the horse, which reared up and deposited its rider onto the ground, where he lay winded.

They searched high and low for Otta and his confederates but without success. Otta had planned to stay in Northumbria for the Witan in the hope of election but, as he'd been recognised, there was now a price on his head equivalent to the weregeld due for killing a king. With such a large sum offered for his capture he was lucky to make it into Mercia safely.

The roads were all but impassable so it was several weeks before he could continue his journey to the coast. From there he sailed back to the Continent and offered his sword to Charles Martel.

Chapter Twenty Four – Osric the Good

718 – 725 AD

'Cenred had the makings of a good king,' John of Beverley told Swefred as they sat together in the bishop's house in Eoforwīc.

Outside the rain pattered on the shutters whilst inside the gloom of the room was matched by Swefred's mood.

'Yes, I'd have gladly killed Otta myself if I could have lain my hands on him.'

The snow had long since melted but it had left the roads a quagmire and now the rain had made matters worse. Swefred had only been able to make it to the capital of Northumbria by sailing down from Bebbanburg. As hereræswa, he had taken over the reins of government and had ruled in partnership with Bishop John in the interregnum.

He'd hoped to have held the Witan by now, but two months after Cenred's assassination it had still proved impossible for everyone to meet. Even sowing for next summer's harvest had been delayed and he worried that the people would starve this year if the rain didn't let up soon.

Two days later it seemed as if his prayers, and those of John, had been answered. The rain stopped and the sun came out. Eight days later nobles, abbots and the two other bishops began to arrive for the Witan.

The seventeen year old Osric was the obvious choice but there were ealdormen who felt that he was still tainted by his relationship to Osred and the assassin Otta. Their candidate was Cenred's brother Ceolwulf. He was now twenty one and, although still a thegn and therefore not present at the Witan, they nominated him in absentia.

One further complication was that a majority of the ealdormen backed Swefred as king.

'After all,' as Beorhtmund pointed out, 'he is the brother of a king, is the greatest warrior alive in Northumbria today and has a son to succeed him.'

'I thank all of you who have nominated me but I don't consider myself an ætheling. I never have and I never will; nor is my son an ætheling.'

With that he sat down. Many present begged him to reconsider but he remained adamant. Eochaid was the next man to stand.

'As Swefred has stated that he is not an ætheling, then, as his cousin, I can hardly consider myself one either. I too decline to stand.'

'There is one other true ætheling whose name has not been mentioned so far,' Bishop Eadfrith said.

At this a hubbub of speculation arose and John of Beverley, who was presiding, had to call for quiet several times before it died away.

'I speak of Æthelwald Moll, Osred's bastard son. Of course he is, as yet, far too young but his name should be entered into the records as an ætheling.'

Swefred swore vividly under his breath. If he'd had his way Æthelwald would never have known about his parentage. Now it was common knowledge he'd have to tell him. He was worried that, at eight, the knowledge that his parents were

King Osred the Wicked and a nun he raped might affect the boy badly; more so even than knowing that he was an ætheling. To Swefred's mind kingship was a curse, and dreaming of kingship was even worse.

'I call upon Osric to state his case,' John said, nodding at the young man.

'My parentage is not in doubt,' he began, inferring that Æthelwald Moll's was. Certainly he never acknowledged him later as his nephew. 'I am as different to my late brother as it is possible to be. Like my father, I would have become a scholar had I not been an ætheling. I am no warrior, but perhaps that it a good thing. Northumbria needs a period of peace and stability in which craftsmanship, culture, religion and trade can flourish.

'We have more land than we can farm thanks to our losses on the battlefield; we certainly don't need more. The land we seem to have acquired in Galloway can't be populated from within the kingdom so we have had to offer it to settlers from Mercia, the Isle of Man and even Hibernia.

'But I digress. If you elect me as your king I will bring an end to the recent turbulence and strive to make you rich. As to the defence of our borders, I have every faith in Swefred as our hereræswa.'

He sat down to cheering and applause.

It fell to Bishop Acca of Hexham to make the case for Coelwulf. Acca was much respected as an accomplished musician and a learned theologian amongst churchmen, but he was little known outside the Church and his own diocese.

'Coelwulf is the late king's younger brother and a man who is a trained warrior but also a devout Christian. Even the

Venerable Bede has praised his piety. A Christian country needs a Christian monarch.'

'Are you saying that Osric isn't a Christian?' one of the ealdormen shouted in protest.

'Be quiet,' John thumped the table behind which he sat with his fist, causing the scribe sitting beside him to smudge the record he was making. 'No one ever interrupts a candidate during his submission. You will have your chance to speak later. Carry on bishop.'

But Acca had evidently lost the thread of what he'd been saying and, after repeating what a good Christian Coelwulf was, he sat down. Unlike the acclaim for Osric his statement was greeted by muted applause.

The outcome was never in doubt and Osric became the last recorded king of the House of Æthelfrith.

~~~

Swefred returned to Bebbanburg to be faced with the difficult task of telling Æthelwald Moll about his parents.

The boy came in to see him with Ulfric by his side. The two went everywhere and did everything together. Swefred thought of sending his son out of the room but Kendra, sitting beside him, touched his arm and shook her head slightly when he glanced at her. She was right, he thought, the boy might need his foster brother to comfort him once he'd heard what Swefred had to say. He cleared his throat and began a little nervously.

'Come and sit down, boys,' he said, indicating two stools. 'Æthelwald have you ever wondered about your parents?'

'Yes, of course. But whenever I asked anybody they would change the subject. I assume I was a bastard and I know I'm lucky you took me in and treated me like your own son.'

'Yes, well. Lady Kendra and I think that you're old enough now to know the truth.'

The boy said nothing but looked apprehensive rather than eager. Ulfric took his hand and gave it a little squeeze.

'As you rightly assumed, you were born out of wedlock.'

When he saw a look of incomprehension on the boy's face he hastily added, 'you are a bastard.'

'Do you know who my parents are, lord?'

'Yes.' He hesitated.

'Are they still alive?'

'Your mother is but your father is dead.'

'Oh, I see. Could I visit my mother?'

'Well, er, it's a bit difficult.'

'She's a nun at Coldingham, Æthelwald,' Kendra put in, seeing her husband's reticence.

'Oh, a nun?' The boy frowned. 'Did she have me before she became a nun?'

'No, Æthelwald. Look, you need to know the truth. She was raped by your father whilst she was a novice.'

Swefred hadn't meant to be so brutal but he didn't know how else to phrase it.

Both boys gasped and Ulfric frowned at his father. Surely he didn't have to break the news to his friend like that. Æthelwald started sobbing and Ulfric put his arms around him and hugged him. Kendra got up and took the boy into her arms and tried to kiss his tears away. Even she looked at Swefred reproachfully. He sighed. He'd made a mess of it, as he knew he would.

Eventually Æthelwald calmed down.

'Who was the rapist,' he spat the last two words out as if they were something foul that he'd eaten. He refused to think of the man as his father.

'King Osred.'

'Osred the Wicked?'

The boy started to sob again and then pushed both Kendra and Ulfric away roughly before rushing out of the hall and down to the beach, where he sat brooding until the incoming tide forced him to move.

Ulfric and he remained friends but the relationship wasn't the same and it remained somewhat strained for a long time. Æthelwald was ashamed of his parentage and built a wall around himself, keeping people away. Ulfric blamed his father and they became, if not estranged, at least not as close as they had been.

~~~

Osric traveled down to Eoforwīc to see John of Beverley towards the end of the year. The bishop's hall was a modest affair sited in the grounds of the monastery and on arrival he was met by the abbot, Wilfrith, a monk from Whitby who had recently been consecrated when John had decided to separate the offices of abbot and bishop.

'Thank you for coming, Cyning,' John held out his hand for the king to kiss his ring. 'Forgive me for sitting in your presence but I'm find it very difficult to stand at the moment.'

'Don't worry, bishop, my only concern is for your health.'

'I fear that my best years are behind me, Osric, which is why I asked to see you.'

'Nonsense, you have years ahead of you yet; this is a passing inconvenience.'

'It is kind of you to say so, but I fear it is far from the truth. I'm sixty seven and I feel fortunate that God had given me so long a life on this earth. Now though I need to prepare for my death. If you will allow it, I wish to retire to the monastery I founded at Beverley and live the life of a simple monk until God calls me to his side.'

'But what will I do without you? I have only been king a short while and I depend upon you for advice and guidance.'

'I commend Abbot Wilfrith to you, Cyning. He is well educated and a scholar who has worked with Bede during his time at Whitby. Your aunt, the Abbess Ælfflaed, thought highly of him and I recommend him to you as my replacement.'

Osric looked at Wilfrith properly for the first time. The abbot had an air of confidence about him without being haughty. He took him to be in his mid-thirties and he was dressed in a plain cream habit with a silver cross suspended from a leather thong about his neck. He decided he liked what he saw.

'I will think about your request, John. Come and see me in my hall tomorrow, Wilfrith, so we can talk properly.'

'He means without me listening and influencing you,' John muttered with a chuckle.

~~~

Life had continued as normal at Bebbanburg after Swefred had told Æthelwald about his parents but the place never felt quite the same to Swefred as it had done in the past. It was as if a cloak of melancholia had enveloped him. When his wife died three years later he sunk deeper into depression and he gave up the post of hereræswa. With the country at peace, Osric didn't appoint a replacement for a while, but eventually he chose Eochaid.

That same summer Bishop Eadfrith died but Swefred didn't bother to go to his funeral; neither did he accept the king's invitation to attend the funeral of John of Beverley a few months later. He was only thirty three but he felt as if he was twenty years older.

However, he did take the two boys to Lindisfarne the following year for them to start their education. Æthelwald was well aware that he had been the cause of Swefred's melancholia and he tried to lift the man's spirits in the months before they left. To some extent he succeeded, and if things weren't back to where they were, at least Bebbanburg was a slightly happier place until the boys left. Unfortunately, Swefred became morose once more as soon as they'd gone.

It was therefore just as well that a week later Swefred had a guest. He hadn't seen Eochaid since Kendra's funeral and he was surprised at how pleased he was to see him again.

'I'm on my way to see Beorhtmund. You've heard that Beli of Strathclyde had died?'

He had heard but it hadn't really registered.

'The new king, his son Teudebur, has allied himself with Óengus.'

'Óengus? You mean King Nectan's son?'

'Yes, apparently there was a plot by Nectan's elder son to seize the throne. He deposed his father and tried to kill Óengus, but he escaped. He raised an army, defeated his brother, and is now King of the Picts.'

'I hadn't heard. But I always thought that Óengus was well disposed towards us.'

'Óengus has ambitions to be King of Alba, as they are now calling Caledonia.'

'Well, that won't sit well with Teudebur, will it?'

'No, of course not. But he probably doesn't know what Óengus is up to. That's why I'm going to see Beorhtmund. We need to find a way to make him aware of the danger he faces from the Picts.'

'Would you mind if I came with you?'

'I was hoping that you'd say that.'

~~~

Swefred realised that what he'd agreed to do was fraught with danger, but he didn't really care. He was doing something useful and he felt more alive that he had done for a long time. He felt a twinge of guilt as he wasn't only just putting his own life in danger but that of Uurad and Oisean, a member of his gesith, as well. He was glad that Oisean had volunteered as he was the only one of them who spoke the Brythonic tongue spoken by the Picts. Uurad went wherever Swefred went without question.

The late autumnal day was fine but windy and there was a distinctly icy tinge to it. The waters of the Firth of Forth were choppy as the birlinn sailed north-west under the power of the wind. Swefred was making for Aberdour where, if the information he'd been given was correct, Óengus was staying at the moment.

'Do you think he'll listen to you?' Uurad asked as he joined his lord and his friend in the bows.

Swefred didn't reply for a moment as he enjoyed the sensation of the prow rising and falling as it ploughed through the waves.

'We used to be friends and for a while I thought he'd choose to stay in Northumbria when he turned sixteen. I even offered him a vill of his own, but he decided to return to the country of his birth once he was free to do so. He's a Pict and that's where his loyalties lie now. Besides, power can change a man, so I have no idea how he'll receive me.'

A short while later they landed and the birlinn left the small jetty to anchor offshore before anyone could think of detaining it. At first no one seemed very interested in the new arrivals so the three men started to walk up to the hall which sat on a small knoll above the settlement. The hall wasn't very large and there was no palisade around it; Swefred was surprised that the King of the Picts had chosen to stay there.

When they reached the hall two bored looking sentries looked them over before one asked who they were and what they wanted.

'This is Ealdorman Swefred, the emissary of King Osric, who had come to see King Óengus,' Oisean replied.

The sentries' air of languid disinterest vanished. They levelled their spears at the visitors and appeared nervous. They had obviously heard of the former Hereræswa of Northumbria.

One of them yelled through the partly open door and a scruffy boy came running out to see what the sentry wanted.

It wasn't exactly true that Swefred was Osric's emissary. The king took little interest in anything other than religion and scholarship. Bishop Wilfrith had proved to be a competent administrator and Osric relied on him to look after his regal responsibilities. Had he been consulted he would have no doubt agreed to any plan that avoided the possibility of war, but he hadn't been. Swefred mission had been agreed by the four ealdormen of Lothian, Eochaid and himself, but that's as far as it went.

One of those ealdormen, Wathsige of Berwic, was now elderly and had no sons. He did have a daughter who he'd had late in life and was now twelve. If Swefred survived this mission he intended to visit Berwic on his return and put a proposition to Wathsige.

The boy reappeared two minutes later and told the sentries that the king would see Swefred on his own, but he was to leave his weapons with his companions. That wasn't encouraging.

He followed the dirty urchin into the hall. He remembered that Óengus had disliked the filthy conditions in which many Picts lived and he was surprised that he employed a servant who stank as much as this lad did. He couldn't have smelled worse if he'd been for a roll in the midden.

The inside of the hall wasn't much better. The rushes on the beaten earth floor were so old that they were rotting and they were full of discarded bones, animal droppings and other detritus.

Óengus sat at the far end beside a man who was presumably his host. Whilst the king was well dressed in a clean tunic and trousers the other man looked as if he hadn't changed his clothes in a month or more.

The king got up as Swefred approached and they gripped each other's forearms in greeting.

'This is the local chieftain, Seathan MacBheatha. I'm here because he has a grievance against his mormaer and I need to hear both sides of the story. I apologise for the state of this place but it's his hall, not mine. It's good to see you again, Swefred but, if you don't mind me saying so, you've aged a lot since I last saw you.'

'The loss of my wife hit me hard,' he replied. He wasn't about to explain about Æthelwald Moll.

'Yes, I was sorry to hear about Kendra.' He paused for a moment and then turned to Seathan and spoke to him for a moment. 'Come outside, let's get the stink of the place out of our nostrils and go for a walk,' he said, reverting to English.

'Why are you here?' Óengus asked bluntly once they were alone.

'Because there is a rumour that you have allied yourself to Teudebur of Strathclyde and we wondered what that means for the peace between us,' Swefred replied, equally bluntly.

'Ah! You're worried about Cumbria's tenuous hold on the Galloway coast?'

'Partly, but also about a rumour that you intend to invade Lothian again.'

'Well, you can forget that. We are still suffering from the number of men we lost the last time we tried.'

'In that case why ally yourself with Teudebur?'

'Because Strathclyde is weak and Dalriada threatens it. I don't wish to see Alba torn apart by internal strife any more than I want war with Northumbria. Look, what I'm about to say is for your ears only. I want your oath that you won't repeat it.'

'Then why tell me?'

'So you don't misunderstand my aspirations. You can reassure Osric, if he really sent you, or whoever did, that they need not fear me.'

'Very well.'

'In the south of England Mercia and Wessex are always struggling for supremacy and it's weakening both kingdoms and draining their treasuries. In Alba we suffer in the same way from fighting amongst ourselves, particularly Strathclyde and Dalriada. I want to put an end to it. Ultimately I'd like to see a united Kingdom of Alba, but we are a long way from that.'

'I'm pleased to hear it,' Swefred said with a smile. 'I have a feeling that, whatever you may feel, any successor who ruled all of Alba would be tempted to push his border southwards.'

'Perhaps, but that's not going to happen in our day.'

'Thank you for being so candid, Óengus. I'll go back and say I have your sworn oath that you have no intention to attack Lothian – or Galloway?'

'Having the Angles rule land north of the Solway Firth makes no sense geographically or politically. However, my alliance with Strathclyde does not include taking action there. It is solely to prevent warfare between them and the Scots of Dalriada.'

~~~

Swefred assured his fellow ealdormen that the Picts did not threaten Lothian, at least not whilst Óengus was on the throne. However, both Beorhtmund and Eochaid suspected that there was something that Swefred wasn't telling them but he refused to say more.

He rode back south with Eochaid and Wathsige of Berwic. He had already told Eochaid that he planned to stay for a day or so with Wathsige so the two friends parted company when they reached the settlement at the mouth of the River Twaid. Eochaid was intrigued by Swefred's decision and jumped to the conclusion that his friend planned to marry again.

If that was his aim, he doubted whether the king would allow Swefred to succeed Wathsige when the latter died. It would make the lord of Bebbanburg, already a large shire, the most powerful noble in the north.

But it wasn't a wife for himself that Swefred sought. He had worried over Æthelwald Moll's future for a while. Once he completed his training as a warrior in three years' time he could join his gesith – or go and serve anyone else if he wished – but he wanted more for him. After all he was the son of a king, albeit an evil one, and he felt that the boy deserved more.

He rode home under grey skies and through frequent showers but he felt happier than he had done for some time. Wathsige's daughter was a pretty little thing and he didn't mind admitting that he would have liked to bed her himself. Her father was interested in the match, especially as it would mean his daughter would be the wife of an ætheling and have an outside chance of being a queen one day. However he wanted to meet the boy and so Swefred headed for Lindisfarne. A place he hadn't visited since Eadfrith had died.

Confusingly the new bishop was also named Æthelwald. Swefred thought him a rather unworldly man whose main concern was to complete and bind the Lindisfarne Gospels written by his predecessor.

Both boys were delighted to see him and Ulfric felt that his father was now happier in himself. Æthelwald Moll had held back when Ulfric had rushed forward to greet Swefred, but now he came and, after pausing for a moment, he threw his arms around him.

The Master of the Novices, who had brought the boys to the bishop's hut, seemed shocked by such a display of affection and stepped forward to haul his charges away, but Swefred shook his head at him and he stepped back. Nevertheless the monk still looked at the two of them with disapproval, whilst the bishop merely looked bemused.

'I need to talk to the two of you, but separately. Wait outside Æthelwald whilst I talk to Ulfric.'

The bishop looked startled until he realised that the ealdorman meant the boy, then he smiled and told the monk he could return to his charges. The man gave the two boys a stern look and left.

'Brother Edward is a good teacher but somewhat too strict I fear,' the bishop commented. 'Leave my namesake with me for now and go and talk to your son.'

'You and Æthelwald seem as close now as you have ever been.'

'Yes, after he learned about his parents he withdrew into himself for a long time but he started to return to his old self before we left Bebbanburg and since we've been here we've become as close as we ever were, perhaps closer.'

478

'Don't the other boys mind?'

'No, we don't exclude them but our relationship is, well, special. They even call us the twins,' he said with a grin.

'I need to talk to you about Æthelwald's future.'

'Oh! He's not going to leave here is he?'

'No, you'll be together until you've finished your warrior training.'

'Good.' He was thoughtful for a moment. 'But after that?'

'He's an ætheling and he deserves the status that goes with his birth. I want him to marry the Ealdorman of Berwic's daughter and I'll petition Osric to recognise Æthelwald as the man's heir. That means he'll become an ealdorman when Wathsige dies.'

'Of Berwic; so he won't be far away.'

'No, in due course you'll be lords of neighbouring shires.'

'Well, I hope that my time to become an ealdorman is a long way off yet; after all, you're not that old.'

Swefred laughed. 'I'm still in my thirties you cheeky rascal,' he replied as he cuffed his son lightly about the head.

'Ow! That's what I said, you're not that old!'

'No, but I want to go to Rome before I get reach my dotage. I have decided that when, or perhaps if, Æthelwald marries Wathsige's daughter and goes to live at Berwic I will ask Osric to make you Ealdorman of Bebbanburg, then I can go on pilgrimage.'

'When will that be? When we're sixteen?'

'Perhaps, or a year later; we'll see.'

'Oh, that's ages yet.'

'It may seem that way to you but it's just three or four years away. It'll pass quickly enough.'

'What happens when you come back? Will you want to become ealdorman again?'

'No, once you're lord of Bebbanburg that's it. You'll marry and have children of your own. You won't want me hanging around.'

He looked around him at the cultivated strips of land, the livestock grazing the pasture and the monastery's few fishing boats out at sea.

'This seems to me the perfect place for me to end my days. I can look across the bay and imagine you and your family in the fortress and spend my time preparing for the next life. After all, by the time I return from Rome I will probably be quite old,' he said with a twinkle in his eye, but his son didn't respond.

'Everything's changing isn't it?'

'Yes, nothing stays the same for ever. You're leaving your childhood behind you, Ulfric. Soon you'll be a man with all the cares and responsibilities that brings. Now, we should get back. I need to talk to Æthelwald.'

Chapter Twenty Five – Epilogue

730 AD

Swefred had become one of Lindisfarne's fishermen in the short time he had been there as a monk. He'd returned from Rome in the summer of 729 and spent a month visiting Beorhtmund, Eochaid and Æthelwald Moll. His final visit was to Bebbanburg to see Ulfric, his wife and their new born son, Seofon. After that he occasionally saw Ulfric on one of his rare visits to the monastery but he never saw the others again before that fateful day at the end of April in 730.

The day had started as normal. It was a fine day with a few clouds dotted around the clear blue sky and the sea was relatively calm with a fresh breeze blowing onshore. The odd white horse appeared on the crest of a wave but nothing indicated what was to follow.

Swefred was out in the area between Lindisfarne and the Farne Islands to the east of Bebbanburg with another monk and a young novice. The boy was gently pulling on the oars to keep the small boat moving slowly as the two monks fished with lines to which half a dozen hooks were attached. First Swefred and then the other monk felt a tug and found that one had caught four mackerel and the other three. They had hit a shoal. For the next half an hour they were busy pulling their lines aboard, unhooking the catch, rebaiting the hooks and throwing the lines back overboard.

All three were so engrossed that they failed to notice the changing weather until the boat started to move about violently. Swefred glanced up from the fish he was removing from his hooks and saw that the blue sky had changed to dark grey. In alarm he looked out to sea and saw even darker clouds approaching with rain visibly cascading from them.

The wind was now getting much stronger and the odd white horse had changed into spume flecked crests which the wind was whipping away horizontally.

'We need to row to shore as fast as we can,' he yelled at the other two, who seemed petrified by the sudden change in the conditions.

They hastened to grab an oar each whilst Swefred swung the tiller to turn the boat towards the beach under Bebbanburg's cliffs. They never made it. A particularly large wave picked the boat up by the stern and flung it to one side so that it was beam on to the wind. The next wave rolled it over and the last thing Swefred was conscious of was something giving him a mighty thwack on his head.

Both the other monks managed to shed their habits and swim to the shore where they lay exhausted. Ulfric had his men search all along the coast but there was no sign of Swefred. They never did find his body.

~~~

Osric lay dying of the plague. The outbreak in Eoforwīc in March 730 had been the worst to date. Wilfrith and his monks had worked tirelessly to ease the suffering of the sick but the disease kept on spreading. The first person to die in the king's hall was Osric's son and a few days later his wife followed him to the grave.

At first it seemed as if Osric might be spared but then he woke up with a black lump in his groin and he knew that he didn't have long to live.

'Wilfrith, I wish to adopt Coelfirth as my son.'

The bishop looked at him in amazement.

'Cenred's brother? But he's three years older than you. Why would you want to do that?'

Osric had a coughing fit and spat bloody mucus into the bowl beside his bed.

'Don't argue, just do as I say. He is to succeed me now my son is dead.'

Wilfrith nodded. 'If you say so, Cyning.'

The king lay back and closed his eyes. He prayed that he would survive long enough to sign the adoption papers.

'Get your scribes busy. I want to sign the deed of adoption today.'

'Yes, Cyning.'

Osric lasted for three more days after he'd signed the deed. He died on the twenty first of April 730, the same day that Swefred had drowned in the shadow of Bebbanburg. So ended the House of Æthelfrith. Although Otta survived he never became king and Æthelwald Moll wasn't acknowledged as Osred's son until much later.

In accordance with the old crone's prophesy one hundred and twenty five years earlier, Æthelfrith's line had lasted for a mere three generations, but it had been a momentous period in the history of Northumbria.

THE STORY OF THE KINGDOM OF NORTHUMBRIA WILL CONTINUE IN

TREASONS, STRATEGEMS AND SPOILS

Author's Note

This story is based on the known facts, but written evidence is patchy and there is some confusion in the main sources about dates, names and even relationships between family members. The main events are as depicted, even if the detail is invented. The chronology of events has sometimes been slightly altered in order to suit the story but this is, after all, a novel.

NORTHUMBRIA AFTER OSWIU

When King Oswiu died of natural causes in 670 AD, Northumbria was ruled by Ecgfrith with his younger brother, Ælfwine, as King of Deira. As he was only nine at the time it was probable that the title was purely honorific. Northumbria continued to flourish under the rule of Oswiu's sons and became culturally important. However, its political decline started with the loss of the territory Oswiu had gained in what would eventually become Scotland.

When Oswiu's eldest son, Aldfrith, died in 705 his eldest son was Osred, a nine year old boy. Many nobles were uneasy about rule by a minor, fearing that he would become the pawn of magnates seeking power for themselves. They therefore chose Eadwulf, an ealdorman and descendant of Ida - the first King of Bernicia - through a different branch of the family. Eadwulf wasn't a wise choice and within months he was deposed in favour of Osred with Bishop Wilfrid and the most powerful nobles as his regents.

However, as he got older Osred exhibited flaws in his character and he alienated many of his supporters. Accounts of his death vary but most assume that he was murdered in 716. He was succeeded by a cousin but his reign didn't last long and Osred's younger brother, Osric, replaced him. He ruled for another eleven years but he was the last of his line and the throne passed to another branch of the descendants of Ida.

After Osric Northumbria's political decline accelerated. There were nine kings in the space of sixty years who were murdered, deposed or abdicated to become monks. The story of what happened in this turbulent period will be told in the next novel in the series – *Treasons, Stratagems and Spoils* – which will cover the period from 730 to 800 AD.

On June 8th 793 a raiding party of Vikings from Norway attacked Lindisfarne. Monks fled in fear and many were slaughtered. More raids followed until eventually the invaders, mainly Danes, settled. There followed a period of Danish supremacy with England divided in two. The Danelaw in the north included much of Northumbria except for the area around Bebbanburg, which remained under Anglian rule, and Cumbria, which had been swallowed up by Strathclyde.

The last two novels in the series will deal with the coming of the Vikings and will conclude with the death of the last king of an independent Northumbria – Aelle.

One of the main characters in these final two novels – *The Wolf and the Raven* and *Blood Eagle* - is the legendary Viking King, Ragnar Lodbrok. However, the story also features Catinus' descendants as lords of Bebbanburg.

ANGLO-SAXON ORGANISATION AND CULTURE

The leaders of the Anglo-Saxons were constantly at war with one another during this period. Borders kept shifting and smaller kingdoms were swallowed up by larger ones. Kings had to pay their war bands and that took money, hence the need to plunder one's neighbours. The peasantry were only there to feed the kings, his nobles and their warriors.

Most kings had a small personal bodyguard of companions – called a gesith – and a warband - that is a permanent army of trained warriors. These were usually no more than a few hundred strong, if that. Nobles and some thegns would also keep a small gesith or warband to protect them, collect taxes and the like. The rest of the army was composed of a militia called the fyrd. It was made up of freemen, or ceorls, who provided their own weapon, and armour if they possessed any. Their standard of training and equipment varied.

When the Anglo-Saxons moved from paganism – about which little is known – to Christianity being a churchman instead of a warrior became an acceptable career for the well-bred. We know that several kings abdicated to become monks. Most other kings died in battle. Oswiu died in bed in his late fifties, but that was a rarity.

The spread of Christianity started with Augustine in the south and the converted recognised the Pope in Rome as their spiritual leader. In the north it was Aidan and the Celtic church who were largely responsible for the religion's growth. Inevitably the two churches came into conflict, resolved in Rome's favour by Oswiu at the Synod of Whitby.

The Anglo-Saxons were a cultured people, as surviving artefacts testify. The standard of illumination of religious tomes, intricate jewellery and well-made ornaments all demonstrate the high standard of their craftsmanship and their culture.

There was a parliament of sorts called the *Witan*, or more properly the Witenaġemot, in most kingdoms. It was an assembly of the ruling class whose primary function was to advise the king and elect a replacement when there was a vacancy. It was composed of the most important noblemen and the ecclesiastic hierarchy, but its membership might be expanded to include the thegns when the most important matters were to be discussed.

Thegns owned land of sufficient size to qualify for recognition by the king as such. A freeman (called a ceorl) could become a thegn by acquiring more land. Their estate was known as a *vill*, which corresponded roughly to the post-Norman manor.

Apart from members of the royal family, nobles also included the *eorls*, and later the *ealdormen*. They were appointed by the king to administer sub-divisions of the kingdom. Later the word was combined with the Norse jarl (meaning chieftain) to produce the title *earl*. However Anglo-Saxon earls ruled what had been the old major kingdoms of a dis-united England (for example Wessex, Mercia and Northumbria). The function of the earlier eorl gradually became that of the *ealdorman,* who was a royal official and chief magistrate of an administrative district called a shire.

ANGLO-SAXON KINGDOMS

In the late seventh century Britain was divided into a number of petty kingdoms. I have listed them here for the sake of completeness, though only a few of them feature significantly in the story. A few others get a passing mention. From north to south:

Land of the Picts – Probably originally divided into seven separate kingdoms and lying in the north and north-east of present day Scotland in the seventh century. By the beginning of the eighth century it became one kingdom. The names of the individual kingdoms seem to vary depending on the source. The names I have used are listed in the Glossary at the start of this novel

Dalriada – Western Scotland including Argyll and the Isles of the Hebrides. Also included part of Ulster in Ireland where the main tribe – the Scots – originated from

Strathclyde – The land between the above two kingdoms on either bank of the River Clyde and extending as far south as the Solway Firth

Lothian – Lothian and Borders Regions of modern Scotland – then subservient to Bernicia and therefore part of Northumbria. Formerly called Goddodin.

Bernicia – The north-east of England. Part of Northumbria. Included Rheged, later divided up.

Strathclyde – South west Scotland

Deira – Essentially modern Yorkshire. Part of Northumbria. Includes Elmet.

Essex – Similar to the present day county of Essex

Lindsey – Lincolnshire and Nottinghamshire, later part of Mercia

Gwynedd – North Wales

Mercia – Most of the English Midlands including the former kingdoms of Lindsey (Lincolnshire) and Middle Anglia (Bedfordshire, Warwickshire and Northamptonshire)

East Anglia – Norfolk, Suffolk and Cambridgeshire

Powys – Mid Wales

Dyfed – South-west Wales

Kingdom of the East Saxons – Essex

Hwicce – South-east Wales, Herefordshire and Gloucestershire. Fought over by Wessex and Mercia

Kingdom of the Middle Saxons – Home counties to the north of London

Wessex – Southern England between Devon and Surrey/Sussex

Kent – South-eastern England south of the River Thames

Kingdom of the South Saxons – Sussex and Surrey

Dumnonia – Devon and Cornwall in south-west England

It's worth noting that the coastline fourteen centuries ago was very different to what it is today. In particular, much of Cambridgeshire, part of Kent and the land around York was under water.

BUBONIC PLAGUE

The first recorded epidemic affected the Eastern Roman Empire and was named the Plague of Justinian after Emperor Justinian I who was infected but survived. The pandemic resulted in the deaths of an estimated 25 million to 50 million people throughout the world over the next two centuries.

In the spring of 542 the plague arrived in Constantinople. Travelling mainly from port to port it spread around the Mediterranean Sea, later migrating inland eastward into Asia Minor and westwards into Greece and Italy. The disease spread along the trade routes.

The so-called Plague of Justinian seems to have arrived in Ireland around 544 AD. There is no conclusive evidence that it spread to mainland Britain, apart from one report that the death of King Maelgwn of Gwynedd in 547 was due to the plague. However, information about this period of history is notoriously scarce and unreliable.

An outbreak occurred in England in the late seventh century which Saint Cuthbert succumbed to, but survived. Deusdedit, Archbishop of Canterbury and Bishop Tuda of Lindisfarne died of the plague in 664 and the next archbishop, Wighard, similarly succumbed in 666. The plague must have lasted for decades as Bishop Eata of Lindisfarne is recorded as dying of the disease in 686 AD. There is no evidence that Ælfflaed contracted the plague, but it doesn't mean she didn't. If she did she recovered. Neither is the cause of Osric's death recorded. As he was still relatively young, probably in his early thirties, I have attributed his death to the plague as well.

Other Novels by H A Culley

The Normans Series

The Bastard's Crown
Death in the Forest
England in Anarchy
Caging the Lyon
Seeking Jerusalem

Babylon Series

Babylon – The Concubine's Son
Babylon – Dawn of Empire

Individual Novels
Magna Carta
The Sins of the Fathers (no longer available)

Robert the Bruce Trilogy

The Path to the Throne
The Winter King
After Bannockburn

Constantine Trilogy

Constantine – The Battle for Rome
Crispus Ascending
Death of the Innocent

Macedon Trilogy

The Strategos
The Sacred War
Alexander

Kings of Northumbria Series

Whiteblade
Warriors of the North
Bretwalda
The Power and the Glory

About The Author

H A Culley was born in Wiltshire in 1944 was educated at St. Edmund's School, Canterbury and Welbeck College. After RMA Sandhurst he served as an Army officer for twenty four years, during which time he had a variety of unusual jobs. He spent his twenty first birthday in the jungles of Borneo, commanded an Arab infantry unit in the Gulf for three years and was the military attaché in Beirut during the aftermath of the Lebanese Civil War.

After leaving the Army he became the bursar of a large independent school for seventeen years before moving into marketing and fundraising in the education sector. He has served on the board of two commercial companies and has been a trustee of several national and local charities. He has also been involved in two major historical projects. His last job before retiring was as the finance director and company secretary of the Institute of Development Professionals in Education.

He now divides his time between giving talks on a variety of historical topics and writing historical fiction. He has three adult children and one granddaughter and lives with his wife and two Bernese Mountain Dogs near Holy Island in Northumberland.

Printed in Great Britain
by Amazon